Praise for The Thorn Healer

"A beautiful, emotionally moving tale of healing, forgiveness, and love's ability to overcome all barriers. Prepare for a late night as you near the end because this story grips you tight and wont let go." ~ Kristi Ann Hunter, award-winning author of *An Elegant Façade* and *A Lady of Esteem?*

"A delectable love story, seasoned with war, epidemics, prejudice, faith, and the beauty of finding healing in the Lord amidst the most broken of circumstances. A book you won't want to miss!" ~ Roseanna M. White, author of the *Ladies of the Manor Series*

"Pepper Basham has penned a story that not only entertains but calls readers to examine their hearts for prejudice and move toward compassion. Full of romance and sweet family, The Thorn Healer's strongest component might just be the hero who tends to the heroine's heart with a steadfast, pursuing love. Not only was I won over by the hero's gentleness, but I ached for the heroine, whose wounds kept her from receiving his love, that is until... well, you'll have to read and find out for yourself. High on romantic chemistry, tenderness, and rich historical research, *The Thorn Healer* will leave your heart smiling and your inner romantic swooning." ~ Sondra Krantz Kraak, author of *One Plus One Equals Trouble*

Pepper Basham's gift of storytelling comes home to the Blue Ridge Mountains in her third Penned in Time book. Intriguing history shares the page with a swoon worthy romance and soul-deep touches of grace. In August Reinhold, you will find a hero of heroes and a tender picture of our Savior's relentless pursuit of our hearts. I've read all three of the Penned in Time books, and I've loved them all, but this one is my absolute favorite! Framed in Basham's exquisite prose, this is a novel that will put down roots in your heart and stay a while. ~ Carrie Schmidt, ReadingIsMySuperPower.org, reviewer for Romantic Times, Blog Mistress Extraordinaire

Pepper Basham writes with a passion for story all her own, braiding timeless romance with fascinating history and spiritual inspiration; *The Thorn Healer* is a lovely example. ~ Rebecca Maney, Avid Reader, Reviewer and Blog Contributor

"From the first page, Pepper Basham will transport you to a different time and the conflicts of post-WW1. I highly recommend this book to lovers of historical fiction." ~ Cara Putman, award-winning author of *Shadowed by Grace* and *Beyond Justice*

"A timely story that tackles deep issues of pain, prejudice, and trusting God through the hard times with a grace that will have your heart sighing." ~ Sarah Monzon, author of *The Isaac Project* and *Finders Keepers*

THE THORN HEALER

Penned in Time-Book III

Pepper D. Basham

Vinspire Publishing
www.vinspirepublishing.com

Copyright ©2016 Pepper D. Basham

Cover illustration copyright © 2016 Elaina Lee/For the Muse Designs

Printed and bound in the United States of America. All rights reserved. No part of this book may be reproduced or transmitted in any form or by any means, electronic or mechanical, including photocopying, recording, or by an information storage and retrieval system-except by a reviewer who may quote brief passages in a review to be printed in a magazine, newspaper, or on the Web-without permission in writing from the publisher. For information, please contact Vinspire Publishing, LLC, P.O. Box 1165, Ladson, SC 29456-1165.

All characters in this work are purely fictional and have no existence outside the imagination of the author and have no relation whatsoever to anyone bearing the same name or names. They are not even distantly inspired by any individual known or unknown to the author, and all incidents are pure invention.

ISBN: 978-0-9971732-8-4

PUBLISHED BY VINSPIRE PUBLISHING, LLC

To Carrie, Rachael, Bonnie, and Meghan

You are examples of how Christ's hope is stronger than despair and His joy shines even brighter through suffering. Thank you for not only being my friends, but constant inspirations.

Chapter One

May 1918

Wounded soldiers returned from war as heroes. Wounded nurses returned as old maids.

Jessica Ross gripped the handle of her purse a little tighter and peered out the dusty train window, eager to catch the first glimpse of her hometown in two years. *Home.* The word swept a sweet balm over the ragged edges of memories rife with the devastation of a world at war.

The Great War, as some called it, held nothing 'great' within its muddied trenches, nothing but dying breaths and a forever-swell of hopelessness. A myriad of named and nameless faces, lost to the senselessness of battle, pinched her thoughts into the much too common headaches she'd developed over the past two years. But now, as she sighed back into the cloth-covered seat, the sweet whisper of home offered her space to breathe and a place to forget.

Her eyes drifted closed and brought visions of her mother and brother to mind, stilling her grin. Home couldn't be the same without their presence. During her last visit to Hot Springs, she'd buried her mother. Less than a year later, a German spy almost killed her older brother, leaving him with memory loss and a mutilated hand. Not the best hope for a surgeon, but David had made it work, despite the excruciating pain of healing.

The hardened fist of hatred tightened around Jessica's heart with a deeper grasp. Trench warfare, treachery, Kaisers?

She was finished with all of it—especially Germans. She hated them. Even German food was out of the question from this point on. All she wanted was to start over far away from the Front Lines.

"Next stop, Hot Springs!"

The clarion call of the train whistle followed the conductor's announcement with a glorious exclamation. A waft of mountain air breezed through the window, dampening the unusual May warmth with the scent of honeysuckles and fresh rain. Hope tickled a dangerous longing, fragile and as broken as she was, but she grasped its promise. A smile bloomed awake. Even if she was damaged beyond the use of war or the makings of a wife, even if nightmares stole her sleep and fear ripped at her peace of mind, one place always promised a sense of belonging—the Blue Ridge Mountains.

The pale summer sky painted a faded backdrop behind the blue-hewn mountains lining the track. As the train curved and slowed its pace, those precious mountains opened in grand theatrical style to unveil the moss-green roof of her hometown's pride and joy, The Mountain Park Hotel. People travelled from all over to benefit from the waters bubbling from Painted Rock Mountain, and the extravagant hotel set the stage for a first-class experience. Not that Jessica had ever benefited from the massages or treatments, or even seen the inside of the marble-pooled bathhouse, but as a child, she'd caught glimpses of the rich visitors and heard tales from local employees.

The white clapboard depot edged into view, and beyond it, the vast lawn of the exclusive inn. Her breath caught with the lurching halt of the train. Were those barracks? She leaned closer to the window, blinking to clear her vision. Rows of long wooden buildings littered the once-manicured lawn. She stood, her hand steadied against the window and gaze transfixed. Men—hundreds of them—moved upon the anomaly of barracks and barbed wire. Had the war followed her home?

Surely not.

This was Hot Springs. Home. Safety.

"Miss Jesse?"

The familiar voice sliced into Jess' living nightmare. She shook off her stupor and looked up to meet the familiar smile of Stanley Donaldson, her grandfather's best friend and station master of the quaint little depot.

"I've checked every train that's come by the last two days, hoping one would bring you home."

Jessica gripped the back of the seat in front of her and pulled herself upright, careful to keep her limp in check. "Stan, if you're not a sight for sore eyes, I don't know what is."

The man blushed at the compliment. "Now, Miss Jesse, I reckon there's a lot nicer sights to see besides my wrinkly face, but you sure do this heart good." He patted his chest. "And your grandparents will be plum tickled to know you arrived safe."

She tipped her chin. "Stan, you don't think a little thing like war is going to keep me from coming home, do you?"

"Land sakes, Miss Jesse." Stan adjusted his wire-rimmed glasses with a chuckle. "Them Kaisers were probably afraid to keep a spitfire like you too close. Afraid you might take a few of them down."

Stan's words doused the welcome, chilling Jessica's skin. She'd certainly taken one of them down. At point-blank range. Her throat closed with the memory. And she'd have taken more of the Hun if given the chance. A shudder quaked her frame and she forced a quick smile. "Don't you remember what Daddy always said about me? 'It's hard to put out a spitfire.'"

"Ain't that the truth?" Stan's smile grew. "And it's a good thing too. Don't think your family could've done with any more tragedy."

Jessica shoved the grief behind a hard-won shrug, ready to leave the tender topic for a more private audience, and then turned to reach for her cane. The scene out the window provided a perfect switch of conversation. "What's happening over at the hotel, Stan? It looks like the war followed me home."

Stan's gray eyebrows shot skyward as color dotted his cheeks at the corners of his moustache. "Your grandma didn't write you about the internees at the camp?"

Internees? Her gaze flitted back to the window and the rows of young men on the Inn's lawn. What sort of camp?

"Let me get you off the train first." He shuffled with his pockets and then reached for Jessica's bag, clearly avoiding her question. "No need for you to stand on that leg any longer than you have to."

She pinched her lips into a tight smile. She'd play along for a few more minutes and then light into Stan like the spitfire she was.

"My leg doesn't hurt much. Some of the nerves were damaged when the bullets lodged in my thigh, but—"

Stan winced.

Jess stepped out of nurse mode. She wasn't on the battlefield anymore. "Anyway, it's a weak leg, but not painful." She offered some levity. "And the limp will only add swagger."

"You know good and well you had plenty of swagger before you left." Stan laughed and took her proffered bag. "Only one bag?"

"There were plenty of women back in France who needed my extra clothes much more than I did."

Stan steadied his gaze on her and a sad grin poked from under his moustache. "Your mother would be real proud of you, girl."

He turned and exited the train, but Jess couldn't move. His gentle statement fell like a brick against her stomach. Loss brought a weight with it, no matter how distant the grief, the unexpected invasion of tears an unnerving consequence. She needed privacy... or some mental occupation, but not silence, and definitely no more talk of loss.

She raised her chin and gripped the cane with purpose, shuffling between the rows of train seats to the doorway. Navigating stairs still made her nervous, especially the narrow and steep train steps. She turned her body and lowered her cane to distribute some of her weight for the first step, then the second, but the sudden appearance of men marching across the platform distracted her descent to the third. They made two lines of khaki slacks and white shirts, the steady clap of shoe-upon-wood in perfect synchrony. She knew it well, even if the sound was dulled from her hearing loss. The men weren't dressed like soldiers, but their stiff spines and focused attention confirmed previous military training.

Four other men, one at each corner of the row, kept in time with the men, and their uniforms set them apart. Guards?

What was happening?

Her weak leg twisted under her poised position, pitching her toward the platform and the oncoming men. She turned her body so her wounded side would take the impact, but two strong arms caught her before the wooden planks did.

Her cane clattered to the platform and her hat tumbled down over her face, blocking her view of her rescuer. Which was a mercy, since her face burned so hot from embarrassment she was pretty sure it resembled Red Delicious apples.

Strong and gentle hands moved to her shoulders to steady her. She tried to overcompensate for her limp by leaning on her right leg and with a swift touch, drew her braid around to cover her injured ear.

A fingertip emerged at the base of her hat and slowly pushed the masses of cloth and fluff back from her face. At first, she saw his firm jaw and crooked grin, then a perfect symmetrical nose which, after treating tons of facial wounds, was quite the sight, and finally, she met a pair of eyes so pale-blue, they looked periwinkle. Paired with his exquisite nose and his lopsided smile, it was the most stunning sight she'd seen since the Blue Ridge Mountains appeared over the horizon.

She fully appreciated the fact the explosion had taken her left hearing instead of her left sight, because she wanted her whole field of vision for this view. Had she ever seen such a man? His gaze searched hers as if he knew her, intimate and not uncomfortable, exactly. Energy zipped between them, taking the heat from her cheeks and sending it downward. His close-cropped hair couldn't hide the swirls of blond curl which softened the soldier-look without diminishing his sheer manliness. Jess' limited experience with attraction left her ill-equipped for the fireworks sizzling in her stomach and the complete loss of words from her head.

His smile softened. "Are you all right, Miss Ross?"

He knew her name? And what was his accent? She'd heard it before. English? French?

"Y... yes. Thank you."

"I was happy to be helpful to you."

Those eyes held such sincerity and interest, Jessica stumbled through trying to identify his voice. Was he Australian? "Well, you've certain done so. I'm much obliged to you, Mr.—?"

His face sobered, his gaze searching hers with an almost pleading expression. "August Reinhold."

Reinhold?

Her heartbeat shot up to machine-gun speed and the beautiful warmth in her chest solidified to a block of ice.

German.

A connection of pure attraction jolted through August Reinhold at his first glimpse of Jessica Ross on the train steps. *Schock.* Black and white photos from her grandparents' home gave a pale comparison to the original. Her hair, the rich gold of alpine poppies, curled up under a green hat the same shade as her eyes, and what eyes—alive and intelligent, swirling with various shades of emerald.

Eight months of stories about her from her grandparents only deepened the connection. In full color, peeking from beneath her hat, her beauty stopped his breath. The faintest touch of curiosity curved her pink lips, twisting his heart with the desire to bring a full smile. His arms steadied her against him, her breath sighed out with hints of peppermint mingled with honeysuckles, and August drowned in a second's certainty. For the briefest moment, they shared the attraction, the interest, both examining each other with mutual understanding of much more than spoken words... until he said his name.

Those emerald eyes widened, and recognition dawned a painful birth.

Kalt.

As cold as the winter winds on the Alps.

He'd known rejection from Americans since the War began, but when Jessica Ross pulled back from him and sent him a look as severe as any slap he'd ever known, pain jabbed to his core.

"Excuse me." She held his gaze and snatched the cane he lifted from the ground. "Thank you."

The acknowledgement squeezed from between her teeth. She blinked and moved past him into the depot without a look back. August pulled his eyes from her retreating back and met Guard Cliff Carter's thoughtful expression.

"I see you've met my cousin."

"I have." August pressed a palm against the ache in his chest. "Indeed, I have."

"Let me give you fair warning before you start conjuring up crazy notions in that head of yours." Cliff patted August on the shoulder and shook his head in solace. "You've won over a lot of folks, August, but you'll not win the likes of her."

August squinted in the direction Jessica had disappeared, Cliff's consolation more of a challenge than a deterrent. After spending months with Jessica's grandparents, he knew enough of her painful war experiences to expect little else. But life had offered him many challenges to overcome, and this one provided the most appealing package. "We shall see."

"Don't say I didn't warn you, friend." Cliff chuckled. "Do you have your pass?"

August turned back to Cliff, his mind catching up with the question. "Ja." August corrected quickly for the kind-hearted guard, keeping to the rules of English with the Americans, and produced the necessary paper. "Yes, I have it."

"Then you'd better be off." Cliff shifted a black brow. "You going to steer clear of Doc's clinic today? It might be wise, considering the morning arrival."

August frowned. "I made a promise to Dr. Ross that I would be available for sutures. He has a surgery today."

"Sewin' up people or suffering the wrath of Jessica Ross?" Cliff winced and took off his cap to run a hand through his dark hair. "Both reasons would keep me far away from Doc's clinic."

August tipped his hat and bowed his head in subtle salute. "Wrath or not, the scenery at Dr. Carter's clinic just improved, you think?"

Cliff's growing smile turned into a full-fledged laugh as he handed August a slip of paper. "Soldier or not, you don't need to be in Europe. You're goin' head first into the frontlines of Hot Springs, and I'm not too sure you're armed for the battle."

August slipped out of the covering of the depot and into the sunlight of the late spring day, his steps marked with purpose. His life had provided one painful challenge after another, so why not charge headlong into one with the best prize so far? He unfolded the paper and read through Dr. Carter's list of supplies. With a whistle on his lips, he took the steps off the platform and glanced down at the sleepy mountain town. Nothing in the meanderings of the quiet street hinted at a battle, but his pulse still hammered from the touch of Jessica Ross' hand and the fascinating hue in her fiery eyes.

A white German shepherd sat by the railway tracks, waiting at the corner near the Iron Horse Station Tavern.

August's lips spread into a full grin. "Guten Morgen, Blitz."

The dog perked an ear at August's voice but didn't move. He might be a German shepherd, but it would take more than eight months to have him comfortable with his German name.

"Come, Lightning." The dog jumped from his spot and ran to August's side, taking a pat to his head with pleasure. "We have a few supplies to collect for the good doctor."

Lightning followed close, passing across the dirt road toward the twin line of brick buildings. Some of the regular townspeople nodded in August's direction and even smiled their welcome. A few of the women averted their gazes, but for the most part, the German occupation of Hot Springs was met with indifference.

Mostly.

The town nestled in a valley surrounded by smooth-topped mountains, nothing like the carved peaks of home but a place which had become increasing more attractive in the year he'd arrived with his countrymen. The quiet streets and serene landscape drew him, a home for his wandering spirit.

He tucked his hands into his pockets and made his way to Kimper's, halfway between the Depot and Dr. Ross' clinic. Lightning halted at the door and looked up, awaiting direction.

"Stay."

Without hesitation, the shepherd yawned and settled himself on the porch by the door. A twinge of regret flickered in August's chest, reminding him of the family dog he'd left behind two lonely years ago. Left behind? No, more like he'd been tossed aside. There was nothing across the ocean for him anymore.

He shrugged off the melancholy and pushed open the door to the popular general store. The usual jingle of bells followed his entry, along with the scent of licorice and sawdust, an odd combination he'd come to identify as solely Kimp's place. A model fighter plane hung from the ceiling, the only apparent addition to the eclectic store's usual fare since August's last visit.

"What do you need, August?" The owner jutted out his square jaw, his look of disapproval as constant a feature as the white apron around his wide frame.

"I've come to collect Dr. Carter's items, sir."

Kimp grunted a reply, took the proffered list, and disappeared to the back of the store. August touched the tip of a few wooden trinkets, 'widdled' by the locals, simple stick and spring devices. His countryman could do much better. In fact, their little 'village' they'd designed on the inn's grounds, a cacophony of discarded wood and metal, proved their talents, if one only took the time to look.

His fingers paused on the wheels of a small wooden train. Would Jessica Ross look beyond prejudice?

A noise from behind and the scent of smoke pulled August's attention around. A stranger, cigarette in hand, watched with a narrowed expression. His dusty, unkempt clothes appeared less hardworking and more uncaring. August nodded but kept his distance. *Arger.* Trouble.

"Not from around here, are ya, boy?"

August measured the man with a look, his gaze steady. "I have been here for almost a year. Are you new to Hot Springs?"

The man's frown snarled, and he blew out a long puff of smoke. "You one of them *friendly* Germans in the camp? The ones taking all our jobs and supplies?"

"I do not know of what you speak."

The stranger loomed a few steps closer. "Oh, I bet you don't. And what are you sending back to your countrymen in all those letters your kind mail off every day?"

"I wouldn't know. I rarely write them."

"Here they are, August." Kimper emerged from the back with a box in hand, his gaze flicking from August to the stranger. "You best get them to the doctor."

"What's this one doing without a guard, Kimp? I thought they all had to be escorted outside the camp." The stranger's gaze never left August's face.

Kimper settled the box on the counter and sifted through the bags, checking the items. "Dr. Carter made an arrangement with the guards since his grandyounguns have been 'crost the Pond.

August, here, seems to keep to the rules just fine. There's been a handful like him, with no complaints from the town."

The stranger released a groan similar to a growl. August turned toward the counter, finished with the conversation.

"I don't like it any better than you do, Davis, but August ain't caused no trouble." Kimper's gaze fixed on August over the parcel, a warning. "And if he knows what's good for him, he won't start no trouble."

August nodded his thanks for the backhanded compliment and to assure Kimper of his assumptions.

"Besides, with Dr. Perry gone to Asheville—" Kimper shot military straight and rounded the counter. "Daggone it, Davis. What have I told you about smokin' in my store? I don't care how long you've been on the rails, my rule ain't changed." He waved Davis toward the door. "Get out before I call the law."

Davis tipped his hat to August as he passed and lowered his voice. "No guards. No witnesses."

August followed the man with his gaze until he left the store.

"I'd steer clear of him if I was you." Kimper held out the box of supplies. "Lost two brothers to the Germans already, and just returned back in town last week from his own wounds. He ain't lookin' to be your friend, if you know what I mean."

The warning stiffened the hair on the back of August's neck, but he forced a smile to the shop owner and took the proffered box of supplies. "Thank you."

There was no sign of Davis outside the mercantile. Morning sunlight blinked between dark clouds and sent shadows across the dusty street. August had hoped most of the dissonance related to the German presence had died down months ago. Evidently not. And all it took was one to stoke the fire of discontent.

He didn't need or want any enemies. What he wanted was...

A flash of green up ahead of him on the street turned his attention in a more pleasing direction. Jessica Ross. Her dress hugged her slim form, but not enough to slow her down, even with the slight limp in her step. An obvious fire of determination added momentum to her stride, or perhaps it was a personality trait.

August's smile spread into a full grin. He'd never backed down from a healthy challenge, and Miss Ross added a dimension to the bond he'd built with Jacob and Lillian Carter, which fueled his curiosity all the way down to his heart. Listening to Lillian read Jessica's letters around the dinner table for the past five months only deepened his interest. They shared many commonalities—the deaths of their mothers to lengthened illnesses, the love of music and family, a fierce loyalty, and the desire to serve God and others. Surely those important similarities could withstand her prejudice?

The memory of distrust in Jessica's eyes returned with full sting. Would her anger cause a breach in his relationship with their family? They'd become as close to him as his own blood, his lifeline beyond the rejection in his past. Could he win her over, at least in friendship, to keep a hold on that connection?

Her grandfather referred to Jessica as a pistol. Her grandmother, as a spitfire.

And from his first glance into her eyes, something akin to electricity shot through his body.

He called to Lightning and walked toward the clinic, the distant sound of thunder an ominous warning. The Great War for Europe's freedom ebbed across the ocean, but a battle brewed at the corner of Bridge and Walnut, and he was pretty certain the enemy wore a tan skirt and green hat.

The thunder sounded again, only closer, and more like galloping horses. August turned toward the sound. A wagon hurried forward in a stampede of orange dust and horses' hooves, a strange sight in this sleepy town.

The few people along the street rushed to get out of the way as the wagon passed them at frenetic speed and nearly jumped the train track. August looked down the road toward the clinic just as Jessica stepped into the street.

Why didn't she turn? Couldn't she hear the wagon?

August's stomach knotted with awareness. Her left side. Her wounded ear.

He dropped his hold on the supplies and darted forward into the line of the incoming wagon. Jessica slowed her pace, stopped in the middle of the road, and then turned toward him. The wagon rattled forward, hammering nearer. Jessica's eyes grew wide and she dropped her bag and cane. With every muscle in his body, he propelled forward, wrapping her in his arms and turning to take the impact of the fall. The roar of the wagon shook the earth as he landed, her body tight against his. One thing was certain. No enemy he'd ever known smelled like honeysuckles and peppermint.

Maybe the wagon had crushed him already, because this was nothing short of heaven.

Chapter Two

Jessica's legs wouldn't move. It served her right for plunging across the street in fury and forgetting she couldn't trust her left ear. When would she learn to think before allowing her anger to erupt in careless words or life-threatening actions?

Her doom blasted toward her in the form of a speeding wagon, two brown steeds leading the way, and she almost laughed at the irony. She'd survived a Zeppelin bombing, grueling months on the Frontlines of France, along with being captured by a German spy, only to die under the wheel of a farmer's wagon?

How uneventful.

The driver strained to veer the wagon from its course, but his forward momentum sealed her fate. She closed her eyes and prepared to meet her mother, when a sudden jolt to her left sent her spiraling through the air. Arms tightened around her, drawing her away from the approaching wheels and into a haven of warm strength. Dying wasn't quite as terrible as she thought.

Reality jarred her as she landed with a thud against something that smelled like fresh pine and was much softer than the ground. She loved pine. It reminded her of Christmas, chestnuts, warmth, and happier times. She smiled into the soft linen, catching her breath and forgetting for a moment she was sprawled in the middle of the road in the arms of a complete stranger after a near-death experience. A startling sense of safety whooshed over her. After the last two years, safety never went unappreciated, and she lingered for a second longer, her erratic breath slowing to drink in another whiff of pine.

His arms tightened, encasing her in a tender hold and bringing her to her senses.

A cascade of loose hair rained over her vision as she pushed up to a sitting position.

"Are you all right, Miss Ross?" The strained voice sounded curiously familiar. So did the accent.

She shoved back her hair with one palm and met the same clear blue eyes she'd seen in the station. Attraction buzzed fresh as lightning over her skin, thickening the air with unwelcome heat. Even his grin spiked an unwanted curiosity. The heat in her face sizzled to fury. What was wrong with her?

His lips tilted into a curious smile. "I've saved you twice in one morning. This proves I'm a good man, yes?"

Jessica swallowed the lump in her throat and embraced the anger with both hands. "Or it proves that trouble precedes you, Mr. Reinhold—a mystery I have no interest to solve."

His steadying palms slipped down her shoulders again and left an unnerving tingle. She shrugged off his hold and sent him a clear warning in her glare. Instead of being offended, as she'd hoped, his grin broadened and the tenderness of his expression only magnified the rate of her pulse. *Men!*

A fluff of white appeared at Mr. Reinhold's side, the nose nuzzling the stranger's shoulder with a concern Jessica certainly didn't share. *Lightning? Her* Lightning? Jessica stumbled to her feet, blinking as if struck. She left for a few years and was replaced by a German?

"That's *my* dog."

Mr. Reinhold squinted up at her against the sun. "He's a very good dog." He patted Lightning's head and stood to join her. "We've become friends."

Jess sent her dog a withering look. *Traitor.*

As if in answer to her unspoken insult, Lightning tilted his head, examined her, and stepped close. Jess lowered herself back to her knees and Lightning bounded into her arms, giving her cheek a sound lick.

"Ah, now you know me?" She buried her face into the folds of his fur, grappling for the sense of safety she'd known in a real traitor's arms. "I missed you."

He whimpered his reply, his nose nuzzling her shoulder. She sighed. *Her* dog.

Mr. Reinhold's gaze drilled into her subconscious, needling like a headache... a strange sort of sweet, tingling headache. To prove he couldn't affect her, she met his stare head-on. His tender grin sent a stutter through her stubborn intentions and defused the edge in her stance a bit. What was it about this man? Jabbing her annoyance at him was like beating a marshmallow.

"What were you doing in the middle of the street, woman?" A harsh voice called from behind and she turned.

Tommy Buchanan jumped from the wagon and punched an accusing finger toward her. "We don't have time to deal with some half-wit female when we—" His gray gaze widened. "Jessica Ross? You're back?"

"Only just."

Her smile stilled as she caught sight of Tom's wife, Alice, in the wagon bed behind them, her face pale.

Jessica moved toward the wagon. "What's going on, Tom?"

Tom blinked out of his stare and raced to the wagon bed. "Dad fell off the barn loft into a pile of wood."

"He's bleedin' real bad, Jess." Alice came into view as Jessica rounded the wagon bed. The woman cradled the older man's head in her bloodstained lap, her dark eyes holding as much concern as her husband's.

Jess took in the scene and stifled a wince. Bright red marked the bed sheets Tom and Alice had used to wrap Mr. Buchanan's abdomen.

"We must get him into the clinic quickly."

"You might need to give us a hand." Tom turned his shoulder, his left sleeve empty. "I can do a whole lot of things with one arm, but carryin' my Dad ain't one of them."

Jess tossed a look over her shoulder to Mr. Reinhold, but he didn't offer to move a step. Of course, why should she expect much else from him? All his flirting was as empty as his chest. Like most of the Germans she'd met—especially the one who nearly killed her and her older brother.

"Of course I'll help." Jess moved to take one side of the sheet. "I'll lift at the feet if Alice will get the head, and Tom, you help with the torso."

They lumbered forward to the clinic door and Mr. Reinhold was there to open it.

"We don't need help from a lousy Jerry." Tom shoved Mr. Reinhold to the side with his body. "If you'd wanted to lend a hand, your people wouldn't have taken mine."

Jess cringed at the voice of bitterness so similar to the one she kept inside, but the angry words bounced off the German without one hint of discomfort, solidifying Jess' previous assumption— heartless. Those periwinkle eyes of August Reinhold, holding such compassion, failed to match the traitor from Jessica's past, Dr. Cramer. Or Lt. Snyder, she later learned. *Spy. Murderer.*

She snatched her gaze from the inexplicable draw to his. No, she couldn't trust appearances.

The smell of alcohol and iodine met Jess upon entrance to the clinic, sheet and wounded still in hand. Though she could walk fine without her cane, her limp became more prominent, placing her wounds on further display.

"What's this?"

Jess almost stumbled at the sight of her grandpa. Two years hadn't changed him. His walnut-colored hair, sprinkled with gray, waved away from his prominent forehead, drawing attention to his pale green eyes, the Carter family legacy. All of her grandparents' letters over the years of her absence from Hot Springs somehow drew them closer, especially after her mother's death. They'd become a lifeline from the barren wasteland of war to something peaceful and secure. To home.

Despite her best efforts, her vision blurred with a rush of tears.

His brows rose. "Jess? You're early."

"I took the first train out of Asheville."

Relief washed over his features and softened the edges of her frustration at coming home to a warzone. "It's good to see you, girl."

Her smile quivered into place. "You too, Grandpa."

Their eyes held, wordless gratitude passing between them for a few seconds before her grandpa switched back to 'the doctor' and turned to Tom and Alice. "Place him here." He took the sheet from Jessica and guided them into the back room, his attention fastened on her. "What happened?"

Jessica followed, snatching some gauze and other supplies as she passed. "Tom said he fell from the barn into a log pile. He has an extensive gash in his abdomen and a smaller one on the back of his head. Entry point to the abdominal wound appears to be from the back and only bypassed the spine by a few inches, from what I could tell."

"Didn't make sense, him fallin'," Tom added as they situated the body on an examining table. "He'd been up there lots of times."

Grandpa stripped back the sheet from Mr. Buchanan's body, revealing the gash on his left lower abdomen. "Was he alert when you found him?"

"Alice came upon him after she heard a crash in the barn." Tom looked to his wife, whose eyes remained red-rimmed.

The woman stared down at her father-in-law's bloody body in shock. Jess touched her arm. "Alice." The connection brought her out of her trance as Grandpa examined Mr. Buchanan's head.

"Did he say anything when you found him? Was he alert at all?"

"He mumbled." Alice's palm flattened against her chest, head shaking. "Didn't make no sense. Sounded like he was drunk or somethin'."

Jess met her grandpa's eyes. Stroke? Seizure? The results of a head trauma?

"We have to stop the bleeding," Grandpa said. "Then we can figure out what caused the fall." Her grandfather scanned the room. "Where's August? He has supplies, and I could use his help with the sutures."

Jessica blinked, her brain sifting through her grandpa's words. "August?" Surely, he couldn't mean... "The German?"

Her grandfather's brows formed a firm line. "Yes, and friend."

"Friend?" Jessica dropped the sheet in her hands, heat shooting into her face.

"No German is going to touch my Dad." Tom's voice seethed with the same hiss of bitterness teeming up Jessica's throat.

Grandpa released a burst of air through his nose, feathering a few hairs on his moustache. "We'll solve this later. Right now, I need your help. Take over here."

Jess jerked off her traveling jacket and pushed back her hair, which still hung loose from the wagon incident. She replaced Grandpa at the table, applying pressure to Mr. Buchanan's wound. The bleeding had slowed, but his pale face, his lips taking on a faint blue hue, sent clear warning. Jess had seen worse—much worse—but she also recognized all too well the chill of death lurking unseen in the shadows of the room.

Grandfather moved to a nearby cabinet and rifled through some supplies. "Whether you like it or not, Tom Buchanan, that German's been a faithful assistant to me for over five months now and he's the one who was supposed to bring in my much needed supplies so I can try to save your daddy's life."

Jessica's insides curled. Why on earth would her grandfather ever build a relationship with a German—especially enough to hire him as an assistant? After all those people had done to her family? After David's injuries and her... her... She closed her mind to the dark thoughts crowding in.

"He's your assistant?" Jess couldn't curb the fire in her voice, even for her grandfather. "A German soldier?"

His emerald gaze flickered to hers, clearly aware of the tone, his brow edged high. "He's no soldier. The men are noncombatants. Mostly sailors, except for the band."

Jess squeezed her eyes closed, trying to make sense of the situation. Sailors and a band housed behind barbed wire at The Mountain Park Hotel? "Band?"

"They were caught at our ports when America joined the war. Only a few were ever soldiers." Her grandfather looked past her. "August?"

"I am here, Doctor." The deep, calm voice rose from the doorway.

Jess pressed a little harder, her eyes narrowed as she peered from the treatment room at the handsome stranger. He stepped toward her grandfather, his arms not only laden with his supplies, but also her cane. Red dirt from the road outside dusted his white shirt and his hair stood in an erratic blond mop on his head, reminding her of their very public encounter on the side of the street.

Her face flushed hot. She focused back on her patient.

Well, at least he hadn't left all the supplies strewn across the street when he'd jumped to her rescue. Her agitation curbed as she inwardly conceded to the fact he'd probably saved her life. She pinched her lips closed on the admission, however.

"August. Thank God you're here." Her grandpa cupped a palm to August's shoulder with a familiarity that only dug the bitterness in Jessica's chest even deeper. "Did the medicines come?"

"Yes, especially the Dakin solution, sir." He placed the supplies on the nearby counter. "I will do whatever I can to assist you, Dr. Carter." The man's gentleness flowed from his words in an unnerving contradiction to every ugly picture against him forming in Jessica's head.

She groaned and leaned forward to hear their quiet conversation, but the voices lowered. Tom and Alice exchanged nervous glances, and Jessica offered them a smile with more reassurance than she felt. "There's no one who can help your father as well as Grandpa, Tom."

Tom grunted but Jessica knew, despite the man's annoyance at her grandfather's unlikely friendship, he was a faithful doctor to the people all over Madison County. And his judgment was usually solid, except when it involved a certain blond foreigner whose piercing gaze pinched her stomach like nervous tweezers.

Grandpa moved back to her side and examined the body, his brow tight. With the slightest of movements, he leaned close. "Have you given a blood transfusion before?"

Visions of her three archaic trials at the Front rushed to mind. Heat drained from her face but she met her grandfather's eyes unswervingly. "Two. Kimpton-Brown."

"Successful?"

She swallowed the growing lump in her throat. "One was."

Her grandfather's lips firmed into a line. "We'll use a modified version of the Kimpton-Brown." He faced the worried couple. "Your father has lost a lot of blood, Tom. Too much to survive without help."

"What do you mean?"

"I need to transfer new blood into him, but you're not going to like the processes."

Tom's palms went to his hips, his face paled. "Will he live if you do?"

"He may, but without it, he'll definitely die."

Tom looked at Alice and then back to her grandfather. "Do whatever you have to do."

Grandfather braced his own hands on his hips and nodded. "I have a few pints of blood saved."

"You've saved some?" Jess attention rocked to him. "Who trained you on the coagulation process?" How on earth, back in the wilds of Appalachia, had her grandfather learned the newest process for storing blood? He never ceased to amaze her.

"A physician from New York came through about a year ago with the latest research." Her grandfather's gaze swung back to Tom's. "But I'll need three trained hands to help me with the process."

"Three?" Tom followed her grandfather's gaze and Jessica's breath seized.

August Reinhold.

The German.

The weariness of her travels, combined with the stress of the procedure, slowed Jess' steps toward the front door of her grandparents' sweeping white farmhouse. Tall and narrow, with a front porch to 'hold a gang', as her Granny said, the house welcomed her forward. A sudden swell of peace encircled her like a hug, loosening some of the tangles in her muscles from the tension of the long surgery.

Whether it proved a success or not, only time would tell. The first twenty-four hours remained the most crucial, which was why her grandfather stayed behind for the night to keep watch over Mr. Buchanan. The memory of the surgery brought another unwelcome reminder of Mr. Reinhold's presence. His quiet demeanor, ready to provide whatever assistance needed, tightened Jess' muscles all over again. Her grandparents had a lot of explaining to do, and there was no time to discuss it while a man's life weighed in the balance.

A gentle hum drifted along the late afternoon breeze from the side of the house—and the perfect person to provide some explanation to all the madness of this day. Her grandmother. Jess pulled her bag securely up on her shoulder and rounded the corner. Tenderness rooted her in place at the sight of the petite matriarch bent over her vegetable garden, a bonnet shading her pale face and ever-present apron cinched around her small waist. Years spun backwards, stabbing into the fresh wounds of loss like the edge of a scalpel. Her mother should have been there, tending the garden alongside her granny. Her throat tightened around a thousand unshed tears.

She almost lost her carefully clenched hold on her bedraggled emotions at the tender sight of something so normal, so simple. A place to which she could never return.

She hesitated to interrupt the sweetness of the scene so she watched, sifting through the ache for the forgotten, wishing for a different middle to this story. Her grandmother finally stood and stretched out her back, glancing up at the cloudy sky. Tendrils of silver and brown swirled beneath the bonnet from the gentle tug of the wind.

The thread of magic broke as her grandmother's gaze settled on Jess's face.

"Jessica?" Her grandmother laughed and rushed forward. "Oh, sweet girl, I'm so glad to see you home."

And in a second, she rested in her grandmother's comforting embrace. "Granny."

Granny pulled back and studied Jess' face, then drew her into another hug, her laugh returning. "Ah, it's been too long. Too long."

As the scent of lilacs surrounded Jessica, followed by an immediate yearning for a mother who was impossible to reach, Jessica wondered if she'd not been gone long enough. Two years melted away with that single scent.

"I made strawberry shortcake to celebrate your homecoming." The little woman slipped her arm around Jess' waist and headed for the back door.

She slid her grandmother a look. "Isn't today a wheatless day? And isn't sugar on short supply?"

"Oh, ye of little faith." Her grandmother tsked. "I baked the cake *yesterday* and I have ten cans of applesauce left to sweeten up my baking, along with a few homemade remedies to keep things tasting scrumptious."

Lillian Carter and her homemade remedies. Jess' grin pulled broad against her cheeks and she released a sigh she had been holding for two years.

Jess followed her grandmother into the house and breathed in the aroma of apples, pine, and sugar. Fresh air ruffled the white curtains in the windows, sending shadows across the sitting room floors.

"I fixed up your old room upstairs." Granny moved ahead into the kitchen. "We rented out your parents' cottage last year to bring in some extra money."

Jess peered out the dining room window as she passed and caught sight of the roofline of the cottage, shrouded by a group of trees. The rock house sat at the back of her grandparents' property, carved from the mountain fieldstone when Jess' parents moved from England years ago. She'd always planned to raise her own family there some day.

She glanced down at her cane.

Former plan.

The cottage was too big for only one person and renting it made good sense, even if it didn't feel good. "Someone local?"

Granny shrugged a shoulder as she pulled the cake from the cake safe and then gestured toward the kitchen table with the plate in hand. "No. A widow who's bringing in good business with her dressmaking. She's not much older than you. Anna's her name."

Jess digested the information, a myriad of questions popping to mind about a widow moving to the secluded mountain town, but weariness kept her quiet. She hadn't stood on her leg or walked so much in several weeks.

"Why don't you take your things up to your room and then come join me for cake?"

And a talk, if she knew anything about her granny. She smiled as she pulled herself up the narrow back steps leading from the kitchen to her secluded room at the back of the house. Scents of honeysuckles and rose petals met with a unique smell of home.

The room looked the same as when she left. A four-poster bed in the center, covered in one of her grandmother's colorful quilts. A dresser to one side of the bed and a nightstand to the other, and on the opposite wall stood her writing desks. She grinned and dropped her bag on the bed before running her hands across the clean sheets of paper scattered over wood. She'd spent hours writing articles for local papers about the rights of women to vote, or own their own property, or earn similar wages as their male counterparts.

And though the process had proved painfully slow, things were changing. What a shame it took a war to push women into the workforce and show men all around the country their value.

She stepped to the window and stared out over the back garden, the cottage a bit clearer from her heightened vantage point. Her father had loved his little sanctuary, with its vine covered rock walls reminding him of England. Her mother had loved it because her father did.

Mother. The loss hollowed out with a deeper ache. Jess lifted her eyes to the guardian mountains on every side and almost whispered a prayer. *Almost.*

She'd grown out of practice with praying. After the days and nights of watching men die in her arms, of piecing broken soldiers back together for an unknown future, of almost losing her brother or having a piece of her innocence stripped away, of nursing her mother until she drew her final breath and then helplessly watching her father grieve... somehow, prayer felt futile.

She ignored the tiny nudge, the call to whisper to the creator of those mountains, and joined Granny back in the kitchen instead.

"Your grandpa sent a message by Joe Gentry's boy that you'd arrived and was helping him with a surgery." Granny gestured toward the kitchen table with a plate of cake in hand. "How'd things go?" She placed the plates down, both brimming with strawberry shortcake.

Jess joined her at the table. "Time will tell. The fact he survived the transfusion is a success in itself."

She sliced her fork through the cake, her mouth watering at the scent of butter and strawberries mixed. "They're still so new, it's difficult to predict the outcome. Mr. Buchanan had a hard fall."

"Well, I'm sure your grandpa was glad to have you there. Experienced help is hard to find since most medical folks are across the Pond."

So, what about Mr. Reinhold? During the entire surgery, he'd stood like a statue, complete with his unnerving calm. Jess steadied a forkful of cake on her fork and peered at her granny. "It seems he's trained one of the internees?"

Her grandmother gave no reaction except the slight pause of her movements as she took a bite. "You've met August?"

"After I stepped off the train to the vision of barracks and barbed wire, as a matter of fact."

Granny placed her fork down on the table and pressed both palms flat, meeting Jessica's gaze with a direct one of her own. "I know you've had a hard time during this war. And I can't imagine what you've had to endure over there."

"No, you can't."

Granny raised a brow. "But your grandpa and I weren't going to risk you not coming home just because you're angry at the entire country of Germany."

Jess put her own fork down and crossed her arms. "They almost killed David, and I've held hundreds of men in my arms who weren't so lucky—all because of those Germans."

"Do you think we ain't felt the sting here? Ten boys lost, so far. About eighteen of the Dorland boys left from the school to head over and we're hopin' they make it back alive." Granny didn't back down. "Each family grieving the loss, or possibility of it, but the men in that camp aren't the ones fighting in Europe. They've been imprisoned since the day America joined the war. First in New York and then moved here."

"You should have told me about the camp."

Granny lowered her gaze, a mild acquiesce to her guilt. "Maybe, but your grandpa and I were afraid you wouldn't come home if we did, and we were selfish enough to want one grandchild here instead of lost to war or England."

A flame of Jessica's anger deflated a little at the recognition of her grandparents' loss, the same shared loss aching through her quiet moments. She sighed out some of her fight. Stay in England? Even with the defilement of the beautiful grounds of the inn, Jess couldn't imagine living anywhere but couched within these mountains.

"I still should have been given the fair choice to decide whether I wanted my neighbors to be Germans or not, especially since one is not only my neighbor but my grandfather's assistant." The fire flickered back to life in her temper.

"You aren't at war with August or any of those men at the camp, Jessica Ross." Granny took another bite of the cake, then pointed the fork at her like a weapon. "You've gathered up your enemies for years, but not from the camp."

"What's that supposed to mean?"

"Not three weeks after your mama died, and you were packing up to return to the war." Her brow edged the words a little sharper. "Running away from your hurt, I'd reckon. And on top of all your grief, you've added these horrible pains of betrayal, David, and the war?"

Jess stood, each additional sentence stabbing fresh reminders, stings she wanted to forget. "And now I should have a daily reminder of what the war took from me by Mr. Reinhold's presence? How can you trust someone like him, let alone have him serve patients?"

"August has been a great help to us since you and David left for the war."

"How ironic then that you found a German to replace us." The words hissed with enough venom to surprise Jessica.

Her granny's gaze, hardened into a convicting gray. "We found a good and kind-hearted man to offer the same compassion our grandchildren used to give to the people of this town. Something a world broken from war needs a whole lot more than a heart filled with blind hatred."

Jess' eyes stung from the swell of tears invading her vision. They came without warning now, overwhelming and unwanted, stabbing at her weakness, reminding her of watching her mother die or her brother, David, be beaten by a German spy. Helpless. Useless. She shoved her chair back into place, her granny's truth and her own scars ripping into her like the terrors haunting her nights. Without another word, she ran from the house.

Chapter Three

August carefully put away the surgical supplies as Dr. Carter checked Mr. Buchanan in the next room. He'd never assisted in something as delicate as a blood transfusion, but the intense nature of the procedure kept his mind distracted from the seething rage burning in the eyes of the green-eyed beauty across the surgical table —or somewhat distracted. Jessica Ross proved difficult to put completely from his mind.

Her skilled fingers had moved from one step to the next, certain, and she only hesitated when she had to interact with him. His confidence wobbled a little from her clear disdain, but thanks to the letters her grandparents had shared with him over dinner, he knew the wounds beneath her anger. Scars held power, their lingering sting bleeding into the present.

Yes. He understood. His past lay stained with them, but time left him a choice—reopen the wounds with bitterness or see the scars as wrongs forgiven. He'd chosen the latter, and as each day broadened the gap between his pain and his present, the wounds hurt less. The Carters and beauty of the Blue Ridge Mountains had been God-sent balms to repair some of his brokenness into a new future. A new home.

A place to finally belong.

And Jessica Ross may not realize it yet, but August knew as certainly as the taste of rain in the afternoon air that she needed him. And he wanted her. The fire, the confidence, the family. His grin returned. He only had to convince her.

"Don't be too put off by my granddaughter, August. She's a good sort once she gets past her pride."

August finished cleaning the tubes used for the transfusion and cast another glance through the doorway to the patient, so pale and weak... with new blood pumping through his veins to replace what was lost.

August's blood.

Dr. Carter had told him his blood type was the perfect donor. O. It could be used for anyone. And so it had, three times. August always found it fascinating and rather remarkable, but from the appearance of Mr. Buchanan, not even August's blood might save the man.

August sent Dr. Carter a keen look. "You should have told her about the camp. About me. She hurts from the shock of her world changed."

Dr. Carter ran a hand through his thick hair and released a sigh, removing his surgical apron. "She needed to come home. I didn't want to give her a reason to stay away."

"She is not a child, my friend." August's grin peaked again. "Definitely not a child."

Dr. Carter shook his head with a chuckle. "You're supposed to keep those thoughts about my granddaughter in your own mind, August."

"I have a hard time with keeping important words inside."

"Well, you're going to find Jess rarely keeps her words inside, important or not. And I'm afraid this war, all this loss, has loosened her tongue even more. She doesn't always think before she speaks."

"Anger hardens the heart and softens the head," August whispered, the admission splintering with the regret he carried like the memories of a mother he'd never see again.

"Words from experience?"

Dr. Carter's emerald gaze, so like his granddaughter's, gentled with compassion. Compassion August had come to crave from this man who provided more of the image of a father than his ever had.

"I did not become a sailor out of clear thinking. I became one out anger." He tapped his forehead. "Soft-head thinking."

Dr. Carter grabbed Mr. Buchanan's wrist, checking the man's pulse again as he would do for many hours to come. "No, you don't strike me as the sailor sort."

"But it has taught me to give excellent sutures, no?"

Dr. Carter nodded and released Mr. Buchanan's arm, his face sober. "Don't you see how God can take our mistakes and turn them around? I'm grateful more than I can say for you arriving into our lives when you did. You done this old man good."

August's vision blurred from the swell of gratitude. He placed his palm to his chest. "And you've done this young man good. God has used you to soften his heart."

"It takes one wounded, hardheaded sort to recognize another. My granddaughter got it honestly, I'm afraid." Dr. Carter shook his head and slumped into a chair near the door to Mr. Buchanan's room. "And it's probably why you feel a kinship with her."

Yes. An unusual 'kinship' born from meeting her through war letters read aloud, from stories told by her grandparents, and an undeniable desire to mend her wounded heart. Something as benign as hearing those letters formed an immediate bond when he finally saw her face-to-face. He'd never nurtured the notion of love at first sight, but when she turned those bright green eyes on him, he lost his heart into her hands. "I doubt the feeling is shared, but I plan to change that."

Dr. Carter raised a doubtful brow. "Well, if anyone can test that steady patience of yours, it's going to be Jessica. You should ask the Reverend Marshall about her. I can't tell you how many times she would argue some point with him about the Good Book until one of them was proven wrong. He said she certainly kept him on his theological toes. There was this one time—"

Dr. Carter took off on a long ramble about how Jessica argued the fact that the Christmas' angel who appeared to the shepherds was named Harold because every year the congregation would sing the carol *Hark the "Harold" Angels Sing*.

August chuckled and finished cleaning up the soiled bandages. "Her humor shone through her anger, even today. Very little, but I saw it."

"I hope so, August." Dr. Carter looked up from his final check, his face sober. "I hope that underneath all of her hurt we can find the girl who left years ago."

"Or a beautiful combination of both girls, yes?"

A smile lit the older man's eyes. "Yes, I want to believe that, son."

Son. The endearment was laced with a mixture of warmth and regret every time, though the more Dr. Carter used it, the less the sting.

"By the way, I'm afraid you're gonna need a clean shirt. The apron didn't protect your sleeves."

August followed Dr. Carter's nod to the white arm of his sleeve and the splattering of blood making a trail from his wrist to his elbow.

"Doesn't this make your third ruined shirt in as many weeks?"

August shrugged with his grin. "I know a good seamstress."

Time and a glimmering hope failed to prepare her for the vision of the chapel's remains. Jessica slowed as she approached the almost hallowed site of so many childhood and family memories, a place as beautiful as the past she cradled close.

But the 1916 Flood had not only taken lives from the little town of Hot Springs, it had also snatched away something else. Pieces of her past. The chapel, once a quaint white beacon overlooking the French Broad River, lay in a tangled heap of white-washed boards and time-worn debris. Once hemmed in on three sides by the forest, now saplings grew up through the center of the broken floorboards. Walls left open to the elements failed to resemble the once beautiful chapel her father had built for her mother before their wedding day. The place where she'd hoped to marry as well.

It housed thousands of precious memories, from the small services held by Reverend Marshall or even Rev Dorland, to Christmas celebrations, to Jessica's own personal recognition of the grace of God. But now, only fragmented boards and weather-beaten rubble remained, a picture as broken and unused as her faith and a visual reminder of all she'd lost.

She stumbled forward, gripping at the trunk of a tree for stability, but her knees gave way and she crumbled to the ground at what used to be the chapel's entrance. Visions of holding her mother's hand at her deathbed two years earlier vied with a mental carousel of David's lifeless face, or the myriad of other men she'd watched die from the wounds of war.

She'd known the flood threatened the building, but she couldn't bear visiting the site after her mother's death so the stark reality of the damage hit an agonizing blow. After all the pain, this one sweet, beautiful thing lay in shambles like everything else? Wasn't there anything unchanging on which to cling? Anything certain?

"Why?" Her question raked across her dry throat. She clawed at the damp ground and turned her face to the graying sky. "Why?" Her voice rose louder, piercing the tranquil forest sounds with a frantic longing. "You've taken so much from me already, did you have to take this too?" Her voice fell to a desperate whisper. "How can you see what's happening and stay so silent?"

A warm wind rustled the leaves above her, cooling the tears on her cheeks, but there was no voice, no calm... no answer. She squeezed her eyes closed and pushed herself up from the ground, hardening her heart against hope. No. She was finished with holding a faith that dangled her on an imaginary thread.

She stepped forward into the rubble, the broken past. A single pew sat in the center of the mess, broken glass and ragged wooden planks scattered all around it. The life she knew in Hot Springs lay as wrecked as the church... or the battlefields of France. It was time to start over and bury the hurt along with countless men and women she'd watched die. And maybe her dwindling faith deserved a place alongside the memories too. Long gone.

Her harsh response to her grandmother came back to mind and hammered into her bitterness. Jess wiped away the remnant of tears and sighed out into the silence. Her grandmother didn't deserve Jess' rage. Oh no, only God should be the beneficiary... along with the entire camp of Germans on the other side of town.

Including August Reinhold.

The further she stayed away from him, the better for all involved.

She turned and started at a march up the overgrown path, ignoring the whispers of wind that called her to enjoy the birdsong serenade. Visiting the demolished chapel proved slowing down opened her heart to loss with enough force to consume her.

She forged ahead, forcing the tears to dry. The stone cottage, her parents' haven, emerged to her right, but she ignored the pull to relax her pace at the once welcome threshold.

Her grandparents needed to become her focus, along with stepping back into the profession which filled her with purpose and occupation. The past offered little for comfort, and her faith? She shook her head. Even less.

She took the porch steps and walked through the back door of the farmhouse. Granny stood in the kitchen, almost as Jessica had left her.

"I shouldn't have taken my anger out on you." She stopped at the doorframe of the room and ran a calming hand down her long braid. "Please forgive me."

Granny walked over and rested her palm on Jessica's cheek, her gray eyes brimming with enough compassion to reawaken those feelings she'd left in the forest. "Jesse, I can't understand all you've endured these years in Europe, but I do know what it's like to grieve."

"I know you do." Jess covered Granny's hand with her own, pride bowing even more to the knowledge that her Granny had lost a daughter, both parents, and a son within the course of her life, not to mention a myriad of friends along the way.

Death was no respecter of persons. Neither was grief.

"You're not alone, little girl. You've never been alone in your whole life." She patted Jess' cheek and stepped back. "Remember that, once the anger fades."

Jess bit back a retort. Granny understood loss, but not the soul-stripping pain of watching tens of men die. Or the utter helplessness of being overpowered by a traitor. Jess couldn't cling to the promises of a God who moved everyone around like pawns on a crooked chessboard and then expected them to still worship Him. A faith with such twisted implications only tightened the knot of acidic anger. Too many scars ripped across her heart to keep her grip on Someone who failed to stop the horrible agonies of war and betrayal. And despite her grandparents' current admiration for the Germans, Jess could never trust them. Not after all they'd done.

But a question whispered over the hardened shell of her heart. Her granny, with all her loss? Her grandpa, with the thousands of people he'd watched die throughout his career as a mountain doctor? Neither seemed weak to cling to, and even celebrate, their faith. How could she reconcile the contradiction? Faith and loss? Strength and brokenness?

She shielded her thoughts against the hope. A deceitful light as brilliant as Lucifer himself. The tenderness in her granny's expression threatened to undo Jess' fragile emotions so she looked out the window, out onto the vast back lawn which reached to the tree line. A movement from the cottage drew her gaze to the inviting red door framed with the earthen hues of field stone.

A man stepped from the cottage. Jess leaned closer, examining the strong, lean form. Didn't her granny say they'd rented the house to a woman? A widow? As the stranger turned, golden hair shining like a halo in the sunlight, his face became clear.

Jessica's stomach pinched.

August Reinhold.

She narrowed her eyes. Someone that handsome *and* German had to be up to no good, and this sneaking around proved her point. She'd catch him before he slid back to town without enough sense to be ashamed of visiting a young widow unchaperoned.

Jess moved toward the back door. "Who did you say rented Daddy and Mama's cottage?"

Granny shot her a look of pure confusion. "Widow. Come down to be close to family."

Family, my eye. Jessica growled and reached for the back door knob, jerking it wide, only to come face-to-face with the fallen angel himself. Complete with that infuriating golden lock brushing over his forehead like a temptation.

August had no chance to knock before the door flung wide and he stared directly into the face that had filled his musings the entire walk. Her wide eyes, emeralds of emotion, narrowed after a moment and she crossed her arms in front of her chest.

"What are you doing here?"

"Do you play lawn badminton?"

The question served its purpose by distracting her from whatever dislike she nursed against him... or rather Germany in its entirety.

Both golden brows fluttered high. "What?"

"Do you play lawn badminton?" He gestured toward the net in the grassy field stretching between the two houses.

Her attention followed the wave of his hand and then moved back to his face, narrowed eyes zeroing in along with her whisper. "I saw you come out of the cottage, so you don't fool me. I know you're up to something."

How could her misdirected fury be so charming? Why not feed the flame, nein? He lowered his voice to hers and topped his grin with a wink. "All sorts of mischief, Nurse Ross. Saving lives and visiting widows."

He'd caught her off-guard, but it only took a moment for her to recover her fire. "Clearly, I'm the only one who can see through this..." She waved a palm in the air toward his face. "Handsome and generous façade. You might have fooled the entire town of Hot Springs, but you haven't fooled me. I've been in the trenches. I know what your kind are really capable of."

He leaned in toward the flame. "Do you think me handsome?"

She groaned and rolled her eyes. "That's all you heard?"

He shrugged. "I like the sound of it better than the nonsense."

Her palms landed on her hips in battle stance, but her grandmother intervened.

"August." Mrs. Carter's arms widened in customary welcome. "What brings you out to the farm?"

He caught a glimpse of Jessica's glare from over Mrs. Carter's hug.

"I came to collect some provisions for your good husband, Mrs. Carter. As well as a change of clothes."

"And why didn't grandpa come on his own?" Jessica tilted her chin as if she'd unraveled some secret scheme of his.

August's grin spread wide, enjoying a boyish fascination with her ire. "Because Mr. Buchanan was afraid I would finish the job the fall started for his father. He trusts me as much as you, I'm afraid."

"You can't win over everyone, August. Though only the blind and foolish fail to see what a joy you are." Mrs. Carter shot her granddaughter a pointed look, inspiring August's smile anew. "I'm surprised you didn't see Jessica on your walk to the farm. She just returned from the chapel."

"Or where the chapel used to be," Jessica murmured, slipping away from the door and back toward the kitchen, her simple blue dress bringing out the golden hues of her hair even more. Yes, in person was much better than letters.

"The chapel? Where your daughter was married?"

"Same." Mrs. Carter nodded toward Jess. "Jess got quite a shock from the mess of it now. A devastated mess." She walked to a hutch by the door and took a picture from its shelf. "Here it is the summer before the flood."

August's chest deflated. Jessica's mother's last summer.

He took the picture, examining it with careful hands. The faces drew him closer. A woman, undoubtedly Jessica's mother, stood supported by a man August recognized from a previous portrait the Carters had shown him of Jessica's father. Jessica stood to the other side as the bookend of support for the mother. The chapel rose behind them in the background, a simple yet delicate construction of painted white wood and hand-carved adornment.

"There is strong craftsmanship." He looked up in time to see grief marking the frown on Jessica's face before she cloaked it behind a well-placed snarl. "Not difficult to reproduce."

Jessica took the picture from him. "No one can replace it."

"Now, I wouldn't toss out the idea altogether, girl." Mrs. Carter moved to her usual place behind the counter and began piecing together a sacked meal. "You see that chair in the corner there?"

Jess gaze slipped from his and followed her grandmother's gesture to the oak rocking chair.

"It was in shambles before August got his hands on it. Broken pieces, torn cloth. I'd kept it in the barn loft to use for kindlin' come winter, but August took it and fixed it up. Did the same to one of my tables and your brother's bed. He's got a real gift for doctorin' up broken things."

Jessica sliced him a look smothered in doubt, renewing the challenge to make her like him... or at the very least, help her find her smile. "It's difficult to break something that is already broken, so of course, I appear the wonder."

"You worked wonders, I'll say." Mrs. Carter waved a fried chicken leg at him before depositing it in the sack. "I gave that chair and table up for scrap."

"I've always enjoyed creating with wood." The admission faltered, shrouded in darker memories. "But a skill not encouraged by mein Vater." He bowed his head in apology, and quickly corrected to English. "My father."

Mrs. Carter's understanding smile smoothed away some of the residual sting of his father's harshness. "Well, it's appreciated here." She placed the sack up on the counter. "I have some fresh cookies you ought to take with you on the walk back to town."

"How is it you have sugar in this time of no sugar?"

Mrs. Carter dusted off her hands and turned to the cookie jar. "Molasses."

August looked to Jessica for clarification, which she gave with a reluctant shrug. "We have a molasses tree on our property, so Granny will leave the jar of molasses open and the top crystalizes into sugar."

"Which allows me to have just a little extra on those ration days."

"You are amazing, Mrs. Carter."

The woman's eyes sparkled. "No, I'm just a woman desperate for sugar. We all have our secret passions."

"Or not so secret," Jessica interjected, the faintest hint of a smile lighting the corners of her pink lips in response to her grandmother's infectious mirth.

The softening produced a beautiful breach in the frown he'd come to recognize as commonplace and kindled a desire to uncover the smile lost behind all of her brokenness.

She looked over at him and the hint faded, and the disapproving frown returned.

It was a good thing August believed in miracles.

Chapter Four

"You were right."

Cliff Carter looked up from his post at the front gate of the internment camp and tipped his grin. "This should not be a surprise, August." He patted August's shoulder as he passed beyond the barbed wired fence into the Lower Lawn of the Inn's grounds. "But to which of my many predictions do you refer?"

"Your lovely cousin."

Cliff's lips took a downward turn and he winced. "Bad?"

August folded his arms across his chest and sighed.

Cliff tipped his hat back and whistled, his gray eyes lighting with their customary twinkle. "Can't say I didn't warn ya."

"I had hoped for a different outcome. Especially after I saved her life."

"What?" Cliffs question burst with humor.

August shrugged away the disappointment and reminded himself of the bits Dr. and Mrs. Carter had shared of Jessica's tragedies in the war, particularly her brother's near-death at the hands of a German, no less.

"She threatened me, too."

Cliff's chuckle turned into a full laugh. He removed his cap to reveal his dark ginger hair. "Yep, that sounds like my cousin. I tried to warn you, friend." He waved the cap toward August before returning it to his head. "Does Jess' warm reception change your plans?"

The teasing tilt of Cliff's smile sparked August's grin. "No, but I should have liked it to be easier."

Cliff gestured toward the expansive complex strewn across the lawn and the remains of a golf course. The inn rose in front of them, overlooking the grounds like a sentry, its mossy green roofs blending into the lush leaves completing the forests on the surrounding mountainsides. "I don't think anything worth having is going to be easy, August."

"I shouldn't mind a few easy conquests for a change."

Cliff's laugh rang out and he thumbed over his shoulder in the general direction of the Carters. "Then you should have chosen a different blonde in town."

August chuckled, shaking his head and walking toward the inn across the massive front lawn of the Mountain Park Hotel. Jessica Ross brought a swirl of contradicting visions to mind. Her stubborn silence during the surgery paired with her calm logic. Her double-edged humor. The softening of gentleness over her stoic expression at her first glimpse of her grandfather.

That look told him more than words. More than wounds.

The breeze whispered warm against his cheeks, ushering in hints of summer on the honeysuckle air. August glanced up into the waning sky, humming with the orange and red hues of sunset. He paused to breathe in the beauty, a new view each evening as the Blue Mountains framed the sky on every side of the small town. Home? Yes.

Rising above a crop of aged trees and the clutter of surrounding barracks, an elaborate complex of board and wire fencing contrasted with the elegance of the elegant inn. August paused in his steps to appreciate the three-story structure as the fading hues of daylight haloed its whitewashed walls with a golden glow. The rich green roof capped the top in pointy spires at each end of the long, window-lined structure, giving it the faintest appearance of a castle.

Though August's home failed to match the size of the 200-room inn, he knew the finery in such a distinguished lifestyle. Servants, the newest amenities, and a father who favored wealth and expectation over family. In hindsight, it was good his elder brother fit the mold his father carved with an iron grasp, leaving August freedom enough to disappoint the patriarch in almost every possible way.

The slow-healing wound awakened the familiar ache, the longing for what might have been. His father fell prey to a generations' curse of wealth, power, and the ultimate corruption—a pattern August used an ocean and a thousand hate-filled words to sever.

Lovelessness.

The pale stone of his family's ancestral home, an estate conquering an entire landscape near Frankfurt, displayed the picture well. Powerful, intriguing, cold... a dying hope. A white-washed tomb.

August bathed the pain in a prayer, accepting the scars left behind from a family life as war-torn as any battlefield, and finished his walk up the lane to the inn. Only the ships' officers enjoyed the accommodations of the inn, but August's service to one of the captains allowed him a place in the barracks near the inn on the Lower Lawn. And though sharing three or more men to a room in the beautiful inn, with its electric lights and steam heat, might have been an adjustment for some of the officers, it was a vast improvement over the bunk-lined barracks heated with stoves. Especially in an Appalachian winter.

August slid in the side door of the inn and donned an apron to assist in serving the officers, a routine duty which also kept him abreast of pertinent information. The white-columned dining hall stretched before him, still with its original elegance though now housing seamen instead of guests. A variety of officers occupied the black leather chairs, mostly men from German and Austrian ships detained in port when America joined the war over a year before. A year as an 'enemy alien,' exchanging the cage of a ship for the wire fencing of the internment camp. His grin curled. The rolling hills of the Blue Ridge Mountains provided a sweet comfort to him the mighty waves never had—healing through the kindness and friendship of the Carters.

"They mean to move us. Soon."

The quiet conversation drew August closer to a table where Captains Nisse and Luther sat in close proximity.

"Bah." Captain Ruser waved away the words, his white brows crimped. "And where would they send us. Why? We've done nothing to bring trouble."

"Most of us did nothing to bring capture on our heads either, yet here we are." Captain Luther gestured to the room. "Prisoners."

Ruser's laughed echoed up to the elaborately ornamented ceiling. "Prisoners? Here?" He patted his belly and caught sight of August bringing fresh coffee to their table. "What say you, Reinhold? Do you think this is the way prisoners live?"

August's grin twitched as he took another glance over the mahogany furnishings and elegant room.

"Ah, see. This is a palace compared to Oglethorpe where the true prisoners go. We are not prisoners. We are..." He waved a hand in the air. "Guests on a leash."

Luther slammed his hand against the table. "I tell you, Ruser, I heard Polk say it himself. The government is making plans to move us, and soon."

The previous calm in August's chest fisted tight. Move?

"Don't fret, Reinhold. Luther's creating a thunderstorm on a clear day. We are safe from Oglethorpe and the other prison camps for now. Let the storm come when it will, but don't seek it."

August met Luther's dark eyes but quickly turned to help in the kitchens. After years of searching and praying for a place to belong, he'd found it nestled between these quiet mountains, and the last place he wanted to go was somewhere else.

―

A shell burst to Jess' right, knocking her to the soggy ground and sending a shudder throughout her damp body. She pressed her hands into the clammy soil and pushed up to her feet, only to quake again at another explosion. Bursts of light flashed in time with the deafening thud of detonation, but she pushed forward, determined to make it to the shelter of the Casualty Clearing Station.

She wiped the mud against her filthy apron but the dampness remained, clinging to her skin more than it should. In the light of the next blast she looked down at her palms. Her skin rushed cold. Bright red stained her hands. Blood. She stumbled back, the light of another explosion glowing off the pale, lifeless faces of hundreds of corpses strewn across the war-torn field. Some she could name. Others blended in to the thousands covered in the memory and mud of a senseless war.

Smoke rose around her, before her, in an unearthly cloud of sickening green. She pulled her apron up to cover her nose and mouth, stifling a scream, but a vision appeared through the cloud. The haunting figure stepped from the smoke, the face free of any mask to protect him as if, by some supernatural power, he withstood the mustard gas. His black eyes bored into her, igniting a tremor and shaking her to her knees. Perhaps he'd always been inhuman. A demon. The shadow lingering in the darkness behind every choice, every fear.

He stalked toward her and she felt his touch while he was still out of reach... his rancid breath, hot and horrible against her throat, his forceful lips against hers. His cold hands moving over her skin, scratching and pawing like the monster he was.

His fingers, stained with the same death-hue as hers, reached out to her, a warning, a promise of the violence to follow. A scream lodged in her throat, dying against the fear snatching her breath. With steel fingers, he gripped her arms, pinching into her flesh. She squeezed her eyes closed to avoid his heated gaze, flailing against his hold as his talons stabbed more firmly into her.

"Jessica."

She fought, but the hands held fast.

"Jessica, honey. Wake up."

The voice, firm but ever so familiar, pierced into the shadows, lighting her mind. A rescuer? The hold on her arms loosened, and she worked to open her heavy eyelids.

"Come on, sweet girl. No one's going to hurt you."

Granny? The darkness dispersed as light seeped beneath her lashes. Her granny's face came into view by lantern light. Sweat dampened Jessica's skin with a sticky chill. She shivered and drew the blankets in to her chest as her granny's palms wiped cool tears from her face.

"It was a dream."

"A nightmare. The same nightmare. Over and over again." Her words dissolved into a trail of sobs and she fought against another chill squeezing between her shoulder blades. "So many faces."

Granny's arms wrapped around her, warm and safe, a comforting respite from the gnawing fear. The weakness—the bone-tired weakness—peeled through her body and pushed her further into her granny's arms.

"I need to be strong, to get through this. Why can't I be strong? Why..." She clutched her granny's arm, a new wave of tears blurring her vision. "I'm anxious all of the time. My heart... it's never quiet. I want to run away from my own skin, but I can't escape."

Her granny's rough palm smoothed back her damp hair then rested on her cheek, guiding her attention into those knowing, compassionate eyes. "You're broken, girl. Filled with so many wounds and scars."

Jessica reached to cover the wretched mark down her neck, but granny shook her head.

"Those aren't the scars that bind you as much as the ones on the inside." She spun a golden lock of Jess' hair around her finger. "You need time and love to help you heal."

Jess pulled back, wiping her fingers over her damp face. "I just want one ounce of peace. One hour of restful sleep. One night without..." A sob closed over her words. "One night without... without the fear."

"Home and love are good places to start with your fight against fear." Granny gave Jess' cheek a gentle pat. "And a way to find your faith."

"Faith?" She bit back a very uncharitable retort and wiped at her face with her hand. Pushing back the blankets, she reached for her robe and sent her granny an apologetic glance. "I'm sorry I woke you."

Granny grinned, but her eyes kept a sober stare. "Don't worry about me. When you reach a certain age, you don't sleep no how. Or at least not the same hours you did when you was young."

Jessica tightened the belt around her waist and allowed a smile to settle on her face. Despite the wrinkles from age and trouble on her grandmother's face, an aura of welcome surrounded her—like a warm hearth on a snowy day... or a refuge in a heart-wrenching storm.

"You know what your grandpa would suggest under such circumstances?"

Jessica's grin twitched a little wider, welcoming the distraction and terrified to release the hope Granny offered in the face of such darkness. How could Jessica grasp such a slippery hope when its promises appeared so fleeting and inconsistent? "A midnight snack sets the appetite to rights, both in body and mind."

Granny chuckled, linking an arm through Jessica's and stepping to the door. "Not much sense in it, I suppose, but it's served your grandpa well these many years. I think we ought to try it."

Jessica stopped at the stairs, the lingering shadows calling her from the darkened bedroom. Moonlight paved the stairway in a beautiful halo of white. "Thank you, Granny."

Granny's jaw took on a fighting tension in the pale light and she tightened her grip on Jessica's arm. "We'll get through this together, girl." Her gray gaze bored deep, holding strength and promise Jessica couldn't find. Couldn't grasp. "You're not alone. Never have been. Never will be."

Jessica hadn't taken much notice of the little town when she'd left the train depot in such an angry state the day before. So focused on speaking her mind to her grandfather and placing as much distance between the infernal Germans and herself, she'd failed to notice a fully repaired bridge crossing the French Broad. Grandpa had spoken of how the Flood tore it down, but there it stood, connecting tiny Hot Springs to the other side of the river.

In the two years since her mother's death, Hot Springs remained the same—a few buildings huddled together along a dusty main street encapsulated by a hedge of mountains. The impressively large depot topped the hill from the Inn, and the street made a gradual decline into town. The Mercantile stood ceremoniously as the most recognizable feature except for the Iron Horse Tavern and the Presbyterian church steeple, the latter two on opposite sides of town for the good of both parties... and the spouses who claimed them.

The smell of fresh-hewn pine—no doubt from Mr. Kimper's widdling habit—and a conglomeration of spices mixed with tin greeted her as she stepped into the familiar shop. A sweet warmth pooled through her at the faithful consistency of the scene. Other than a few new items on the shelves, Kimper's Mercantile looked exactly the same as she'd left it—a grab-bag of necessary items all in one place.

Shelves to her left displayed canned food of all varieties, with the coveted flour and sugar housed safely behind Mr. Kimper's counter. A few ready-made garments hung on a rack to the right. Nothing like Madame Rouselle's famous boutique back in her father's childhood town of Ednesbury, but impressive for the small mountain town. Jessica's sister-in-law, Catherine, would love the opportunity to revolutionize the fashion of rural little Hot Springs.

Hot Springs wasn't prepared for that sort of fiery revolution.

Jess' smile spread at the thought of her spirited sister-in-law and her gentle brother. What a combination! A perfect complement of personalities in the most unexpected of ways.

A toy fighter plane hung by a string from the ceiling, encouraging little American boys to play the war from home. Jessica grimaced. Too many boys lost that game in real life.

Only a few people shopped in the mercantile. The top of a man's head rose over a shelf in the back, and a woman waited by the counter. The quiet, predictable small-town life unwound the tension in Jess' shoulders.

"Jessica Ross?"

The thick-shouldered clerk, Mr. Enoch Kimper, gave an enthusiastic pat to the counter which caused the waiting woman to jump.

"Good morning, Mr. Kimper."

"I heard you'd arrived. Why, Stanley Donaldson's already spread the news from Marshall to Asheville, if I know him."

Jess had often heard other people refer to Kimp as a gruff sort, but she'd only known the welcome side of the mountain-of-a-man. Grandpa said it was because Jess tutored Kimp's son, Frank, in reading and math while they attended the little two-room school.

"I'm certain you exaggerate." Though most likely not.

He laughed, a loud, hearty sound filling the shop, and then he tipped his head in her direction. "I have something for you."

The glint in his eyes gave his intentions away and unfolded Jessica's smile in anticipation. Kimp reached into the icebox and unveiled an ice cold Dr. Pepper. Jess mouth watered from the sight. It had been two years since she'd tasted the sweet fizz of her favorite drink. An unexpected laugh bubbled from her throat.

"Mr. Kimper, you are my current favorite person."

He popped the top of the glass bottle and handed it over the counter. "You've done too much for my son. This is the least I can offer."

She took the offering and raised it to her lips, the soda pop almost too sweet to her taste buds—but so good. "Thank you, Mr. Kimper. And how is Frank?"

Mr. Kimper's face fell and he finished ringing up the woman waiting before he answered. "Sent a letter that he'd arrived safe in France." He hesitated, leaning against the counter. "Is it really as bad as they say?"

Jess paused, contemplating her answer. Soften the blow? She pinched her eyes closed and sighed out a long stream of air before meeting the man's gaze. No, families needed to know the truth. "I won't lie to you, Kimp. It's worse."

Kimp looked down and braced his palms against the counter. "Oh, God, help him."

She covered one of his hands with her own. "But with America joining, this war should be over much more quickly, and then Frank and our other boys can come home. We need them there so Germany wouldn't take over the whole world like it's taking over our town."

Too late. She hadn't caught her bitter response in time, and Kimp's brows responded to the fury.

"I'm sorry. You know me. I speak before I think sometimes."

"Seems only right, you having a hard time with them being here. Especially since they left you crippled."

Jess reached for her braid and bit back a verbal tirade against his choice of words. She wasn't crippled. Wounded, but not crippled. Those were two very different things. "How's the town handled them?"

He shrugged his big shoulder. "We had a little trouble in the beginning—nothing big, but enough to bring attention—but for the past eight months, nothin'. Been good for business, in fact. I'm sure it practically saved the Inn from closing down as much money as it was losin' before the war."

Jess ignored any thoughts of good coming from Germans invading her little town. "Well, I'm glad the Inn is safe."

"But it's a wonder your grandpa can serve as a doctor for them folks, knowing what you and your brother have been through.

Even hiring one of 'em to help in the clinic? He must be closer to God than me, 'cause I don't reckon I could stomach helping any of 'em if they hurt one of my kind."

Jess took another drink of the Dr. Pepper and avoided meeting Kimp's eyes. As much as Kimp's statement burned a deeper line in her own resentment, she couldn't harbor ill will towards her Grandpa. His sturdy, consistent kindness and ready generosity beat against her anger like a steady rain, cooling the flames.

"Grandpa's always tried to look for the best in people. I can find fault in many things, as you well know." Kimp's smile returned, no doubt conjuring up memories of his many childhood exploits in correcting all the wrongs of Hot Springs. A warm rush blushed her cheeks. Saving the world turned out to be much more painful than a ten-year-old could imagine. "But I can't fault with his goodness."

Kimp shook her head. "No, I reckon not."

Jess offered him the list her grandmother provided. "I'd like to pick up Granny's order."

Kimp quickly gathered the items together and placed them in a small box, glancing down at her cane again. "Are you certain you don't need help with these?"

The warmth in her cheek brightened. "No, thank you." She released a stream of air through her clenched smile, calming herself. "But I appreciate your offer." She toasted him with her Dr. Pepper bottle. "And thank you for the pop."

"I'll keep a stash for ya, Jesse-girl, rations or not."

The previous irritation fled with her grin. "Like I said, Kimp, you are one of my favorite people."

His chuckle followed her to the front of the store where a stranger appeared from the left and pushed the door wide. A brown Fedora, tilted in a fashionable way, topped his wealth of wavy hair. He'd loosened his tie to release the tension on his white collar, and his well-made suit jacket hung open. He wasn't from Hot Springs.

Jess looked up into eyes as dark as fresh molasses. His swept-back hair ran a shade darker, bringing out rich black rims around his irises. "Thank you."

He touched the tip of his hat, his grin sloped in the flattering way she'd witnessed among hundreds of soldiers. She squelched an eye-roll and maneuvered through the doorway, only to wobble at the threshold between managing her cane and the box of supplies, spilling two items to the floor.

"Let me get those for you." He swept down to retrieve them. "I wouldn't envy you returning home without this." He held out her coveted bag of sugar as if he offered a glass slipper. "Your husband will miss his sweet bread."

Oh, he oozed charm like an expensive cologne, and his accent only enhanced the air of sophistication. English. But why on earth would an educated man from across the globe show up in her little town? She'd play his game to find out. "Probably not, since I haven't met him yet."

"How unfortunate for him."

She stepped outside and turned back to face the handsome stranger. "I have every hope he'll make up for his tardiness."

"If he doesn't, I'd say he wasn't meant for you." The stranger stepped out of the shop along with her, closing the door behind him.

"Clever." She propped her cane against her leg and offered her hand. "Jessica Ross."

She looked down, expecting him to take her offering, only to see he didn't have a right hand—amputated, full up to his elbow.

She lowered her palm. "I'm sorry."

"German shell." He shrugged. "A nasty by-product of war, as you are keenly aware, I hear."

His gaze dropped to her cane. Charming and an eavesdropper? The faintest hint of warning rose its ugly head. For months, maybe even years, she'd fought a battle with an undercurrent of paranoia. Ever since one of the doctors she worked with at the Front turned out to be a German spy, capturing her and her brother, strangers produced an unsettling suspicion. Having a whole internment camp of them nearly stabbed like hundreds of knives into her nerve-endings.

"Jasper Little, at your service, Miss Ross."

She surveyed him with fresh eyes. A soldier and Englishman? Already they had an entire backstory in common.

"What happened?" Her directness might have put off a civilian, but not those who'd seen the terrors of war. Candor came as a welcome alternative to uncomfortable stares and nervous glances.

He breathed out a sigh and removed his hat, running a hand through the dark masses of his hair. Despite his obvious and life-altering wound, he bore an easy confidence. Charismatic. A noteworthy accomplishment, at any rate.

Or maybe it cloaked some insecurities.

War left many scars, unseen.

Another commonality.

His dark eyes gave nothing away. Steady. Unswerving, with a certainty she admired.

"Gangrene set in from a wound to my palm. There was nothing else to be done."

She nodded and turned, beginning her walk to her grandfather's clinic. He kept in step. "And how did an Englishman find his way to our small town?"

His eyes widened with the first sign of authenticity she'd seen in his face. "You know the accent? From your work in the war effort?"

"My father is English." The question in his gaze urged her to explain. "My mother was from this town, but my great aunt bestowed on her the gift of education. My parents met when she studied abroad."

"I can see how the mountain culture can bring with it a certain appeal."

His attention never left her face and another uncustomary blush stole into her cheeks at his poignant perusal. "I doubt the mountain appeal is what brought you to our particular part of Appalachia."

He chuckled and placed his hat back on his head. "You do get back to the point, don't you?"

"Makes it easier to dodge bullets when they're coming at you."

His dark gaze zeroed in on hers, serious and unreadable. "True." He looked ahead of them as they came to the Spring Creek Bridge. "It's rather an interesting story, really. Before the war, I was a history professor. American culture, particularly Southern American culture, was a unique interest of mine. I'd started studying the works of various researchers on the topic, its music and language—which mirrored much of the English culture."

"Older English culture." Jess added with a grin.

"Exactly. When I was called up to serve in the war, my history degree was little help, but I worked with one of the medics and began serving in some ways with him. It was difficult work, but rewarding in its own way."

She stopped to cross the street, studying him for a hint of duplicity or any authentic emotion whatsoever. "So you've come to the tiny town of Hot Springs to... be a medic?"

He pulled her arm through his and started across the dusty road. Jess stiffened against his touch, uncomfortable at his quick familiarity. Though she'd spent years among young men of various personalities and types, she'd packed any dreams for romance behind a myriad of disappointments. With her wounds, the dreams evaporated into forever. But she couldn't deny the pleasant warmth accompanying his touch and attention. After all the doubt from being damaged goods, could there be romance in her future?

Hope proved a precarious perch at best, a path to despair at worst.

"Actually, I've resorted to my previous interests. Your culture." He helped her up the curb. "I stumbled upon Cecil Sharpe's recent publications and am trying to follow up on his research."

It was her turn for surprise. "On balladry?"

He nodded, his smile coming unhinged once again and drawing hers out. He continued walking with her as she maneuvered down the side street to her grandfather's clinic. "It's an easy transition. Your English background should strengthen your knowledge of the history. Most of the ballads woven into the fabric of our culture stem from our English and Scottish ancestors."

"Exactly." His dark eyes glinted with excitement. "And should Mrs. Jane Gentry still be alive...?"

"Oh, she's very much alive and running a boarding house down the street." She stopped in front of the clinic.

"Excellent." He tipped his head toward her. "And I'd like to be of assistance to your grandfather, if I may. I don't have formal training, of course, but I'm willing help."

A smile shifted from an evolving idea directly to her lips. Perhaps a little encouragement for her grandfather to accept Mr. Little's help might naturally lead to a cessation of German influences in her family's life. Particularly August Reinhold's presence.

Perhaps Jasper Little was the perfect excuse to keep Germans, and their influences, behind their blessed fence and out of her life for good.

Chapter Five

August finished wrapping a fresh bandage over Mr. Buchanan's leg wound. The man's deep, even breaths gave no indication of the healing taking place within... or not. It had been a long night for the good Dr. Carter, and August moved quietly across the wooden floor as the doctor snored from a chair in the corner of the room. Though August attempted to fix his attention on the work at hand, Luther's warning cast a shadow over his thoughts. Eleven months ago, when the train first deposited him in this tiny town, he'd craved a way out, even contemplated escape, but not now.

From the welcome morning sky rising over a wall of blue mountains to the friendly townspeople to the hushed evening birdsong and cricket calls, this place breathed of home, of life.

He stood from his place, careful to keep his movements quiet to ensure Dr. Carter's continued rest, restoring various bottles to their places on the shelf. As he lifted the last container to its designated location, a movement outside the window caught his attention. A couple, arm-in-arm, walked down the lane toward the clinic.

He tightened his grip on the bottle in his hand. Jessica Ross looked dazzling in a pale blue frock, her large white hat tilted to one side so that only a section of her face brimmed from beneath. She smiled—a small smile with a clever twist to one side, but more than she'd offered to him.

And who was this stranger? A medium-sized fellow, lean, smartly dressed, and extremely close to August's future bride. August's fingers clattered over the bottles, sending one nearly toppling to the floor.

"I'm not liking the look of this head wound, August."

August pulled his attention away from the pair in the window and back to Dr. Carter, who stood over the pale patient fighting for his life.

"Maybe, if he makes it through one more night, we shall see a change, but I dare not leave him yet."

August glanced back over his shoulder at the pair getting closer to the clinic and his agitation burned in the pit of his stomach. But what right did he have for jealousy? Nein. He could claim no hold on her interest or her future, let alone her heart.

"I'm sorry for the prolonged anxiety, good friend." August would not succumb to the failures in his past. God had brought him beyond those glaring accusations and supported him with acceptance beyond his flaws. "You have worked tirelessly and there may yet bear fruit from your labors."

Dr. Carter bestowed his kind smile, a welcome balm over August's agitation. "And there you go, as usual. Bringing sunshine into the storm."

And yet, still left in the rain alone, it would seem. What a fool! To imagine there could be a romance between the two of them? He'd known her, through those letters, for months, but she had no idea who he was… and even more, hated him because of his Fatherland. How could he win with such an offense against him?

He shrugged off the melancholy and braced himself for the ensuing thunder with lovely blonde hair.

"Patience is certainly the miracle-worker at times, this is true. Patience and consistent care."

And a miracle seemed the only option for Mr. Buchanan's survival and August's intentions for Jessica Ross. Patience and consistent care? *Oh, God, help him!*

The door jingled with its opening, bringing Jessica, the stranger, and a cool breeze inside. Her emerald gaze scanned the room, taking inventory, it seemed, and finally landed on him. A frown slipped the previous smile away.

"Good morning, Grandpa." She graced August with another look and tipped her head. "Mr. Reinhold."

August responded in kind but Dr. Carter moved across the room, wiping his hands off on his apron as he approached. "Granddaughter." Dr. Carter turned to the stranger. "And this is?"

"Jasper Little." Jessica continued, her welcome smile returning.

August nearly dropped another bottle. Her smile lit her entire face... entrancing. Oh, to have it land on him.

"We met over at Kimp's. He's only now arrived in town and I wonder if Mr. Little might not be useful to you."

Dr. Carter exchanged a glance with August and then placed his palm to his chest. "To me?"

Something about newcomer bit into August's optimism like a storm cloud in a blue sky, and it had to be more than a bout of jealousy at the way Mr. Little looked at Jessica.

"He assisted medics at the Front and now he's come to follow up with Mr. Cecil Sharpe's balladry research," Jessica said.

"The Englishman who recorded Jane Gentry singing all those folk songs?" Dr. Carter gestured toward the wall on the same side as Sunnybank Boarding house, where the kind woman lived as proprietor and Hot Springs' vigilant storyteller.

"Precisely." The man spoke for the first time, stepping forward and sweeping his cap off his head. "Before the war, I was a history professor, you see, but I'm certain to have spare time as I interview some of the mountain folk. I'd be happy to offer any assistance I can."

Mr. Little's voice pearled with culture and the beloved accent of the English. No, he'd not be shunned or ridiculed as the Germans. All he need do was open his mouth with silver-tongued elegance and see women melt into a ridiculous swoon. August swallowed a groan. *English!*

"August has been a great help to me." Dr. Carter's smile curbed some of the edge in August's internal monologue. "But he has a new project to see to, so this might be the perfect time to take some more help." Dr. Carter reached out a palm to the stranger, which was when August noticed Mr. Little's absent hand. Dr. Carter hesitated. "I'm sorry."

Mr. Little grinned and offered his left hand. "I still have one useful hand the Germans didn't steal, Dr. Carter, and am keen to serve. The war didn't steal my determination to do the right thing."

The man's gaze met August's with like-suspicion, his lips twitching into a smile that failed to reach his dark eyes. *Unruhestifter.* Trouble maker. Why would this stranger hold such venom against August—a man he'd never clapped eyes on until this very moment? The pinch in his spirit twisted more tightly.

August hated intimidation. He offered his left hand and smiled his greeting, without looking away. "August Reinhold."

The slightest hestitation caught in Mr. Little's greeting before he grasped August's hand. "Reinhold?" The stranger pinched August's hand before releasing, never breaking eye contact.

Trouble.

"August has been working with me for a good eight months. One of the best assistants I've had since Jess left."

"You've always been a supporter of free labor?" Jessica's brow arched with a pinpoint of purpose all too clear in her entreaty.

Dr. Carter placed his hands on his hips and nodded. "I do my regular rounds on Tuesdays and Thursdays. What say you come with me Tuesday next?"

Jessica's brow crinkled with her frown. August pinched his lips to keep his grin from sliding wide. Frontlines or not, traipsing through the wilds of Western North Carolina was not for the faint of heart. He slid Dr. Carter a glance from his periphery. The clever doctor knew how to test the sincerity and stamina of strangers. He'd taken August on the same journey when he'd first shown an interest in providing assistance—a welcome alternative to staying behind the tall fence of the camp.

"I shall be there."

Dr. Carter's moustache twitched, but otherwise, his expression gave nothing away—and August admired the man all the more. Clever.

With a sudden crash, the door of the clinic burst open, slamming into the wall as it swung. Afternoon light framed the silhouette of a child—a boy, probably no older than seven. A hound stood to his right, awaiting the next move.

Dr. Carter pushed between Jessica and Mr. Little to greet the lad.

"Jude Larson?"

The little boy stepped forward, his hair a shaggy batch of brown and his clothes as tattered as the shoes on his feet. The dog stayed at the threshold, a sturdy, lean animal of brown and white. "My mama needs a doctor."

"I see." Dr. Carter's shoulder dropped with an unnamed weight. He ran a palm over his face. "The baby?"

The boys' hands went to his hips, displaying more maturity than his slim size warranted. "I reckon so, and I've been gone too long now. Doctor Peck ain't nowhere to be found on the outside of the fence, so I come to you."

Dr. Carter turned to August. "Dr. Peck is up on the ridge tending a family with scarlet fever. He can't make it back in time to help Eliza." He moved to the cabinet and began placing items into his black bag. "I can't leave Mr. Buchanan."

"Somebody's gotta come help my momma." The lad's voice broke with his plea.

August moved to the ready, catching Jessica's frown in the process.

"And somebody will do just that." Dr. Carter crossed the room to the boy and knelt to his level, cradling the boy's shoulder with his palm. "I can't leave my patient, Jude, but I'm sending the next best thing."

Dr. Carter nodded his head toward Jessica. "I'm sending my granddaughter. She and your mama went to school together."

Jessica took her cue, joining her grandfather's side.

Jude examined her with more suspicion than any child ought to muster, his chin tilted higher. "And she's birthed babies afore?"

"Yes, sir. She's had practice birthing babies, but even more than that, she's had practice taking care of wounded people." Dr. Carter took Jude's shoulders, meeting the boy at eye level. "And we both know your mama's not been feeling good for a long while."

Jude stared at Dr. Carter and offered a deliberate nod, the boy's eyes holding a greater burden than his small body should carry. A weight of responsibility August understood. "She's needed lots of help since Daddy died in the war."

"And you've been a great help to her. Miss Jessica will take good care of your mama, and my friend here, August, will go with her." He nodded back toward August, a wary look in his eyes steeping August's caution. "He'll be there to do whatever's necessary."

The foreboding response bit like pinpricks up August's spine.

"But, Jude, you gotta listen to them, son. No matter what they ask you to do. Having a baby is hard business on a woman, especially a woman who's been sick. I don't know how much of it she can take."

August turned a sharp eye to Jessica, and for a moment, a fragile fear wavered her exterior confidence. She looked away, back at the boy.

"But we'll do all we can. I promise you," Jessica said, conviction marking each word.

"I reckon you better. She was hollerin' something awful afore I left." The boy turned to Dr. Carter, his gaze unswerving and not fully comprehending the devastating implications in the doctor's words. "I'll do whatever ya'll need me to."

"Good lad." Dr. Carter patted his shoulder and stood. "I need you and Scraps"—he gestured toward the dog—"to run back home as fast as you can and start up a fire."

"But it's hot as blazes outside."

"True. But we're going to need hot water to help birth the baby, and you'll get home faster than any of us."

The boy's eyes widened and he backed toward the door. "I'll be right on it, Doctor. I can make it there in no time if I don't stop none."

"Then get to it."

The boy rushed from the building, Scraps on his heels. Dr. Carter released a long sigh.

"What is it?" Jessica's question broke the silence.

Dr. Carter's attention moved to his granddaughter. "After news of Paul came back from Europe, Eliza's never been the same. Practically gave up on living. Growing thinner and thinner each time I saw her in town or took a turn to visit her on the ridge in Dr. Peck's stead."

Jessica's face paled, her emerald gaze searching her grandfather's face. "Surely she'd fight to live for her children's sake. One doesn't die from a lack of will to live."

"You've been in Europe. Seen countless deaths, my girl. The lack of will is only one deciding factor in a struggle against sickness and sorrow."

Jessica pinched her pink lips closed, a 'spitfire' of determination marking her soft features. She marched to the counter, continuing her grandfather's work of packing the bag.

August ran to the shelf with the bandages and bottle of morphine.

"See here, Dr. Carter, I can assist Miss Ross instead of this—" Mr. Little curbed his words. "Mr. Reinhold. I've actually had medical training."

August's hands paused on the bandages. Dr. Carter stopped in his walk toward Jessica, and even Jessica turned to stare at Mr. Little.

"I appreciate your willingness, Mr. Little." Dr. Carter placed his fists on his hips, studying the young man. "And I mean no offense, sir, but I don't know you."

"Pardon?" Mr. Little blinked as if he couldn't comprehend the words.

"I have no doubt you're a trustworthy sort of man, but I need to know you much better before I leave you with one of my critical patients... or my granddaughter."

"But sir..."

"You just got off the train today, Mr. Little. *Today*. You're still wearing your traveling clothes. You came here for songs and history, but you don't know the forests and people of the Blue Ridge, and they certainly don't know you. I need people familiar with this region and the hardships right now, but I appreciate your willingness, as I said."

The man's lips pinched and white fire sparked to life in the glint in his eyes. His jaw tensed. "You would allow this"—he gestured toward August— "enemy alien to go? You trust *him*?"

The label given to the Germans, the harshness of it, failed to wound August anymore, but the Mr. Little's sudden fury told an unnerving tale of the man's hatred.

Dr. Carter pointed to August, his profile as stoic and tense as Mr. Little's. "This foreigner isn't a stranger. I'd trust him with my life." The moment stretched like the tautness of a drawn bowstring waiting to snap. And then Dr. Carter smiled. "Don't worry, Mr.

Little. With the hundreds of people living in the nooks and crannies of these hollows, I'm certain you'll get plenty of opportunity to serve." The soft words cushioned the edge in the room a little but not enough to steal the glower when Mr. Little glanced at August.

What had happened to the man besides the loss of his hand? The loss of a loved one? Whatever it was brought enough vengeance to remain volatile.

"Go. Now." Dr. Carter turned back to August and Jessica. "And may God be with you both."

August locked gazes with the doctor and offered an internal prayer. He was charged with taking a little boy to the bedside of his dying mother while assisting a nurse who hated him, all the while under the shadow of some German-hating Englishman? If there was ever a time for prayer, it was this moment.

Chapter Six

From his first walk through the forests surrounding Hot Springs, August had felt drawn in by the lush beauty of the sloping mountains. Of course, his first trek had been on a rainy evening, helping a small band of guards search for the camp's first runaway, but even then, the pull of the mountains' quiet call ushered him to linger... to live.

Now, as he marched at a steady pace up the hill, with Jessica at his side trying to ignore him, the tree-lined path cast late afternoon shadows in front of him, keeping his thoughts away from the darkness of the past. Reminding him of fresh beginnings—hope brought to life by Dr. and Mrs. Carter's kindness along with their welcome into their family.

Peace. A presence almost tangible in the quiet woods. God's fingerprints stamped across the horizon, carried on each birdsong, and within each fleshy leaf on the trees.

Jessica kept silent as they made the steady climb, just as she'd done in the automobile ride to the bottom of the hill. What was she thinking? Was she entertaining thoughts of Jasper Little? August grimaced and cast her another glance from his periphery.

Perhaps he truly was playing the fool, but somewhere within all those letters, woven through their stories and memories, there beat a kindred heart. A loyal, faithful resilience. Though it bent and twisted beneath the heavy hand of pain, he'd not only heard about her kindness and strength, he'd already witnessed it.

He'd learned hard lessons on patience—lessons, no doubt, she'd push to the edge if his first few days with her proved typical. But he'd found his home in Hot Springs. He'd never known what it meant to belong somewhere until he'd run to the assistance of Dr. Carter when a woman collapsed at the train depot a few months after his arrival to the camp. From that moment, the gentleness and forbearance, the trust, offered by Dr. and Mrs. Carter began the long and sweet healing August's heart needed.

A place of belonging.

And Jessica's entrance, along with the three-inch block of resentment on her shoulder, threatened to wedge distance between August and his beloved Carters. If nothing else, he had to win her indifference, but he wanted much more.

"You have had a busy entrance, no?"

She slid him a glance from her periphery and continued moving forward without a response.

"It must be difficult returning after so long. Much has changed for you but stayed the same for your small town."

Her sudden exhalation of air broke the quiet and she shot him a heated look. "My small town hasn't stayed the same from where I'm standing, Mr. Reinhold. The flood. The camp." She focused ahead. "Not the same at all."

"The spirit of your town is the same. Kind people, like your grandparents, and the beauty of the —"

"You need to understand something." She stopped on the trail, her palms planted on her hips as she turned the full brunt of her fiery gaze on him. "We are not going to be friends."

He combatted her statement with a shrug. "I am an optimist."

She groaned and resumed her frantic pace up the hillside, slowed only by the limp in her stride. Silence moved between them like a wall. August glanced up at the afternoon sky, awash with a mixture of clouds and sun. He had to return to camp by dusk or he would endanger the freedom his good name allowed.

"Just because you think you know my grandparents doesn't mean you know me." Jessica's words erupted in a harsh whisper, fueling her steps to an even faster rhythm.

He kept the pace. "No. But knowing the kindness and the welcome from your grandparents has made me wish to know you as well. They assure me you can be kind."

She turned the power of those emerald eyes on him, her mouth dropped wide. "Of course I can be kind. I'm a nurse, for heaven sakes."

"I would not see the two as related." August shoved his hands in his pockets, holding his grin in check. At least he had her talking. "Nurses have always brought needles and stings to me."

Her brow tilted skyward. "Perhaps you deserved the needles and stings."

The grip on his smile loosed completely. "No doubt, Nurse Ross. No doubt."

Her gaze hesitated in his before she jerked her attention back to the path ahead and tightened her jaw into a line of defense. The fiery glint in those large eyes fascinated him. He knew the gentleness and longing braided through her letters, the dry humor and compassion infused onto the pages. But those eyes added a dimension of depth he'd failed to anticipate. Fascinating. Challenging.

The quiet of the forest slid in between their labored breaths as the path grew steep. August had learned to embrace the earthy stillness and gentle solitude, but had Jessica's mind and heart become so full of the sounds of war, she'd lost the ability to hear the quiet of a serene afternoon, the stillness of peace? He remembered a time when the noise from his pain drowned out all peace.

"Eliza's cabin's at the top of the ridge."

August nodded.

"How do you know English so well?" She asked the question with a reluctant edge.

"My father worked with Englishmen so he learned the language first and taught it to me, my brother, and sister, but then I took classes at the camp."

For some reason, the answer paused her steps. "The camp offers classes?"

"Yes." He had her attention. Even as she began walking again, she studied him. What did she see? "We've even created a small town inside the fence. New Heidelberg. Nothing like the true city, but a little taste of home."

Her frown curled. "Taste of home, is it?"

"I am not like the people who hurt you."

She stepped forward, her finger pointed like a weapon. "You know nothing about the people who hurt me."

He held her gaze, as unswerving as hers. "And you know nothing about who I am."

"Ya'll need to git a move on." Jude's face emerged at the top of the trail, his hound at his side. "Mama needs ya."

Jessica stabbed him with a glare and then grabbed the front of her skirt, running as best she could up the hill, her limp becoming more evident.

The path ended in front of a tiny log cabin, much like some of the other houses August had seen while assisting Dr. Carter. It stood in need of repairs, but as August had learned, men were scarce and widows received help in filtered opportunities as hands were able. By the state of this cabin, it had been a long time since workman shadowed the door of Eliza Larson's doorstep. The short-hewn log home clung to the hillside as if the next puff of wind might send it toppling over the edge.

A pitiful moan broke into the afternoon from the open door, sending Jessica up the crooked porch steps and through the door. August stopped at the threshold, his chest deflating at the sight.

A woman, sallow-faced and pale, sat on a low, straw-tic bed, her hands clawing at the care-worn quilt barely covering her frail body. Based on Dr. Carter's warning, he'd expected a weaker vessel to greet him, but not one already holding an otherworldly countenance.

His throat tightened. He knew the shadow lurking in the corners of the room. An icy chill slid up his spine, unearthing darker memories of his grandfather's deathbed and the lifeless body of his sister's newborn daughter. He cringed against the tremor, but Jessica seemed untouched by the sense of doom hemming in on all sides of the dimly lit room. She moved to the bed, taking the woman's wrist to feel a pulse and pushing back the woman's damp hair from her face.

The intensity and compassion marking every feature of her inspired August into action too. "I'll help Jude with the hot water, yes?"

Jessica met his gaze with the slightest hint of surprise. "Yes."

"I already got it a'goin'," Jude answered from the doorway.

"Jessica Ross?" The voice rising from the ghostly figure on the bed pooled as fragile as the gown draping her shoulders. "You're back?"

"Yes, Liza." Jessica's tones smoothed into a gentle touch, stilling August's movements to stare in wonder. "I came back just in time to help you meet your newest family member. Wasn't that nice of me?"

The woman's gray eyes searched Jessica's face. "It's a sign."

"A sign?"

"I was waitin' for a sign and here you came." Her voice quivered as her smile grew. "Now... now, all is as it should be."

Jessica looked up to August, and for the first time since he'd met her, the fire steeling her gaze bowed to a vulnerability. Fear. Uncertainty. He took another step forward, ready to fight against whatever distress raked at her strength.

Another contraction wracked through the woman's body. August turned to the little boy whose somber gaze fastened on his unsettled mother. Emotions squeezed August's voice low as he knelt in front of the boy. "Jude."

The boy turned those piercing blue eyes, his countenance much older than his years. He'd stepped into his father's position at home as his father stepped into war. "Yes, sir."

"I believe Nurse Jesse has an occupation for you, isn't that correct, Nurse?"

Jessica pulled her attention to the pair, dazed. "Yes... yes, that's right. Do you know what the basil plant looks like?"

The boy perked to attention and shot a gaze back to the bed where his mother collapsed from the exertion of the activity. "Mama uses it for cookin'. I've got it for her before."

"Excellent. Will you run grab some for me? We'll make some tea for your mama."

His nose wrinkled with his doubt. August's did as well.

"Ain't meanin' no disrespect, ma'am. But my mama's wantin' to have a baby, not drink no tea."

Jessica placed her palm against the woman's arm, a gesture of support, as she gave the little boy a gentle smile. "It's to help with the baby, Jude. It fights infection."

His thin body perked to attention. "Yes, ma'am." He took another look at his mother and backed up to the threshold of the door. "I won't be long." He placed his little hands on his hips and set his jaw with a defiance. "'Cause I plan to be right here to keep Mama safe."

"Most of the time menfolk stay outside until the baby comes, Jude." August entered the conversation from his quiet corner, lowering himself to one knee. "Women need privacy for such as this, and if need be, I'll help as I can."

"I can't trust no stinkin' German to put his hands on my mama."

August didn't even flinch. The boy had lost his father due to Germans, so why wouldn't he absorb the anger shared by his mother? The lostness.

"Do you trust my grandpa, Jude?" An unlikely ally emerged in Jessica Ross.

Jude stared back. "Sure do. Ain't no better man on the mountain."

Jess' lips tipped at the compliment. "Well, my grandpa trusts Mr. Reinhold enough to send him here with me to help your mama. Do you think if my grandpa trusts him, you can too?"

The boy examined August from head to toe. "All right." The boy drew out the words. "I'll trust ya, then."

August's smile spread and he offered his hand. The boy shook it, sealing the deal, his gaze sober, fingers squeezing tight. Somehow August felt certain he'd gained a friend with the help of the persnickety Jessica Ross. "Go on, now, son. See to the basil for Nurse Ross."

"Take Scraps with you so he won't be in the way," Jessica called after, but Scraps already ran out the door at the boy's heels.

"You're a good liar," August said, glancing over at her as he reached to check the water.

Jess sent him a sideways glance. "I never said *I* trusted you. I said my grandpa does. It wasn't a lie." Her attention flickered to his, and for the briefest moment, softened the hardened edges around her face. Beautiful. She cleared her throat. "Now, if you don't mind, I have to check Eliza, so I'd appreciate if you and your smirk would slide right out that front door."

"I need you to promise me, Jesse." The mother's voice moaned into the conversation as her body writhed against another contraction and sweat beads pearled across her forehead. "Please."

August snatched a cloth from the lukewarm pot over the stove and waved it in the air to cool. He'd assisted in his sister's delivery of his tiny niece, a whisper of a child who barely lived two months. Any small service of assistance mattered at this crucial time.

In a few strides, he crossed the room and placed the cloth in Jessica's hand.

"Thank you," she whispered, touching the linen to Mrs. Larson's skin as her tension subsided into a shivering sigh against the pillows. "The pains are close, Eliza. It shouldn't be long now."

"That's right." Mrs. Larson grabbed at Jessica's free hand, drawing it to her chest. "Not long. So... so I need you to promise, about the younguns." Her breath punctuated each word. "You'll promise me, won't you?"

"Promise you what, Eliza?"

"You'll take 'em." The mother's voice moaned out the phrase. "You'll promise to take keer of my young'uns."

Jessica's eyes pinched closed for a moment and August began to put the pieces together.

Jessica tried to pull back. "I need you to fight, Liza. For your children."

The woman, as frail as she seemed, held Jessica in a vice. "Joshua's already called me home. I've seen it in my dreams. I'm going to him."

The superstition of the mountains crept into her voice and waited in the wings, cloaked in a black robe and a sickle. August stayed the chills with a prayer.

"You know as well as I that sometimes, dreams are only dreams." Jessica shook the hand Eliza held. "God expects us to use good sense too. He's given you these children, and He knows they need a mother."

"He wants you to be their mother."

"What?" Jessica replayed the sentence whispered by her high school friend, but the words and meaning came back as almost incomprehensible.

Mother? Jessica? No! She'd never been good with children and she didn't plan to practice on two would-be orphans at a mother's dying request. Eliza Larson had to survive.

"I seen it in my dreams but I didn't know it 'twas you, Jesse. All make sense now." Eliza sighed back into the pillows for a momentary reprieve from her pangs but tensed again almost immediately.

Jess tried to loosen the woman's hold, but her fingers gripped as tightly as the desperation in her eyes. Jess groaned and severed her gaze from Eliza's, searching for some help—anything from anyone, even traitor August Reinhold.

His eyes captured her with their tenderness, sending strength and a sweet taste of calm over the coils of tension under her skin. An unwelcome flutter slid in between Jess' internal panic and utter disdain.

She stifled a grimace at the memory of Jude's honest declaration about August being a 'stinkin' German.' Paired with his gentle nature and ready smile, she found it more and more difficult to hate him. As much as every scar inside her cried out in protest, she couldn't tend to a dying mother and a grieving seven-year-old by herself.

Eliza tensed through another contraction ending in a jolt of quiet. The woman's weak breaths rose and fell in shallow puffs. Her complexion looked pasty, and Jess acknowledged the familiar shades of death fingering closer with each passing second.

"The baby's comin'." Eliza moaned and sent Jessica into motion.

She barely heard August slip from the room to leave them in privacy. Eliza pushed, but the effort weakened her even more, barely moving the baby along.

"Stay with me, Eliza. The baby is almost here. I need you to give me one or two more pushes and we'll be finished."

"I can't." The woman's cry puddled out on a whimper.

"Did your dream say the baby was going to die too?" The statement snatched the woman's full focus. "Because that's what's going to happen if you don't get him out of the birth canal very soon."

The edge in Jessica's words punctured whatever state left Eliza powerless, and with a cry loud enough to shake Jess' bones, the woman pushed the baby clean out of her body. Jess caught the crying bundle in a towel by the bed, staring at the tiny person in wonder.

This... miracle never grew commonplace.

"A girl." Jess whispered and looked up. "You have a girl, Eliza."

"Good. She'll make you a fine daughter." Eliza's voice fainted into a whisper, her breath rasped and ragged.

"No, no." Jess leaned forward. "You need to get well and be the mother for this little one." Jess pressed the baby into Eliza's arms, hoping the tactile awareness would shake Eliza's hold on her gloomy end.

The woman touched the baby's face and with a sluggish familiarity, moved the little one to her breast to quell the desperate cries. After a few attempts, the quiet sound of suckling hummed in chorus with the crackling fire. Jess breathed a sigh of relief and went to work, finalizing the birthing process.

As the placenta expelled, another burst of blood followed.

No. How on earth could the woman have known she would hemorrhage?

Eliza moaned, a pitiful sound, and Jessica sent a frenzied look about the tiny cabin for anything cold. Something to perhaps slow the bleeding? Her view offered nothing.

The contented hums of the suckling baby couldn't overshadow Eliza's breaths, growing shallower.

"Do you need anything, Nurse Ross?"

August's face appeared in the doorway, but before Jess could send him away, Eliza grasped Jess' arm in a feeble hold. "I feel my life leavin'. Promise me you'll take care of my young'uns."

The request hit Jess in the stomach all over again. If she didn't think she'd hasten the woman's decline, she'd shake some sense into her, but the shadows beneath her eyes and the pallor of her face kept the edge out of Jess' voice. "You want to give me a helpless newborn and an impressionable seven-year-old? You've known me my whole life. I've never been very good with children."

Eliza smiled in a resigned, knowing sort of way, as if Jessica had accepted the awesome responsibility without question. She patted Jessica's hand before her fingers dropped to her lap. "I have every faith you're the one for my sweet young'uns." Her eyes lit with a small spark and she moved a weak finger down the baby's cheek. "Faith." She drew in a shallow breath. "Call her Faith. May she be a stronger woman than her mama."

"Eliza, please—"

The woman sank further down into the bed, her shoulders slumping low and her energy waning with the loss of blood. Dying. Helpless. Fire exploded up through Jess' middle. All she could do was watch Eliza die, just like she'd done hundreds of times with the soldiers in her care. Why did she have to feel so helpless all of the time?

"Where's Jude? I need to talk to Jude." Eliza's words teetered to a higher pitch, rising on Jude's name.

"I'll get him," August replied from the doorway, turning to leave.

"No." Jessica stepped forward. "He shouldn't be here for this." She gestured back toward the bed. "Not for this."

August's pale blue eyes took on a steely glint. "His mother has asked for him. I will not refuse her request."

Jess stepped closer, lowering her voice. "She has less than five minutes at the rate she's bleeding out. A little boy doesn't need to—"

"No. He should be with her." His words hardened in command and Jessica stepped back.

After the light-hearted banter he'd shown since she first met him, his curt reaction took her by surprise. Before she could respond, he'd ushered the little boy into the room and to his mother's side.

Jude never hesitated but took his mother's outstretched hand with a sweet smile. And Jessica's heart pinched in knots from the site of the contented baby in Eliza's arms and the little boy facing a man's heartache.

How could God allow this? What earthly good could any of this do? Her heart fisted tight against the remnants of her childhood faith. Nothing.

"Come close, boy." Eliza urged Jude closer with a gentle tug. "This is your little sister, Faith. Help take care of her."

Warmth invaded Jessica's vision, blurring the scene into fog and whispers.

"I will, Mama. I always try to help you."

Jude's simple reply nudged a tear free and the dam of self-control threatened to burst with so many unshed tears she nearly turned and left the house, but August's presence at her side kept her firmly in place. She couldn't leave a strange man alone with this dying mother.

Eliza's smile quivered with the fight to speak, to breathe. "You've always been a good boy and I... I have a special job for you now."

The words grew softer, frail as the baby's tiny fingers flexing open and closed against the blanket as she suckled.

"Your daddy's calling me to join him so I must go."

"Is he callin' me too?"

Jess pinched her eyes closed against the scene but the question lingered with longing. Oh, the poor, sweet boy!

"No, he 'spects you to grow up and be... be a strong man, like... him." Her voice faltered, and her hand dropped its hold on the boy's. "You and Faith is going to belong to Miss Jessica."

Jude raised those clear gray eyes to her, the stare searching for answers Jessica didn't even have the strength to voice. Words and promises scratched her throat for release. Anything to comfort the confusion on Jude's little face.

"Love ya, boy."

"Mama?"

But there was no response.

Chapter Seven

Thunder hounded her steps down the mountain trail, like gunfire reverberating in her skull and skittering a violent cold sweat over her skin. The limp in her stride and newborn in her arms slowed her pace, but nothing could ease the erratic taste of fear gripping her breath with each thunder clash.

Visions burst at every explosion. A dying nurse in her arms, bleeding from an abdominal wound from a shell. A soldier fighting for breath from the ravages of a gas attack. Dark German eyes piercing hers before seizing her mouth in a violent kiss, stripping her of the distance and strength she'd coveted for years. Three pulls of a trigger as she fired a pistol into the head of a man trying to kill her brother. One. Two. Three.

She cringed against the hateful, haunting memories and attempted to quicken her pace, only to stumble.

August caught her by the arm, steadied her, and then quickly released her. She nodded a reluctant thanks before forging ahead, the sound of August's gentle voice as he spoke to Jude about the hound, Scrubs, at the boys' side whishing a gentle distracting to her terror. She focused on August's voice, attempting to allow the comfort and calm of his mellow base drive the panic away, but another boom of thunder jolted her pulse.

The darkened sky promised a deluge. Soon.

"We need to hurry."

August turned to her, those eyes so pale and gentle, they somehow softened her scowl. She couldn't shake the memories of his care for Eliza's body as he quietly helped her wrap it until Granny Painter or one of her midwife apprentices came to prepare it for the wake. She'd notify Clive at the general store, and then mountain people would crawl out of the hollows and cabins to pay their respects. And, of course, someone would have to dig the grave. Eliza had no family, no kin apart from the two children who now belonged to Jessica.

She tried to wrap her mind around that thought, but a closer boom of thunder blasted her mind with white fear, sending a seizure-like tremor through her and waking the baby. The farmhouse rose before her around the tree line path, across the field. Pinpricks clawed at her spine, like the cold steel of a pistol at her neck. Her throat strangled. She hobbled faster. The baby started to whimper, but Jess couldn't stop.

An overwhelming panic rose above logic and understanding. It gripped her senses and left her practically paralyzed... unless she could get to the house before the storm grew any closer. Before she lost her last remnant of control.

Another clap of thunder nearly crippled her to the ground, but August caught her again.

He looked down into her face, his brow crinkled with concern.

"I need to get inside." Words squeezed through her tightening throat. "Please."

August looked up at the sky, then to the front door, and back at Jess' face. She didn't have time for him to sort out the problem, or her weaknesses. She'd already swallowed two gallons of pride saying "please" to the man.

She attempted to jerk free from his hold and take the final steps to the house before her body became immovable, but August swept her and the baby up in his arms and crossed the final expanse to the back porch steps just as the sky opened.

He placed her down on the porch, his unnerving stare almost distracting her from the panic lacing each breath she took. She slung the door open, ushered Jude inside, and turned to August, who stood at the threshold, unmoving.

Her fingers dug into the wood of the door, but she couldn't quite take her gaze from his.

"You are safe."

His whisper, the compassion softening the sharp edges of his jaw, clashed against her assumptions and desperate need to hate him. Safe?

Lightning flashed behind him and the thunder cracked in unison, lighting the sky and reigniting the terror.

"Thank you," she managed to say before slamming the door in his face. Maybe she said it. The blackness on the fringes of her thoughts sifted memory and present into a murky mess. She needed to hide.

"What are you doing?" Her grandmother's voice filtered in through the coming fog.

Jess turned to her and pushed the crying baby into her grandmother's arms and then, as the darkness started closing in on her vision and the sounds of gunfire eclipsed all other noise, she fumbled up the stairs to her room, opened the tiny closet, and closed herself inside.

August walked up Spring Street over the well-worn train tracks glistening with fresh rain. He'd learned summer rains arrived in a hurry but ended as quickly, leaving the earthy smells of wet grass and flowers mingling in the damp air. He stopped at the corner of the Hot Spring's depot and drew in a fresh breath of honeysuckle air. The small town stretched before him, buildings huddled around a narrow, dirt-stained main street, which had grown only a little since his people had 'invaded' this tiny corner of the Blue Ridge Mountains.

Behind him extended the long bridge over the French Broad, a steel edifice he and his comrades succeeded in repairing after the flood left the bridge gnarled and broken. The mountains, shields of gray and blue, rose on every side, cradling the town and its five hundred natives.

August shoved his hands in his pockets and completed the short walk along the twelve-foot wooden fence to the entry gate. His feet hesitated each time he crossed the threshold back behind the fence, the temporary freedom of the day stolen with one step. He looked back over his shoulder before entering his confinement for the night. His thoughts turned back to the afternoon's tragic scene and Jessica Ross' behavior—her fathomless emerald eyes seized with terror. Confinement came in all shape and sizes. For some, it was wooden fences and barbed wire, for others... bitterness and fear.

The woman posed an interesting quandary. For a few moments, she'd softened her defenses, allowing him to see behind her protective wall of resentment. Gentleness and a deep-set compassion flowed from her interactions with and her glances to Jude. She carried a strength, an almost indomitable courage in each step she took, even against the pull of her limp. But her strength bowed to the weight of helplessness, both during Eliza's birth and then... during the storm.

Everything within him stood to assistance, readied to give whatever she needed to snatch the fear from those evergreen eyes. What haunted her? August knew some of the stories her grandparents shared, but had something much worse ripped through her strength to inspire such terror?

A movement along the fence line, shadowed gray clouds in the storm-waning sky, slowed August's pace toward the camp gate. The silhouette crept along the fence, head bent low as if searching for something lost along the ground.

There was a distant familiarity to his gait and lean physique. August moved toward the man, but the shadowed figure must have heard his approach and scampered away until he disappeared over the edge of road down toward the river.

August waited, watching the shadows a little longer to see if the man might emerge. Though his countryman's arrival in Hot Springs came with a general sense of good feeling, or at the least indifference, there were always those whose losses and fears bent their sensibilities toward a darker turn.

Sinister? Dangerous?

One last glance over his shoulder afforded an orange-hewn main street. A figure leaned against the Tavern wall, smoke trailing from his cigarette, his dark eyes trained on the camp. On August. Davis, the man August saw in Kimp's store, the one with such a severe grudge against him and his countrymen.

August steadied his gaze, refusing to bend beneath the glare, and then turned the corner into the Lower Lawn gate of the camp.

"In for the evening, August?" Cliff's voice drew him from his thoughts.

The man, about August's height, stepped from behind the guard office and met August at the bottom of the steps to the small building.

"It's been a long day, my friend."

Cliff placed a comforting palm on August's shoulder. "You're wearing the weariness in your face. My cousin beat you down?"

August chuckled, appreciating the welcome bond he'd developed with the camp guard. "More related to the sadness in my work with your cousin than your cousin herself." Though the entire Jasper Little scene still irritated his worry. "Eliza Larson died in childbirth today."

Cliff's broad shoulder bent with his sigh. "I'm sorry to hear it. I went to school with her husband. Good, hardworking fella. What about his young'un?"

August raised two fingers. "The baby daughter survived. They are with your cousin."

Cliff's mouth dropped. "Jessica?"

August's weary grin sloped in response to Cliff's astonishment. "Yes."

"Well, that's evidence enough of Eliza Larson's state of mind. Leaving two children in the hands of my cousin who has been fairly terrified of children ever since she watched two brothers nearly drown?" Cliff shook his head. "Seriously, August, the woman ain't held a baby since then unless under duress."

Which explained a great deal of her behavior from the time she wrapped the baby in a worn-out blanket, somewhat nervously, to the tension as she walked. It still didn't explain her increased fear as they descended the mountainside, but certainly seemed to add to it.

"Why?"

"Those two brothers were boys she'd helped tutor in school. Took to them something fierce. Doc almost lost one of the boys—lips turned plumb blue." Cliff shook his head. "You don't know her like me, friend, but she's more protective than any mama bear I've ever seen. Her family. Friends." Cliff released a low whistle. "She might act like the devil may care, but she holds a depth of feeling on the inside nobody sees."

"Then the children should be in good hands, yes?"

Cliff's eyebrow snagged with the corner of his lips. "Good? Well, I reckon good and capable are two different things, ain't they?" A cloud shadowed Cliff's features. "Childbirth takes more women in this part of the world than the war would ever steal the menfolk."

August allowed the silence to settle and Cliff's gaze to return to the present before speaking. "Your wife?"

The brawny man cleared his throat and set his palms against his hips. "And the babe. A daughter."

August touched the man's shoulder, a prayer of comfort in his mind. "I'm sorry, friend."

"It was three years ago, but some days... when I learn of another situation, the years disappear and I'm back in my house, holding my wife and praying for a miracle."

Grief held a curious dagger, striking at the most unexpected times in unlikely ways. Oh, yes, August knew. And during these times of war and change, death stalked as close as a breath, touching each home with its chilling grasp. Cliff Carter embodied a certain breed of mountain man. Intimidating in size and strength, but underneath the rough edges beat a tender heart. A faithful heart.

August grinned. Cliff Carter was cut from the same mold as August's grandfather.

August glanced ahead of him across the massive lawn framed in by a few barracks. At least his kinsmen preserved some of the beauty of the inn's landscaping by leaving the massive holly trees and oaks in the front lawn and keeping the larger portion of the grassy area free for activity.

"General Ames visited today."

August looked up and pushed back his straw hat to get a better view of his friend's face, the implication clear. If the government sent Ames, something was getting ready to happen.

"He's come to inspect the camp, look over policies."

Warmth rushed back into August's body and he relaxed his shoulders with a sigh. "Routine, yes?"

"Yes." Cliff grinned, but his face quickly sobered. "But, August, there's talk of a change. I don't think it's going to be much longer."

Silence blanketed Jessica's early morning steps as she held onto the stair railing. As she reached the bottom step, her grandmother's quiet shuffling greeted her from the kitchen. Jessica's head ached from lack of sleep, from the weariness of warring against ghosts and nightmares—faces of dying men, horrors mixed with mud and blood.

She ran a palm over her face and quelled another shiver. How could she have expected life to return to normal after all she'd seen? Shadows haunted her as rabid as death, and they'd followed her home. *Home.* The one place she thought she'd find peace... but it had deserted her, just as God had done. Leaving her to battle alone.

She fisted the railing and reigned in the tears, gripping her anger in an iron hold. She knew how to fight.

A lantern lit the dim kitchen. Grandmother sat by the window, a bundle of blankets in her arms, but as Jessica drew closer, she realized her grandmother held a baby. Jess stopped her forward motion, memories from the previous day flooding back through her mind in full, excruciating clarity. Eliza. The children.

Jess blinked down at the baby. *Her* baby? Surely not. She couldn't take care of a baby—or a grieving little boy.

"August sent some supplies from town I'd asked for. Some bottles and things." Her grandmother's voice soothed gently into the silence. "Told me about Eliza."

Jess stepped closer, peering down at the infant with the same caution she'd experienced around every baby. The tiny mouth moved on the bottle nipple and the quietest of swallowing sounds created a wispy pattern. How could someone so small terrify her so much?

Granny looked up in examination. "Blake told the preacher and he's been spreading the word. I'm sure the Marshalls and Painters will see to the wake."

"And the children?"

"I fixed Jude up in David's old room. He thought he'd entered Paradise itself from the look on his little face when he crawled in that big bed."

Jess rubbed her eyes, half to wake up and half to keep the residual tears from spilling. She slid into the chair opposite her grandmother, her heart still pumping with a sudden flight response. She her arms around her shoulders, warding off the chill of the storm and her nibbling insecurities. "You'll take care of them, won't you?"

Granny's brow tilted before she looked back down at the baby. "I'll help *you* take care of 'em, but they're not my young'uns." Her gaze pinned Jess to her chair. "They're yours now."

Her grandmother's words locked with a finality Jess repelled. She knew nothing about taking care of children, especially newborns. How on earth could anyone think it was a good idea, especially her grandmother?

"What happened yesterday? To you?"

Jess leaned her face into her palms, avoiding those searching eyes. "It's more proof why I'm not fit to be a mother." She sighed back into the chair and swallowed past her tightening throat. "I... I don't know how to explain it. Sometimes, I'm seized by this... terror I can't control. What you saw?" She pointed to the front door to provide a memory cue. "What you saw was a good response. I caught myself in time to be alone for the... episode." Her voice cracked as another sweep of warmth surged into her cheeks. Sheer panic still spiked the pulse in her throat at the thought of the storm. The thunder. The swelling fear. "I... I can't stop it, Granny."

Granny stared at her, her gaze penetrating deep. Jess had no idea what her granny deciphered, but whatever it was somehow meant placing that fragile little baby into Jess' unsuspecting arms. Clearly, her grandmother failed to listen well.

"What are you doing?" Jess whispered, her entire body stiffening from the effort to hold the small and moving parcel.

Granny pushed the bottle into Jess' free hand. "I'm fixin' breakfast."

With that, she turned and walked right out the back door toward the barn and chicken coop. Jess wanted to run after her and trade. She swallowed the lump in her throat and looked down atced the little face, the round eyes staring right back at her almost as if she questioned Jess' ability too.

"You *should* be terrified right now," Jess whispered. "I have no idea what I'm doing."

The baby's tiny mouth moved with a breath, so small and fragile like everything else about her, but otherwise, she didn't seem too afraid. Jess lowered the bottle into the tiny rosebud mouth and the little one took hold of the nipple, knowing exactly what to do.

Tension rolled off Jess' shoulders. Okay, so far so good. The swallowing pattern returned, a consistent, peaceful sound. Small fingers reached up and took hold of Jess' braid, squeezing, then releasing, in time with her suckle.

A sweet warmth, like nothing she'd ever known, spilled over scars and scrapes around her heart. Tenderness squeezed against her tension, taunting her to release a hold on the fear engrained in every breath she took.

She touched the baby's little cheek. "Afraid I'll go somewhere and take that bottle with me?"

The baby's eyes drooped lower in response.

"I guess not." Jess chuckled, her voice loosening its hold on the little one's name. "Faith."

If there was a God, he wasn't all-knowing, otherwise he'd never entrusted something so fragile and... precious to a woman with enough ghosts to impress Old Man Langston and his tall tales. But as the tenderness spread through Jess' chest and the little baby fell into a sleep Jess envied, Jess embraced her promise.

If God wasn't going to help these children, then she certainly would.

Chapter Eight

"I think the baby is sick."

Jess rushed into the backyard, holding a crying Faith wrapped in nothing but a towel. Her grandmother's head turned away from a plant she nursed in the kitchen garden. "I... I think we need to take her to Grandpa."

Granny stood and stretched out her back, not nearly as panicked as she ought to be. "You're a nurse. What do you think's wrong?"

Jess stepped closer to ensure Granny heard her over the crying. "She's... she's sick to her stomach, I think."

Granny's gray and gold brow rose. "How can you tell?"

"Her stool... its..." Jessica cringed. "Yellow and... much more than it should be."

"She's been takin' a lot of milk, and you added a little water to it last night, didn't you?"

Jess pointed back toward the house which held the offensive diaper. "That much... stuff should not come from something so small. She has to be sick. She's going to dehydrate from that much loss."

To Jess' complete astonishment, her granny started laughing. And no light laugh, either. She placed a palm to her stomach and held her head back, barely catching a breath between another burst of amusement. Jess failed to find any amusement in the fact that this little baby in her care was probably going to become dehydrated and possibly die by the time her grandmother stopped laughing.

"I don't see how this is funny, Granny." Jess gave a gentle bounce to the bundle in her arms, soothing the cry away. What a technique! She'd remember it for later. Bouncing the baby soothed her.

"Oh, honey, to be so smart at nursing, you sure do have a lot to learn about mothering."

"One of the reasons why I was trying to steer clear of it." Jess narrowed her eyes with every intention of showing her grandmother exactly what she thought of that statement, but her granny only chuckled at the desired blow.

"You've always liked challenges. I reckon this'n will be the hardest one yet."

All Jess needed was to feel even more helpless than she already did, but she growled and turned back toward the house. Clearly, she'd come to the wrong person for compassion.

"You're going to be fine, girl. There ain't one baby I know in these parts that's bested her mama yet." Her granny's voice dissolved into another fit of chuckles and Jess marched up the steps into the house without looking back.

"Your granny isn't very nice right now, Faith," Jess murmured down into the little face. "And I don't think either one of us should talk to her for the rest of the day, regardless of what kind of cake she makes."

Jess finished cleaning up Faith's mess, took much too long to get the little thing into a gown and diaper, then ignored her granny again as she fumbled through fixing Faith's bottle. When she finally placed a drowsy baby down on Jess' large bed, it was midmorning, and Jess' body ached like she'd tended patients all day. How could that even be possible? She leaned back into the rocking chair for just a moment and breathed out a sigh, the tension in her muscles uncurling. Her thoughts smoothed into a foggy blanket, the rocking motion lulling a mindless rhythm accentuated by the gentle hum of Faith's breath.

A cry shook Jess from her slumber. She shot to her feet and blinked the room into focus. Her room... and a crying baby? Another cry shocked her brain into motion and lit memories from the previous day back to the present. She stepped to the bedside and squinted against the afternoon light pouring cheery warmth through the window. Afternoon? She'd slept through to afternoon? As her memories from the previous day clashed with her present, a cool rush of fear zipped through her entire body.

Jude!

Her breath caught in a whimper. She scooped a squirming Faith up from the bed and made an uneven march down the stairs to the kitchen. Perfect. She hadn't even been a mother for twenty-four hours, and she'd already lost a child.

She turned the corner of the stairs and moved into the kitchen, bouncing a whimpering baby in her arms. How could she possibly get a bottle ready and look for a missing boy?

"Whoa, now. Where's the fire?"

She looked to her granny and then scanned the room. "Jude! I haven't seen him all morning. Not even a full day and I've already failed at motherhood."

"Don't worry, girl, you'll get plenty of practice at failin' much worse." She moved to the stovetop and poured tap water from the new system into the pot for boiling. Only cold water, unlike her brother's home at Beacon House in Ednesbury, England. But running water was much better than what she'd grown up with in Hot Springs—a well and nearby creek.

Jess' shoulder slumped. "Where did all of that grandmotherly encouragement go?"

"It's camouflaged behind hard work at the moment." Her granny grinned, pouring milk into a glass bottle and setting it in the pot of water on the stove. "Don't worry, I reckon it'll resurrect when you really need it."

"Aren't you at all worried that I misplaced a seven-year-old?"

Her granny's chuckle fueled Jess' scowl. "I sent him off with Cliff and August to Eliza's. They're helpin' Preacher Russell with diggin' the grave since Eliza didn't have no family."

Jess' panic vanished at the sound of August's name. One hand flew to her hip and the jostling of poor, hungry baby Faith came to a complete stop. "You sent Jude with the German?"

Her granny turned from her pot on the stove and shot a gray-slitted look that sent a chill over Jessica's skin. "Jessica Ross, I know you've been through heartache and grief. Hurts no one should know, but you're not the only one who's known their share of pain." Granny's brow edged sharp. "You're trying to be angry at the whole country of Germany when more than half of them men in that camp are civilians, including August the German."

Granny folded her arms and continued to stare. Faith lost all of her patience and burst out into a pitiful cry. Jess had the slightest inclination to join her. Granny's fury sent the bravest, craziest, or most stubborn, cowering.

"Place your finger in that baby's mouth for a minute before she gets so worked up she won't eat."

Jess complied and Faith began sucking on the little finger with surprising suction. Poor little thing. Jess groaned. She'd lost one child and left another to starve. Stellar mothering skills.

"And stop doubting yourself." The bite in Granny's voice drew Jess' attention back to her face. "If God's given you these young'uns, he's gonna make sure you can take care of them."

He hadn't done very much to help her out recently. Why should she expect it now?

"Can you watch Faith for me?"

Granny's eyes narrowed again but she nodded, taking the fussing bundle into her arms and turning back to the bottle on the stove. "And exactly what you are you plotting?"

"Nothing." Jess started braiding her hair as she walked to the door. "Just going to check on Jude and collect any clothes or keepsakes from the house for these children."

"I'll tell you one thing, girl." Granny's voice paused Jessica's exit at the back door. She half-turned, bracing herself for some deep-meaning words of wisdom waiting to pounce guilt on her again. "August Reinhold is a kind, generous person. You ain't gonna find whatever meanness you're looking for in that boy."

Jess took a deep breath, keeping her rebuttal behind clenched teeth. If her granny had seen the atrocities, experienced the utter betrayal Jessica knew from the battlefield, she wouldn't be so quick to see the blessed goodness of these blond-headed foreigners. And now, a poor little boy... She swallowed down a lump. *Her* poor little boy was at the mercy of the foreigner and her gregarious cousin? Jess quickened her steps to the door. "I certainly hope you're right, Granny."

As Jessica passed her parent's rock cottage, a woman exited the red-painted front door. Her hair, a rich caramel color, crowned her head in a mass of intricate braids, like none Jess had ever seen. She offered a tentative smile, her eyes a gleaming pool of periwinkle, familiar in a way that forced Jessica to scratch the back of her mind for a memory to match.

"Miss Ross?"

The greeting welcomed with a hint of foreign accent. Jessica's spine tensed straight to the defense. "Yes?"

The woman held out a pink, blue, and lace bundle. "For the baby."

Jessica took the offering slowly, running a palm over the intricate designs of various infant gowns beautifully sewn. An expert seamstress.

"Thank you." Jessica tried to place the woman with her porcelain complexion and delicate features.

"I cannot imagine finding yourself a mother so unexpectedly."

German. The tenant living in her parents' old home was German. Jessica sucked in a slow breath through her teeth and attempted to curb her internal disdain with a forced smile. Yet another detail her grandparents failed to divulge in their letters. "I don't believe we've met?"

The intelligence behind the woman's expression shone with an understanding Jess wanted to ignore. "Anna Fischer."

Jess offered a stiff hand to grasp Mrs. Fischer's. The door to the cottage opened and a brown-eyed little girl appeared, her hair a lighter sheen but other features making a familial relationship between the two undeniable. Despite her annoyance, Jess softened at the sight of golden curls, violet ruffles, and a dimpled smile.

"This is Sylvie, my daughter."

Jess looked from the woman to the girl and back to the clothes in her arms, attempting to hold to her resentment despite the disarming generosity before her. Forgiving the past? How could she forgive the past without somehow condoning all the atrocities of it? The injustices?

"I... appreciate your kindness." Jessica turned her attention away from the smiling cherub and back to the woman's face. The words faltered on her tongue but she swallowed the churning hatred. "Thank you."

The young woman dipped her head in acceptance of the meager offering, and the tip in her smile hinted that she held a knowledge of Jess' struggle. Somehow.

"Are you to go to the wake? To the house of your children's mother?"

Jess blinked at the reference, still unfamiliar and somewhat terrifying. "Yes."

She nodded and raised an index finger for Jess to wait. "One moment, please. I have something."

She rushed back into the house and the little girl, swaying to a tune only she seemed to hear, danced forward on the rock path, her sweet smile pointed down to the bluebells at the path's edge. The tension in Jessica's frown loosed to the scene, so gentle and free. Oh, to protect such a world. Such an innocence.

Sylvie's purple frock, simple in its design but exquisite in its embroidery, fluttered in the afternoon breeze until she stopped in front of Jessica, apparently suddenly aware of a pair of different shoes. She looked up, her large eyes a shocked shade of blue—dark, almost purple, haloed by the golden locks. Jess stared in pure fascination at such a heavenly sight. There was a glow, an intelligence, in her expression, and in a moment of such tenderness, the cherub bestowed a double-dimpled smile.

Jessica's smile unhinged in response, slowly, as if rusty from disuse. She looked a year or two younger than Jude, maybe. Jess lowered herself to the ground and offered her hand. "Hello, Sylvie, my name is Miss Ross."

The little girl's attention dropped to Jessica's mouth, focused and intense.

Her glittering gaze moved back to Jessica's eyes and she took Jessica's outstretched hand. "Sylvie Fischer." The sounds materialized with an odd quality, blurred and tunnel-like.

Anna Fischer appeared at the doorway, a shirt in hand, watching the exchange.

"This is Jessica Ross, Sylvie." Anna tossed the shirt over her shoulder and moved her hands in intricate ways as she talked. "She is Mr. and Mrs. Carter's granddaughter. A nurse."

Sylvie's smile returned, compete with dimples, and she made a movement with her hands as she spoke. "Nice to meet you."

Anna nodded to the girl and turned to Jessica. "Sylvie cannot hear. She lost her hearing during an illness two years ago when she was four."

"What were you doing?" Jess waved toward her hands.

"I've spent the last two years trying to learn and teach Sylvie sign language, both with her German words and her English words." Anna's grin broadened. "Some are homemade signs, but she is very smart. She's learned quickly and even attempts to keep talking as much as she can. She wants to talk. She knows it is how others can hear her."

Jess tried to keep her distance, reminding herself of the grudge she nursed like life-breath, but the tenderness, loss, and love all pieced together by the vision before her crumbled her bitterness beneath a steady downpour of... hope. A terrifying hope. One shivering for freedom beneath all the open wounds of her heart.

"She's beautiful."

Anna's pale gaze shot to Jessica's face, her smile a little guarded but kind. "Yes. Both in heart and in body. She has been a great comfort and joy to me, as you will learn from your new children."

Jessica's breath hitched on the thought again, so new and strange. *Her* children. Which reminded her of her purpose in finding the disappearing Jude. "I must be going. Thank you for the clothes."

"Yes, and please, deliver this to August? He will need it."

Anna Fischer took the shirt from her shoulder and held it out to Jessica. A man's shirt. The previous sweetness puttered into a sour aftertaste. Was this August's sweetheart? Jess had heard of several German wives following their husbands to this remote town to be near the camp, maybe staying at Jane Gentry's or Lance's boarding houses. Many even enrolled their children in the local school.

But Anna Fischer didn't have Reinhold as her last name so... what was August doing secretly visiting the young woman at the cottage? No, things didn't look too pristine and perfect for Mr. Reinhold at the moment, and despite her desire to gloat a little at her prediction, a piece of her bent beneath disappointment.

Life at its basest. Disappointing. She should be used to it by now. Now, she had proof to place directly in August Reinhold's handsome face.

"Of course." She took the shirt and pressed on a smile. "Thank you for the gowns for the baby. Have a good day."

Jess turned back to the trail but not before Sylvie waved a joyful good-bye and then proceeded to run to her mother with a bouquet of flowers. Jess focused ahead, but her heart stuttered into a softer rhythm. There was something inextricably tender and poignant about seeing that little girl harboring such unfettered joy in the face of difficulties—far from home in a strange new place, loss of hearing...

A gentle voice whispered over her musings. *Peace I leave you. Hope I give to you.*

The leaves overhead rustled in time with the voice, brushing a cool breeze like a caress over her warm face. A touch awakening a promise she used to believe. She pinched her eyes closed, pushing forward up the trail and gripping her cane tight as a bearing and a reminder of her loss. Her pain. All the ways hope failed.

But the breeze kissed her cheeks again, refusing to be ignored. Her mind fought a weary battle, a constant struggle between the visions of a war-torn battlefield, dying men, and unwanted affections. Her heart ached through each beat from fresh and old wounds, unhealed and deep. Peace? If only she could find such an elusive paradise. If only the joy little Sylvie knew within her quiet world somehow materialized in adulthood.

Heat stung her eyes, blurring the sun-splattered greenery around her. No. She couldn't give in. Trust a vaporous promise. She forged ahead, blocking off her rebel thoughts and wavering on the edge of a nervous precipice between longing and running. But all she felt for certain was a constant fear of falling.

The sound of voices emerged through the wood before Eliza's house came into view. Voices? Jessica strained her ears to pick up the various nuances of pitches and patterns. Women. Mountain women, with varied cadences but similar style. The hard edges of the Appalachian accent, thicker and more prevalent the further into the hollows and hedges one traveled, cascaded down to her in the fluid tones of gossip.

Jessica sighed. Not all women were as careful and wise in their conversations as her grandmother, and from the passionate tenor of the voices lisping downwind, these probably weren't the wisest.

"I heard the doves calling yesterday morn. Ain't a good sign a'tall."

"I'll be surprised if the babe survives the week," another voice responded, deepened with age.

Jess' stomach roiled in revolt.

"And a full moon besides. I wouldn't go naming the babe for a few months yet. Not with a start as she's had."

Jess crested the hill and came to an abrupt stop at the entrance into the swept yard. The ramshackle house stood even more forlorn-looking in the afternoon light than it had in the later shades of day. What must Jude have thought of her grandparents' well-maintained home, with its secure walls without one hole in them?

She glanced the breadth of the yard and came to a stop at a sight below the house. Her cousin, Cliff, stood digging a hole, and his partner in the grisly act was none other than August Reinhold. Cliff stood above the gaping hole, while August shoveled from within. Jessica marched forward, ignoring the calls of the superstitious gaggle near the house, and closing in on the reason she'd come a bit early for the funeral.

August's white shirt clung to his skin, damp from his hard work, and highlighted the strength of his shoulders and arms. Those same arms which had swept her up without one hitch and rushed her to her grandparents' house in the storm. Strong. Capable.

Her throat went dry and she slowed her pace, uncertain now.

August looked up then, his pale blue gaze reaching across the space and igniting an inextricable pull... like the first time she'd seen him. A single golden lock spilled over his damp forehead and softened his sheer strength, beautiful raw manliness housed within such a gentle gaze. Who was this puzzling man?

Jude stepped from the forest, shovel in hand, and broke the unnatural link between Jess and the gentle German. Right. He'd stolen her... son. She should be throttling him instead of stargazing.

She strained a deep breath through her tightening throat, tipped her chin up for battle, and stepped forward in the fray. "The next time you decide to take off with Jude, I'd appreciate some notice."

August's eyes shot wide and he reached for Cliff's hand to help him out of the grave. "It would be ungentlemanly to interrupt a lady's sleep."

"It's worse by far to wake up and find a child missing."

He gained his balance along the edge of the grave and placed a palm to his chest, his head lowered a little but his eyes looked up at her through a lush array of lashes. Jessica's throat tightened all over again.

"I had permission from Mrs. Carter."

Jessica stepped closer, lowering her voice so Jude couldn't' hear. "He shouldn't be here, August." His name slipped off her tongue without a hint of discomfort and both their eyes widened in response. "Um... Mr. Reinhold." She ignored the warmth rising into her cheeks at the easy familiarity in which she'd addressed him. Ridiculous. "He's not even eight years old. And digging his own mother's grave?"

He stared back, unflinching, a quiet fighter. "He's taking care of his mother till the end, as he wants to do. Do not despise it. This service will do him good, not harm."

"Good? How can this"—she waved a hand from the grave to the house of mourners—"do him good?"

His gaze gentled. "You know, as well as I, the blessing in personally saying goodbye. Yet..." His gaze faltered, deepened with hidden wounds. "I know the long ache of an unspoken Auf Wiedersehen."

Her anger waned, and she almost placed a comforting hand to his arm to abate the grief wrinkling his brow. Yes, she'd nursed her mother to her dying breath. Dressed her body for the funeral and watched as her father, brother, and Cliff dug the grave. The goodbye was excruciating but softened by the opportunity to serve and... love her mother to the end. Even in the final breath. She knew, felt keenly the blessing of closure, of giving as her mother had always given.

A kindred wound tightened some invisible bond to him—a man whose very blood pumped with the same as the villains she'd known. Even now, she knew he made clandestine visits to Mrs.

Fischer, despite his gentle flirting with Jessica. She fisted the cloth of her skirt to keep her fingers away from him.

He was as false as the man who attacked her. "It's a difficult burden for someone so young."

August nodded. "Yes, but let the boy complete the care he began the day his father left. It will do his heart good."

"Leave poor August alone and tell your cousin hello."

Jessica rolled her eyes toward Cliff Carter and sighed. "Hello, Cliff."

Her stance slackened a little in the face of her cousin's lopsided grin. She'd missed him. He provided the other side of healthy banter in their childhood, since her brother David gentled every good argument with his peaceful demeanor. It was infuriating. Sometimes, a woman just needed a healthy argument.

Cliff rarely failed to provide one.

"I'd hug you, but I'm pretty sure you don't want all this stink on your nice yellow dress, especially with the funeral in a few minutes and all."

She followed the gesture of Cliff's chin and saw Reverend Russell appearing through the grove of trees, his hat firmly on his head and Bible in hand.

"I suppose I'll have to forego that stinky pleasure for now."

"Don't tease too much, little cousin. You're standing right between two hard-working men who could turn you into a stinky sandwich any minute."

A laugh waited to erupt in her throat. A true laugh. One she hadn't indulged in... years? Her smile tremored from the effort to keep her control. "Tempting, but I have an aversion to crowded and stinky spaces since coming back from Europe. Besides, I'm a meat and potatoes type girl, so you can keep your sandwich-loving self on the other side of that ditch."

August's broad laugh pulled her attention back to him. It sounded so free and pleasant, her smile unfurled completely before she could catch it. To cover her immediate discomfort at her clear loss of control, she pushed the clean, white shirt into his chest. "Mrs. Fischer asked me to deliver this to you for the funeral."

His face didn't mirror one glimmer of shame. Not a hint.

"I suppose you must be very close to the *single* woman to privately visit her and have her mend your shirts?"

August's gaze met hers and his smile even tipped in complete rebellion to the embarrassment he should display. "Very close."

Jess' breath hitched and the lightning connection lit afresh between them. She nearly growled against it. For such a man!

"Mrs. Painter warmed up some water for us to wash off a bit before the service." Cliff broke into the tension and pointed to a basin and cloth sitting atop a stump. "It looks like we ought to get fit for it, August. Preacher's ready, and Carl's boys just entered the house with the coffin. It shouldn't take long for the gaggle to get Eliza's body fit for burying."

August started to unbutton his dirty shirt. Jess turned her back, heat climbing up her neck at the very idea. "It seems your Mrs. Fischer takes very good care of you."

He chuckled. *Chuckled*. Cliff stood in front of her, making a vain attempt to cover his smile with his hand, and he shrugged out of his shirt to reveal his undershirt.

"What are you snickering at, Cliff Carter?"

"His sister takes very good care of him."

"Sister?" Jess turned to needle the truth out of August, only to find him bent over the basin, his back bare and his sinewy muscles tightening and flexing as he poured water over his skin. Jess ought to turn around, but neither her eyes nor her feet cooperated. Instead, she kept staring like a child gaping over the candy varieties on the shelves at Kimp's store.

For heaven's sake! She acted like she'd never seen a barechested man before. She'd sutured and completed surgery on plenty, but this man? Somehow, despite her perfectly manicured indifference to the schoolgirl-ish wiles of romance, she fell completely entangled in its surprising hold.

He looked up, patting his face with the towel, and caught her in her humiliating bewilderment. His grin tilted up at one side and made a slow slide to the other, beguiling and twisting every one of her stomach muscles into a knot.

She cleared her throat and spun back around, steadying her breaths. Her cousin's humorous expression pestered a deeper annoyance, but she readily ignored it and focused on the little boy she'd come to rescue from the German's evil clutches.

He stood nearby, staring down into the massive hole he'd helped dig. His mother's final resting place. The heat of her anger died on her cheeks and her heart nearly broke at the sight. Such a small boy. Such a big burden. "Jude?"

He blinked from his stare and looked up, sun-drops of freckles sprinkled over his small nose. She hadn't noticed those yesterday, but their presence made him appear even younger. More vulnerable. She stepped closer to him, taking his little shoulder into her hand. "Do you have a fresh shirt you can wear?"

He nodded, his chin stiffening with his task. "One more, but these is the only trousers I got with no holes."

The strings around Jess' heart tightened to the aching spot. She bent to his height and gave him her most encouraging smile. "Those'll do just fine. Could you go find that shirt in the house and change so you'll be ready?"

"Yes, ma'am." He ran the short distance to the house, the tattered bottoms of his trousers encouraging Jess to task as soon as she returned home. She couldn't do as many domestic things as her brilliant grandmother, but she could sew.

August moved beside her and her treacherous gaze took in his broad shoulders as if the fresh shirt didn't exist. She fought every flicker of heat entering her face and stared back at him, determined to control this ridiculous attraction. "Sister, is she?"

"Perhaps, Jessica Ross"—his voice smoothed over the words as he leaned a little too close for comfort— "I am a very different person than you suspect?"

And she had the sneaky suspicion that getting to know him any more than she already did might be a detriment to her hard-won bitterness... and her terrified heart.

Chapter Nine

"If I didn't know better, I'd say there's a lighter bounce in your step, August."

August sent Cliff a cautious grin as they walked down the mountainside toward home. If Cliff Carter had learned one thing about his friend, it was that within August Reinhold beat the heart of a pure optimist.

"Your cousin's stare burned a little less than usual. Perhaps I'm growing on her, yes?"

Cliff chuckled and raised his gaze upward, marveling a little at his cousin's gentling toward his foreign friend. Cliff had heard enough from his aunt and uncle to know the war stole more from her than her smile. Or her hope. Some German stole a piece of her purity, while another nearly stole her brother.

"I have to admit, you've rattled her, that's for sure. I don't think I've seen her this distracted since Jake Morris almost beat her at badminton."

"Badminton." August held a plan in his grin.

"Your thoughts can't be any good from the looks of it."

August's palms came up in defense. "Nothing to bring worry, good friend. Only some healthy competition?"

"Well, that's an idea. She always was one to like a good challenge, especially against the boys." Cliff shook his head and followed August out of the shelter of the forest. "Seemed to have a constant need to prove herself."

"Did many boys wish to court her?"

"Court her?" Cliff couldn't reign in his waiting laugh. "The poor boys were terrified of her. A few of the younger ones she tutored spent a whole lot of time moonin' over her in secret, but actually tell her about it? No doin'. She's not exactly the warm and cuddly sort."

August kept silent, slowing his pace as they entered the clearing of the Carter farm. "I see a lot of warmth. She cares for Jude."

As shocking as it seemed, maybe that little boy and newborn were exactly what his cousin needed. Something to distract her from the wounds festering inside—to draw her out of her pain.

Her gentleness with Jude during the funeral and the way she carefully went through the house with him to make certain he collected anything he wanted to take—even an old rope his father had used to teach Jude how to tie knots—showed the Jessica he'd known from years ago. She'd never rushed the boy, allowing him time, Scraps at his heels, carefully gathering up as many treasures as he and Jessica could carry.

Despite her spitfire personality, she'd always given with an enormous amount of generosity and patience. Cliff always thought that was why nursing suited her so well. Underneath the sometimes brash, prickly façade beat the heart of one of the most loyal, tenderhearted, and strong people in his life. "I saw it too, and I reckon if she's going to be his mama now, he couldn't be in any better hands. Once she cares, it's somethin' fierce."

August paused, tilting his head a moment as if digesting the statement.

Now, if Jess could find it in her heart to care for a foreigner like August? Cliff scratched his head. He wasn't too sure, but she couldn't do better. Over the past eight months since Cliff started working as a camp guard, their acquaintance had grown into a real friendship. The man lived a life of consistency and kindness, and though he didn't shove strength on people like Jessica did, there'd been enough times in the camp where August's quiet strength forged an unshakeable line between right and wrong.

But even with August's immense patience and determination, did he really have a chance with Jessica? Was it possible to break down the bitterness barring her in? Despite his cousin's generosity, she could hold a grudge better than January held onto winter. Cliff wasn't ready to enter that discussion just yet, for August's sake alone. "What do you think of Colonel Ames' visit?"

"The colonel makes predictions I do not wish to hear."

"August." August looked up, his usual grin gripped into a frown. "You've known all along that you and your countrymen wouldn't stay here forever."

"I had high hopes we would outlast the war. Then I would be free to live wherever I chose."

Cliff shoved his hands into his pockets and steadied his gaze on his friend. "Maybe after the war ends, you can find your home here, but unless it ends within the month—"

August raised a palm to still Cliff's words. "I know, friend. I know." They came to the pebbled walkway to the cottage door in silence.

What were they doing at Anna's Cottage? Cliff adjusted the collar of his shirt and stared up at the place in which he'd passed many childhood hours with Jessica and David. As an only child, they'd become his playmates, his adopted siblings. It was a familiar and beloved home, even though it still carried the sadness of his aunt's death within its walls.

But now it also held a dangerous flicker of something Cliff hadn't experienced since his wife died... and he wasn't too sure what to do about the clawing in his stomach and sweat on his palms.

A vision of gold and lavender appeared at the window and then disappeared, only to rush from the doorway like a cherub in a spring garden. Sylvie Fischer ran directly into August's arms, her giggle lighting up Cliff's heart with an internal squeeze of bittersweet. His own little girl wouldn't have been quite as old as Sylvie, if she'd survived, but Cliff imagined her glowing with the same childish joy.

Sylvie placed her palms on each of August's cheeks, clasped him close, and planted a kiss directly on his lips.

"You want tooties?" Her little voice lilted, the words muffled with a strange intonation Cliff had learned to understand. Cookies.

"Of course," came August's ready reply. "Apfel cookies, perhaps?"

Sylvie tilted her head, her curious eyes examining her uncle's mouth, her mind working out his words. "Ja, apple and timmamon too."

Apples and cinnamon could not be as sweet as Sylvie Fischer.

Sylvie peeked over August's shoulder and bestowed a dimpled smile on Cliff. His smile immediately responded. "Mr. Tarter, you want tooties too?"

Her mispronunciation of Cliff's name drew a soft palm landing over his heart to keep the feeling close. "I love cookies."

Sylvie watched his face and seemed to understand because she hopped out of August's arms and ran back into the house.

"That girl."

August nodded. "She steals hearts everywhere she goes."

"I understand you want some cookies?" Anna Fischer poised in the doorway, her long honey-colored hair in a thick braid over the shoulder of her blue dress, the same color blue as her eyes.

Cliff swallowed through the lump growing in his throat when her gaze landed on him, her smile tilting in such a way his heart stumbled into a drumroll. "You too, Cliff Carter."

He fumbled through removing his hat and followed August into the cottage.

"She likes you."

Cliff frowned at his friend's teasing glint. "I'm gonna pretend you just spoke in German and I didn't understand a word."

August chuckled. "I think you have an excellent chance to win her."

Cliff lowered his voice to a whisper as they entered the house. "You can start giving romance advice when this whole scheme of yours with my cousin works out."

"Standing in the doorway whispering is a bad habit, gentlemen." Anna's voice pulled Cliff's attention to the kitchen, where she stood with a plate of cookies and a look just as sweet.

For three years, memories and regret kept Cliff's heart buffered from the tow of attraction... until Anna Fischer moved into town with her adorable daughter. It was like waking up from a foggy dream, his senses dulled by grief, but then she arrived, following her brother into the wilds of the Blue Ridge Mountains. And somehow... right into his life.

He couldn't help but notice her. She lived at his aunt and uncle's farm, a place that'd become as much home to him since his daddy's death five years earlier, and was sister to an internee who Cliff claimed as friend.

And she was elegant and beautiful. Like sunlight. Cliff cringed at his glossy thoughts.

"I met your Miss Ross." Anna offered the plate to August, her slender brow slanted at a teasing tilt. "You are either brave or crazy."

A laugh shocked Cliff's shoulders at Anna's blunt response. "I've told him the same thing."

Anna shared a smile with him and it somehow lit a fire through his chest. "He is a stubborn sort, here." She tapped her forehead. "Hard-headed."

"But soft-hearted," August interjected, taking a seat and gesturing toward one for Cliff.

"Mind that soft heart of yours, brother. I would not see it broken." Anna waved a cookie at him in reprimand.

It was the most adorable thing Cliff had seen in a long time. Yep, he was a lost cause.

"Now, I don't think Jess would ever try to break your heart. She's not mean. She's just..." Cliff pinched his lips closed and thought. "She's a little prickly, but her heart's in the right place most of the time."

"I see that."

"She gets it honest, Mrs. Fischer." Cliff took a cookie from the plate, trying to keep his attention away from those interesting eyes of hers. "Our whole family is a little rough around the edges until you get to know us."

"Anna." Her correction pulled his gaze right into hers and the cookie got stuck in his throat. "You may call me Anna. You've been coming by with August for four months now. Don't you think we can be friends?"

He looked away from her pretty face right at August's grin. Four months of sheer emotional torture. He should win an award or something. "Yes, of course, thank you, Mrs..." Heat exploded in his face. "Anna." The name, spoken aloud, somehow fumbled up the rest of everything else he thought about saying. He stood to his feet and cleared his throat. "But I need to get back to the camp." He lifted the remains of his cookie in the air. "Thanks for the cookie."

Sylvie caught him on the way to the door, her tiny hand grasping his. "You need mil with your tootie, Mr. Tarter."

He bent to one knee so the little angel could watch his face. "Not today, Sylvie." And then he lost complete control of his senses and placed a finger to her soft little cheek, right beneath her dimple. "Maybe next time."

She rewarded him with a brighter smile and his air strangled in his lungs. Was he brave enough to risk his heart again? On both of them? He'd barely survived the first loss, turning to liquor instead of God as an escape. But now? After the years and the healing? Was he strong enough?

He looked up long enough to get caught in Anna's fascinating eyes once again—beautiful, tender, offering him a second chance. His heart pounded behind his ribs. He nodded another goodbye and turned.

"Cliff, wait." August ran out the door after him, his smile a bit too bright for Cliff's comfort.

"I can't stay right now, August. I'm this close to turning into a blubbering mess in front of your sister."

"Then why don't you end your suffering and make your feelings known?"

Cliff glanced back toward the cottage and lowered his voice. "It ain't right for a brother to try and get a man to start sparkin' his sister, August. If you knew the thoughts goin' on in my head, you ought to be runnin' me off with a shotgun."

August tapped his head. "Intelligent. When the right man for his sister arrives, then he should encourage this sparking. She's had many heartaches too."

"I just don't know..." The admission caught in his throat. "I don't know if I'm ready to try."

"Would you let fear keep you from finding love again?"

"When you hold your wife and baby in your arms and watch them slip away to a place you can't reach? No matter how strong you are or how hard you pray?" The ache swelled up in his chest as the memory gripped him. "It makes a man realize how weak and powerless he is."

"It also shows the capacity for great love."

Cliff shook his head. "The painful kind."

"The only kind." August's gaze bore into Cliff's, urging him to step out into the frightening unknown. "God will be your strength, and perhaps you are the one my sister has been praying for these years since her husband's death. She's known loss, but she has not known love."

Cliff ran a palm down his face and growled. August's declaration stung with truth and hit Cliff's attraction to Anna on target. "You sure are persistent, you know that?"

"Yes, and I am right." August's eyes glinted with mischief. Cliff braced himself. "I have a good wager for you, friend."

Cliff rubbed his forehead and looked back at the cottage, the slightest scent of hope burrowing beneath the fear. "I'm afraid to ask."

August's grin tipped higher. "When I win your cousin's heart, you will spark my sister."

Cliff almost chuckled at August's misuse of the word 'spark.' "When? You're pretty confident."

"I believe it is right too." He shrugged and put out his hand for Cliff to take. "Besides, it's no hardship for me. It has been my plan all along. You just need a nudge to take the risk, ja?"

"I ain't making no promises, August." He took the man's hand. "But I'm certainly looking forward to watching what Jess thinks of your plans for her future."

Jess peered into the small room from the doorway. It used to be her brother David's room, with its yellow and white striped wallpaper and large window overlooking the forest. Jude sat on the white, rod-iron bed, dim lantern-light casting a glow toward the book he held in his lap. The dressing gown Granny had given him hung loose on his thin frame, shrinking him a few years.

It'd taken her an hour to convince him to take a tub bath, but now, with his hair still damp from the water, curls formed and framed his forehead. He was so young yet stoic in the face of his loss. Jess clutched the doorframe and lifted her eyes heavenward, the sudden weight of responsibility sending a tremor through her.

"Did you find a book to read?"

Jude looked up, his usual somber expression in place. "Mr. Carter let me read his book on animals and places."

Jess stepped into the room, knowing the book. One of her childhood favorites, with colored pictures of all sorts of animals and their habitats. As a child, Jess marveled at the great variety of wildlife but even greater scope of the world. She placed her hands on the railing at the foot of the bed. "I remember that one. Have you gotten to the desert pictures yet?"

A faint glimmer of interest lit his eyes. "The one with that big ol' lizard?"

Jess moved to sit on the edge of the bed, his interest fueling her conversation. A little boy waited beneath all of the heartache and responsibility of a grown man. "Exactly. Have you seen the one of the tiger yet?"

His eyes grew a little wider and he shook his head, holding the book out to her.

"Oh, you'll love that one." She flipped through the pages and finally landed on the right one, turning the book so Jude could see. "And in the background you can see a deer."

"I bet the tiger is gonna eat him."

"I bet so too. Did you know tigers are one of the few types of cats who actually like to swim?"

"Really?"

A sweetness stilled over Jess' concern at this connection and the ability to bring this wounded little boy out of his shell. "Something else... look on this page." She turned to the following page and pointed toward the giant, gray animal displayed there.

"What is that?"

"An elephant."

He pulled the book close and stared at the picture in silence.

"My old teacher, Miss Kraft, said that elephants give themselves baths by pulling water into their trunks and then spraying it over their bodies."

His lips curled into a grimace. "Like a giant sneeze?"

Her smile loosed. "A clean sneeze. Just water. Like the bath you had today."

Jude looked down at the sleeves of his dressing gown. "I don't think I've ever been so clean afore." He ran a hand over the quilt covering his legs. "And soft. I reckon Mama would have loved a bed like this."

Jess hesitated before covering the little boy's hand with her own. "I'm sure she's glad you have the chance to sleep in one."

He examined her a moment, the lantern light playing off of his face. "You think so?"

Jess heart squeezed to the point of pain. "Mamas should always want good things for their children."

"So that's why mama picked you for my new mama."

The statement, uttered so innocently, seared through Jess' defenses like lightning through a dark sky. *Mama.* The word cradled such tender memories for her, a woman of courage, strength, and grace, who won the heart of an Englishman while studying abroad. But Jess wasn't like her. Gentle? Gracious? Strong? She almost scoffed. The hard edge around her personality before she left for war had sharpened and thickened with the harshness of life. Was the joyful dreamer still buried beneath the scars somewhere?

Jess patted Jude's hand and then stood. "I've never been a mama before, so I have a lot to learn, Jude."

He shrugged and offered her a lopsided grin. "That's all right. I've had a mama before, so I reckon I can help you with your learnin'."

The tenderness and compassion of her own mother proved a sweet example too. Warmth swelled in Jess' eyes. "I reckon you can." She stepped to the lantern, dulling the wick into darkness except for the pale glow of moonlight flickering into the room. "First order of mom-business is bedtime, I guess."

His lips twitched into the smallest smile in the night's glow. Jessica's responded to the tiny victory in this overwhelming learning opportunity. "Well, I reckon you got the bath time part right too, 'ceptin' I got my whole body in a tub instead of just a cloth. I should be clean for a whole week."

Jess' smile spread wide to still the internal laughter growing with a surprising warmth inside her. In her experience, little boys rarely stayed clean for a day, let alone an entire week.

"We know what we need to do in the instance you don't." She approached the bed, uncertain. "Good night, Jude."

"You gonna say prayers, Miss Jesse?"

The warmth slid into a chill. She'd prayed over hundreds of soldiers, several nurses and doctors, and even her mother's deathbed, to no avail.

"It don't have to be a long 'un, I don't guess. Mama's were awful short. She said God knew her heart already."

Jess drew in a deep breath. "How about you pray tonight, Jude, with your mama in mind, and then I'll pray tomorrow night?"

Silence followed for a second and then the little boy hopped from the bed and knelt to the floor. "I s'pose I've heard enough prayers to know a thing or two 'bout 'em."

Jess braced herself with the bed as she lowered to her knees beside Jude. Heaviness pressed down on her with incredible force, bringing the heat of tears back into her eyes.

"Oh, Heavenly Father in Heaven."

Tears tipped over Jess' eyelids at the sound of the little voice in the dark room and his redundancy.

"Thank you for our food and a warm bed. In fact, it's the warmest bed I 'bout ever seen. And thank you that Mama and Daddy are together again."

The warmth spilled down her cheeks at his innocence and gratitude, only days after his mother died. Sweet gratitude in the face of brokenness. Pain seared through her chest. How?

"And thank you for Miss Jesse' and Mr. and Mrs. Carter for being so kind to take me and Faith on, especially since Miss Jesse ain't had no motherin' experience."

Jess' smile returned despite her tears.

"I reckon you must know best about these things and I reckon you placed me in Miss Jesse's life for as good a reason as you placed her in mine. If you don't mind none, would you help us learn how to be a family like Mama wanted? And help Faith sleep better for Miss Jesse."

Jess covered her mouth with her palm to hold back a sob.

"I know there's gotta be a heap of people who need you worse 'n me, but I appreciate you listenin'. Amen."

Jess stood as the boy crawled into bed, barely able to trust her voice. The tears cooled on her face but didn't stop, thankfully hidden by the darkness.

"Good night, Miss Jesse."

With quick movements, she leaned over and kissed the boy's head. "Good night, Jude."

Jess slipped from the room and leaned back against the wall at the top of the hallway. How? How could Jude Larson hold such a thankful heart in the middle of his grief? She tried to explain it all away as a simply a childish innocence, but a piece of her heart bucked against the easy dismissal. She'd believed it all once. Cherished her faith and the Keeper of it. But how could she cling to such a love filled with loss and grief and scars? How could she take the hard providences as His good work in her life? The betrayals?

Her wounds cried out for revenge. Her heart ached from the weary battle to maintain control.

"How?" She whispered into the moonlit darkness.

You are not alone.

Chapter Ten

Jessica hurried to town, her grandpa's Model T bumping along the dirt road made sloshy by the morning rain. As soon as the sun broke through the gray skies after dinner, Jess asked Granny to watch Jude and Faith while she dashed to town for a few supplies, particularly baby needs, as well as a lollipop for Jude. After watching the pure ecstasy on his face at tasting Granny's cinnamon-apple cookies for the first time, Jess couldn't wait to see his response to a lollipop. Her smile spread. Or a Life Saver. If Kimp carried them, she'd purchase a whole pack so he could taste each flavor.

"Mr. Lawry saw you coming down the street and brought some mail to you." Kimp handed over two envelopes and then proceeded to ring up Jessica's items.

"Thank you." She glanced down at the top envelope and smiled. Her father's handwriting. Oh, how she missed him, her brother, David, and even David's wife, Catherine.

She slid the mail into her skirt pocket. "Any news from the war?"

"Same old," Kimp answered, sliding the groceries to a young girl on his left to place in a paper bag. "Seems there's talk it might not be much longer, but they've been saying that for months now."

And by the time news reached Hot Springs, it was at least a month old.

"Who is your fine helper, Mr. Kimper?"

He passed the girl a look from his periphery. "This is my niece, Amy McKinney, come to live with us and study at the school."

"Dorland Bell?" Jess surveyed the young girl, whose simple attire and pale features gave off a Jane Eyre quality—well, everything except for the spindly curl to her dark hair, hair so unruly it would not be tamed into a bun and instead sprung down either side of the girl's face in ringlets. "I've heard excellent things of the school, Miss McKinney."

Her smile transformed her entire face, and her rich brown eyes even sparkled. "They've been very kind to me."

"And have you learned a lot?"

"Oh, yes." A brightness filled her hazel eyes. "I'm ever so thankful for Uncle Kimp taking me in so I could attend there."

Kimp grunted in a good-natured response, typical of most of the menfolk in town. Tenderness was a private emotion, not public. Very unlike her father, despite his English upbringing, who doled out affection like morphine in a Clearing Station.

"I'm glad you are in such good hands."

"I've heard you are a nurse." Miss McKinney held out the grocery bag, her smile growing to an infectious degree.

"Yes, I am."

"I hope to study medicine too." The girl nodded, her jaw firm with confidence. "Maybe even become a doctor."

"Don't talk nonsense, girl. Girls don't become doctors 'round here."

"Now, Mr. Kimper." Jess leveled the man with a stare. "Careful, or I'll assume you think your niece can't become a doctor."

Kimp placed his hands on his hips and shook his head. "I ain't gonna start an argument with you about the rights of women. I couldn't win 'em ten years ago and I don't reckon I could win 'em now." He gestured toward his niece. "But it ain't good to put notions in simple girls' heads. She ain't got no earl for a daddy."

"My father wasn't an earl when I went to school. He was part of Hot Springs and worked hard to put food on the table like every other man here, but he also believed I could achieve just as much as my brother, if I wanted." She smiled over at Amy. "And so can Amy. Who's to say she can't be a doctor if she has the mind and will for it?"

Kimp barely held back his grin as he shoved the other grocery bag toward Jess. "You've caused enough trouble in here for one morning, Jessica Ross. You'd better git out before Amy takes the notion to run for president."

Jess took the bag and twisted her smile into submission. "What an excellent suggestion, Mr. Kimper. I'm glad to see you're a visionary."

Kimp rolled his eyes and shooed her toward the door. She caught Amy's grin and added a wink to the exchange before she stepped from the store.

"We meet again, Miss Ross. My day has greatly improved."

Jasper Little strolled toward her. He looked quite fetching with his straw hat, walking cane, and Cheshire cat smile, each sending the slightest thrill through her middle.

What woman didn't enjoy a little harmless flattery from a handsome man? Even a woman who was perfectly capable of taking care of herself.

"I see you've not been frightened away by the natives yet, sir."

His smile spread. "Despite their best attempts, I remain. I'm quite stubborn in my way, you understand."

"I'm cut from the same cloth, for good or for bad." She shrugged and loosened her grin. "But mostly good, of course."

"I wouldn't imagine otherwise."

She reveled in the freedom of such harmless flirtation, especially with a man of equal wit and interest. Many of the good-hearted boys of Hot Springs were either much too intense to appreciate healthy banter or too involved in their farm lives and work to provide conversational variety.

"Let me assist you." He took her bags in his arms, maneuvering with more ease than expected without his hand.

He'd learned to live with his wounds as she'd done. Survivors. Fighters. Yes, he understood in ways others couldn't.

"Thank you."

"Whatever excuse necessary to enjoy your company, Miss Ross."

A rush of heat stole into her face at his compliment and she started toward her car down the street to avoid his poignant stare.

He fell into step with her, bringing with him the sweet scent of licorice.

"You've indulged in some of Kimp's sweet treats, I see."

His brow tilted with his enticing grin. "I have the money to pay for such inflated sweets, which Mr. Kimper readily took without complaint."

"No doubt." She snickered, indulging in the giddy swell of controlled attraction. "And how goes your research?"

He groaned and shook his head, his expression fading into a grimace. "Slower than anticipated, I'm afraid."

She stopped and turned to him, lowering her cane to the ground now that her arms were free. "It's a big world behind all those forests, isn't it?"

He looked away, staring ahead. "Quite."

She could only imagine. Eliza's death and funeral whisked Jess quickly back into the culture of her upbringing. As a whole, the Appalachian people, particularly the ones further back in the mountains, kept to themselves and wore suspicion like a coat. Of course, there were exceptions, and most of the people were quick to offer generous aid to those within their community, but newcomers? Many times, that was a very different story.

"I'd suspect not everyone was very welcoming."

He squinted into the cloud-covered sunlight in the faded afternoon blue sky. "Indeed not. Part of the culture?"

"Lots of natives of the mountains are suspicious of outsiders, but I'm certain that's no surprise to you based on your studies."

"Of course not."

"I can go with you some time, if you like, and help bridge the gap? Perhaps bring grandfather along."

His smile wavered, but quickly returned. "I appreciate your offer and will be happy to employ your assistance when next I venture forth into the great unknown hollows."

She laughed and shrugged off a sudden sense of discomfort, commencing her walk up Main Street toward the Railroad depot and the camp. "I'm certain Jane Gentry gave you bushels of insight. She's usually very good at that."

"Indeed. Bushels, as you said, but at least someone was helpful."

"Any of the other ladies I mentioned?" she prodded, searching for their previous fluid and congeal conversation. "Certainly not only Jane has helped you? Most of the older ladies near town enjoy reminiscing as much as they enjoy their rocking chairs."

His smile didn't return, his brow crinkled. "One or two, but I can't recall their names. Unusual names, I believe."

The uneasiness dampened a bit. "No doubt it was Bellzora or Zipporah?"

He laughed. "Ah, yes. Weren't those ladies on the outskirts of town, as you said?"

"Yes, and you'll have opportunity to meet more when you accompany my grandfather on his rounds in the future."

"Ah." He stopped at the railroad crossing and waited for direction. "Which should begin in only a few days, if I remember."

"Yes, Tuesday morning." Jessica sighed, feeling a little sorry for the handsome English stranger. No doubt his upbringing had not prepared him for Hot Springs. "I'll apologize ahead of time. If you thought traipsing about the mountains nearby were daunting, wait until you join Grandpa on his rounds. It certainly provides an education into the culture."

"Why did that sound more like a warning than an offer of encouragement?"

She paused in his gaze. There'd been a few men over the years, nothing serious. Much like this, the conversations kept to a shallow ease, never piercing beneath the surface of convention and pretense. Never dipping into depths August Reinhold's gaze threatened to unearth with tender tilling.

Why him? Of all the people in the world, or even in Western North Carolina, why a man who came from the heritage of her attacker, and even resembled him in some slight way. Why?

More of God's humor doled out for her good?

"Probably a little of both." She nodded across the street near Iron Horse's Boarding House where she'd left the car. "There's my car. I appreciate your help and company for the walk, Mr. Little, but I must get back home to help Granny with supper. What are your plans? More investigating?"

His dark gaze locked on hers, more intense. "Um... yes, investigating." He sighed and his brow puckered with a frown. "I suppose I'll return to the boarding house for this evening. I find myself quite lost after dark, except for the excitement offered inside the tavern."

"Oh, I'm certain there's a whole variety of excitement there." Folks rarely stepped too far across the law in town, especially with the upright and serious Officer Lawson at the helm, but a tavern was still a tavern. "If you have no plans for Monday evening, perhaps you'd like to join me and my grandparents for supper? It would give you a chance to ask my grandfather questions before he leads you into the great unknown on Tuesday? Unless your usual cohorts at the tavern will miss you?"

His gaze wavered before returning with an added smile. "I suppose they can do without me for one night. I'd be delighted to accept your offer."

"Good." She turned toward the street. "Then I best get these items home and share the news with Granny. She loves feeding people." Jess steadied her cane as she stepped to cross the street, making certain of no oncoming carriages or rare automobiles.

"Do you think you could walk unaided by your cane as you near the camp?"

The question sent her a little off balance, with or without the cane. She *could* walk without the cane, but the exercise always made her limp more pronounced.

"You could hold to my arm instead, perhaps?" he added, quickly, his attention flicking to the camp gate and back.

Jess followed his gaze to the camp, where a few internees stood in a line at the camp gate, most likely preparing to cross back to the Upper Camp to the barracks for the evening. "I'm sorry, Mr. Little, but I don't make it a habit of linking arms with a man on a regular basis. People would think we're courting."

His smile spread, tight and false. "And that would be a problem?"

"At this point, to make a habit of it would be false advertising."

He groaned and followed her out into the street. "But couldn't you go without your cane near the camp? You mustn't let them know how they've wounded you. I'm certain they'll find a way to take advantage of your weaknesses."

A chill crossed over her skin at the unintentional foreknowledge in his topic. She walked a little faster. "Come now, Mr. Little, the men are behind a clapboard fence near town and a barbed wire one along the remainder of the periphery."

"Not all of them."

His implication clipped with bitterness. August Reinhold. Jess reached for the anger to apply to the very thought of the golden-headed stranger, but its potency staggered as mental visions of him clamored to the surface. Could he have deceived her entire family for this long? What could he gain by showing kindness to Jude during and after Eliza's death?

Her grandparents were soft-hearted but not ignorant, mountain-born but seasoned with life's wisdom. Would they be so easily taken in by a duplicitous foreigner?

She looked toward the camp as a careful line of internees marched across the street to the barracks on the other side. They paraded tall and proud in khaki trousers and white shirts stained with hard work. She shook off the chill of Jasper's warning.

"I appreciate your concern, Mr. Little, but I've taken care of myself for a long time, Germans or not, and I mean to continue the practice." She took the bags from his arms and placed them in the Model T.

"Unless you find someone who would willingly take care of you?" He leaned against the vehicle, his gaze moving from her face down to her shoes and back. She flinched.

"Or I find someone who needs my care?" she challenged with a grin and refused his assistance into the car to prove her point, taking her place behind the steering mechanism. "I appreciate chivalry, Mr. Little, as any thoughtful woman should, but I also value an equal partnership of minds and strengths. A couple, to my mind, should not only desire each other's company, but find relief in their complementary strengths."

"Of course." He tipped his hat.

"Now, if you'll excuse me, I must be off to let Granny know of your visit. Despite the delicious fare served at the Iron Horse, I suggest you prepare yourself for a feast of Appalachian cooking as only my granny can offer. Good day."

She turned the car into motion and glanced over to the camp, only to catch the last glimpse of August' face before he disappeared behind the fence. Had he seen the exchange between her and Jasper?

Jess sat a little straighter and stared ahead. No matter. Why should she worry about the thoughts of August Reinhold?

"We will have a formal visit from General Ames again in three weeks, at which time we are to have the entire camp ready for an inspection."

August stepped into the dining hall in time to hear the tail end of Captain Ruser's announcement. The older but stalwart captain stood at the front of the long room, his presence as commanding as his voice. The hundreds of officers in the room sat to attention.

"If we are to leave our mountain camp, we will leave honorably and without cause for shame. If the U.S. Government wishes us to prepare the camp for departure, then we shall work toward the goal until they remove the last man."

August caught Captain Luther's attention and approached the man as the other officers began their meals. "What is this news, sir?"

The lean man, a young captain, trained his gaze on the task of opening his serviette. "The same as has been expected for a month or more. The government plans to move us soon."

Heat drained from August's face taking his smile with it. How soon? Would he have enough time to complete the project he'd promised to Dr. Carter? For Jessica's sake?

Of course, from the way Jessica had smiled into the face of the Englishman, August might have lost his chance to win her heart already. He grimaced. But to such a man? The dark, shifty eyes? The saccharine charm? Nein.

"And the timeline, sir?"

The captain sat back in his chair and stared up at August. "Colonel Ames is to arrive within the month to announce plans, but until then, we are to work."

Not even a month? August closed his eyes and allowed the frustration to escape in a rush from his nostrils. Another sweet dream snatched from his hand? *Oh, Lord, please make a way of rescue. Of escape.*

"Do they have a specific place in mind to send us?"

"The only logical conclusion would be Oglethorpe."

The word soaked warmth like an icy blast. Stories strained through their ranks regarding the dreaded prison camp. Its very presence brought the stench of shame, along with unending tales of beatings and brutal work. A treacherous life for accused traitors. Prisoners.

August looked around the room. Few of the men reclining at these beautiful tables held the heart of a traitor or murderer. They were not the sort of men turning Jessica's thoughts against him. No. Not the same man who attacked her and her brother at the Front. Would these men have fought for their country? Yes. And proudly. But traitors? Nein.

"And once the government men come?" Captain Nisse tipped his glass toward Luther. "What do you say our camp becomes less... relaxed than it is now? These hardworking men pulled from the fields and forests of these mountains to sentry us are not soldiers. They are more friend than guard. They've ruled with a firm yet generous hand."

Being a castoff from his family never waned in its grief, but August had healed in so many ways from that wound and grown to accept the hard-heartedness of his father and the indifference of his elder brother. But now, to be ripped from another haven, another home, warm with its people, faith, and beauty? An unleashed cry crept for release in his throat. *No, God. Please.*

Luther nodded, his frown deepening the lines in his brow. "I can assure you, gentlemen. We will not get such treatment when the government sends their trained men. No." He tilted his gaze up to August. "Take your freedom now, August. Enjoy it. It will not last much longer."

Jessica dug up another potato and placed it in the bag at her side. She'd gotten straight to work as soon as she'd returned from town, an uneasiness propelling her into mindless activity. With Faith slung across her chest in a makeshift carrier, she'd managed to collect enough vegetables from the garden to supply Granny with food for the next four days, and then some. She needed to keep busy, employ her wayward thoughts, especially away from introspection with her own heart.

She paused in her work, staring up at the blue-hazed sky. She'd been impulsive in inviting Mr. Little, almost compelled to force a connection her heart didn't readily make. Why? She covered Faith's little head nestled against her chest with her palm, in some way grounding herself in the moment, and a tiny awareness tucked behind her fear awakened. August. She was terrified of the vibrant connection. The need to look for him. The unlassoed curiosity and something deeper than attraction, something luring her away from her assumptions, against her will and hate.

But what was it? And why him?

"The kinder... children have discovered one another."

A shadow fell over Jessica and she looked up to see Anna Fischer standing at the edge of the garden. A straw hat, only a few shades lighter than her hair, topped her head boasting a single green ribbon for decoration—the same color as her skirt.

Jess followed her gaze to where Jude stood nearby, talking to Sylvie, apparently nonplussed by Sylvie's different communication style. They bent close, their heads low over some interesting item in the grass. Sylvie, in her delicate yellow dress, her rich golden hair tied back in a matching bow, stared up at Jude, his dusty overalls covering an oversized white shirt. Her cherub face was intense, her gaze watching with fascination and curiosity over their shared adventure.

"I saw them start talking a few moments ago and hoped it would be good for both of them," Jessica said, placing her palms on her back as she rose. Faith might be small but her little weight didn't go unnoticed for an unseasoned adoptive mother's back. "I can imagine Sylvie can become lonely for children out here with only my grandparents as neighbors."

Anna's smile softened and she turned her curiosity full on Jessica. "Yes. And not everyone is patient enough to keep trying when they hear her differences."

Jess sighed and switched her attention back to the pair. Jude held a caterpillar in his hand and Sylvie ran a finger over it, jumped back with a giggle, and returned, all the while switching her attention back to Jude's face. The little boy who'd lost his family offered kinship to a little girl from the countrymen who killed his father? No hindrances. What would their generation bring? A place of peace between two worlds?

The biting claw of conviction scraped across her soul. She pulled her attention away from the innocent scene and hoped her smile held a welcome she wasn't sure she felt. "I think they both need the friendship."

"As we all do."

Jessica adjusted the cloth sling wrapped around her body as Faith's little eyes, bright and blue, watched from her cocoon. Her dearest friend, Ashleigh, had lived an hour's train ride from Hot Springs when they became friends in nursing school, and now she lived across the world in Ednesbury with her brother. Jess even missed Catherine, her enigmatic sister-in-law. Though their relationship began in animosity, at best, time and change had molded it into a sweet kinship, but here? In Hot Springs? Many of her former friends stayed busy with their married lives or had moved away from Hot Springs altogether. Friendship? Yes, she missed friendship.

"How do you like living in our little town, Mrs. Fischer?"

"Anna, please." The woman stepped forward, this time offering her hand again.

Jess drew a deep breath, wiped her dirty palm against her apron, and took the offering. "And you may call me Jessica, if you like."

"It is a beautiful and restful place. I am glad to have come and to be away from the town enough to enjoy the quiet."

Jess almost followed with another question, one too personal for a second conversation, but Anna caught the hesitation. "You wonder why I am here, Jessica?"

"Your husband is in the camp, I suppose?"

"I did not move to the States for my husband. He died in combat two years ago."

The news stopped Jess as she reached for the bag of vegetables at her feet. "In France?"

"Yes." Anna's face gave nothing away. No sorrow or anger.

Jess filtered through the names of every German she'd treated but a 'Fischer' didn't emerge from the clouded dust of memory. "I'm sorry for your loss."

"He was gone in heart a long time before he left our home." Anna reached down for the other bag of vegetables. "My father chose my husband for me for his wealth, not his kindness. I am sad for what *he* lost in having such a hard heart more than it grieves me to have lost him."

Jess' gaze wavered beneath Anna's direct stare, her confession beating at Jessica's will. "Then I'm sorry for a different reason. For you and Sylvie."

Anna placed her palm to the back of her hat and looked up at the sky with a sigh. "Time has healed a great many wounds. Time and your grandparents' kindness."

"Your father sounds like a real pill."

Anna's lips slipped to a grin. "Yes, the kind that would stick in your throat."

The unexpected humor inspired a chuckle. "Those are the worst kind."

"Indeed." She covered her smile with her palm. "But I should not speak ill of the dead." Her periwinkle eyes continued to glimmer with mischief. Maybe there was more to Anna than Jess wished to see.

"Your father chose your husband for you?"

"Yes. He chooses all of the children's spouses. We were from a very wealthy family, August and me."

"Were?"

She shook her head. "Come, I will tell you more inside with a glass of the lemonade your grandmother taught me to make. You will like that, yes?"

Jess looked back toward the house, then to Jude who continued to entertain Sylvie, and then down at baby Faith. She'd need a bottle soon, but Jess had a few minutes... and Granny was completely out of lemonade.

"Thank you."

She followed Anna to the cottage and froze at the first step over the threshold. Despite the two years, the faintest hint of lilacs drifted out of the recesses of the house. Her mother's scent. Sunlight bathed the familiar furniture with a hallowed glow and pulled her forward into memory. Her childhood home, and the place her mother died.

"Here, I also have some of the molasses cookies Mrs. Carter taught me to make."

Jess swallowed the knot of tears in the throat and reached for a cookie from the plate Anna offered. Her fingers trembled.

"I am sorry, Jessica." Anna set down the plate and took Jessica's hand into hers. "I did not think. This must be hard for you. Do you wish to leave?"

Jess slipped her hand free of Anna's hold, gripped the back of a nearby chair for support, and stiffened her smile. "No." Her voice formed in a rasp. She cleared her throat. "No, thank you. I'm fine."

"Admitting you grieve is not a weakness." Anna took a seat nearby. "My mother died last year as well. In May."

Jess looked up and recognized the same grief in Anna's eyes, the same heart scar. "I'm sorry."

Anna sat back in the chair, her gaze softening to memory. "She was a lovely woman. Kind. Gentle. All of the things my father was not. I tended to her until her death, and then found no reason to stay in Germany any longer. With August cast out from the family and my father determined to marry me to another wretched man, I decided to start afresh."

"And you came to Hot Springs?"

"I can think of worse places to start afresh, can't you?"

Again, a smile teased the corners of Jess' lips. "True." Jess studied the dainty teacup in her hand, a unique design of orchids framed its scalloped edges. Beautiful craftsmanship and artistry. "Your brother was cast out?"

Anna's smile veiled more than it uncovered. "I understand from August that you are not fond of Germans, and I can appreciate your hesitancy since you were so intimately involved in the war, but some battles are not faced on the battlefield. Some are fought through an entire childhood without protection of armies and soldiers, and leave as deep a scar."

Ashleigh, Jessica's closest friend, came to mind with her childhood secret of abuse. Yes, there were more, but they didn't invalidate the wounds and humiliation of those she'd incurred during the war. Faith made a smacking noise, her fist in her mouth. The lemonade wouldn't last much longer.

"I'm sorry for whatever happened to you and your brother in your past." She stood, placing her cup on the small table at her side. "But I've returned home to find the one place I considered safe to be overrun with more Germans than I'd seen during the whole war. Do you expect me to embrace this like the rest of Hot Springs? I've witnessed atrocities at your kinsmen's hands. I've been the brunt of their—" She snapped her lips closed and stepped toward the door. "I'm sorry, Anna. Someday, I might accept this friendship you offer, but not today."

Chapter Eleven

"You've been awful quiet this afternoon."

Jess stopped at the bottom of the stairs to meet her grandpa, still working to control her emotions from the earlier conversation with Anna. Something in her head, the rational part of her, shouted out the ridiculousness of her prejudice. The utter lunacy of such narrow-minded assumptions. But her heart ached with the weighty cost of another man's lust and the reigning grief of hundreds of lost lives in a devastating war.

"Coming home is harder than I thought."

He nodded, tugging his pipe from his pocket. "I'd imagine so, and it's not been so easy this first month."

She rubbed her forehead. "No, Grandpa. It hasn't."

"Let's go for a walk, like old times." He gestured with his chin toward the front door, hinting to their weekly path along Spring Creek they'd taken when she was a child. "You just put the baby down for a nap and Jude's helpin' Granny with some biscuits." His brows wiggled with playful temptation and loosed her resolve.

"Sounds like a good idea."

They checked with Granny before stepping off the large front porch for the tree-lined trail. There was something magical about this path with its rosy dogwood entrance framing the way into a mountain laurel wonderland. The rhododendron, hiding among the fleshing leaves of the laurel, bowed to the newer blooms of summer, only to have both eventually fade to the brilliant quilt of autumn leaves. Home.

Scraps and Lightning bounded after them, dancing about each other like two overgrown rabbits. They'd found kinship with each other too.

Grandpa and Jess walked in silence a while, the vibrant whistle of the busy birds serenading a lazy summer afternoon. Honeysuckle air brought a cool touch to Jess' cheeks as their easy pace crumpled old leaves underfoot.

"I don't imagine we'll have much more afternoons this cool with summer closing in."

"Probably not."

The stillness seeped deep, whispering to her battered soul, calling her from her solitude. Her grandpa's intent, no doubt. She breathed in the sweet air and almost felt a prayer slip from the recesses of her pain. A child's cry. A weary reach for help.

"When I lost my parents three months apart from each other, I sought out the comfort of God in these forests. Your granny and I would take long walks, and sometimes, we wouldn't say a word, only listen. Listen for God to speak to our hearts. Touch us with comfort."

They took a few more steps. "And what did He say?"

Grandpa offered her a grin from his periphery. "Well, for a long time, I didn't hear him say anything at all. Same thing happened after your mama died. I was overcome with sorrow, too busy listening to the sound of my own voice asking God why."

The words came with a gentle sting.

"But then, after the pain started to subside and I began to see clear again, He spoke. His comfort came from the same place it'd always been. In his Word. I read, *He heals the brokenhearted and binds up their wounds.*"

The irony. As a nurse, her occupation, by definition, was to heal, to bind brokenness, so why couldn't she cure her own shattered insides? She craved healing, the soothing freedom of a quiet heart, but feared it at the same time. It came with a cost.

What would she lose if she relinquished her anger, her fury at the man… and his people who had caused such harm to so many? What price would God require her to pay in exchange for an ounce of peace?

Wounds hollowed her out. Fear prickled the remains. How could she keep living this shattered life? This ghost-walk of an existence? Two choices rose from the silence—either a hard heart or a mended one.

"That same Psalm goes on to talk about God's greatness. He names the stars and calls down the snow. Makes the wind blow and the rains come. But none of those big things make him happier than His children finding hope in His steadfast love."

Jess stopped and faced her grandpa, her gaze searching his. "Steadfast? How can his love be steadfast when there is death and destruction going on in every corner of this world? What kind of love lets thousands of young men die in a senseless war? Or leaves two children orphaned to whoever will take them? Or… or allows a drunken German soldier to steal the innocence of his captive?" Tears blurred her grandpa's face, but he moved, embracing her in his thick, strong arms.

She buried her face in his shoulder, breathing in the scent of his two worlds. Pine and lye soap. Pipe tobacco and the faintest hint of peroxide.

"I'm sorry, little girl." His deep voice rasped with the pain, searing her middle. "I'm sorry I couldn't stop those wounds from finding you. So sorry you were the victim of a broken man's evil. I can't tell you why it happened, but I can tell you that the temptation to wall yourself up inside will only hurt you worse. The anger will harden you to any good feelin' of the sweetness of this life and the tender touch of love."

"But how can you trust Him? When all these bad things happen? How can He be steadfast?"

"Steadfast means that His love stays the same though the whole world falls apart. He promises to hold you, especially when your heart breaks from hands of broken people. He's holding you right now, girl. Better and more certain than I ever could, because he holds your soul. As scarred and crumbled as it feels, His fingers are gliding over it, healing and molding and shaping it into something new. Something stronger because of His love. Steadfast doesn't mean the storm ends. It means there's unshakeable safety in the middle of the storm."

"I hate storms." Her words trembled.

Her grandpa wiped a tear from her cheek with his wrinkled palm. "Then let Him be your shelter. The world can be mad all around you, but your heart can know His peace no matter the storm. No matter the pain others put upon you. He promises to heal you."

She clung to Grandpa, weeping into his shirt until the sobs subsided in a withered breath.

His soft, deep voice rose into the quiet. "Dear God, you who named the stars and set the planets in place. Who formed those destined for good and those for ill. Oh, God of the broken and lonely, scarred and rejected. Father to fatherless and home for the foreigner."

She stiffened at his reference, but then breathed out some of her anger on a sigh.

"Comfort my girl. Take this burden she keeps holding, a burden too big for her to carry, and drench her hatred with your sweet mercies. Overwhelm her with your presence so she will see the goodness of your hands and the greatness of your love. And..."

The hitch in his voice pierced her so deeply, a fresh wave of tears warmed her eyes.

"And, Father, give her the strength to forgive the unforgiveable so that she can be free from bitterness. Open her eyes."

She pulled back and looked up at him. "Open my eyes?"

His palm bushed away another tear. "Oh, honey, grief and anger make us blind. You're so busy staring at your empty hand, you've failed to see how full the other one is."

He squeezed her shoulders and offered his own teary-eyed grin. "We all miss your mama, but her strength is still alive in you. Her courage is too." He kissed her forehead. "You're braver than you think you are."

Jess looked down at the trail, her heart wrestling for peace, for truth.

"I'm going to go on back and help your granny with the young'uns. Why don't you take a little while and come on home when you're ready?"

She nodded.

"And maybe you can bring in a few of them apples on your way back. I bet we can convince your granny to cook up some apple turnovers for breakfast. They always made you feel a little better when you were small."

Jess grinned and wiped at her nose like a little girl. "They did have some magical qualities to them."

"What would she say about those sour apples and her dessert?" He looked up at the sky. "Some sour and some sweet..."

"Make this apple treat complete," Jessica finished.

He raised a brow and gave her shoulder a final squeeze. "Food for thought, I'd say."

With that, he walked away, disappearing behind the curve in the path toward home.

She couldn't recall how long she stayed there among the flowers and squirrels, waiting for a peace she used to know but which lingered just beyond her grasp. What did her grandfather mean by her hand being full?

She looked down at her left hand. A residual scar from the explosion made a curve from her wrist to the middle of her palm. She'd lost friends, almost lost her brother, lost a piece of her innocence, lost a friend in childbirth, lost her ability to walk without a limp or hear well from one ear. She turned over her right palm and looked at it, the hand smooth and unhindered by the effects of war. What did she have left?

She balled up her fist and stared upward. Paint strokes of white clouds breezed along in the faded blue sky. "I... I don't know how my grandparents can see your love inside this pain and I'm not inclined to go along without good cause, so..." She glanced around the forest, waiting, wondering, and the little girl inside of her hoping this fairytale might be true. "So, if you are in the middle of all this mess, show me."

Jessica tucked a final apple into her burgeoning apron before stepping out of the forest in sight of the farm house. Whether from the crying on her grandfather's shoulder or the fresh air of the day, the heaviness from earlier had lifted a little. As she came to the front porch steps, the sound of laughter from behind the house piqued her curiosity. She unloaded the apples onto the porch and made her way around the side of the house, stopping at the back corner to take in the sight.

August Reinhold stood, holding Sylvie's arm with a badminton racquet, while Jude waited across the net with his own racquet in hand. Evidently, from the gentle instruction and occasional laughter, he was trying to teach the children badminton. Sylvie kept trying to turn around to see his face. Jude's intense focus caused him to hit the birdie too hard. All the while, August kept attempting to teach, unscathed by the complete futility of the effort.

Jess leaned against the house, watching him from her shadowed perch. He crouched behind Sylvie, his khaki slacks and white button-up still giving him a fashionable look despite his current occupation. A special sort of tenderness enveloped him in some strange way, a gentle strength. The way he cupped Sylvie's hand with his own against the racquet, his cheek pressed to hers as he helped her practice her swing, most likely to help her feel the vibrations of his speech at her ear. Gentle.

So different from her attacker.

Lt. Snyder, the true name of the spy who captured her and her brother, never stooped to dirty his clothes for the pleasure of a child. Not while he playacted as a Belgian doctor on the Front lines and certainly not after he'd revealed his true identity to Jess and David at gunpoint. He'd been harsh, forceful, taking exactly what he wanted from those subordinate to him. And though he hadn't been able to completely violate her in his attack, he'd done enough to leave a stain of shame on her soul. She pinched her eyes closed at the naked memory... his rough hands on her skin... his heated breath scraping across her lips to her neck.

She forced her attention away from the ravaged remains of those memories and frantically searched for hints of duplicity in the countenance of the man before her. Sylvie snatched the racquet from him at one point, tossed it to the ground, and grabbed his face in her hands, fussing at him in an animated fashion. August's deep laugh drifted to her from the field, pricking her frown to respond.

Her lips complied and her heart pushed against the boundaries of her hurt.

Sylvie pushed at August until he fell from his crouched position into the grass and after a second's hesitation, Jude joined Sylvie in piling on top of the vulnerable sailor. August's laugh continued, warm and inviting, intermingled with Sylvie's infectious giggle. Jessica lost her hold on her smile as it spread wide, pinching into her cheeks.

In that moment, as August stood from the ground, Sylvie hooked to one of his legs and Jude clinging to his neck in a vain attempt to bring the man down again, his gaze found hers across the yard. His unfettered smile, broad and alive, froze. He raised a brow, his gaze beckoning her to enter his world of laughter and children and unbridled joy.

And something her heart understood that her mind didn't.

She paused, grappling her expression back to neutral, waiting as Jude's weight finally won against August's balance and they both toppled to the ground again. She emerged from the shadows of the house and walked forward, each step closer to the cheerful bunch.

"I've never learned this rule of badminton, Mr. Reinhold. Is it part of the German version?"

He sat up, picking off Jude then Sylvie carefully and placing them on the grass with a tickle or two in the process. It was very difficult to remain cross with such a man.

"I'm afraid my students became distracted."

She folded her arms across her chest, examining him as he rose to his feet. "Clearly."

He dusted off his trousers with his hat and then replaced the latter back on his head, peeking at her from beneath the rim. "You could do better?"

"Probably. At this rate, it will be winter before you have one rally."

"Is that a challenge, Miss Ross?"

She laughed. "I don't need to challenge you, Mr. Reinhold."

He matched her pose, his arms folded. "I could best you, I think."

She slipped her palms to her hips, giving his full body a cynical perusal. "From what I just witnessed, that's doubtful."

"You play me?"

"No."

He grimaced and then some thought must have spurned a mischievous smile. "You are afraid I will best you?"

Her laugh spilled loose again, and the residual warmth of his teasing ushered her own response. "Oh no, I won't lose, dear Mr. Reinhold. I just don't like to see grown men cry."

His grin spread wide again in a way that let her know what she said pleased him, though she couldn't figure out how. Her sassy comments rarely evoked much except scorn or a reprimand.

"Bold words." He ushered his palm toward the playing field, then slid her a look. "I promise to be easy on you."

Her smile faded and she stood up straighter. "Easy on me?" Her lips pursed tight and she stepped closer, hoping her glare singed his perfect grin. "Because of my leg?"

"Oh no, Miss Jesse." He stared back, his brow raised in pure innocence. "Because you are a woman."

A shock of air burst from her lungs. She held out her palm. "It's a challenge, Mr. Reinhold."

He took her hand, his grin tilted in his mesmerizing way, and she suddenly realized what had happened. She'd walked readily into his trap, and for some reason, she wasn't half as infuriated as she ought to be.

"But the match will have to wait until... later?"

"Ah, I see. You've suddenly realized you've overcommitted yourself?"

He removed his hat, unveiling his rebel curls. "Oh no, my dear Miss Jesse. I promised Sylvie and Jude a treasure hunt before I return to camp this afternoon."

"A treasure hunt?" She crossed her arms again, the fire of a new argument animating her tongue. "How convenient."

He raised his palms in admission of his blamelessness. "I speak the truth. You can ask Jude or Sylvie. We have a very special treasure hunt to make."

"It sounds highly suspicious, Mr. Reinhold."

She bestowed her most narrow-eyed gaze. He didn't even flinch. In fact, his grin teased wider. "You are right." He leaned close enough that his breath taunted chills across the skin at her cheek. "We are on a secret mission to collect information for the Kaiser, all hidden within the woods of your fair town."

She rolled her gaze up to his, his face close, his scent of pine even closer. "And you just shared your vital information with your enemy."

"You are not *my* enemy, Miss Jesse." He wiggled his brows. "Until you are across the net from me."

She shoved his shoulder to created distance from his enticing warmth. "Fine. Go off on your treasure hunt."

Those periwinkle eyes held her attention for a moment longer, the gentle tug toward him opening a dormant curiosity. Trust him? Her breath hitched at the terrifying possibility. Trust a German? Again?

Mercifully, August turned his attention to Jude. "Jude, collect Sylvie for our walk. Our treasure hunt is too exciting for Miss Jesse today."

She stared at the back of his head, hoping her vision left the slightest mark. But it would be a shame to scorch such lovely hair. "I like adventure as good as the next person, but I have work to do. Dinner, in fact. And a baby to see to."

She gestured up toward the porch where Granny sat with Sylvie in her arms.

"Don't mind us none, Jess honey. We're fine as can be."

Jessica's shoulders slumped. Granny was no help at all with excuses.

Jess turned back to the trio, but they were already walking away from her, starting for the path through the woods toward the chapel. Sylvie rode on August's back like an oversized and adorable knapsack in frilly rose. Jude walked beside him, one strap of his overalls falling over his shoulder, reminding her of how young he really was. Vulnerable. And *hers*.

Her heart squeezed as they disappeared into the forest. Afternoon sunlight filtered haloed hues through greenery, creating a golden archway of shade and sun, beckoning her to follow.

August Reinhold was an infuriating man. Argumentative and abrasive men, she understood, even overtly flirtatious and obvious like Jasper Little, but calm and quiet confidence? A man who appeared to hold the same tender heart she loved in her grandfather, father, and brother, yet with a distinctly more distracting smile? No, she wasn't quite sure what to do with that.

She glanced up to the porch. Granny grinned, patting Faith as she slept on her shoulder.

"Well?" Her granny's brows rose.

Jess released a body-shaking sigh. "Fine. I'll be back soon." She raised a finger to her grandmother to make her point. "Very soon."

Chapter Twelve

Sylvie and Jude moved among the broken remains of the chapel, cheerful comrades in August's plight for restoration of the broken building. He grinned down at them, Jude directing Sylvie to different things among the rubbish with a patience uncommon to most children his age.

August checked on the fresh boards he'd put in place as a framework for the new chapel—barely a skeleton, but enough to start taking shape. He stepped back to view his handiwork, grateful for the opportunity to practice his lifelong love of building, a passion scorned by his father.

"What... what are you doing?"

August turned to the sound of Jessica's voice. There she stood at the entrance of what used to be the chapel doors, poised amidst the sunlit greenery and lavender rhododendron in a simple dress as green as the foliage framing her. When he'd seen her staring at him from the corner of the house, she'd captured him. Her hair, usually pinned in a braid, had been kept loose in the back, flowing in waves of gold around her shoulders. She stepped into the sunlight, as much a fairie of the forest as ever he'd imagined. Golden and alive, with a glint in her eyes enough to mesmerize any man. His grin spread in full appreciation. And he'd gladly succumb to her fiery spell, should she cast it his way.

"Pardon me?"

She exaggerated an eye-roll and gestured toward the children rummaging around in the chapel's remains. "What are you doing *here?*"

He stepped through the clutter toward her. Though he'd removed some to make space for his new creation, he still had a lot the ruins to remove. This place called to him. A broken, forgotten place. He knew the vacancy of being cast off, and he also knew the beauty of transforming remains into what it was meant to be all along. His calling and gift.

The foundation still held true to this building. The pictures gave him guidance. All it needed was restoration, a word with vibrant meaning in his shadowed past of failure and rejection. Hope rising from the ashes of despair.

"A treasure hunt, as I told you."

Her palms landed on her hips again and her eyes grew narrower as he drew closer. "This place is a disaster. A remnant of something beautiful." She stared around the small space, lost in memory, before snapping back to the present. "But now it's destroyed and filled with... broken oak and splintered pine. What treasures could you possibly find?"

He studied her, his head tilted in question. Was that her view now? Of brokenness and desolation? Had war and pain sent hope scurrying into the shadows so she saw the world through a veil of loss? Grief? No wonder she walled herself in with her sharp wit and deflection.

"Don't you see, Miss Ross? Sometimes, you must look beyond the rubble to find a treasure that has been hiding all along." He turned to Jude. "Jude, would you show Miss Jesse your treasures?"

She sent August a sizzling glance but unsheathed her smile on the little boy. The sheer beauty of it stopped his breath. Ah, what a smile! Could it be that a smile harder won brought greater joy? He was determined for her to bestow the glow on him.

Jude raised up a cloth sack for her view. Inside, mismatched and broken, lay various pieces of stained glass, charred remains from the windows found in the little chapel, brilliant colors of rich red, vibrant green, a dark royal, and pale yellow.

"They're broken pieces."

He held her stare, his smile offering a bridge of understanding. "We cannot recreate the memories, but we can salvage the beauty of what was."

She looked up at him, doubt crinkling her brows into a 'v.' "How on earth can you make something beautiful out of shattered glass?"

He tipped his head toward her, lowering his voice. "Wait and see. It will be a grand surprise."

Her cheeks bloomed pink and beautiful. "Did... did Grandpa hire you to do this?"

He nodded. "And I was happy to comply. This holds more of my talent than medicine, as I'm certain you could appreciate from my many stumbles during surgery last week."

The tension in those lips softened at the edges. A small victory. "But who will help Grandpa now, with or without the stumbling?"

"I thought you had worked out for Mr. Little to procure that specific responsibility."

She blinked and lifted her chin—a gesture, he was quickly learning, which meant she was readied to fight. "That is a distinct possibility, of course."

"I finished," came Sylvie's joyous call. She held out the cloth sack, half the depth of Jude's, her cherub-smile triumphant.

"Sylvie, schau mich an. Look at me." He tipped her chin and her glittering eyes focused on his face. "You say, I *am* finished. Ya?"

"I am finished," she repeated with added intensity and then her smile flashed bright again.

"Very good." He turned to Jude. "Have you enough treasure, Jude?"

The boy looked down into his bag and shrugged. "I'm fine with stayin' or leavin'."

The stoic independence of these native mountaineers bled through their bodies from childhood. Even in his few interactions with Jude, his strength and pride came as a surprise. But gentleness hovered beneath the serious demeanor, especially when it involved Sylvie. No doubt, the boy had shown such care to his mother in her final days. Old grief contracted his chest. He looked away only to find his gaze locked with Jessica Ross', her guarded expression gentled into one of curiosity.

He cleared his throat. "Shall we return to the house so I can best you at badminton, as promised?"

"As promised?"

"I am a man of my word."

One golden brow shot up like a weapon mercifully dulled by the subtle glint in her eyes. "Pride goeth before a fall, Mr. Reinhold."

"Fine words, Miss Ross. I suppose you listened to them very intently as you spoke them, yes?"

And those pink lips softened even more before she turned and began to walk back down the forest path. Jude grabbed Sylvie's hand and forged ahead, her dress flapping around her as they went and her giggle leading the way.

August fell into step with Jessica, allowing the silence to encourage her conversation. Or at least he hoped it would. He still felt as if he walked on uneven ground in her presence.

"Why did you leave Germany?"

Not the introductory question he'd expected. He braided his fingers together behind his back. "Do you mean to say I do not look the very model of a sailor?"

Her brow tipped again, teasing him with the lighter side of her personality. The side he'd seen in the letters and glimpsed in her conversations with her grandparents. "I'm certain you could do the part, but you don't strike me as the sort. Craftsman? Caretaker, perhaps? But not the sailor or soldier."

"Neither was I a staunch businessman, at which my father was most acutely disappointed." He shook his head, a painful chuckle escaping. "I forget I know you better than you know me. I've had months to learn of you. I am still a stranger to you, and an unwelcome one at that."

Her pace slowed, her head bent thoughtfully in his direction. "Then I suppose the only way to bridge the gap of my river-wide suspicions..." She sighed as if she released some internal grip of defiance. "Is to get to know you now."

He attempted to rein in his smile, to keep the hope shielded for a little longer, but he utterly failed to contain the surge of joy. His attempt to cling to patience faltered as every small victory boosted hope.

Hope in a faithful romance from a lady of conviction.

He knew rejection, the icy sting of duplicity, and the cutting edge of betrayal. Here stood a woman of authenticity, the clarion call of a loyal heart, even to her own detriment. He'd prayed to find a woman of such steadfast persuasion, even if now, her misguided convictions kept her at a distance.

He drew in a deep breath of patience, the one constant in his life of change and misfortune, and shoved his hands in his pockets as they walked. "I'm afraid I did not have the luxury of a kind father. My elder brother fit the mold my father wished of his son. He was not an enthusiast of compassion."

She looked over at him, her gaze fixed on his—searching for clarity? Sincerity?

"And what did he admire?"

"Work first." He grimaced, attempting to imitate the furious disposition of his father. "Money second. And somewhere beneath many other things, came family and faith, unless one served a purpose he could... um... exploit."

"And I gather you didn't quite meet his convoluted expectations?"

August's smile fell as he stared up beyond the trees into the waning afternoon sky. "No, I was quite the failure. First, in business and then in marriage."

Jess stopped altogether and faced him. "You're married?"

His laughter erupted before he could catch it. "You are very quick to make assumptions, Miss Ross. First, I am a murderer, then I am seducing a widow, and now I am married before I can even finish my tale?"

She sighed, the attractive rose color filling in her cheeks again as she resumed their walk. "You're right. I'll reserve my assumptions until after you finish your tale."

"At least then, your misguided assumptions will be flavored with some truth, yes?"

He caught the tempered smile on her profile but otherwise, she kept quiet, so he continued.

"I *was* to be married to a woman of my father's choosing. Wealthy and prestigious. In truth, I cared for her, but she broke the engagement to marry a man with more money than I. My father blamed me for failing to keep her, but quickly found another woman to be my bride. However, this one had the personality of a fish."

She grinned up at him, full and unhindered, and his whole world slowed to take in the outstanding vision. "And not even her money would sway your heart?"

"I suppose I'm old-fashioned to long for camaraderie and love, yes?" He gave a playful one-shoulder shrug and her smile spread a little wider. "One of my many failings, I assure you, and certainly one which incurred my father's wrath. Despite my ailing mother's plea, he disinherited me and sent me away." The remembrance of his mother, standing at the door, weak and tear-stained as she watched him leave, blocked up his throat and strained his air.

"And you found yourself swept out to sea?" Her comment, paired with a guarded look of compassion, added a balm of levity into the depths of his despair.

"Lost would have been a more accurate description." He nodded as the path turned the bend and the farmhouse came into view. "Until I found myself in this quiet part of the world and in the unexpected care of your grandparents."

Their pace slowed again, the badminton net a sign of the end to their more serious conversation. "I have found more freedom and acceptance here in this foreign place than I've ever known. To my father, I was not hard enough... too gentle, too kind. To my fiancée, I was not... what would you say, charming enough for her social demands?

He studied her to see if his word choice proved correct.

"I'm not sure that's the right word, but I get your meaning."

He gestured toward the farm, the woods, and the welcoming mountains framing them. "I prefer a quiet life. These mountains, these people, have become my own."

She stopped by the net, her hair a halo of spun gold in the sunlight. "So, if you could be free, you'd stay here?"

He drew his stare from the beauty of her hair and back to her eyes. "If I could, yes. If I had the freedom to walk up the trail and keep walking and not return." He gestured toward the forest. "Start over. August Reinhold could disappear and I would become someone else. But this I could not do. I would spend my days as a hunted man, wondering if someone would discover the truth that I lied and shamed my kinsman. No, this would be wrong."

"There's no other way for you to be free?"

"Besides an end to this war? No, nothing but death, and I am not keen to experience that anytime soon, though it would be a less shameful freedom than running away."

Her smile emerged with a challenging glint in her eyes. "Unless, of course, it's a death to your pride?"

He tipped his head closer, examining the layers of evergreen and emerald intermingled in the swirls of her eyes. "I admire your confidence, but I have no plans of being a casualty to your hands, Miss Ross."

"We'll just have to see about that, Mr. Reinhold."

The man was positively infuriating. Two matches of badminton, and he'd pummeled her without breaking a sweat. She found very little consolation in the fact he'd dirtied his otherwise pristine appearance with a good fall to the ground, but it failed to dampen his good-natured smile.

Oh, that smile! She growled. Most likely, he told her the story about his fiancée to soften her fight because his history paired with his boyish grin became her ultimate undoing. Her leg slowed her, of course, and being out of practice didn't help, but she'd blame the smile.

She wanted to nurse the distrust for him. Every scar left behind from Snyder fueled the need, but August contradicted every rationale or even irrational argument she conjured. He oozed with a unique charm, one Jessica found hard to counter. Not like Jasper, with his playboy grin and silver tongue. She never felt the draw to speak authentically or deeply with him, only to indulge a shallow flirtation with a slight hint of danger—but August? He wore tenderness and gentleness in his expression, mining beneath her prejudice to unearth a buried need inside. How had he slipped beneath her defenses so effortlessly? It terrified her.

"Mr. August is very good at badminton," Jude said, piling another spoonful of potatoes onto his plate, the dictionary underneath his bottom giving him enough of a lift to reach the food bowls on his own.

Jess pulled her thoughts away from the afternoon events back to supper. The beef dried out in her mouth but she smiled at the little boy. "Yes, very good."

Her grandfather's moustache twitched with the effort to tame his smile. Jessica shot him a glare. His moustache twitched again.

"I think you'll do much better after you have more practice, Miss Jesse."

Jessica swallowed down the mountain-sized lump of pride in her throat and held her grin intact, despite her grandfather's sudden choking attack... which sounded suspiciously like laughter.

"She used to best every boy in town." Her grandmother sent her a wink as she passed a bowl of beans. "Even her father, at times."

Father! Jessica pushed up from the table. "I forgot! Father sent a letter yesterday and I completely forgot about it. How could I have forgotten?"

"You've been busy lately, Jessica, not to mention having a hard time getting a full night's sleep. Motherhood has a way of causing women to become a bit more forgetful than usual." Her grandfather nodded, and a forkful of potatoes hung in mid-air on its way to his mouth.

"But don't worry, your mind will come back to you for a few years before old age begins to weedle it away all over again," her grandmother added with a chuckle and then waved her spoon in the air. "Go on. Git the letter so we can have some news from across the Pond."

Jessica rushed up the stairs as fast as her limp would take her and slowed before entering her room. A tiny grunt from the corner of the room alerted her to Faith's sleep status. Awake for an hour, perhaps, and then she'd sleep a good two hours before Jessica would wake her for her last daytime feeding before, she hoped, a longer stretch of sleep for the night.

She'd found her fist, sucking on it hard enough to make a smacking noise. Jessica grinned down at the little face. "Are you hungry, sweet one?"

The sucking paused a moment, her round, blue eyes looking up to find Jessica's face, and then she resumed with more vigor.

Jess took the little bundle into her arms without a hitch, cradling the tiny head in the crook of her elbow. "Hungry already? I don't think it's been a full two hours yet."

The sucking stopped again and tenderness soaked through Jess' chest like tepid rain. Faith knew the sound of her voice? Jess' eyes burned, stinging with emotions on the brink all of the time. Whether from her lack of sleep or the bubbling concoction of untied wounds, or an unhealthy combination of the two, her heart teetered as precarious as the tears on her lashes.

She scooped the letter from her desk and placed a kiss on the tiny bald head before collecting her wayward emotions and heading down the stairs.

"Well, I see you found more than the letter to entertain us." Grandpa stood before Granny and stepped close to Jess, peering down at the baby. "She's looking healthy."

"And hungry," Jess added, moving to the stove to start warming a bottle.

"She's sure hungry a lot." Jude took another bite of fried chicken. "To be so little, she's got a heap of an appetite."

"Well, she's got a lot of growin' to do to catch up with her big brother," Granny said, walking to the stove and taking over. "Go on and read that letter. I'll get this goin'."

Jess slid back into her chair at the table, adjusted her hold on Faith, and turned over the envelope to open it. The Cavanaugh seal, a lion holding a sword, stamped the back of the envelope with its expensive putty. Ednesbury Court, the estate and title her father had inherited as the only living biological heir to the Cavanaughs. He'd been cast out of the family when he'd chosen to marry Jess' mother, a poor mountain woman with a vibrant imagination and a generous heart. He'd called it love at first sight and had never looked back. But by some miracle of time and circumstance, all of the other heirs to the Cavanaugh legacy died without producing a male heir—all except her father.

He'd stepped into the role with the same ingenuity and generosity as he'd always shown, building up the village of Ednesbury from what the previous generation had torn apart. She smiled as she broke the seal and removed the high quality paper. Her brother, David, would make an excellent successor—he and his wife, Catherine.

Jess lost complete control of her smile at the thought of her strong-willed and sharp-tongued sister-in-law. Oh, what would Catherine think of Hot Springs? And of Jessica's instant motherhood?

"Well, what does it say?" Her grandfather's words knocked her from her musings.

She unfolded the paper and frowned at the brevity of the note.

My dearest daughter,

You have only been away for a few weeks and already I miss you too much to keep the distance.

Jess looked up at her granny and then quickly back to the words.

It's been much too long since I've traveled to Hot Springs and I feel the estate is now established enough under my care to survive without my immediate supervision for a short while. My man, James, is quite capable as steward, and I feel the freedom to leave all manner of concerns to him for a few weeks so that I can come and see you. If it is too much trouble for your grandparents, I will be happy to board at Lance's, should it still be there, or the inn, but at any rate, I am coming.

And I do not come alone.

The words barely formed on Jess lips before she sped to the end of the note.

David, Catherine, and little Addie will accompany me. A holiday from hospital work will do them all a great day of good, so I have forced their hands. And, as you know Catherine, it was no small feat to convince her to leave.

We embark on June 8 and should arrive in Hot Springs by the 15th. I am eager to see those mountains, but most of all, I am hungry to see you, my dear.

Affectionately,
Your father

Complete silence greeted the end of her letter. Granny looked to Grandpa, then they both turned to Jessica. Jude continued to shovel potatoes into his mouth, eating like the hungry child he must have been once, and Faith's grunts took a downward turn toward a whimper.

Granny brought the bottle and shrugged. "Well, they're goin' to stay here, of course."

"Is there room?"

"'Course there's room," Grandpa added. "Jude can bunk up with you on the rollaway bed so Alexander can take his room. And David, Catherine, and the baby can sleep in the front room."

"It shouldn't take too much work to clear out the space for them." Granny nodded with more sureness. "They're family—and they should stay with family if they can."

Jess tightened her smile, not quite feeling her grandparents' confidence. Her father, the earl, with her brother and his fashion-forward wife, in the small Appalachian town of Hot Springs that hosted a German internment camp? Hot Springs wasn't prepared for the intriguing beauty and charismatic charm of her sister-in-law. And what would August think?

Chapter Thirteen

Jude rode alongside Jessica down the street to the Mercantile in Grandpa's Model T. Grandpa rarely used the auto car, since it couldn't reach patients back in the mountains. Horse and buggy still worked for those visits, and sometimes, for the steeper hollows, only old-fashioned walking would do.

Jude sat wide-eyed, holding to the front of the car with both hands, and bubbled with non-stop questions. What made the car go forward? Why were there three pedals?

Though both a part of the same culture, their lives had been so different. He'd grown up in the mountains, barely coming into town more than once a month to get supplies, living off whatever they found in the forest, keeping one cow and pig, which now resided at her grandparents'. She'd been raised a mile from town, next door to her grandparents, couched in an environment of hard work, plenty, and love.

With some extra change in her pocket, Jess barely contained the little-girl excitement at letting Jude pick out his own candy from Kimp's. As they walked across the street toward the store, Jess caught sight of Jasper Little's familiar profile. Straw hat at a fashionable tilt, he leaned against the brick wall of the Hardware Store in conversation with another man. Who was it? Casper Davis?

She ought to warn Jasper against developing friendships with the any unsavory sorts in Hot Springs. There were few people in

Hot Springs who carried a sour expression, and worse, sour intentions. Casper Davis and his family were the minority in a town of five hundred, but a minority worth their own warning.

She ushered Jude through the door of Kimp's and into a rush of commotion. A woman wailed from the back of the room where a group of four huddled close. The bell above the door chimed Jess and Jude's entry, and Kimp looked their way from his kneeled position on the floor. His eyes widened and he stood, marching toward them, his face red.

"Thank God you showed up, Miss Ross."

Jess squeezed Jude's hand and met Kimp halfway across the room, her instincts on alert. "What is it, Mr. Kimper?"

"Ryan, Mrs. Lester's boy, just had a fall."

"I couldn't hold him." A woman in the back murmured against a little boy's hair as she cradled him against her. His pain-filled screams rivaled her voice. "He wiggled right out of my arms."

"Face first on the hard wood floors."

Jess pushed past the man and into the small group, dropping Jude's hand to get a closer view. The boy, no more than two, lay limp against his mother's chest. Amy, Kimp's niece, stood. "I checked him as soon as it happened. The bulge on his head popped out instead of sunk in, which is 'spose to be a better sign from what I've read. Is that right?"

Jess nodded to the girl, impressed with her intelligent calm and awareness. "Most of the time. Did he lose consciousness at all?"

"No," came Amy's quick reply. "From what I can tell, he kind of got stunned for a second and then started off a wailin'. I got some icings right away to reduce swelling for the bulge on his head."

"Excellent thinking, Amy."

The girl's smile beamed, appreciative. Jess knew that smile, the appreciation of good work.

She knelt down to the mother's level. "Mrs...?"

"Landers," the woman sniffled, face red from crying. "Edith Landers."

"Mrs. Landers, my name is Jessica Ross. I'm Dr. Carter's granddaughter but also a nurse. Would you allow me to examine your son a moment, please?"

"He just jumped from my arms, going after the toy airplane." She nodded toward one of the model biplanes hanging in tempting display from the ceiling. "I... I couldn't hold on to him."

Jess pried the little boy from her arms, his face bright pink from crying, but the screams were dying to a whimper, enough that he opened his eyes to see who held him. Dilation looked equal and normal in both eyes. Jess moved her head back from side to side, and his little eyes tracked her movements without a hitch.

"Mr. Kimper, would you mind bringing a lolly?"

The man rushed to the candy shelf and returned within seconds with one of the largest red lollipops Jess had ever seen. Had they gotten bigger since she was a girl?

The little boy's eyes grew as round as tires and his whimpers dissolved into a series of sniffs. The bulge on his head swelled to an impressive size, but Jess had seen much worse. Painful, and certainly noticeable, but nothing life-risking. To be sure, she moved the lollipop in front of his face and watched as he reached up for it.

"What is this...?" Jess looked to the mother in search of the boys' name?

"Thomas."

"Thomas, what is this?"

He reached for the candy but Jess kept it just a teensy bit out of reach.

His dark, round gaze switched to hers, a bit annoyed, and back to the candy. "Lolly."

"Yes, that's right." Jess moved the lollipop toward her mouth. "Is it for me or your mother?"

His gaze switched to his mother in response to her name. Yes, no sluggishness in those big brown eyes. A very good sign. "Mine."

"Ah." Jessica grinned, the tension in her body ebbing with her sigh. "I think you've certainly earned it from the goose-egg on your sweet head."

Whether from her recent motherhood or the passage of time, Jess found new comfort in holding the little boy and talking with him—one she'd never experience when helping at her friend Ashleigh's orphanage.

Mrs. Landers' panicked gaze met Jessica's. "Will he be all right?"

Jess handed the boy, lolly in hand, back to his mother. "I think so. The bump on his head is going to be there for a while. At least a week, but I wouldn't let him nap today. Not until late afternoon, at least. And when he does take a nap, don't let him sleep long without stirring him to the point he can answer a few questions for you. If all goes well, he should be fine going to bed tonight at his usual time."

"Thank you." Mrs. Landers gathered her sniffling boy back into her arms. "I'm so happy you happened to be by."

Jess tossed Amy a grin. "It looks like you were already in good hands."

Amy's smile responded with instant gratitude. Jess felt the kindred tug toward this young girl's dream, a desperate hope to climb from the world she'd always known to something beyond, maybe even something greater.

She stood and Amy rose with her. "Do you have any of your days free, Amy?"

Her brown eyes, almost a cinnamon color, widened. "What do you mean?"

"Would you like some training? Outside of your classes, of course, but a chance to learn from a real doctor?"

Amy's palm covered her chest and her pink bottom lip swung loose. "Would I?"

"I can't make any promises, you understand, but my grandfather could use another hand."

Mrs. Landers walked past them, carrying her content, sniffling son out of the shop, and Mr. Kimper stepped forward. "I don't know if that'd work, Miss Jesse."

"Why not?" Jessica's gaze took in Kimp's wary expression and then switched to the sudden dejection on Amy's face. "The school would object?"

Amy shook her head, a slight wobble in her bottom lip before it firmed into a frown. "Uncle Kimp means my bad blood... or my family's, at any rate."

Jessica knew the phrase, a title tarnished with the sins and superstitions of generations. Seldom did it prove true, except as a self-fulfilling prophecy for a child who couldn't move beyond the stigma of having a debauched parent.

Jessica turned to Jude, offering him a smile. "Jude, would you go over to the cloth at the far corner of the store and try to find some white thread for Granny?"

Those eyes, filled with much more knowledge than they ought, scanned the faces of the three adults and then, with a nod, he moved to the other side of the store. What went on behind those eyes? Perhaps, as she sorted out how to be a mother, he'd let her know.

"Why?"

Amy looked to her uncle and, with a movement of his chin, he released her to speak. "I came here to live with my uncle and aunt because all my family's dead or... gone."

"Gone?" The way she hesitated on the word brought its own shadows.

Kimp took a look around the vacant store and lowered his voice. "Her mama's in the asylum. She plumb lost her mind."

Tears glistened in Amy's eyes, giving them a golden hue among the cinnamon. "She killed my brother and daddy first."

Jess' palm flew to her stomach as the declaration hollowed her like a blow. "What?"

"I was with my Papa. He was dying from some sort of lung infection is all I can tell from my readings, so I didn't know until I..." Amy stopped talking, her lips pinched tight against her emotions.

"The boy was found drowned in a feed sack," Kimp whispered, placing a hand on Amy's shoulder. "Her daddy... well, there wasn't much left to know what happened to him after the fire."

Jess glanced back toward Jude, the mere thought of someone hurting him inciting a wave of nausea and rage. She turned back to Amy. "I'm sorry, Amy. I can't even imagine how much you're hurting."

"Thank you, Miss Ross."

"Jessica." Jess put out her palm. "Call me Jessica."

Amy shook a tear loose from her lashes and smiled. "Thank you, Jessica." She took Jess' hand, lowering her head. "I'm sorry I can't take advantage of your offer to learn more about medicine."

"Why not?" Jess laced her arms across her chest and defied any argument. "Why can't you? I don't buy into this rubbish about bad blood, and I'm certain there are other people who won't either.

Besides, it's high time people started thinking with their heads instead of their superstitions."

"Do... do you mean you'll still have me?"

"Have you? Amy, I have a particular fondness for helping young women believe in themselves. Bad blood? Good blood?" Jess shook away the ridiculous notion. "I see smarts and talent, and the world needs more people willing to take those skills in hand and refine them to serve others. If your uncle has no objections to me talking to my grandfather?" She sent Kimp a look.

"I... I don't see why not." He pushed a thick hand through his hair. "If you're sure?"

She focused her attention back on Amy, her smile spreading. "Oh, I'm sure, and I'll make sure Grandpa's certain too."

She looked over her shoulder to *her* little boy. "Jude, how about we pick out your very first lollipop." She paused and smiled at Amy. "Make that two lollipops. I feel like celebrating a small victory in a really big war."

"I know your heart is in the right place, Jessica." Her grandfather moved across the clinic, putting away the supplies he'd used to set a broken finger after Mr. Chase hit it with his hammer. "But there are some battles too ingrained to try and fight."

Jessica cast a look over her shoulder at Jude, who she'd given the job of rolling up some of Grandpa's unraveled gauze. He'd come to help her at the clinic for the past few days, doing menial chores to pass the time, and they both seemed to enjoy each other's company.

She turned back to Grandpa and lowered her voice. "I'd say it's high time we performed some much needed surgery on the mindset of a few sects of mountain people."

"Insanity is hereditary. You, as a nurse, are well aware of the fact." He raised a brow, edging his doubts into her certainty.

"I'm also well aware that more times than not, this fear of hereditary insanity is used to condemn many an innocent person to a life as an outcast. I don't think Amy carries her mother's illness."

"Which may not present itself until adulthood."

Jessica gritted her teeth at her grandpa's reluctance. If God was watching this scene, wouldn't He try to bring some sanctified reasoning to her hard-headed grandfather? She tossed her gaze to the ceiling for a brief and half-hearted plea for help and a sudden idea formed. An argument... no, an appeal.

"Then what a better person to look for signs, if there are any, of her having the same illness as her mother. You're a doctor. You'd notice the red flags. You'd be able to predict if she was dangerous or not. There's no safer place in all of Hot Springs for her to be than working for you."

Grandpa bestowed her with a long-suffering stare. "I see you've lost none of your cleverness, my dear girl."

"It's especially handy with hard-headed men."

He growled and shook his head. "Have you thought about her? How the rejection might impact her?" Her grandpa stepped closer. "There will be plenty of people who won't even talk to her, let alone let her treat them."

"Then for those who will, who see beyond superstition and bad blood..." She grimaced around the words. "For those people and for Amy, we have the opportunity to set the right example—to start a new way of thinking." She waited until he looked back up from his work. "You wouldn't let this culture hold me back from going to college, from traveling across the world to help serve in a war that wasn't even mine yet."

"That's different. Your father was English and you... you were from a different type of family." He faltered over his words. "You weren't born back in those mountains, Jess. You were born here, where there is a little more opportunity, to parents who stretched beyond the borders of what they'd known."

"Then help me bring that same kind of opportunity to these mountain girls."

"The mission school is trying to do that."

She released a burst of contained air and looked down at the floor. Yes, her grandpa grew from generations of mountain people, but innovative and creative mountain people. Big thinkers. Dreamers. That was the only reason he had the vision to send Jess' mother abroad for schooling after she'd finished a surprisingly eclectic and solid education at the little two-room schoolhouse in town. Surely, she could reach beyond years of staying in these mountains to touch to his creative heart. "Our mountain school is a wonderful mission. And women will be much more prepared to take care of their families when they complete their studies. But what about those who desire even more? What about those who feel called to something else?"

Grandpa took her by the shoulders, and his green-hued gaze rimmed his firmness with tenderness. "There's no need for you to put ideas in these girls' heads. Lots of them are content with being mothers and wives."

"And I'm only beginning to understand what a beautiful opportunity motherhood is. One of the highest callings of any woman's heart." Her chest flooded with a painfully sweet warmth, spreading wider more and more each day, as she thought about Jude and Faith. "But there are other callings too. I'm not trying to change anybody's mind."

His raised eyebrow challenged her statement.

"I'm serious. I don't want to stop some girl who finds contentment in being a wife and mother. I'm glad my mother was able to be with me my whole childhood, even as she pursued her writing career from her mountain home. But she still fed another dream." She sighed. "I only want these girls to know that if they harbor another dream inside them, they are as capable of making it happen as any man."

"No, Jessica, they're not. Man or woman, there are dreams in people's hearts in these mountains that will never be able to find a place in reality." He gave her shoulders a small shake and dropped his hold. "You've been across the ocean in the middle of a war, and you've gotten used to a really big world, with access to things that we won't see in these parts for twenty years or more. But this world here"—he pointed to the window—"is still very small and wrapped in its own superstitions and beliefs and values."

"But that big wide world has already started coming here. First, with the railroad and now, with fewer and fewer of our people living off the land and relying on foods provided from outside these mountains. Why should we wait for that world out there to impact us when we can impact it?"

Grandpa smiled, his moustache twitching with a look of resignation... and a hint of pride. "You sure can argue a point, girl."

She held her smile in check, softening her voice. "I know this world can't go back to the way it was before the war, and we'll receive the good and the bad from those changes, but the world Jude and Faith walk into in fifteen years is going to look much different. And now, since this war and the railway and the radio have made this world so much bigger, don't you think it can encourage us to dream bigger too?"

"You know you can't change the mindset of a whole community and you can't meet the dreams of every young woman in this town."

Her breathing came in forced intervals. "Then how about we start with the dreams of one?"

"I can see you are very good at this game, Miss Jesse. I must work hard to keep up with you." August tipped the birdie back across the net and Jessica bolted for it.

She'd worn a dress with a shorter hemline today, pale blue, and even more flattering than some of her other regular frocks. August could only suppose the length kept her feet from entanglement, but the dress itself also provided a tempting view of her silhouette. It cinched at her waist, showing off her curves in a way he'd failed to observe. He certainly didn't miss the opportunity now.

Caring for her personality through letters came with a somewhat benign attraction, but in the flesh, the fiery and beautiful flesh, his attraction twisted into a severe distraction. He missed the next shot.

"Are you growing tired yet, Mr. Reinhold? I can give you a rest if you need one." Her smile mocked him with a sweetness her gaze contradicted. Good-humored teasing.

Her previous disdain had disappeared after their conversation at the chapel, and perhaps her suspicions would run the same vein. At the very least, she tolerated his presence, but he hoped time would curb her indifference.

He caught her watching him as he went to collect the birdie from the grass. His grin hitched. Perhaps things were already changing? "I am merely distracted by the lovely view, Miss Jesse."

She opened her mouth to respond with something witty judging from the defiant tilt in her chin, and then she seemed to catch his hidden meaning. A swath of pink rose into her cheeks, her gaze faltering on his before she recovered. "Whatever advantages I need, you understand, Mr. Reinhold."

"Your advantage or mine?" His poor attempt to tame his smile transformed into a full grin, and another ribbon of pink shot into Jessica's face.

With her golden hair loosed from its bindings around her heated faced and her evergreen eyes bright from her physical exertion, August couldn't imagine an advantage or vantage greater than his at present.

"Are we going to play or talk? Or perhaps you're stalling because you need the rest?"

They followed with two more long rallies, both of which August won. Jessica leaned forward, catching her breath.

"Would you like to stop for today?"

"No," she answered too quickly. "I'm one point from passing you."

He stepped close to the net, bending down to see her face. "You must truly love the game."

She slit him a glare. "It's beginning to lose a bit of its luster."

"You would not be a bad sport, would you, Jessica Ross?"

She stood straight, her lips wrestling with a smile. "Honestly, Mr. Reinhold, I'm a horrible sport, but I'm putting on a good face for that little boy over there."

She nodded toward Jude, who sat on the porch with a lemonade in hand, watching the entire exchange. Her smile turned ruthless. "I hate losing."

"Another rally then?" he offered.

She fought ferociously for the next point and it seemed impossible, but August dove for it, barely touching the birdie with his racquet before crumbling to the earth. He watched from his grassy bed as the birdie flew through the air and, as if sprouting wings, tipped over the net to Jessica's side.

With a relieved sigh he collapsed back to the earth and suddenly, the most remarkable thing happened. From the other side of the net, a chuckle bubbled into full-blown laughter. He turned his head as she rounded the net, her clapping exaggerated.

He could do little but stare at her—her eyes glistening, her smile broad, and everything about her drawing his waiting heart into her very unpredictable hands. Beautiful.

"Mr. Reinhold, I rarely see such commitment in an opponent." She reached down in an effort to help him to a stand. "Quite impressive."

Without hesitation, he took her offering and she helped him to his feet. "I'm pleased I've impressed you in some way, my dear Miss Ross."

Her smile faded, her emerald gaze locked with his, and a jolt of connection, as fierce as the first touch in the train depot, shocked back to life between them. Her breath faded, and for the faintest second, her attention dropped to his mouth.

A violent heat scorched through him at the sudden awareness... desire. He dared not move, breathe... do anything to break this unexpected link of her initiation. Her gaze flickered back to his, curious and confused. To have a battlefield of experiences, her understanding of romance mirrored more of a schoolgirl's than a woman's. Uncertain. Timid. Or at least it did with him.

She blinked and dropped his hand, stepping back. "You are quite the anomaly, Mr. Reinhold."

"And this is a compliment, yes?"

His gaze searched hers until her smile twitched up on one side. "I'm not quite sure how to figure you out."

"I am simple, really." He opened his palms and shrugged. "As you see."

Her survey swept the length of him, leaving a lightning trail in its wake. "You are many things, but simple doesn't seem to hold the appropriate description."

He halved the distance between them, drawing upon the recent, tangible attraction of their touch. "No?"

Her breath hitched. "No," she whispered, and then stepped back, clearing her throat and returning those palms to her hips. "However, competitive certainly does seem to describe you. And determined."

"So, we are not that different, you and I?" He shrugged. "Except I am still winning and you are not."

The singe in her glare stung a little less. "Stop gloating."

"Gloat? What is this word?"

"It means..." She waved a hand in the air as if the answer might magically appear. "Showing an expression of pride that you're winning."

"I *am* proud I am winning."

She sighed. "You are so infuriating."

"Jessica, Mr. Little just arrived." Granny called from the back porch. "I think you might need to come on in and make yourself presentable."

She pinched her eyes closed and placed her palm against her forehead. "Oh, goodness, I completely forgot. I need to go."

He made a poor attempt at pitching down his smile and kept in step with her. "Would you like me better if I let you win?"

"No." She groaned, shooting another glare from her periphery. "I'm going to beat you fair and square."

He moved in time with her steps.

She pivoted toward him with a groan. "Why is it so important that I like you, anyway?"

"Because I like you. It's much more pleasant when it's mutual."

She slowed her pace and turned to him, the crinkle of confusion resurfacing on her face. "I don't know why you would like me. I've not been very nice to you."

Her honesty and the pain in her admission drew him closer, teased his need to comfort her. "But that is not the real you. I have learned about the real you through the letters, and have seen glimpses in your love for your family."

She braced a hand on the porch step railing and looked away, toward the door. "And you think somehow you know me because of those letters?"

Her tone took on an edge, curbed with a tinge of sadness.

"Mostly. There was much of you in those letters." He leaned closer, drawing her attention back to his face. "But I know you better now, and better with each day."

She pushed her hair back from her face and stared up at him, those endless eyes mining deep for something he wasn't certain how to give. "The woman you met in those letters..." She swallowed and looked away, squinting against the afternoon light. "That woman disappeared in Europe. She's gone."

"No." His response brought her attention back to him, and he suppressed the overwhelming urge to touch a loose strand of her golden hair waving down her cheek. "Merely misplaced, I think." He gentled his voice, desperately trying to draw her out, gain her trust... touch her heart. "Underneath all the wounds and grief of war, but I have every faith we will find her. In fact, I caught a glimpse of her today."

"Miss Jesse." Jude called from the back door. "Granny says you need to wash up somethin' quick."

Jess stepped back, clearly shaken, and stumbled up the porch steps. He reached to steady her, but she tugged her arms free gently, almost in a daze. "Good evening, Mr. Reinhold."

And with that, she disappeared into the house, but not before glancing back. Yes, he'd caught a glimpse of her, seen her guard lift and the beauty unearthed beneath the pain. Somehow he knew, in finding her, he'd uncover a part of his heart buried and waiting for resurrection.

Chapter Fourteen

"How is your research going, Mr. Little?" Grandpa offered Jasper another biscuit

"Slower than expected, but I hope some of your influence tomorrow will help me make the inroads I need to secure more of Mr. Sharpe's research."

"Well, I can't promise they'll warm up to you real quick, but the help of a native might thaw them a bit."

He chuckled, a pleasant sound, much like the rest of his demeanor. He charmed, from the dark curls of his hair to the tip in his smile. Jessica couldn't help but compare him to her fair-haired badminton competitor. Without a doubt, Jasper brought with him a magnetizing energy. Paired with his dashing looks, it seemed impossible not to feel some sort of interest in him, so why was it the ridiculous badminton match with August Reinhold which brought the unquenchable smile?

She shoved another bite of chicken in her mouth to give her lips something to do beside grin at the preposterous memory. She should focus on Mr. Little. He was English. Flirting with his attention was a much better use of her time than allowing her mind to wander to the complete impossibility of August Reinhold. Even the mere internal conversation made her angry. She shouldn't like August Reinhold at all. Besides being German, he'd beat her twice at badminton.

"Are both you and Mrs. Carter natives to Hot Springs?"

Jasper's question drew Jess back into the conversation and to his dark eyes. He tipped his glass toward her, his dashing grin in place.

"Well, I'm from Marshall," Grandpa answered, scooping a spoonful of potatoes on this plate, and then nodded to Granny. "But Elaine's family have been in Hot Springs for three generations. We moved here years ago when her mama became sick to tend to her."

"Don't you ever wish to travel outside of these mountains?" He glanced to both of her grandparents and halted his attention on her. "Or for you to return to your family in England?"

"I've had my fill of travel for a long time, Mr. Little." It always took outsiders by surprise when they learned of the natives' contentment havened in by these rolling hills.

"And I've done some traveling." Granny's brow rose with her smile. "Not as far as your country, Mr. Little, but a few places in this one. It was nice to see them, but there's no place quite like home for my heart."

Faith's cry broke into the momentary quiet of enjoying Granny's spread of baked chicken, potatoes, beans, and squash. Jess excused herself from the table and retrieved the little bundle, talking her down from the screaming ledge with soft reassurances.

Jess returned to a conversation about how Jude and Faith came to live at the farm.

"It must be difficult for you, returning from the war to instant motherhood."

Jess reached for the prepared bottle she'd set on the table and cast a glance to Jude in the chair beside her. The little boy carried enough weight of responsibility. He didn't need an added guilt. "Jude and I have been learning from each other quite well, haven't we, Jude?"

His little smile quivered full. "We sure have."

"Although I'm sometimes a slow learner."

A glimmer lit the boy's eyes, a tightening of their growing bond glowing in his smile. "I've seen a heap of a lot worse."

Grandpa burst out in laughter. "Boy, you've got that quiet, quick wit like August. You just never know when it'll break the silence of a room."

"August?" Jasper's brow rose, his expression tightening. "Your German... friend?"

"Well, the boy is more like family than just a friend." Grandpa leaned back in his chair. "But yes, he's one of the men in the camp."

Jasper touched the napkin to his mouth. "As close-knit a community as this is, I suppose the arrival of the Germans caused quite a stir." Jasper kept his eyes downward. "Not everyone is as generous or obliging as you, I'd suspect."

The tinge of warning resurrected again in Jess, but she couldn't place the shadow with the man before her. His dislike of the Germans didn't cause him to be a dangerous sort. After all, he was here to research ballads, not harm anyone, but the slight turn in his frown brought a sudden pause. Was she so quick to criticize? So all-encompassing with her judgments?

Her grandparents' generosity shone a stark contrast on the recent attitude of her own heart. Hadn't she learned anything from watching her sister-in-law, Catherine, transform from a fallen woman to a powerful entity of grace? Her own thoughts pounded in on her heart, reviving doubts she'd pushed underneath her broken heart and biting shame.

"At first, but most people soon got used to their presence." Grandpa poured some milk into his cup. "But as you can see for yourself, they've not brought any trouble with them."

"I've heard from several men in town who aren't too pleased with your town's acceptance of the prisoners, even allowing some to walk free among the town." He gestured toward her grandpa. "Work for them."

"There will always be those sort, don't you think?" Granny's words came out as sweet as the strawberry cake waiting for dessert, but they held a hidden reprimand. "But we don't have to be part of them, do we? We can show a better way."

Jasper didn't even flinch from the slight reprimand, but Jessica felt it to her core.

"Yes, I'm certain." Jasper smiled, an odd-looking expression crossing his face before he took another bite of the potatoes. "Of course, these sailors were caught in the wrong place at the wrong time. The only trouble they would've caused was being able to return home and join the Kaiser's forces, I suppose."

How many were like August? Men running away from wounds of their past and caught in the middle of a war's decision? Not soldiers. Her stomach crunched. Not enemies. "I'd suspect many of them would prefer freedom instead of living behind barbed wire, no matter how lovely the view."

Jasper chuckled. "It could be worse for them, you know. It's almost like they're on holiday from what I understand about the Mountain Park Hotel and grounds. A swimming pool? Golf course? Three-hundred room inn with heating and electricity?"

"It is a grand place, that's for certain," Granny answered, offering Jasper another piece of chicken which he waved away. "After the first one burned to the ground, this one emerged as an even greater spectacle."

Granny's excellent diversion transferred the conversation to safer ground.

"I'd love to see it some time." Jasper looked to Grandpa. "Do you think it would be possible? Mr. Sharpe stayed there a few nights when he came for his research and effused praise of its beauty."

"I don't see why not. If you're with me, you should be fine," Grandpa answered.

A knock at the door broke into the conversation, and August's face emerged from the doorway.

"Speak of the devil." Grandpa stood, not realizing how his phrase might fuel the animosity Jasper attempted to hide behind his perfect smile. "You done for today?"

"Yes, sir, I am almost finished with the framework. I returned your tools to the barn."

"You're a wonder, August. I can't wait to see what you have in mind for the finished product."

He bent his head in acceptance of the compliment and then looked up through those lashes of his to find Jessica before switching his attention back to Grandpa. The hooded glance, complete with a tipped grin, left a singe across her skin which took full bloom in her face. She'd have reached for a sip of milk for her dry throat if both hands weren't full with a baby.

"It is my pleasure to restore something important to this family." He patted his chest. "And it does my craftsman's heart good to create."

"You're just in time for dessert, August." Granny stood and walked to the counter for the cake. "Care to join us for a slice?"

August's gaze flitted to Jasper and back to Jess, from hardened to soft, and then he unleashed his gentle smile on her granny. "I appreciate your kindness, Mrs. Carter, but I'm expected back at the camp."

"Well, you might as well take a slice with you." Granny sent him a wink of encouragement which melted any argument the poor man could have mustered.

How could Granny do that? Diffuse conflict and sway people with a word or wink? Jess looked over at Jude and down into Faith's sweet face. Oh, she had so much to learn about life!

"You are most kind, as usual, Mrs. Carter. I could not refuse your excellent cooking."

Granny's face perked with rose from the compliment, brimming Jess' own smile. And then she got caught back in August's stare. His ushered a sweet calling to her heart, filled with tenderness, a playful camaraderie, something sifting deep inside of her for an answer she refused to investigate. Her breath pinched against the call despite her pulse running headlong toward it. Caring for him, falling into this attraction, battled against every scar-stain on her heart.

"You remember Mr. Little, don't you, August?" Grandpa stood along with Jasper.

The men exchanged nods, and the tension pinged as tight as a banjo string.

"And what exactly has these kind folks singing your praises, Mr. Reinhold?"

"August is rebuilding our family chapel destroyed in the flood last summer. Without much help around here, and the needs of my clinic, I hadn't gotten to the repairs, but it just so happens to be August's specialty. Restoring things."

"So you're a sailor and a craftsman, Mr. Reinhold?"

August took the wrapped slice of cake from Granny and then turned to Jasper on his way to the door. "Circumstances forced me to become a sailor, Mr. Little. But my heart calls me to be a craftsman. I'm certain your love for music helps you understand the beauty of art, yes?"

Mr. Little's smile took a somewhat ruthless turn. "Of course."

"Yes, of course." August's eyes lost none of their gleam as he offered Jess a smile on his way to the door. She really tried not to grin back, but her mouth took on a response of its own. He stopped and raised his parcel. "Thank you, Mrs. Carter. Good day."

Jess stifled an infuriated growl and stared back down into Faith's face, those big blue eyes staring back as if she knew exactly what her fumbling mother was hiding. *Mother*. The word and thought jumbled through her in a wave of sweet acceptance.

Granny placed her world famous strawberry cake on the table and she thought the little boy's eyes might pop clean out of his head. Her boy. *Her* boy.

"Eat it slowly, Jude. You'll want to appreciate the taste of that on your lips for the first time."

He nodded, staring as Granny sliced a piece and placed it in front of him.

"What is this masterpiece Mr. Reinhold is restoring for you?" Jasper asked, taking a forkful of the cake. "And this looks divine, Mrs. Carter."

"It's as close as we can get during sugar rations, Mr. Little. So let that give you an extra dose of enjoyment as you eat it." She laughed in her good-hearted way and returned to her seat, but only a shadow of Jasper's light-hearted mood returned. A mock recurrence.

"We have a photo of the chapel in the parlor." Grandpa left the room and reappeared with the photo in hand. "You can see it here."

To the Englishman, her family's little country chapel probably looked like a quaint but rustic edifice. Without the stories behind it, how could Jasper appreciate its simple beauty?

"It's charming."

Ah, the word that meant nothing.

"Please excuse my surprise, but I still find it difficult to comprehend how you would allow the same countrymen who are endangering the lives of your people across the world to work for you in your home. Even referring to them as friend, or family? Don't you worry about the possible repercussions of such actions? Can you truly trust this August Reinhold?"

"We're not the sort to blame the wrongs of a few men on the heads of the many." Granny's words cut into Jess' guilt with a potent slice. "They're our neighbors here in Hot Springs, just as you are."

"I am not like them." Jasper seethed, and then quickly tempered his response. "And I beg your forgiveness if I am slow to warm up to them as my neighbors. I lost both of my brothers at the hands of the Germans. Was left like this." He held up his amputated stump as a grisly reminder of the gravity in his situation. "And have seen more friends than I care to mention die or left crippled by the barbarity used in this war. The torture." His voice broke, his hand balled into a fist on the table. "There are some actions which are unforgiveable, and certainly unforgettable."

A sober silence met the gruesome vision his words painted. Jess knew it, had experienced the utter devastation. Jude's fork clashed against his plate.

"Jude, dear, since you're finished, would you take your plate to the sink and wash up for bed?"

He stood but stopped by her chair, leaning to her ear. "You'll be comin' up shortly, won't you, Miss Jesse?"

The fear in his eyes, most likely from the images Jasper described, beckoned her to follow him. "Of course, once Faith finishes her bottle and I bid Mr. Little good night."

He nodded and left the room, casting a glance over his shoulder before disappearing up the stairway. Those visions of the past still haunted her dreams, but not as much as they'd once done. Now... now, she had other memories to push back at the terrifying and heart wrenching battalion of ghosts from the battlefield. Traitors. When had these children begun to smooth the edges of her broken heart?

"I am sorry for your loss, Jasper." Granny responded, her voice hushed to keep it from carrying up the stairs. "But generalizing your hate to a whole group of people isn't going to help heal your wounds or stay your grief either. It will only deepen the pain you harbor."

"And as you said earlier, these men were caught in the wrong place at the wrong time." Grandpa added. "They don't care to hurt anyone."

Jasper looked from one face to the other and then bent his head. "Of course, you're right. My experiences have colored my vision. Surely, those men behind the fence do not carry the same animosity in their hearts toward your country as the ones on the battlefield, nor would the one you trust most care to wound such a generous family by turning as treacherous as his kin."

Though his words glistened with understanding, a darker current slithered with warning. Mistrust. And no wonder. Jessica knew the hatred full well, but something had changed for her. She felt it. Recognized the pulse of a greater voice pushing back the ashes of her anger with the fire of truth. She did not have to care about Mr. Reinhold to show kindness to him.

The conversation turned to more benign topics until Jasper took his leave. Jess handed Faith off to Granny and walked Jasper out the front door to the porch, the horizon painted with the orange and red hues of sunset.

"Please thank your grandparents again for their hospitality, won't you?"

"Of course."

"And apologize again to them for me, please." His brow crunched. "If I spoke untoward and dampened their evening."

"They're not easily offended, Mr. Little. I think you can safely trust in another offer to dinner."

He chuckled and placed his fedora on his head. "I'm not too certain Jude will appreciate my arrival again. I think my annoyance left him unsettled."

"I'll smooth things over. He's an observant little boy with a lot of hurt to manage, but he's very strong."

"How long will they stay? Until the baby is able to travel to an orphanage?"

"Orphanage?" Jess blinked up at him. "No, they'll live here. I have no plans to send them to the overcrowded and underfunded orphanages when they can receive love and family right here."

"I mean no offense, of course. I'm only thinking of the future." His smile softened, rekindling the dashing man from earlier in the evening. "Are you certain your grandparents are the best caretakers? They're not so young as would be beneficial for a rambunctious boy and baby girl, are they?"

"My grandparents?" Ah, Jess saw the turn of conversation now. Was that what everyone in town assumed too? She raised her gaze to him, readying herself for the admission aloud for the first time. "I assure you, they're quite capable of taking care of these children and giving them a beautiful life, but Jude and Faith do not belong to them." She drew in a strengthening breath. "They belong to me."

His dark brows rose almost to his hairline. "You... you mean to keep them?"

"Yes, I made a promise to their mother on her deathbed and I intend to keep my promise."

His hip slacked and he shook his head. "No one would expect you to rearrange your life and become a mother based on a deathbed promise, Jessica."

The use of her name, so intimate and careless, inspired a sudden need for distance. She barely knew him, but more than that, his changefulness tipped an imaginary scale of caution, causing her to reevaluate the glossy allure.

Her pulse snipped into a scared-rabbit run. "Mr. Little, I rarely concern myself with what people think. However, what matters a great deal to me is honesty, and keeping my word when I give it. Those children, though they aren't mine by blood, have become mine by heart."

Hearing the declaration from her own lips, spoken with such certainty, firmed the resolution all the way to her soul. She'd chosen them as her own.

As I have chosen you. The words poured over her spirit, offering comfort like the arrival of a long-lost friend. A balm she'd forgotten... or rejected?

"But can't you see how this choice will impact your life? Don't you care what a future suitor might say?"

"Suitor?" She laughed. "I didn't hold a great deal of hope for a suitor before I left for war, Mr. Little. But now, to return as a wounded woman, I imagine my prospects have taken a distinctive plummet. However, should I find myself in a situation where matrimony lingers in my future?" She shrugged. "My husband—my future husband, that is—would need to be as welcoming to these children as he would be to me, because they're mine."

Jasper had the good sense to look sorry, and he wore the expression quite well. "Yes, of course. I do apologize for my rash words." He grabbed one of her hands, drawing her a few stiff steps toward him. "Please, forgive me. I envy your family's generosity of heart."

She slipped her hand from his, another churn of warning sliding between his smooth touch and her shaky trust. Generosity of heart? She'd doled out kindness to August Reinhold through a sieve, yet welcomed Jasper Little as if he'd been a missing link to her world. Why?

Was it truly as simple as bitterness towards Germans and desperation to counter her fear in this incomprehensible attraction for August? Her head hurt from the inner war of past and present. Fear and faith.

"I hope generosity will always win out, Mr. Little."

"As do all of us who've survived the stings of war."

The distant sound of *Let Me Call You Sweetheart,* played by the German brass band in the camp, drifted on the late afternoon air, accompanied by the cricket calls.

"I'll bid you good evening, Miss Ross." Jasper tipped his hat, but his dark gaze latched onto hers. "But within all of your generosity, keep caution close to heart. You know as well as I how changeful our German neighbors can be." He moved a few steps down the porch. "I would hate for any of you to feel the betrayal of their duplicity once again."

His warning sent a chill shimmying down her spine, unearthing the tiniest prayer. She was a broken woman, haunted and afraid, and now determined to raise to orphans as her own. The weight of it all, overshadowed by Jasper's ominous caveat, entangled her freedom, drawing her down to drown in her fear.

She braced herself against the post of the porch and stared out into the coming night. The horizon, a painted sky of brilliant hues, softened the earth with a halo of tempered auburn. From deep within, braided among the scars she tended so well, a fragile thread of hope unfurled.

I have chosen you. I will not let you go.

And for the first time in a very long time, she didn't squelch the soul-whisper. She closed her eyes. "Help me."

The gentlest calm fingered over her scars with a healer's touch, bringing with it the undertones of a much-coveted peace. She didn't know how to recover from her past, or how to trust in her future, but, perhaps the Savior who'd rescued her heart as a child could mend the leftover pieces as an adult.

Jess startled awake to Jude's face in the darkness of the bedroom.

"Oh, Jude—honey, what on earth are you doing?" She emerged from the mental fog of a deep sleep, uncommon but becoming more so as the weeks passed.

"I... I can't sleep."

She sat up and glanced over at Faith's crib. Jess had gotten a full four hours of sleep in a row yesterday, free from both nightmares and nightly feedings, which felt like a massive accomplishment.

"What's wrong?"

"I had a bad dream and..." His little voice pitched higher. "I'm skeered."

His bottom lip wobbled and her heart melted for her brave little man. She pushed back the blankets and patted the bed. "How about you scrunch up here with me for a while? Do you think that will help?"

He nodded and slid beneath the covers. Jess wrapped her arms around his little shoulders and whispered into his hair. "I know about bad dreams."

His head moved. "I heard ya callin' out one night. Granny said you'd have 'em some from the war."

Jess rested her cheek against his head. "I do, but they're happening less."

"Mama used to say that she was God's arms in this world for me. When I'd have a nightmare sometimes, I'd run to her bed and she'd wrap me in her arms just like you're doin' right now."

Heated tears gathered in Jess' eyes, tipping onto her pillow. "Mama's are good about that."

His little head bobbed again. "She'd say, 'we pray for God to make us strong, but sometimes, we just need some arms to remind us that we're loved, so that's what I'm here for. I'm God's arms.'"

She squeezed Jude closer and buried another kiss into his hair. "That's a good reminder, Jude. I'm happy to be God's arms for you, sweet boy. You don't have to be afraid."

Chapter Fifteen

"Sylvie may still have some hearing, Anna."

Jess looked from her grandpa to Anna Fischer. The woman's bottom limp dropped limp.

"Now, I wouldn't get all my hopes up. It's still a large loss, but there's something..."

"It can be amplified," Jess finished.

Anna sent a frantic look between Grandpa and Jess, and even included Amy in the search for clarification. "Amplified? What does this mean?"

"There are devices called electric hearing aids we can attach to Sylvie's ears that will make the sounds louder for her." Grandpa tried to simplify the words.

"So perhaps she will be able to hear something again."

Anna stared again, the information slowly seeping into comprehension with the return of her tremulous smile. "Truly?"

"We won't know until we can try a hearing device on her," Grandpa warned. "I've never used them on children, and they can be cumbersome, but she's a clever one."

"Da," Anna said, clasping Sylvie's face in her hands and placing a kiss to her little forehead. "She is clever."

"How long would it take for the device to arrive when you order it?"

Amy's first words during the entire situation brought Jess' attention back to the young girl. Ever since she'd started working with her grandpa the day before, she'd held a wide-eyed look of pure fascination. But Jess instincts proved on target. Amy's learned quickly by observation, asked insightful questions, and came with her own self-researched knowledge. Jess couldn't help but see a little bit of her younger self shining in the curiosity behind Amy's caramel gaze.

"I'm not quite sure with the war on and all." Grandpa rubbed his chin. "A month or more, I suspect. And then we'll have to see how they fit, and if Sylvie can manage them at her age."

"She can." Anna responded, immediately. "I will make certain she can."

"I'm going to go to the post office directly and place the order." Grandpa nodded to Amy. "Take the catalog with the latest options from Seimens and I'll show you how it's done."

Amy's ready smile beamed with the joy of feeling useful.

"If you're fine, Grandpa, I'll take Anna back home in the car and help Granny with the children as we prepare for the Ross family arrival."

"She'll appreciate it. I know she's still trying to clean out the front room."

"Do you need the cottage?" Anna drew Sylvie from the examination table into her arms. "We can stay in town until your family leaves if you need the space."

"No, thank you, Anna." Grandpa walked toward the door, Amy at his heels. "Mrs. Carter's family managed a houseful in that farmhouse for a century or more. Besides, it'll be nice to have a full house after all this time."

Jess followed them out, locking up the clinic and leading Anna and Sylvie to the car. Her gaze immediately swept up the street to the camp and took an unwanted turn toward a certain German. What was she doing? Though Jasper softened after his warning last night, it was clear raising someone else's children wasn't even on his list of possibilities. Why on earth would she even consider contemplating a relationship with any man, especially some German who unnerved her more than anything else?

She grimaced. Well, he *did* ignite quite a few other things inside of her, but she didn't like to think about them, let alone name them. If she'd hovered on the edge of spinsterhood before the war, as a single mom of two, she completely catapulted over the cliff.

What man would want her? Wounded, outspoken, and a mother of two orphans? Best to bury that dream along with countless others and embrace the growing sweetness of her current life.

"You fight very hard against liking him, don't you?"

Jess turned to Anna's soft voice as they topped the street and turned toward the car. She took a few steps in silence, grinding her teeth to unravel a response. "I don't see why my opinion matters all that much. I'm certain my somewhat abrasive personality will wear away his interest soon enough."

Anna chuckled and placed Sylvie in the middle of the car seat, then took her place on the other side. "I do not think you understand my brother or how he views you. He appreciates your strength, your single-mindedness. His past is littered with people who were swayed by society or selfishness more than conscience. You are quite different."

Jess pressed the starter and the engine rumbled to life. "Quite different, hmm?" She released her frustration in a mock laugh. "Well, that makes the most sense for an attraction than anything else."

"You do not see, do you? You should reread those letters you sent to your grandparents. Hear the stories they tell of you, with such love and laughter."

Jess kept her eyes forward, restraining a massive eye-roll. "People don't fall in love through letters, Anna."

"It depends on the letters." Humor lit her words. "Some great romances occurred through letters, or at least were encouraged by them."

Jess sighed against the tempting tug of Anna's optimism. "Name one."

"My grandparents. The day they met in person, my grandfather proposed to her, but they'd corresponded for a year. My mother kept them as a reminder that there are men in the world such as my grandfather."

The memory of Anna's confession about her former husband's cruelty tempered Jessica's response with curiosity. "And what was this grandfather like?"

"Gentle. Strong." Her voice quieted with reminiscence. "He countered our father's harshness with a quiet dignity. My mother carried the same quiet strength in her. That and her faith were the only things holding her heart together in the face of our father's brutality. He only had enough love for one child. One rule. One dream. And if we did not fit into the dream, we were cast away. If you did not harden to him and take on his ways, he had little use for you. My husband was father's protégé, both in business and in personal matters, but August..." She smiled. "He is much like our grandfather."

Jessica paused on the sentiment before continuing. Quiet strength? With a slight begrudging hold on her dislike, she'd agree. He carried a strength, an internal calm. "And what about your other family? Don't you want to return to Germany for them?"

"There is no other family. When August left after disinheritance by our father, I remained close to care for our mother. After her death, the bond holding me to my homeland broke. August and I have learned to rely on one another, as we've done our whole lives. Both outcasts. Misfits in an expectation of perfection."

Jess digested this new information as they drew close to the farmhouse. Her childhood and the Reinhold's stood in complete contrast to one another. Anchored within a loving family, blanketed with encouragement her whole life, she couldn't fathom a home destitute of tenderness or laughter.

"How can you just accept your father's behavior? Having to uproot your life? Your brother's exile from home?"

"I have fought my battles against my heart and my past, Jessica. So has August. Life is filled with scars from others, and we can choose to pick the scars and keep them bleeding, or tend the scars with faith and forgiveness so they will heal."

She stopped the car and turned to Anna, her eyes and throat on fire. "What happens then? What happens if I forgive?" She pointed out the window to the sky. "How can I just release all of this wrong when someone should pay for it, or at the very least He should explain himself for all that's happened?" She pinched the steering mechanism in her grasp, fighting the onslaught of tears.

Anna lifted a brow and covered one of Jessica's hands with her own. "Don't you know? Someone has paid for it. All the wrongs done to us, by us, for us. All the wounds we cause or excuse. The injustices we scream. Christ has already paid for it." She reached for the car door and nodded to the back yard where Jude worked to hit the birdie back across the net to August.

August raised his straw hat in welcome, his grin almost infectious. "My opponent has finally arrived?"

Jess pulse twittered into another rhythm and she looked away, right into Anna's clear blue gaze. "Open your eyes, Jessica. Open and see."

―

"Why do you keep torturing yourself through these matches with her, August?" Mrs. Carter whispered as Jess and Anna approached from the car. "Are you a glutton for punishment? She'll play you until she wins."

August matched her volume, keeping his eyes on the beautiful prize walking his way. "That's why I must keep winning."

Mrs. Carter chuckled and placed a palm on his shoulder, drawing his attention to her warm, gray eyes. "You clever boy. My granddaughter is stubborn, but she's no fool. When she comes around, and she will, she'll reward your patience. She's fiercely loyal." She shook her head. "You just have to get past her wicked stubbornness to reach the heart of gold."

He pressed a palm to his chest, an ache forming at the thought. "Time is not on my side, Mrs. Carter. Perhaps I should relinquish my pursuit before I wound her."

"Wound her? Jess needs to learn the risk is worth the reward. Besides, time may not be on your side, but it's well in hand for Him." She gestured skyward. "I'd let him worry about those details, and keep your eyes on the goal."

Which wasn't a hardship by any means. She wore a cream blouse with short sleeves paired with a long, green skirt reaching down to the tops of her boots. The cinched waist of her skirt drew attention to her curves and the length of her legs. The sun added an extra scorch to his face, but he took his time appreciating the view. What would it be like to have all of her energy and determination turned to loving him? He'd certainly like to find out.

"Allow me to change my shoes, Mr. Reinhold." Jessica's smile challenged him. "I'm feeling rather lucky today, so prepare yourself."

His grin stretched wide and he gave a sweeping bow in response. "Hope is an excellent virtue, Miss Ross."

Evergreen glittered with mischief. She raised her golden brow. "There's always hope."

He held her gaze. "And that is exactly what I'm counting on."

The teasing fell from her expression, replaced by a wave of uncertainty. He stepped forward, searching for a reason in this sudden shift, but she backed toward the house, recovering her grin. "Just so you know, I'm excellent in math too, so counting might not be your best defense either."

His gaze followed her until she disappeared through the back door, her skirt swaying the entire way.

"You leave very little for her to guess, don't you?" Anna shook her head.

"She's had enough guesses the past two years." He shrugged, glancing back at the porch, more certain than ever to keep his direct approach. "I will offer truth or I will offer nothing at all."

Despite her firmed frown, the lines around Anna's eyes gentled. "And what about that heart of yours?"

He patted his chest, attempting to cloak his sister's worry with some levity. "As I told Mrs. Carter, I'm playing to win."

The game kept a frenetic pace from the first serve. Jessica played like a woman with a ghost on her heels, pursuing each step, and August struggled to keep one pace ahead of her. She moved with a bit more fluidity, and ran for the most unexpected shots. It wasn't until about halfway through the match that she unleashed her natural charm from behind the cautious and killer quiet from which she'd attacked him.

All of her hair slipped from its pins, cascading around her in a rain of gold and completely distracting him from his winning shot. The birdie spun out of bounds and Jessica laughed.

"You shall not have that game point, Mr. Reinhold. I mean to beat you this time."

He couldn't pull his gaze from her face—the color in her cheeks, the smile lighting her emerald eyes. Her lips parted as she breathed in the afternoon scent of honeysuckles. Would those lips taste as sweet as honey?

"It looks as though you have something devious on your mind." She moved to the net and placed a hand to her hip. "Are you worried about the game? Have I tired you out? Come now, share your thoughts."

"I wondered if your lips would taste as sweet as honey."

Her eyes shot wide and all color fled her face. She didn't speak for a few seconds. His grin itched to respond.

"You shouldn't say things like that to me."

He met her at the net. "Why not? I think things like that about you."

She stumbled through another reply, clearly off-set by his directness. If he had to practice patience, perhaps he could enjoy the process.

"But... but we are not..." She waved a hand between them. "Together."

He glanced around the yard. His sister had retired with Sylvie to the cottage long ago, and Mrs. Carter had taken Jude inside to help tend to Faith. Nothing but the birds and the sunbeams offered any audience. "It looks as though we are. Together. Right now." His voice dropped as he tilted his head closer, wiggling his brow in playful invitation. "Alone."

Her narrowed eyes held a fiery sting. "You need a good beating, Mr. Reinhold, and I mean to win this game."

"And you need a good kiss, and then we'd both win, yes?"

Nothing but a helpless squeak came from her open mouth.

"I see I'll need to wait until you are ready, Miss Ross. Kisses are powerful things."

She firmed her lips into a decided frown and marched back to her place, racquet to the ready as if a weapon. "You'll be waiting a long time, then."

August whistled on his way to his place at the line, then turned to prepare for his serve. Jessica looked everywhere else except at his face, and the racquet in her hands bounced like Jude's new rubber ball.

He tamed his smile and served a beautiful ace, barely crossing the net without a touch. She struggled to reach it and got her racquet on it, but the birdie spun up into the air and out of bounds.

"Match point, my advantage." August winked and she quickly looked away, a deeper shade of rose darkening her cheeks.

Jessica took a ready position, her lips as pinched as her brow. "That smirk does not become you, Mr. Reinhold."

He unleashed a laugh and her frown tipped in the opposite direction. A little. Not enough to encourage him to march across the court and satisfy the curiosity about the taste of her lips, but enough to hint at a certain softening behind her apparent disdain? His lips hitched wider. Perhaps he was winning in more ways than one.

The next rally proved the longest, a battle of stamina and speed, until he tipped the birdie over the net with the slightest touch and she couldn't get to it in time. He stood, breathing hard, and offered his hand of sportsmanship.

Her stare bore into his as she walked toward the net and wrapped her cool fingers around his in a vice. "You cheated."

"Cheated? I assure you, I did not cheat."

"Yes, you did." She rounded the net, a pointed finger punctuating each word. "With what you said."

What he said? The previous conversation and her current rosy cheeks punctuated his clarity. He feigned innocence with a full shrug. "About winning?"

"No." Her lips thinned against the words, hesitating before lowering her voice to a whisper. "About the kissing. I couldn't concentrate."

"Very flattering, my dear Miss Jesse." He leaned in to match her volume. "But if it didn't matter to you, it shouldn't distract you."

She stared back, wide-eyed, so he continued. "Besides, as long as you're near, my thoughts will eventually turn to the topic without much difficulty."

Her gaze dropped to his lips, sending a tingle shooting across them before they spun into a smile.

She blinked from the daze and stood straight, distancing herself with a step. "I'd say you need more work to do because clearly, your mind has too much free time."

"No, no. My thoughts are properly ordered. Quite in order."

"You, Mr. Reinhold, are insufferable." She marched across the lawn toward the house.

He ran to catch up. "What does this mean? Insufferable?"

She stopped at the bottom of the porch steps, her head down. "It means you're impossible. Nearly unbearable." She enunciated each word as she turned to face him. "You should take this interest you have and lay it at the feet of some woman more interested in your persistent adoration."

"I have a feeling you've succeeded in frightening away many suitors." A sudden awareness drew him closer, in search of the truth. "You are afraid."

"Of you?" She scoffed.

"Nein, of releasing your heart, I think."

"Very clever, Mr. Reinhold, but the heart isn't trustworthy." She looked away under his scrutiny. "Better to use one's head and experience."

He covered her hand on the railing with his, snatching back her attention. "Ah, you know what you want? What is best for you?" He searched her face. "But He knows." He tipped his head to the sky. "He knows what you truly need in your head and your heart, and you might be surprised by His choices."

She tugged her hand free to cross it in front of her chest. Her expression laced with suspicion, a little humor... and maybe the tiniest bit of curiosity. "And I suppose you are what's best for my head and my heart?"

"Alas, I am not strong enough to get through to your head." He placed his racquet by the porch steps and shoved his hands in his pockets, the tug to take her in his arms almost overpowering. "But I think I might be getting through to your heart."

She pinched her palms tighter in a hug and the sardonic smile slid from her lips, though she tried to keep the strength in her stance, the barrier. "Oh really?"

"Yes." He shrugged, holding her gaze, memorizing her silhouette against the farmhouse with the backdrop of blue sky. "But just like a good kiss, I will wait. I'm very good at waiting."

"I did not write the letter, sir. I give you my word." August stood to attention in front of Ruser, readied to find whatever proof necessary to clear his name. After such a rewarding afternoon, his face still warm from his invigorating conversation with Jessica Ross, August thought he'd turned a corner of disappointment. Her eyes held such hurt, such mistrust, but the wall was beginning to crumble. Little by little. Could this dream for which he'd prayed truly solidify into flesh and blood? Was it possible God would not only give him a future in Hot Springs but also Jessica Ross' heart?

But he'd barely made it through the threshold of the Lower Camp before Cliff took him directly to Ruser's office.

Ruser scanned over the paper in his hand and then removed his wire-rimmed spectacles, examining August with the same scrutiny. August stared back, unwavering, the letter in Ruser's hands a pure act of ruthless fiction.

The letter contained information about the Allies movements in France, hidden within a flimsy code any grade school child might decipher, and signed with August's name.

"And you have no knowledge of this Lieutenant Schleigle to whom the letter is addressed?"

"No, sir."

"Your father is mentioned." Ruser pointed an accusing finger at the page.

"Only by the last name, which could be written by any person who knew my surname," August argued. "Is this the only such letter discovered?"

Ruser placed the paper down on the desk and braided his hands together to rest on the desk. "No, this is the third, but the first within the past two weeks."

"And the other two?"

Ruser sighed and leaned back in his chair, his frown deepening. "Written anonymously by someone who means to stir up discord for us."

August sighed down into the chair Ruser had offered him in the beginning of their meeting. "Then you know I am no traitor."

Ruser's moustache twitched. "August, there are some men in my camp for whom the title could most certainly fit, but not you." His frown returned. "However, it seems someone is attempting to bring trouble to our camp, and I mean to find out who it is."

August leaned forward. "So you do not blame me for this?"

Ruser matched August's position, his eyes narrowed in scrutiny for a moment until his brow cleared with a smile. "I have been in war and life for many years. I've learned to recognize the difference between an honest man and a traitor, no matter how virtuous the intentions. You are no traitor, but I would keep a watch on others around you, whether inside or outside the camp. Somewhere, we do have a traitor, and I hope his intentions are limited to ill-planned letters." Ruser picked up the paper and waved it in the air before depositing it back on his desk. "And nothing more."

Chapter Sixteen

Jess barely touched her supper. After Anna's unwitting reprimand, Jess' heart spun on a carousel as fast the one the Germans had constructed inside the camp. Her shoulders bent, wearied from the struggle to capture peace but determined to hold to her cause. Her pain deserved justice, just as the man who'd almost killed her brother and then defiled her deserved whatever justice he received beyond the grave.

The thought caught. What justice did he face at this moment? She'd killed him in self-defense, sent him to his eternal destination. A shiver trembled over her skin and strained her emotions, raw and aching. Tears teetered for release, as they'd done since her conversation with Anna. She couldn't keep living like this.

Even her struggle to distance herself from August grew more difficult with each passing day. Everything about him, from his gentleness, to his quiet strength, to the teasing glint in his morning-blue eyes, called to all the bruised places in her heart for a shelter. A refuge from the chaos of nightmares and harbored grief.

Her smile bloomed, starting around her heart and moving upward. And she enjoyed his conversation.

She kicked against the resignation, the old argument rising to battle her weaknesses. She didn't need a man's protection. Faith nestled close, staring back at Jess with unwavering confidence. Trust.

But every little girl needed to know the strength of a daddy, as she'd known. The presence of someone who'd stand up to all the monsters or bullies in the world. And that desire still wove into grown-up girls' hearts, though molded into a different sort of hero.

A hero she didn't necessarily *need*...

Jess sighed deeper into the dining chair. But a hero she *wanted*.

The internal admission turned the few bites of chicken she'd eaten sour in her stomach, but her heart pulsed a stronger beat. The very thought of sharing her burdens, blessings, dreams, and cares with someone who might also buffer the trials of life alongside her encouraged a welcome whisper of daydreams.

But certainly not August Reinhold! His camp would transition out of Hot Springs, on to Georgia, and then back to Germany. Despite what August or Anna wanted, staying in America after the war seemed unlikely.

"I hear you didn't get to introduce Mr. Little to the finer points of mountain life yesterday, Uncle Jacob?" Cliff took Jessica's plate from the table, tossing her a mischievous smile. "I reckon my company was a great disappointment compared to the sophisticated Englishman."

Jess exaggerated her eye-roll, grateful for his levity intruding into her thoughts.

"No." Her grandfather finished up his meal at the end of the table. "He had an unexpected meeting with some professor in Asheville, so he left on the early train. Told me he'd like to reschedule for next week, but I'm not sure what our week will look like once Alexander and David arrive."

"I know Jessica's been sparkin' him, but I'm not too impressed with the fancy fellow."

"Cliff Carter, I'll have you know I've not been sparkin' anybody." But her familiarity with Jasper Little annoyed her usual sensibilities. Why had she warmed up to the man so quickly? The unfamiliar response bounded against her typically cautious nature.

"What does sparkin' mean?" Jude's voice rose above her grandpa's chuckle.

Jessica's eyes fluttered closed.

"It means Miss Jesse has a particular interest in Mr. Little's company." Cliff snuck a maple cookie from Granny's offering on the counter and pointed it at Jessica. "In the hopes he'll take a particular interest too."

"Oh, don't be ridiculous, Cliff."

"I don't like Mr. Little." Jude's little nose wrinkled with his admission. "Why don't you spark August instead?"

"That is one fine question, Jude. Why don't you spark August instead?" Cliff leaned against the counter and tilted his head, his gaze needling her response while he took a bite of his cookie.

Jess stood and snatched the remaining cookie from Cliff's hand, then pointed it at him like a weapon. "Cliff Carter, you are the most exasperating man on this planet. Don't put ideas in Jude's head."

"Just because you don't appreciate my certain brand of charm, doesn't mean I'm exasperating." He reached for another cookie without hesitation. "And don't try to change the subject. Your boy asked you a very thoughtful question."

"What does exasperatin' mean?"

Jess smiled at 'her boy.' "It means Uncle Cliff needs to mind his own business."

The daggers she shot her cousin bounced off his self-satisfied smirk. He glanced around her. "And just why do you think your mama ought to spark August, Jude?"

Grandpa's chuckle didn't help one bit. "This brings back memories."

"I'd better snatch Faith before they get worse." Granny wedged in between Jess and Cliff to pry little Faith from Jess' arms. "You remember the time she jumped on Cliff's back and held on by his hair?"

"Granny! I was seven." Jess reluctantly released her little, squirming bundle.

"I wouldn't be surprised if you didn't make it to blows again, the two of you." She eyed them both, a laugh in her smile, before returning to her chair to coo over Faith.

Jess returned her attention to her annoying cousin. "I don't feel the need to be sparkin' anyone, at present."

"I saw Mr. Little talkin' up a storm with that Davis man, and I don't think he's good through-and-through."

"Smart boy."

Jess smacked Cliff's shoulder.

"Now, Cliff, just because he's talking with the Davises doesn't mean he's a problem." Granny's sweet reprimand came out with steely undertones.

Cliff hitched a brow as if he didn't catch one hint of Granny's tone. Stubborn man. "Doesn't mean there isn't either." He turned to Jude. "What do you like about August, Jude?"

Jess groaned and rubbed her forehead. Trouble maker. "Leave the boy alone, Cliff."

Jude swallowed the last bite of potatoes in his mouth, unaware of Uncle Cliff transforming into a complete nuisance.

"You already know," came Jude's reply. "You done seen it too."

Jess turned completely around to face her 'little boy' as Cliff called him. She liked the sound of it. "Seen what?"

"All the good things about August." Jude reached to take a cookie from the plate that Granny had moved to the center of the table, seemingly oblivious to the mystery his words evoked.

"Like what?"

Jude munched on his cookie, barely casting a glance to the adults listening in. "You know, he smiles with his whole face, and he sits on the porch with me."

Jess slid back down into her chair, trying to make some sense of Jude's simple statement. "Sits on the porch with you?"

"Yes, ma'am. Like Grandpa and Cliff do. They don't mind sittin' on the porch steps to tawk."

Jess exchanged a look with Granny. Did Jude have memories of his father? Had he known long talks on a porch step or a family game of badminton? The simplicity in his statement spoke volumes and opened the hurt for him in her heart even more. He had no idea how his words pierced the room.

"And you don't have to ask if he's good or not. Mama says the best folks do good even when no one's lookin'. I seed him work hard. Make purdy things with his hands. Help folks, even when no one's lookin'. I reckon that's worth somethin'."

He took a drink of his milk and looked up, staring from one face to the other, and finally landing his attention on Granny. "These are real good cookies, Granny."

"He *is* a smart boy." Granny tossed Jess one of those looks Jess really wanted to ignore but found her gaze inextricably linked to

Granny's against her will. "There's a whole lot of truth in those words."

Jess shot back a glare—a respectful glare so as not to incur wrath—and stood. She walked to the sink and rinsed off her plate before placing it in the tub of soapy water for washing, avoiding everyone's curious looks. "I don't have a particular interest in anyone except Jude and Faith at present, so all of these painfully obvious hints are a waste of good scheming, if you ask me."

Grandpa stood and stretched out his back, taking his plate up to the counter to slide his scraps into the pummy dish. Jude's dog definitely didn't go hungry too often, but with Jude's arrival, the scraps decreased significantly. The boy ate like a man.

Jess took the plate from Grandpa's hands and scrubbed it with more force than necessary. He'd practically licked it clean.

"Speaking of August, we ain't seen him in two days. Do you know if he's all right? He rarely passes by without stoppin' in."

Cliff's expression took a distinct turn, and Jess put the plate aside. Something was wrong.

"Jude, would you run out and give some of these pummies to the dogs?"

"Yes, ma'am." He shot up, delivered his plate, and disappeared out the back door.

Jess wiped her fingers on her apron. "What is it?"

"August is down at the chapel working today."

"We didn't see him pass," Grandpa said.

"Why didn't he come by and get some dinner?" Granny stood too, Faith now asleep in her arms. "What's happened?"

Cliff braced his palms against the counter and raised his gaze to Jess', hesitating. Her stomach tightened for the awaiting blow. "I reckon you'll hear about it soon enough, but I didn't want you to jump to the wrong conclusions."

"What are you talking about?"

"August is afraid of what ya'll will think about him since he's recently been falsely accused."

"What?" Her grandparents' response came in unison.

"Seems someone wrote letters to contacts in Germany sharing particular information about Allied movements on the Front. August and two other men were framed for the job."

Everyone grew quiet. Her grandpa placed a hand to Granny's shoulder.

Not again. Not another traitor hurting people she loved! It didn't make sense. Anna's story about their childhood and August's disinheritance? August's apparent kindness to her family and especially the children. Her faith faltered. But she'd been wrong before. Worked alongside a doctor serving wounded and dying soldiers who'd betrayed them all, and nearly killed her brother in the process. What if... what if she was wrong again?

Grandpa shook his head, his hand coming down on the counter with a thud. "That makes me plumb mad. We've been gettin' on just fine in this community with these men for a year and someone comes along now, at the end of their stay, to cause trouble? And for August, of all people?"

Cliff picked up his jacket and hat from a seat nearby and started for the door. "I'm just glad Ruser and the other officers know a lie when they see one. Now, I gotta get back. I'm working the evening shift tonight, but I sure do appreciate a good supper, Aunt Lillian."

Granny palmed Cliff's cheek with her customary love-pat. "You can stop by any time. You always gotta place here, boy."

"So does August." Grandpa added. "Tell him that when you see him."

Cliff looked her way, his expression beckoning her forward. "Walk me out, Jess. Will ya?"

Jess followed Cliff to the porch, late afternoon light waxing long and orange across the backyard. He stopped by the steps and tilted his head to examine her face. "I saw it on your face in there. The doubt. You're worried August is guilty."

"Anyone's capable of treachery if given the right incentive, Cliff." Her defenses riled against him, the old stings reviving her anger. "Even someone as seemingly sweet as August Reinhold."

"The only thing August Reinhold and Lt. Snyder have in common is where they were born." He jerked his hat off and ran a hand through his hair. "Good grief, Jessica, whatever else you suffered from the war, please tell me it didn't steal your common sense. Use the clear-headedness I've always admired in you and see the truth."

"I don't have time to listen to your platitudes, cousin." She turned toward the door but he caught her arm.

"Stop it. Just stop it. The world is filled with hurting people, but that doesn't give us the right to sentence innocent ones to the same fate as the guilty. August had nothin' to do with what happened to you in Europe, but you've been punishing him since you got home for crimes he didn't commit."

Cliff's words propelled her to the attack. If nothing else, she had to defend herself, protect her anger. "And you've been encouraging Jude and even my grandparents to welcome him in like a long lost son. What do you really know about this stranger, Cliff?"

"He's not a stranger. He's my friend, and if your head wasn't fogged with bitterness, you'd see the truth as plain as Jude does."

"You have no idea what happened to me. What I've been through."

"No, I don't know all you've suffered, but do you think I don't understand what it feels like to be betrayed? By God? That raw wound of utter loneliness and pain of thinking God would allow something so unjust to happen to me?"

He spoke directly to her heart, naming her scars. She nearly buckled from the agony of the fight. Every logical thought in her head recognized her irrational assumptions and screamed 'foul,' but her stubborn heart refused to release the pain and fury.

Cliff jammed his hat back on his head. "When Elizabeth and our baby died, I knew. I could have competed with your screams at God." His fist rammed into his chest. "I still hurt from that loss on a daily basis, occasionally weep for the family I don't have, but there comes a time for mourning to end and life to start again."

"And condone what happened?"

"That's crazy talk. Your hurt and grief's jumbled up your thinking. You're so blind by what you think God's done *to* you, that you've forgotten what God has done *for* you."

Anna's words from earlier came back to mind. Jess fought against their accuracy. Cliff's too. "He's allowed some of my friends to die, thousands of young soldiers, almost my brother, and then—" She stopped before confessing Snyder's horrible assault.

Cliff shook his head. "Listen to yourself. You keep using the same argument over and over. You're digging your own hole to nowhere."

She folded her arms across her chest and grimaced at him.

"The only thing bitterness does is change you, not Him. God doesn't need you. He doesn't need me." He stepped closer and gentled a palm on Jess' shoulder. She stiffened against the unwanted sting of tears at his compassion. "But, Jess, he does even better than that. He *wants* us. He chooses us. He left Heaven to rescue us." Cliff shook his head, his own eyes swimming with sunset-tears. "Because when the heartbreak comes, we can see there's something bigger than our pain. His love gives us strength to let go and trust Him for the purpose."

She recoiled, jerking her arm free from his touch. "I can't let go. There's no justice in letting go. The death, the utter waste of life, the treachery? If I let go, who will grieve for those who've lost their lives? Who will fight for them? Who will seek to justify the wrong that's happened to so many?" *To me.* She pinched her eyes closed, the nightmarish visions, the unwholesome betrayal striking a fresh sting. "It sounds easy to say God will take care of it, but when it comes down to the truth—"

"You want to seek justice on your own? Revenge?" His words seethed, his eyes alight. "Then what, Jessica? Will *your* justice bring you peace then? Can you bring back the dead? Restore whatever inside of you that's lost?"

He stepped close and tugged her into his arms. "You're still going to feel as empty and lost, even if you find whatever 'justice' you've defined as the answer." His words breathed over her hair, burdened with a fading sorrow. "You have a choice. To trust God for the peace you crave and this justice for your soul, or to continue to live in the turmoil of 'unfair.'"

He drew back from her, searching her gaze with a watery one of his own. "Life is unfair. But even in that knowledge, our measurement, our gauge, is skewed."

She ran the back of her hand across her eyes. "What do you mean?"

"What is fair? What is unfair?" Cliff squeezed her shoulders to punctuate the questions. "The only way we can truly answer those questions is to be able to see the vastness of time and how each choice, each decision, plays out in eternity." His grin quirked despite a tear slipping down his cheek. "I don't have that ability or knowledge. And unless something remarkable happened to you over in the war, you don't either."

His words hollowed her out, clawing at the anger she clung to. "Then what do I do?"

"You already know, that's why you're fightin' so hard, because you don't like the answer. Trust has always been hard for you." He shook his head, stepping back to bestow a comforting smile on her. "I'm not sure why, but it always has, and this war made things worse. There's a voice inside of you, calling you back to the peace you once knew. It can calm this fury and quell your thirst for justice, because He's already taken on all the injustices for us. Only He can set your torn heart back to rights."

Cliff distanced himself with another step and tipped his hat. "It's your choice. Your justice... or His peace. You can't hold onto both."

Jess stood on the porch long after Cliff disappeared down the road. She wanted to block everything he said, push it away from infiltrating her justified resentment, but the truth seeped through the cracks in her faulty logic.

The trail to the chapel beckoned her to follow, abate her curiosity, and perhaps confirm the pestering truth about who August Reinhold really was. Was she ready to accept whatever answer met her down the leaf riddled path?

She walked forward, leaving behind the house and her fear of being wrong. The afternoon sounds of busy forest animals and birdsong came to life around her, awakening her dormant soul to the music of the wood around her... and the God intrinsically connecting it all together? Cliff's sermon preached a harsh gospel to her anger, but deep inside, she felt the cleansing peroxide of truth, burning at hatred and hollowed-out fear.

This struggle against peace wearied her to her soul. She fisted her will and looked up to the trees branching together overhead like an arbor.

"I can't do this on my own. I don't know how, but if you'll help me let go, I'll try to trust you. So, please help me...." She took a deep breath and stepped out into the clearing.

Her breath caught.

What had only been a skeleton of her beloved chapel a week ago now emerged from her memories in actual size and form, only better. The steeple tower framed the entry way, as it had before, except a gaping hole waited above the doorway for some special addition. A window, perhaps.

A beautiful ribbon of carving, the design an intricate weave of ivy, dripped down the edges of the doorframe in an immaculate fashion, as lovely as her father's massive country estate or her sister-in-law's beloved Beacon House.

Jess stared, lost in the amazement of rediscovery, as if her prayer materialized before her in tangible proof. She glided forward, entranced, emotions bubbling to the top in complete abandon. This chapel, filled with memories so excruciating and sweet, stood almost restored to something even more beautiful than she remembered. How was that possible?

A consistent thud pinged from inside. Hammering. *August.*

With quiet steps, she approached, taking in the unfinished but carefully fashioned work of a dedicated craftsman, a lovely restoration of something mangled and destroyed.

I will restore your heart.

A prayer caught in her throat with a sob.

August bent low, the muscles in his back moving with the swing of his hammer, revealing his strength. His golden head, uncovered, glistened in waves from his hard work in the silence of the forest. Alone.

Jude's innocent comment swept through her. *The best folks do good even when no one's lookin'.*

The hinge in her spirit swung wider—to God, to hope, and to the possibility that this man was much more than she'd allowed him to be. Someone she... *wanted.*

August nailed another floorboard into place. Only a few more and the oak floor, though unfinished, would be complete. Much like the framework, with its walls and temporary holes for the windows he hoped to add shortly, the chapel had taken form, almost a replica of what stood previously except for a few additions of August's own design. A grander steeple capped the entryway with a pinnacle surprise waiting to finalize its simple beauty.

He almost smiled but for the aching reminder of his loss. Even if the Carters appreciated his finished product, with the rumor of his letter paired with Jessica's natural distrust, could they trust him?

Not Jessica. He'd only recently earned a smile and some heartwarming banter, but her trust still dangled beyond reach, trapped in wounds he couldn't touch, no matter his patient pursuit.

Dear God, what would you have me do?

A crunch of leaves paused his work. He waited for another sound, another hint to the creature invading the quiet of his sanctuary, but silence greeted him, so he finally abated his curiosity and turned. Jessica Ross stood in the doorway, her hand on the frame as if posed for a painter. Her straw hat veiled part of her downturned face, but not enough to keep her mesmerizing gaze from finding his.

The green of her blouse brought out the paler hues in her eyes, captivating him until only force of will drew his attention back to his work.

"You have heard of the letter?" His words echoed back to him off the oak walks.

"Yes," she replied, barely above a whisper.

He hammered another nail to fill the silence, the skin on his back tingling in awareness of her presence. Was she taunting him? Laughing at him? Reveling in how right she'd been not to trust a German?

He gripped the hammer, giving the nail an unnecessary beating until he dented the wood. With a sigh, he placed the hammer down and stood, turning to face her. "Why are you still here? All your suspicions are confirmed, yes? I am the traitor you hoped."

She didn't flinch. Her expression remained impassable except for those large unfathomable eyes. They delved into his with a curiosity and... compassion he'd not seen before. She took another step into his handiwork, her gaze never leaving his.

"You have my grandparents in an uproar of worry, August Reinhold."

His fist clenched at his side, waiting for the blow of accusation.

"Do you realize how much food my Granny cooks on a daily basis to make sure you eat some of it?"

He blinked, taking in her question. Her... acceptance. His fingers unwound and the tension in his body fled.

She stepped closer, her countenance serious despite the levity in her conversation. "And Grandpa thought you were dying of some horrible disease because he hadn't seen you in two days, so

I advise you to stop by the house on your way back to camp to assure them you are well."

His grimace relaxed as he searched her face. "I'll be certain to do so, Miss Ross."

She examined the chapel, her look of appreciation deepening the warmth in his chest. Blonde curls framed her face like a softened halo, begging his work-wearing fingers to test the texture. She accepted him? Even after the letter? He almost shouted in triumph and took her in his arms.

She placed her hands on her hips. "Now, we have a few hours of daylight left." Her grin spread with a tip of her brow. "And I think you could use some help."

Chapter Seventeen

The train hissed to a stop in front of the small Hot Springs depot and Jess adjusted her gloves, feeling conspicuous in her Sunday best on a Thursday. A few people waited on the platform with her, some dressed in their finest, and others less so, but each giving Jessica a solid look as they walked past her.

A flash of coral and embroidery descended from the train steps, fitted to the elegant figure of her sister-in-law, Catherine Ross. Jess enjoyed the responses of the bystanders as much as seeing the feisty and familiar face.

People actually stopped in mid-conversation, probably wondering if some actress from the moving pictures or a cover model from *The Delineator* or *The Ladies World* graced the small-town with her presence. In fact, it might have been the most interesting sight since the Germans took up residence next door.

Catherine's sapphire eyes searched the platform and finally landed on Jessica. Her red lips slid into a genuine smile, lighting her entire face. "Well, it's nice to know you haven't lost your sense of style, sister dear."

Jess laughed and rushed forward, wrapping Catherine in a hug—or as close a hug as their mutual hats would allow. "I can't tell you how glad I am to see you all."

"Three months is a long time for a father."

Alexander Ross followed Catherine down the steps. All at once, Jess was wrapped in the warmth of sandalwood, sweetness, and her father's arms. She buried her face into his shoulder, pushing her hat to the back of her head, but she didn't care. Her vision blurred so she closed her eyes to pinch back the tears.

"Hi, Daddy."

He tipped back her hat even more and pressed a kiss to her forehead. "I know I'll detract from the style, but a father is allowed such liberties."

"And ready forgiveness, as he often reminds me," came Catherine's quick reply, paired with a playful tilt of her dark brow. "Which is fairly easy to give, I must say."

Father squeezed Jess' shoulders once more and then gestured toward Catherine. "She works very hard to fill the void of your spirited presence."

"You know as well as I that her particular brand of determined was there well before I left."

Catherine's smile turned impish along with her smile. "And it's served me well. There's absolutely nothing wrong with spirited, determined women, isn't that so?"

"I, for one, am a grateful recipient of both."

Jess failed to hold back her tears at the sight of her brother holding his two-year old daughter, Addie, in his arms. Her fashion rivaled her mother's, with a dark lavender travel suit and matching hat to top her dark curls. Jess basked in her brother's grin, their shared blond hair and green eyes a proud trait.

Every time she saw him, a vision of holding his bleeding head in her lap flashed through her mind and crushed air from her lungs. The fact that he lived and recovered most of his memories proved a miracle all on its own. The war cost her so much, but at least God had given her this one miracle. Her brother, alive, whole, and from the smile in his eyes, happy.

Catherine swept David a look that left Jess in no doubt of their mutual affection.

"It's quite annoying to be surrounded by such overwhelming romantic contentment, my dear." Her father offered his arm, not looking one bit annoyed. He leaned close, his voice soft. "She takes splendid care of our boy."

"And I've no doubt the adoration is mutual."

"I've heard rumors from your grandfather that a young man holds a similar adoration for my daughter?"

Jess pulled back and examined her father's face. Saints alive, Grandpa was dabbling in matchmaking now too?

"Actually, I do have a particular fellow who's won my heart." She announced it loud enough to garner Catherine's undivided attention.

"And you failed to mention him in your last letter?" Her red lips slit into a smirk. "Scandalous and very unsisterly, Jessica."

David slid his arm around Jess and stole an embrace. "Father and I must approve, you know."

"Well, there's very little not to approve. He's extremely handsome, smart, witty, a great judge of character."

"And his occupation?" this from Father.

Jess paused, sifting through a proper descriptive. "At present, he's part student, part apprentice."

David and Catherine exchanged a look of pure confusion. Oh, the delights of a secret.

"Walk with me to the car and I shall explain everything on the drive." Jess tossed a grin over her shoulder. "But I can assure you, you'll meet my prince at supper and he'll win your hearts too."

He'd never seen her like this.

August stood by the barn, collecting some additional tools for his work on the chapel, when the Carter automobile pulled up to the house, crowded with people. The Carters had told August of their family's arrival from England, so he'd expected a change in his ability to visit as unexpectedly as usual, but no one had prepared him for Jessica Ross dressed in her finest.

She stepped from the car, laughing, fitted in a deep rose day suit and her hair pinned back underneath an ivory hat crowded with some simple rosebuds. Her laughter drifted across the morning breeze and squeezed his heart with its lilt. The sound brought a smile.

In fact, he'd grown to like more and more about her since she'd shown up to help him with the chapel a few days earlier. She'd join him in the late afternoon, after working with her grandpa at the clinic or taking care of the children. Most of the time, Jude came as a welcome tagalong.

August stayed in the shadow of the barn door, watching for a glimpse of these new arrivals. From the passenger door stepped a distinguished looking man, streaks of grey at his temples glistening within his blond hair. The man matched a photo the Carters had. Dr. Alexander Ross.

August stood a little taller, wondering how the good doctor might respond if he knew August's intentions toward his daughter. He grimaced and moved deeper into the shadow. No, perhaps it wasn't the best time to make himself known on the first day.

A younger version of Dr. Ross came around the car with a dark-haired child in his arms and opened the back door. David Ross, no doubt. David and Jessica shared a remarkable family resemblance. Unlike August and Anna. Thankfully, she took after their mother's softened beauty with her round face and small nose. They shared the same pale blue eyes, and, he hoped, the same compassionate heart, but August had taken after their father with his sharp, angled features and lighter hair.

August's grin angled wider as another lady emerged from the car. Jessica had told him, 'Oh, you'll know Catherine when you see her. And you will see her. No man can really help but notice her because she is one of those rare beauties that cause people to stop and stare.'

She wore a coral suit, her straw hat tilted fashionably and laden with flowers and lace. Jessica had been right. Catherine Ross was a striking beauty, with thick, dark hair and slim, elegant features. Her laughter trickled across the breeze and she held her stomach from the force of the exercise.

"It really isn't that funny, Catherine," he heard Jessica say, attempting to rein in her own grin.

Catherine nodded. "Yes, it is. It's hilarious. You, a mother of two?" Her chuckles broke through again as she reached to touch the cheek of the little girl in her husband's arms. "If that isn't irony, I don't know what is."

"Your faith in me is underwhelming."

Her gloved hand came up in defense, her voice carrying across the lawn with another laugh. "By all means, I have a great appreciation for irony and God's sense of humor. Who else would pair the village flirt with the upstanding and quite remarkable village doctor?"

David Ross took his wife's fingers and raised them to his lips. "Only remarkable because of the company I keep."

August remembered David and Catherine's story from Jessica's letters. The fury with which Jessica had denounced her brother's relationship with a woman expecting a child from another man. Her impassioned plea at her brother's obvious lunacy came back to August and encouraged a grin. Clearly, from the overt affection between the pair, lunacy worked well for them.

His gaze pulled back toward Jessica as she linked her arm through her father's. Did she long for the same endearing relationship as her brother? Did she even wonder about such things or was he caught in a one-sided daydream?

He leaned against the door frame, enjoying this uninterrupted observation. He liked her directness and sincerity. No coy displays of indifference. No game-playing with a man's affections. And completely beautiful from the tip of her head down every curve of her body.

What was he thinking? He was leaving Hot Springs and should distance his heart from the magnetizing draw. If not for his own ache, then for the one she would have if her feelings ever turned toward him, and then... he left.

"You might as well come out of hiding and meet everybody."

August jumped from the shadows and turned to face Dr. Carter, who looked very much like a boy hiding his own secrets. He stepped around August and peered toward the house and the small crowd disappearing inside.

"I see you found a good vantage point to keep an eye on my granddaughter."

August bent his head but couldn't tame his smile. Dr. Carter's gentle teasing came as a welcome comparison to years of abrasive criticism. He looked back at the feisty blonde, taking in the view with renewed appreciation.

"Yes. In fact, I kept both eyes on her."

Dr. Carter patted his shoulder. "Smart man. You'll need both of them for the likes of her." He nodded toward the crowd. "Granny's planned a massive supper. Come on and join us in about an hour or so?"

"I would not interfere with your family."

"Boy, you *are* family." He squeezed his hold on August's shoulder, giving it a little shake. "In all the ways that matter. Besides, you'll be needing to meet Alexander Ross sooner or later if your sights are still set on a certain feisty blond."

August swallowed through his tightening throat, sending the group one last look before they disappeared into the house. "I will think about it, Doctor." August smiled. "And thank you for your invitation."

Dr. Carter's gaze turned intense. "August, you are always welcome. Remember that, boy."

⁓

"She's so beautiful." Catherine pulled Faith up into her arms and examined the little face. Faith's bright eyes fastened on Catherine's, most likely trying to sort out who this new woman was. She looked up at Jessica, her quizzical expression from the afternoon returning, and then she chuckled. "I still can't believe it."

Jess shook her head and rubbed a palm over Faith's soft head. "It's..."

"Life changing."

Jess sighed and moved to sit on the bed. "Completely."

"Well, it seems as though you're succeeding at it." Catherine cooed down into Faith's face. "The children are still alive and you appear as mentally fit as you ever were."

Jess rolled her eyes with her growing smile. "Which isn't saying a great deal."

"I find a healthy mind always dances on the edge of uncertainty." One dark eyebrow jutted north with a glimmer in her sapphire gaze. "It seems to be one of the requirements of motherhood. Sleepless nights. Aching body. Doting on someone who will leave more of a mess behind than sweet-smelling fragrances."

Jessica laughed, each description poignantly true. She looked down at Faith's face and her eyes, round and wondering. "And yet... somehow, they've moved right into my heart as if they'd always belonged. Like... like my spirit had a hollowed out space waiting for them to fill it." She shook her head. "Does that sound ridiculous?"

"Not at all. I felt that way with Addie, but even more so, I felt it with David."

"David?"

Catherine nodded, slipping Faith into the crook of her arm. "I'd sought acceptance and affection in the wrong people and things. It wasn't until I understood God's love and then saw how his love worked through David's gentle regard for me that I recognized what my heart sought all along."

"I came to terms months ago, when I was wounded, that marriage wasn't in my future." She tilted her chin high, accepting her life as it was. "I don't need a man—a romance—to fulfill my life."

"Of course not. God is enough." Catherine ran a finger down Faith's round cheek, inciting the smile she'd only begun to share with world.

Jess heart fluttered each time, a beautiful connection of the soul within shining out to the world.

"I certainly could have raised Addie on my own, and thought that was to be my lot when I became pregnant by that idiot Drew Cavanaugh." Catherine looked over at Jessica, her gaze piercing. "I could have raised her and found happiness in doing so. And no, you do not *need* a man to find happiness, but with the right man, you'll *want* him. God designed him to touch your life and fill that hollowed-out anticipation like no one else can do, but you have to be willing to risk your heart, just as you're doing with these children."

"I don't know if I'm willing." Almost losing her brother? Losing her mother? The pain surged through her with an unending ache and lingering loneliness.

Catherine stared at her, those curious eyes taking in the silence and Jessica's reluctance without condemnation—or worse, pity. "The best things in life come with a choice, and a terrible risk. I almost lost David too, and I realized in those weeks of trying to help him remember me, that even if he never remembered who I was, I would never wish away having been loved by him." She slid down on the bed beside of Jessica. "The right love is worth the risk."

Laughter reached beyond the walls of the Carter house and teased August a step closer. Dr. Carter's invitation nudged reconsideration of his plans to join Anna and Sylvie for supper instead of facing a room of strangers with possibly the same distaste for Germans as Jessica.

No, he needn't disturb their reunion.

He returned the tools to the barn and made his way past the porch, meeting the edge of before a voice stopped him.

"I didn't suspect you as a coward, August."

Mrs. Carter didn't look up as she scraped a few leftovers into a bowl at the bottom of the steps with Lightning and Scraps gladly waiting for their turn to enjoy the feast.

He sighed and turned on his heels. "I didn't wish to intrude."

"Oh, you won't be intruding." She gestured toward the door with her head. "You've been the topic of conversation for a good half hour."

August took a step back, feeling the sudden urge to become the coward she accused him to be.

"Don't you worry none. Dr. Carter's talked down the menfolk from causing any permanent harm to you." Her gray eyes twinkled. "Now, they're mostly curious, is all."

August met her at the bottom of the porch steps. "And you wouldn't have encouraged this particularly topic of conversation, would you now, Mrs. Carter?"

She gave him a pointed look and waved her spoon at him. "August Reinhold. I'm plumb shocked you'd suggest such a thing." She nudged him with the spoon toward the door. "Now, come on. I found enough berries to make a good cobbler and you don't want to miss it."

He looked down at his work clothes. "I'm not fit for your table."

"Hogwash." The weapon-spoon pushed against his shoulder again. For such a small woman, she was certainly persistent. "Go on in and wash up, then join us."

He opened his mouth to add another protest, but her look sealed his lips. He'd surrounded himself with bossy, headstrong women. His grin perched. And he liked it.

"I will not have you dressin' up as a coward. Now git to washing off in the sink or I'll send Grandpa out after you."

August did as he was told, making himself as presentable as sawdust and hard work allowed. He ran a damp hand through his hair and stood back in front of the door.

God, I know this seems like a small prayer in your grand universe, but would you bring favor and direction? Favor from Jessica's family and direction for my heart.

Jessica's will contorted like a pretzel as she fought her growing interest. August slid into the family dinner conversation as if he'd always been there, even joining in to tease Catherine about going without a children's nurse for the two-week-long visit.

"If I cannot take care of my own child for a few days without the assistance of a nursemaid, then I should reconsider my fortitude." She shook her head and fed Addie another bite of potatoes. "Servants and nursemaids are not as commonplace among the Blue Ridge Mountains, and I wouldn't care to cause a scene."

"You cause a scene wherever you go, my dear." David assisted with keeping Addie entertained during the meal, his tenderness for his little family evident in the permanent glow of his smile.

The sight and its sweetness pierced a chink in Jessica's self-induced emotional cage with yet another hit of possibility. Even as she searched for more reasons to dislike August, more excuses to keep him at arm's length, the curiosity swelled into an intolerable need. The fact that he looked even more handsome than usual added salt to the wound.

"Well, I've not always been the product of high society. Jessica knew our family when we lived in our Grandmama's home and employed only two servants."

Jessica caught her laugh in her hand. And she'd grown up in a home with no servants or indoor plumbing. She'd never gotten used to the servants in David's new home at Beacon House, but the indoor plumbing made life much easier and more sanitary.

Thankfully, her grandparents had modified since her last visit, though the water only ran cold.

She examined August's profile as he spoke with her brother. In fact, her attention kept pulling back toward him the entire meal, watching for his response, waiting for his laughter... almost wishing for him to look her way. What a miserable, soft-hearted reaction!

What could the Almighty be thinking? One day, she trusts Him with her future again, and the next, He awakens her heart to this infuriating interest?

August's gaze met hers across the table and the playful glint spiked her internal temperature into a fever. Ridiculous. Utterly ridiculous. And yet she couldn't look away. That smile, those eyes, pried her fingers loose from her stranglehold on her heart. What would letting go feel like? Falling into such a love, such a terrifying unknown?

Her breath held.

Over the past week, as she'd spent more time with him, he'd proven to be as authentic as her grandparents believed. His lively wit tempered by subtlety, his fond glances—they served to unravel her pent-up suspicions with a thread of hope.

So many memories imprisoned her against releasing her past, her pain. So many wounds pounded like enemy fire in her brain, urging her to wall up her heart from this whirlpool tug of attraction.

Love was worth the risk.

Was it really? The risk of being betrayed again? The risk of feeling life-altering wounds again? She balanced the choice. No one would force her to step over that ledge into an abyss of uncertainty. And she hated uncertainty. The war had only served to harden her suspicions, taught her to shy away from the unknown, from loss. Because beyond all the warm feelings and tender glances, the truth still remained.

August was leaving.

Why should she leap into a relationship with him when he would only disappear from her life as so many others had done? How could love be worth a risk like that?

"You've never been in military service?" This from her brother, David, who remained amiable, which was no surprise. David always remained amiable.

"No. My father would have preferred me choose the military instead of the profession I chose."

"And what was that?" Catherine asked, drawing Addie into her lap. "You weren't born to be a sailor, Mr. Reinhold?"

He smiled. "Sailor was more a forced occupation than a calling." He opened his palms. "I find great pleasure in creating things with my hands. Restoring things that need care."

"Like the chapel." Grandfather added. "I can't wait for you to see it, Alexander."

Father nodded. "I've heard great things of your work." Her father looked her way. "And you've been helping him, Jessica. What do you think of Mr. Reinhold's craftsmanship?"

Jess avoided looking at August as she answered. "It's beautiful, truly. He's done a remarkable job." His stare bore into her to such an extent she finally glanced up, which was a bad idea because she hesitated too long in those gentle, periwinkle hues. She quickly flicked her gaze to her father. "You'll be pleased with his work."

"Will I?" Her father passed a glance between the two of them, his grin twitching. "Could you take me out to see it after supper, August?"

"I'm sorry, sir, but I must return to the camp before nightfall. Curfew is strictly enforced, and I have no wish for them to revoke my daily freedoms. Perhaps tomorrow?"

"Tomorrow, then." Father sat back in his chair and examined August. "What are your plans then, August? When the war is over and our countries are no longer enemies?"

August glanced her way long enough to place warmth in her cheeks, and then moved his attention back to her father. "I have no plans to return to Germany."

"So you'll stay in Hot Springs?" Catherine asked, making no attempt to hide her amusement.

"That would be my choice, but it all depends."

"Depends? On what?"

August lifted his gaze to Jessica. "If Hot Springs wants me to stay."

Chapter Eighteen

August tipped his hat to Cliff as he passed the gatehouse on the way out of the camp. The mid-morning sunlight burned a path along the road, guiding him back to the home he'd left the night before.

His smile stilled before spreading fully. A part of him wished to savor the sweet camaraderie of last night's dinner with the Rosses and the Carters, but another part accepted the untimely reality of his departure from Hot Springs, a truth carving away at his good intentions and dreams.

The news had been announced this morning to the whole camp: Next week, the deportation of the sailors to Oglethorpe would begin, and he wielded no power to stop it.

He wasn't so much concerned about finishing the chapel. It would only be a few more days and that piece of his heart and hard work would remain a fixture in these mountains. A reminder to the Carters of him, he hoped.

But what about Jessica? He'd been foolish and selfish to attempt to win her affections when the inevitable fog of departure lingered over each day. He removed his hat and ran a hand through his hair, pausing at the crossroads of town.

He knew the answer. It was time to begin the process of distancing himself and his emotions from Jessica and the Carters in preparation for the final split. An ache, deep and raw, started with the announcement and only intensified as he stared down the street, a path as familiar to him now as the honeysuckle air.

With a hesitant sigh, he accepted his decision. Create distance to the ones he loved to ease the pain of leaving. And love them, he did. As certain as the hues of blue in the surrounding mountains and the shades of reds and pinks in the wild roses along his path. He'd found a home, and now... he was ripped away from it again.

"I see they've let the traitor out of his cage again."

Jasper Little sauntered across the street toward the crossroads, his hand tucked in his pocket, his broad smile plastered with insincerity. August cloaked his expression. There was little benefit in nursing a confrontation in the middle of the street, despite the certain satisfaction for August in besting the man.

"I see no point in conversation that starts with accusation, Mr. Little. Good day." August turned toward the Carters in an attempt to create space between him and Mr. Little.

"I've heard about your little letter exploits. So this façade you present to the people of this town will be uncovered. Your people have no place here."

August pivoted on his heels and faced the vile man. "Despite how badly you wish to instigate a confrontation, you will not find one here. With me. Your personality might hold a melodramatic bent, but I care more for the eyes watching how gentleman behave than I do in creating a theatrical."

"I think you're concerned they'll hear the truth. That you're an imposter."

His voice took on a different quality, fluctuating between two styles. English and American. Warning replaced the flint of jealousy. Jasper Little was not at all who he seemed.

August examined the man with fresh eyes, taking in the subtleties. He stood with the posture of a soldier, so that part of his story was most likely true, but an Englishman?

"I'm not certain I am the one who is an imposter, Mr. Little."

The man's gaze flickered to the camp and then back to August with renewed fire. "Are you nervous at my accusations? Turning the blame on me, an innocent bystander to your treachery." He closed the gap between them, a snarl his companion. "What do you have planned next for the people of this town?"

His volume grew, drawing attention from passersby, which was no doubt his intention.

August stared at the man, declining to dignify his accusation with a response but refusing to back down. Mr. Little sent another glance over his shoulder, ensuring his audience stayed within earshot, but August was done.

"Mr. Little, our conversation is over. Good day."

The man spouted off something else as August strolled down the road, making certain his usual stride kept in step with his convictions. He had nothing to hide, and if he knew most of the people of Hot Springs well enough, they'd see Mr. Little's accusations for what they were. Pure drivel.

But something worse lured beneath the exchange. Why was Mr. Little pretending to possess an English accent, and why was he really in Hot Springs?

August had slipped into the barn, taken his usual tools, and disappeared into the forest without one 'hello' to Jess' family... or her. She'd watched from the kitchen window, waiting for his usual greeting to make them aware he was working. Of course, he didn't have to tell them, but he always did.

Except this time.

Her father had followed down the chapel trail about half an hour later, but Jess couldn't shake the fact that something was wrong. She frowned at the forest, as if it hid a secret to her quandary. This concern, this need to make certain of August's well-being, annoyed her because, despite her best efforts, it proved she cared about him.

She sat down on the porch steps, watching David play with Addie while Jude and Sylvie attempted to help. A faint breeze warded off the promised heat of the day and clouds gathered overhead, hinting at an afternoon rain. She hoped the summer thunder stayed away, but the rain would cool off the day.

"Jude and Sylvie seem to have Addie well in hand." David approached, joining her on the step, shoulder-to-shoulder. "He's a good lad, Jess."

"That he is. His mother couldn't give him much, but she gave him the most important thing. Love."

"And you've taken up her mantle beautifully. You've always loved ferociously." David nudged her shoulder with his own. "Stubborn to a fault."

"Must be why you fell in love with Catherine." She grinned, nudging him back. "You'd gotten used to stubborn, headstrong women."

"I don't know that any other woman could have managed the difficulties we've faced over the past few years and come out stronger for it. She's remarkable." He looked over at Jess, tenderness in his smile. "As are you. That is why these children are in good hands."

His strong voice sounded more certain than her inward one, but she'd trust that this God she knew as a child kept his promises. He had to. She needed him to keep his promises since nothing else in this crazy world held fast and sure.

She watched Jude and Sylvie bring dandelions to Addie, entertaining her as they blew the flowers into hundreds of white, flying wisps. Her laughter trilled toward the house and nestled around her heart in a sweet warmth.

"How are you doing? Really?" He turned to face her, his eyes examining her face as he measured her well-being. Ever the doctor, but even more the brother. "Coming back from the war, to this? It can't be easy."

She stared off into the horizon and breathed in a pine and honeysuckles. "The nightmares are fewer. And I'm finding new thoughts and memories to replace the haunting ones. It's just been difficult and slow."

His hand covered hers and he gave it a gentle squeeze. "Of course. Time is undervalued in its ability to heal." He released her hand and leaned forward, his elbows on his knees. "I suppose there is mercy in my head injury because I don't remember many things about serving at the Front."

She pinched back a cringe at the memory of her brother, limp and lifeless in her arms, and offset the ghost with a grin. "Granny would call that a blessing dressed in suffering."

"And she'd be right." His smile responded.

"Have you recovered most of your memories?"

He nodded and returned his gaze to the children. "I have pictures in my head of my wedding to Catherine and flickers of our time together before the war, as well as a few scenes of being at the Front, but otherwise, they're like shadows."

"And you're fine with those lost memories?"

He shrugged. "I must be fine with them." His grin turned roguish. "Besides, Catherine has more than made up for any memory loss."

Jessica hit his shoulder with her hand, warmth rising all the way to her hairline. "Clearly, your wife's influence is rubbing off on your boldness."

"And I'll share another bold declaration, though it's a secret. Catherine means to announce it tonight at supper." He leaned close, lowering his voice. "We have another little Ross arriving in the New Year."

Jessica laughed and threw her arms around her brother. "Oh, how wonderful! What a wonderful surprise."

"Yes, though Catherine touts her skills as a mother—and she is a wonderful mother—she'll be pleased to return to Beacon House and enjoy the help of our small group of servants. They dote on Addie and I'm certain will be a great help with our newest addition."

Catherine and David's solid relationship still amazed Jessica. For David, the quiet, gentle, bookish sort, and Catherine, the witty, dramatic, passionate sort, stood out as opposites, and yet complimentary in a beautiful... She sighed, accepting the link. Divinely appointed way.

Her gaze drifted back to the forest. How could she relinquish this fear to a possible romance? It ate at her, memories crashing into the scars and reopening them in the silence of the night. Lt Snyder's hands, rough and strong against her skin. His hot and hard mouth her only comparison to a kiss. She flinched, tamping down the grief. Her mind knew it was different between two people who loved each other, but her heart stumbled against experience. Raw, stolen experience.

"Mr. Reinhold seems a good chap, Jessica. I don't know why you leave the man in such uncertainty about your regard."

She shot her brother a frown since he'd jumped into her thoughts unwelcome. "My regard?"

"You may not wish to care for him, but it's clear to me that you do." His sly grin slid into his profile. "You're a fighter, I know, but you don't have to fight so hard. Sometimes, it's okay to let your emotions win."

If she released all of the emotions she pinned down into her gnarled heart, she'd likely explode and take a few people with her. "David, you ought to count yourself blessed to not remember the Front. I almost watched you die. In my arms. After we'd been tortured and forced to serve Lt. Snyder for months, barely being fed." She pressed her fist into her chest. "I have so many emotions right now that they're tearing me apart inside, like they're already winning."

He took her fist into his hand and rubbed his fingers over her knuckles. "I'm sorry for the hurt you remember which I cannot. I know the stories you told. I've seen the grief you bear. And in some way, I understand that fear, because when I awoke from the haze of my head injury to a world I didn't understand, filled with irrational fears and explosive anger, I wanted to crawl inside myself and hide." He squeezed her hand. "But... I needed help to find my life again. To gain strength and faith I'd lost in the suffering. There is no weakness in letting others help you heal. I can't imagine my life if Catherine hadn't been there to love me through my injuries. Of course, I had you and Father, but there was the special connection she made with my wounds that somehow helped me be brave and heal faster than I could have in the hands of anyone else."

Jessica's grin twitched alive on one side. "Not even your amnesia was going to stop Catherine. I'm sure the wounds bowed to the power of her wrath and passions in complete terror."

David's full smile responded and the glow and the gentle light of his love for his bride both pained and soothed Jessica heart, and burst wide the ache in her soul from something so sweet.

Her brother's face sobered, his gaze growing intense. "Love heals, Jessica. Catherine couldn't bring back the memories I'd lost. I've recovered lots of them but not all of them. And there are wounds inside of you that no one but God can fully heal. Scars remain. But those scars are reminders that we've survived, and that we fought to survive. Those wounds only overcome us if we forget that He's held us through all these trials and brought us out to the other side. Safe. And stronger than we were before."

And she had. She'd pushed beyond her fear on hundreds of situations to use her God-given smarts and will to survive. He'd strategically placed people in her path to help her, guide her, and sometimes, remind her of whose she was and His ever-present hand even in the storm. Now, her heart pushed her yet again, trembling and uncertain on the precipice of a place she'd never been. A hope she'd pushed beneath her pain, justified by her disabilities, and closed off with her fears. A leap? A fall? One step across a threshold where she willingly offered her dreams, failures, and hopes to another person?

David seemed to read her thoughts. "Sometimes, God sends a special someone along to love us in a way that mends our scars and our hearts as none other can."

She tugged her hand free from his hold and swiped a rebel tear from her cheek, sending her brother an annoyed smile. "Do I hear you joining the ranks of everyone else who thinks this August Reinhold is the one who will help me heal? For goodness sakes, you've been here a grand total of three days and everyone's already sorted out my future?"

He chuckled. "It does seem a rather large consensus, doesn't it? But I will not choose your future. You're smart enough to figure it out on your own, and you're brave enough to risk whatever you need to make it yours."

"I'm also stubborn enough to let it pass." She pinned him with a look. "Which might be the smarter choice."

He lifted a challenging brow. "Or the more cowardly one."

Cowardly? Oh no! She may be a great many flawed things, but cowardly wasn't one of them. She marched through the forest, leaving Jude with a laughing David and Faith with a curious granny. August Reinhold wasn't a man to inspire fear, and she'd prove to everyone she was quite capable of managing herself with him... maybe even take a baby-step toward this tremulous attraction.

Maybe.

But she wasn't afraid.

Her steps faltered as the chapel came into view. August's modification involved a small steeple with a new cross-shaped hole near the top that he hadn't filled yet, but she could see from the sides as she approached that he'd placed the windows, three on each side of the small wooden building.

The thrum of male voices rumbled from inside, an odd mixture of cultures echoing off the bare walls in chorus. Her father's deep and pristine English accent and August's smooth baritone flavored with German tones, all set in a little Appalachian chapel.

Who says God doesn't like variety?

The internal declaration pegged her brother's previous conversation with added punctuation. She paused in the doorway, watching the two men, their backs turned toward the dark, stained altar. August had added intricate carvings along the curved back wall surrounding the altar, scenes engraved into five wooden sheets and then nailed into the wall to create the chronological story of the five days leading up to the resurrection of Christ. He must have kept them at the camp and brought them to the chapel when he'd finished as a grand unveiling for the simple country church.

"Fine job." Her father nodded. "And you're adding the beams this week?"

August looked up to the ceiling. "They were in the photos I saw. I've placed two in already and hope to add two more, today along with a surprise gift for your daughter I hope she will like."

"If you haven't figured it out, I'm not a huge fan of surprises," Jessica said, crossing her arms but allowing a smile to contradict her stance.

August turned, his gaze taking her in from head to toe. His smile slid from one side to the other and captured her completely. Her skin lit with a responsive flame.

Okay, maybe she was a little afraid.

"But you are a woman who appreciates advancement. Certainly, you can progress to take some pleasure in them?"

His verbal dip into her history of women's rights piqued her smile despite her best efforts.

Her father patted August on the back with a laugh. "Well said, August. It's good for Jessica to see men who appreciate the former plight of women's rights." Father turned to her. "Since she's won her right to vote, now perhaps she'll enjoy her right to live well?"

"I've always lived on purpose, Father."

He walked toward her, his emerald gaze showering her with a paternal radiance. "Perhaps it's time to live with joy too." He turned and tipped his hat to August. "I have to send a telegram in town, so I will be off, but I appreciate the tour of the chapel. Stellar work." He winked at Jessica. "And I can't wait to learn of this surprise."

And with his exit, leaving her alone with August, her father gave his stamp of approval. He trusted August... with her?

She looked across the chapel to him, pale light straining through the glass panes dusty from woodwork. August stared back, his hair windswept and his strong, lean body posing a striking figure at the center of the chapel.

She squeezed a breath into her lungs and raised a brow to show she was still in control. "So, about this surprise?"

He took a few steps forward, his attention never leaving her face, and then, as if his thoughts turned into less pleasant realms, he frowned and stopped. "I must speak to you."

"Then speak."

"The camp is moving next week."

Her forward momentum died with a sudden sickness in her stomach. "Please tell me that's not your idea of a surprise for me."

A smile softened the tension on his face. "I may have a thick head"—he tapped his forehead—"but it is not *that* thick."

The levity took some of the sting from his announcement. "I'm sorry, August."

He tilted his head, captivating her with his searching gaze. "Are you?"

Her gaze faltered under his and she took another look around the chapel. "Of course. You don't expect me to know how to finish this chapel, do you?"

"I suspect if you put your mind to it, you could accomplish almost anything."

Her attention shot back to him and she suddenly recognized one thing among many she'd failed to see during their acquaintance. He saw her as the woman she desperately wanted to be. The woman she thought she'd once been before war and betrayal weakened her from the inside out.

"I'd rather not resort to such extreme measures if I don't have to." She steadied her palms on her hips. "So, what if we get to work?"

He took another step closer, his beautiful smile returning to entrance her all over again. Perhaps having courage also meant utter lunacy because she suddenly had difficulty keeping her mind clear of periwinkle eyes, strong shoulders, and a dashing smile. What had become of her sensibilities?

"Your answer deserves the surprise. Are you ready?" He didn't wait for her to answer but almost ran to a small door in the chapel she hadn't noticed. It stood at the steeple's base, and from Jessica' quick view, it led to a small stairway with a skeleton of a spiral staircase twisting the one story upward to the steeple—and the mysterious, framed cross-hole.

With careful movements, he drew something from the shadows of the closet and carried it to her. At first, she couldn't make it out, but as he neared and the fading light reflected off of his cumbersome package, Jess recognized it. A patchwork cross? Dark wood framed a cross shape filled with tens of small, colorful shards of stained-glass pieced together like a puzzle in the form of a cross. August bent beneath its weight, the window a little over half his height. The mingling shades all merged into one setting and cast rainbows against the chapel floor in a myriad of faded and beautiful hues.

"Where did you—" She gasped. The treasure hunts? Digging through the muck and remains the flood left behind to retrieve lost pieces of the church's former stained glass windows? She grappled for her voice, for words. Some response to match the beauty of this gift. "It's... it's beautiful."

"Nothing is too broken that it cannot be restored with the proper care."

He spoke to her at the soul level, guiding her from the cocooned safety of her cage.

She met his gaze, trying to absorb this growing awareness, this tenderness. He was everything he appeared to be and so much more. Her breath shallowed, and her heart took a tremulous response forward. "Thank you."

He bowed his head in acceptance, looking up through those luxurious lashes and spiking her pulse into arrhythmia. "My pleasure, Miss Jesse." He gestured with his head toward the steeple. "Are you ready to set it?"

Her shoulders relaxed from the tension, the awkwardness of embracing emotions she'd tied off like a tourniquet, and embraced the distraction of work. "Yes. Please."

The work moved forward in companionable silence and with a great deal of distraction in the form of her work partner. Suddenly, her senses came to life with everything about him... his breathing, the way he turned his body to keep sawdust from falling toward her, the spun gold links within his blond hair, the cleft in his chin. And the one feature which was quickly growing to be her favorite—his ready smile. She'd always thought people who smiled too much or too quickly held secrets, were false or oblivious, but August carried a genuine joy ready to emerge to the surface in a beautiful, breath-altering smile.

Her newfound fascination with him was her only excuse for ignoring the signs—the scent of wet trees in the air, the coolness of the advancing breeze, the darkening sky. They'd barely placed the stained glass cross securely in its new home when the first burst of thunder nearly toppled her from the stairway.

August steadied her, but she jerked free, stumbling down the remaining stairs until she reached low ground. Her pulse stampeded in her ears, competing with the thunder. The chapel walls closed in as the thunder intensified, calling her back to exploding shells, dismembered bodies, and fiery, hate-filled eyes.

She paced the perimeter inside the chapel, prowling like a cat for a hiding place.

"I will get you home."

"There's no time," she shot back. "No time. The storm is already here. I have nowhere to go. Nowhere. I'm caught. Trapped. I can't hide. I can't." She placed her hands over her ears as another blast drew closer, shattering through her until she stumbled.

"No." August's arms enveloped her in warmth and pine-scent. He swept her off her feet, cradling her against his strong chest, and marched across the chapel to the tiny stairwell closet. "You cannot hide. But you are not alone. I will be with you through this storm, Mause. I will not leave you alone."

Chapter Nineteen

Jessica's face paled and she paced like a caged animal from one corner of the chapel to the next, her gaze darting from wall to wall. Another clash of thunder echoed through the mountains, closer now, and she whimpered, her large, emerald eyes taking on an almost wild look.

"I... I need a place to hide." She rounded the inside of the chapel again, murmuring to herself. "Where is somewhere to hide?"

August moved toward her, trying to gain her attention. Break the panic. "I will get you home."

She glanced at him, her body tensed, awaiting another blast. "No time. The storm is already here. I have nowhere to go. Nowhere. I'm trapped and it's coming for me."

He'd heard from some of the older, former soldiers in the about their violent reactions to noises or seemingly insignificant situations as they recovered from war. To watch this strong, beautiful woman convulse into tremors before him pushed him into immediate protective action. He charged forward, sweeping her into his arms as she crumbled beneath the next thunderous crash. In four strides, he opened the narrow door leading to the steeple stairwell. Darkness shrouded them except for the faint myriad of colors reflecting off the walls from the stained glass window above.

She gripped him close, shuddering into his chest like a terrified child. He enveloped her and the feelings to protect her, holding her against him and attempting to shield her from the storm. She shivered uncontrollably, burrowing deeper into his arms with every blast of thunder.

August palmed the back of her head and tipped it to the side, pressing her cheek against him so that her good ear rested against his chest. "Focus on my heartbeat, Jess. Not the thunder."

Her tremulous breathing and her sobs stopped at his words. Her entire body tensed.

"Hear how slow and steady my heartbeat is. I will protect you. You are not alone," he whispered against her honeysuckle-scented hair. "Breathe in and out, slow and relaxed, like my heartbeat. My voice."

Another thunder crash shook her with a shudder, and she gripped his shirt more tightly.

"Hold on as tightly as you need. I will not leave you." He rested his cheek against her hair and covered her other ear with his palm, dampening the sounds outside. "You are safe, Mause."

Her shoulders shook but her struggling slowed and her breath released in a long, sniffling sigh.

They sat in the dim stairwell as the storm passed and the shadows shifted from dark to light. Her breathing slowed and became even. Her grasp loosened, and yet he cradled her. His protective hold slipped into a gentler embrace, his palm sliding up her back until his fingers brushed against the soft blush of her hair.

His throat constricted at the intimacy in the touch and he returned his palm to her back, training his thoughts into submission. Would she wish for such caresses from him? Something had changed between them when she'd arrived that afternoon. The previous suspicion had faded, her attention had lingered on him, softened... enough to encourage him with hope, but she'd never flirted or flattered him. He grinned into her hair. Of course, she wasn't exactly the sort to do either, anyway. And that was one reason he liked her the best. No pretense.

She'd grown still in his arms, almost as if she'd fallen to sleep. He peeked down at her face in the dimness. Her eyes still pinched closed, long lashes sweeping down over her pale cheeks. With a careful shift in his movements, he pushed her damp hair back from her face and allowed his fingers a second's linger against her cheek. Her eyes flickered open and held him captive, dark jade in the shadows of the little room. She studied him, fear dwindling into uncertainty and curiosity... and something else. New. Sweet.

The chill in the air faded into a thick heat, moving down his throat and expanding through his chest. She sat up slowly, her gaze never leaving his face, the wisped air of her shallow breaths piercing the darkened space. His other palm slid up her shoulders, over the thin cloth of her pale blue blouse, until both hands cradled her jaws. Those jade eyes still glistened with the tears she'd shed during the storm, shining now like jewels. Her lips, parted slightly, held him captive, spiking a renewed curiosity of how they'd taste. Bitter like her words had been to him in the beginning? No. Not now.

Now, he wondered just how sweet one taste could be.

He'd shielded her, encapsulated her in his arms for the entire storm, as if it was the most natural thing in the world. There was no judgment at her child-like terror, no disgust as she clung to him with an embarrassingly desperate hold that now brought a flood of warmth into her face.

His palms rested on her shoulders as she pulled back from him, his face half in shadow and half haloed in the rainbow-light cascading down from the stained-glass cross. His pale gaze took in her face, searching for her well-being, and her heart trembled anew in a very different way than at a passing storm. It pulsed with a trepidation, a yearning new to her.

His palms moved to cup her cheeks, the calloused touch from his hard work surprisingly gentle. Wordless power, an invisible tether, drew her toward him, spiraling her insides with a swirl of energy and warmth. Her gaze dropped to his lips against her will or understanding. Would he kiss her?

Air blocked in her throat as his breath exhaled against her mouth, drawing closer. She closed her eyes, trying to brace herself for whatever might come, but the only other kiss she'd ever known was stolen from her by a ruthless German. His face surged into her thoughts, replacing the swarming warmth with a frigid stillness. Ice. Fear. Her stomach curled as the stark memory of his lips and teeth raking over hers stripped her of all curiosity.

She jerked back. "I... I can't."

His hands dropped back to her shoulders and he blinked. "Why do you fight so hard? I know you feel this... this same draw."

She slipped from his hold and gripped the stair railing to pull herself to her feet. "I can't. I can't be with..."

"Someone who is German?" His voice hardened and he ran a hand through his hair, his gaze moving to hers, pleading and fiery, but most of all intensely fascinating.

He stood and stepped from the small stairwell out into the chapel.

"You don't realize. It's not as you think." She followed him, searching for a way to answer. How to admit this shame undergirding her insecurities and second-guesses?

"You've made your intentions quite clear from the beginning, Miss Ross. I was only too dim-witted to believe it." He marched to the far side of the chapel and began gathering up his tools. The pain lacing his voice sliced through her.

"August—"

"I have spent my life not meeting other people's expectations." He slammed the hammer into the tool bag. "I was not rich enough for my fiancée, I was not brave enough for my brother." He shoved a box of nails into the bag, accentuating the word 'not'. "I wasn't strong enough for my father."

He turned on her, those usually gentle eyes now aflame with indignation and hurt... hurt she'd caused. "I know the truth now, but then... then the knives of their rejection carved out my heart." His palm rammed into his chest with a thud. "Now, my fiancée is unhappily married but very wealthy, my brother, in all of his bravery, has left his family because he cared more for self-glory than his own blood, and my father?" A chaff of air burst from him in a joyless laugh. "My father is dogmatic and powerful, but incredibly lonely." He raised those wounded eyes to her, searching her face, his jaw tense. "Now, I will not meet your expectations because of the nation of my birth? It is good, then, that God does not hold the same lofty arrogance as you, for I would be a hopeless cause, as I once was but for His grace. When did you lose your understanding of grace?"

"In the treacherous arms of a German lieutenant who wanted much more from me than the medical assistance he captured me to provide." The confession slipped out, battling against his accusations with as sharp an edge. "Who overpowered me and found pleasure in doing so, leaving me seared from his kiss and touch." She shivered as the memory took hold again, words adding stings to the secret. "It's not you. I know that. But... but I have no other comparison. I... I... can't know—"

"Oh, Mause." His endearment erupted on a gut-wrenching sigh. "My poor Mause." He dropped the tool bag and crossed the chapel floor toward her, the fire in his gaze replaced by a probing tenderness. "Don't you know? I am not that man. I am the man who would walk miles only to play badminton with you so I could hear you laugh." He grew closer. "I am the man who pieced together a shattered window to show you that you are not too broken to be beautiful." He bridged the gap, his gaze never letting her go. "I am the man would capture the thunder in his hands, if he had the power, so you would not be afraid." He stood before her, so close and certain.

She soaked in his confidence, his... care, embracing it in the only fumbling way she knew how. Completely. "I know. I know you're not him."

He held her gaze and brought his hand up to brush away a tear from her cheek. Her eyes fluttered closed at the touch, the strength in his promises. He shifted close enough that she noticed a darker rim of navy around the paler hues of periwinkle in his eyes. His caress slipped across her cheek to rest on her chin and she swayed toward him, entranced by his gentle entreaty.

His kiss? Would it be powerful enough to replace the nightmares of Lieutenant Snyder's? Memorable enough to overcome the pain of his touch?

August's thumb slipped across her bottom lip, his gaze following the gentle line of his movements. Her skin responded like the flickering of electric lights buzzing to life with energy, with anticipation for something her body seemed to recognize as wholly different from the wretched lieutenant.

His attention pulled to her eyes. "I have made a rule, though it pains me greatly." The tip of his lips tilted. "I will wait for you to kiss me first."

She blinked. "What?"

"Yes. You are a woman who appreciates initiation."

Her cheeks blazed. "August Reinhold, it is not appropriate for a woman to... instigate such an action."

He chuckled. "Where is my lovely suffragette now? Do you not believe in equality?"

"Of course I do."

"Then you have equal the right to kiss me as I have to kiss you. What better way to ensure you are prepared for such a powerful experience than to initiate it yourself, yes? Unless you do not think you have the strength?"

He was baiting her again, and despite the trepidation still quivering her stomach, her smile responded and she moved back into his space, daring him with her unswerving stare. "I've always been efficient at finding strength when I need it, Mr. Reinhold."

His eyes sparkled and then smoldered, reigniting the heat in the room. "I have no doubt, Miss Ross."

She'd never been so fascinated with a pair of lips in her life. And she'd seen plenty. She was a nurse, of course, even sometimes assisting with reconstructive surgery, but this... this was an interest far beyond professional.

Her curiosity began a steady climb to overcome her fear, and his lips were a significant motivator in the fight. She placed a palm against his chest and bridged the gap between them, slowly, battling the irrational fear of a nightmare repeating itself.

He didn't move, only encouraged her with a daring smile she found increasingly more tempting with each breath. Challenging her. Pushing her to step outside her panic and soiled expectations.

"Mama Jesse?"

She spun around almost falling from the unexpected shift in her balance for her weak leg. August steadied her from behind, his closeness sending tingles of awareness up her spine. She forced a smile at Jude who waited in the doorway of the chapel, adorable in a set of new overalls she'd bought him last week.

"Jude?" She cleared her throat, August's closeness fogging up every thought in her head.

What on earth was wrong with her? "Is... Is everything all right?"

He propped his palms on his hips and studied her, his intelligent gaze shifting from Jess to August. "Grandpa sent me to check on you 'cause of the storm."

Jess created distance from August and moved to the doorway, hoping the heady influence of the handsome German might lessen with distance. "I'm fine, thank you. I..." She glanced behind her to where August had returned to the tool bag. "August stayed with me so... so I wouldn't be afraid."

Jude gave a nod of approval. "Well, I reckon that's what people do when they love ya. They stick with ya through the hard times, like you done for me."

August's eyebrow twitched up with the hint of his smile. Jess' stomach produced a responsive twinge to the sheer attractiveness of the man.

She could drown in such affection. Paired with his gentleness and strength, she wondered how on earth her stubbornness kept her vision so skewed.

Pride. She frowned. And a healthy dose of *bitterness*.

Jess drew her attention from those pale, mesmerizing eyes and knelt down to Jude's level. "That's exactly right. And like you've done with me." She squeezed one of his shoulders and then stood, tousling his hair as she did so.

He stood a little taller. "Then I reckon we all got enough lovin' to go around. Ain't that right, August?"

August's attention moved from Jude back to Jessica, and her knees wobbled from the intensity. "Most certainly, Jude. Plenty to go around."

Jess pinched her eyes closed to still the lightning bursts of heat flashing through her and then drew in a deep breath, focusing her full attention on the adorable face before her. "Is everyone back at the farmhouse all right?"

"I reckon so. They was just worried somethin' awful for you out here in the storm. And then that dark-haired man with the mean smile come for a visit. Showed up in the middle of the storm like a loon."

Man with the mean smile? Jess looked back to August for clarification and the grin hardened on his face. *Jasper Little?*

"Mr. Little showed up during the storm?"

"Yep, asked if he could help Grandpa with his doctorin' visit at the camp today. Crazy man. Was soaked clean through. More like a rat than a man."

"Jude, that's not kind to say about Mr. Little." She rested her hand back on Jude's shoulder and tossed August another glance. "I'll talk to you later?"

He threw the tool bag over his shoulder and walked out with her, drawing the church door to a close. "Take care, Mause."

"Mause?"

His frown softened around the edges of his eyes. "It is an endearment."

"I'm not a big fan of mice." She focused ahead on the trail and Jude leading the way. Her smile fought for release. "Troublesome little creatures."

"Ah." He came into step with her, lowering his voice until the hair on her neck rose to attention. "Then it is perfect, Mause."

Her glare hit his grin without one effect, except to add a broader hint of mischief. What could she call him? Rascal?

"You think you're quite clever, don't you?"

"I have to be clever to keep up with you, and fast. You are good at running away."

She tilted her head up to the sky and sighed. "Well, Mr. Reinhold, I've just decided I've grown rather weary of running." She glanced in her periphery at his windswept profile. "In fact, I've realized there's no place like home."

He took her arm and drew her to a stop, his gaze sweeping over her face. "Be mindful then, dear Mause, you do not run into the claws of the cat with Mr. Little."

"Jealousy does not become you, August." Although she didn't mind it as much as she thought.

"Jealousy only fuels a small portion of my concern. I am afraid he is not what he appears. Be careful. Be smart."

"I will."

~

The Ross family caused quite a stir at the little Presbyterian Church downtown on Sunday morning. Jessica grinned. Well, mostly it was Catherine who caused the stir. She didn't intentionally evoke such responses with her slim, fashionable styles, but a woman of her exquisite beauty, clothed in dark blue and wearing a hat of her own design, swept into town like a moving picture star. Even unflappable Amy gawked, unashamed.

Despite the somewhat humorous distractions, Jess found the sermon confirmed all the small conversations her family had shared with her over the past few weeks. God's fingerprints marked every turn of her life. Her heart might grieve forever over what she'd lost, but His love carved a steady path through every moment, covering and comforting her in the most barren places. Even as her heart ached for her mother, trembled from fears still scratching at her peace, and cringed from a stolen innocence... even in her hateful pride and raw bitterness at the turn of his will, He'd loved her.

As the pastor called everyone to pray, Jude slid his little hand into hers, and God's truth burned a clear line through her hungry heart. She stared down at his little fingers wrapped around hers and then looked at Faith's angelic face as she slept in Jess' embrace. Her grandpa's words rushed back to her. *You're so busy staring at the empty hand, you can't see how full the other hand is.*

Tears crowded into her vision as gratitude swarmed over her. Here she sat, surrounded by family... and both of her hands, as well as her heart, were full. Pain had stripped her world, but God's mercy still brought sweet comfort and the promise of healing she'd refused to see for a long time.

Could this God whom she'd blamed truly forgive her with such a generous hand after all of her suspicions and scars? She quieted a sob as a new revelation shed light on the inner workings of her heart. *August.*

God couldn't bless her with someone like him too? His tenderness and patience. His teasing spark and quiet strength. She'd battled so long against releasing her fears and trusting this possibility... or even more, trusting God for her future, but in one quiet whisper, she breathed out her fight and the need to know why. And breathed in the fragrance of peace she'd missed for far too long.

"It's such a quaint town, isn't it?" Catherine said, as they walked from Branson's to the car. David walked ahead of them next to their father, carrying sweet Addie in her perfectly matched green frock and hat, with Jude and her grandparents in between.

"Much smaller than Ednesbury."

"And that's saying something." Catherine grinned. "For Ednesbury is only slightly larger than a hamlet." She glanced around Main Street. "But pleasant, isn't it? All it wants is a dress shop."

Jessica laughed, a new lightness in her step and heart. "I don't think Hot Springs is prepared for the style you'd impose, my dear sister-in-law."

"Oh, rubbish. Anyone can do with extra style." Her dark brow teased high.

"Miss Ross?"

Jess turned to meet the dashing grin of Mr. Jasper Little. He wore an impressive brown suit and hat, but she'd failed to notice him in their little sanctuary. Perhaps he attended one of the other four churches within walking distance of town. At any rate, he looked quite dapper, but after her experience with August in the chapel, Mr. Little's charm had lost its glimmer.

"Mr. Little. Good morning."

His attention turned to Catherine and the interest in his expression took a heated turn. "And who do you have with you this morning?"

"This is my—"

"Catherine," Catherine interjected, offering her hand and shooting Jess a playful grin. "Catherine Ross."

"Miss Ross." He took her hand and kept his gaze fixed on her. Any attentiveness Jess might have held for Mr. Little left with the obvious fluidity of his interest. But what was Catherine up to?

"I've heard of you, Mr. Little. Research here in town, isn't that right?"

"Yes." His dark gaze shimmied down Catherine's entire body and settled back on her face.

Jess grimaced. Had he always been this obvious and she'd been too blind to see? She almost groaned. Oh, she'd been blind about so much. Arrogance paired with bitterness created a fog of self-importance that left a sour taste in her mouth. Much like the lurid glances Mr. Little overtly imposed on her sister-in-law. "I suppose you've heard of balladry in this part of world?"

"A little, but I'm originally from a town closer to Asheville. Balladry seems to be more transfixed in the deeper recesses of Appalachia." Her smile remained welcoming, but her eyes sparkled with caution. "And where do you call home, Mr. Little? I can't help but note your accent."

"Yes, I'm originally from a small town in Derbyshire."

"Truly? And what did you do in that part of the world, Mr. Little?"

For anyone who knew Catherine, the warning signs shone clear. She was baiting the poor man, but why? First, August's warning, and now, Catherine's behavior? What had Jessica missed?

"Well, before the war, I was a professor, which I've returned to now."

"Delightful. I'm a great proponent of educating those in desperate need of awareness." She turned to the men who'd stopped their walk a little distance away. "Father, dear, I have someone for you to meet."

Jess looked from her father to Catherine and back to Mr. Little whose grin widened at Alexander Ross' approach.

"Mr. Little, this is my father-in-law, Lord Alexander Ross of Ednesbury Court in Derbyshire."

Catherine rarely introduced father with his title, and why in this little town of Hot Springs to Jasper? Jasper's face paled. "Your... your father-in-law? Lord?"

"Mr. Jasper Little, Father, whom I believe both Mr. Reinhold and grandfather mentioned to you earlier."

"Yes. A pleasure, Mr. Little." Father offered his hand which Mr. Little took once he'd shaken off the look of shock on his face.

"Mr. Reinhold?" Jasper whispered, his frown taking a sinister turn.

"Yes, a pleasant chap. Quite the woodworker."

"Mr. Little hails from Derbyshire, Father." Catherine stepped back, linking her arm through David's. "I wondered if you might have any common acquaintances."

"I doubt it," Jasper rushed to answer. "I would not have been in your circles at all."

"Your accent is interesting for the locale. What part of Derbyshire do you call home?"

The whole scene was like watching a moving picture show where the little nuances and expressions took on a whole new meaning.

Mr. Little's tone changed to reserved and distant, and even his accent wavered. He backed away and offered a paper-thin smile. "We moved quite often in my younger days, so I am uncertain where my accent truly fits."

"Of course." Father kept his approach kind, but Jess had known Catherine long enough to see the devious click of her thoughts.

First August, and now Catherine? Their suspicions sharpened Jess' senses.

"I must bid you good day." Jasper tipped his hat and backed away, barely grazing Jess with a glance before walking down the street and away from them.

Catherine stepped to Jessica's side. "I know his sort, and he's rotten—from the top of his smart hat to the heel of his second-hand shoes."

"How can you know that? You only met him five minutes ago." Jessica took a battle stance, even as doubt crept into her confidence. Hadn't she begun to sense something darker behind Jasper's conversations? A deep anger burning beneath his smile?

"He isn't English," her father said, resuming their walk to the car. "He attempts an accent, and somewhat admirably, I must say, but August voiced his concerns to me earlier and he was right. Something is amiss about Mr. Little."

"And the way he ogled me?"

"You do make quite an impression, Kat." David's eyes sparkled. "I'm certain the poor man could hardly help it. I know I'm at a loss."

Her red lips slit in response, sharing that intimate smile she'd seen between them for the year she worked in their hospital in Ednesbury. "Yes, but you're the only man I wish to ensnare, my dear Dr. Ross. I find no gratification in being ogled."

"As your grandfather spent time with him yesterday, he grew concerned when Mr. Little continued to ask in-depth questions about the camp and the men inside it." A chill of warning accompanied her father's stare. "Whatever he's up to, I'd give him a wide berth, Jess. And I wouldn't trust him."

Chapter Twenty

He heard Jude's sweet voice on the path before Jessica's shoes met the chapel steps. He'd only arrived a few minutes earlier, half hoping she'd seen him make his usual stop in the barn to collect tools. The fact that she watched out for him kindled his grin. God saw fit to put him out of his misery of heart sooner rather than later.

What sweet mercy.

She'd stepped off the train over two months ago. After eight months of learning about her through letters, of slowly being endeared to the dry humor, the loyal love for her family, and the deep-set compassion in her words, he'd prayed her heart might warm to his pursuit.

Dared he hope it was so?

"Mornin', August." Jude's words echoed off the wooden walls, glossy from August's recent staining. "Granny sent you a biscuit with jelly."

Jude placed a small parcel of cloth in August's palm and grinned up at him with a rather toothless smile.

"Thank you, sir." He tapped Jude's nose. "And I see you have been careless today?"

Jude's little head tilted. "Careless? I carried that biscuit all the way here with both hands so I wouldn't drop nary a crumb."

August lowered himself to one knee. "Losing one tooth is understandable, but losing two?" He whistled low and shook his head. "That is rather careless."

Jude's grin returned, recognizing the joke. "Can't help it none when the apple's tougher than my teeth. Took a bite at dinner and out one popped. Got stuck right in that apple. The second one wasn't far behind."

August laughed, sending a look over the boy's shoulder to his mother. She'd worn her hair long in the back and pinned at the sides, a rare style for her. Did she do this for him? He stared so long a hint of rose bloomed in her cheeks. She still kept long strands of hair pulled over her shoulders to cover the scar he'd caught glimpses of, but the sight of all that glorious hair, haloed by the afternoon sunlight, nearly had him wondering if an angel visited.

"What work you got for me today, August?"

He patted the boy's shoulder and stood. "Would you walk around the outside of the chapel and find any nails left in the grass? We would not wish for someone to step on a stray nail."

"We want 'em to have holy hearts, not holey feet." Jude snickered at his own joke and Jessica joined in.

Her light laugh drew August's attention back to her and as their gazes met, her laughter stilled from her lips but danced in her eyes. She captivated him. "I think his humor is starting to grow."

"Must be the company he keeps."

Her brow shot high, leveling him with a pointed look. "Exactly what I was thinking."

"I reckon it happens often enough around the Carters. They're always carryin' on about somethin' or other." Jude shrugged his little shoulder and started out the chapel door. "Might as well join in."

The closing door echoed into the silent chapel and August set down the tool bag he'd been holding during the entire conversation. It clattered to the dark wooden floorboards.

Jess averted her gaze and stared past him. "You didn't have those support beams up earlier. Did something happen to the lovely rafters you set that you'd need to support them?"

August turned to see a thin plank, long enough to reach from the floor to one of the large, wooden rafters, almost as if it propped up the beam. Odd. He'd finished both of those beams the day before and removed any props.

"Has your grandfather been here?"

"Not to my knowledge," she said, her voice closer. "He was busy giving Mr. Little a tour of the camp yesterday."

August half-turned but didn't comment.

"It seems the whole family is up in arms about Mr. Little and his fake accent."

August turned completely around and faced her. "Your grandfather said as much?"

"Catherine and my father. It seems your misgivings perked their interest enough to put Mr. Little to the test." She stepped closer, placing a hand on his arm. "But certainly you don't think he's up to something sinister. He's angry, but so was I, and I had no designs to harm anyone."

He covered her hand with his. "Underneath all your anger beats a generous heart and an intelligence. Not everyone can emerge from fury with a clear mind, Mause."

Her lips quirked at the endearment, a softening which tempted him to break his promise and give her a kiss to wipe the barbarian who'd hurt her from her thoughts forever.

"You know, Mr. Reinhold, I'm beginning to think you're either fiercely optimistic or a little mad to pursue me when I've been rather unkind and stubborn to you."

"What if I told you that I saw beneath all your anger to something beautiful? Would you believe me?"

She studied him, those jade eyes taking him in with new vision—gentler. Her smile shimmered with something tender, strengthening the bond growing between them. "I don't understand it, but I believe you." She looked away, back to the rafters. "But what I don't understand is all of your kindness. Your service to my grandparents goes far beyond this chapel. You've made repairs for them, served them."

"I did not restore this chapel for them, Mause." He took her fingers into his hand and raised them to his lips, watching her sudden intake of breath at his touch. Her breathing hollowed and her jeweled gaze pooled with wonder. "I did it for you."

"Me?"

"This building may be only boards and nails. Pretty and serene, but as you know, not lasting." He squeezed her hand and rubbed a thumb over her knuckles, taking in the softness of her skin. She rested her fingers in his, trusting. His smile took on a whole new brightness. "It's what lives on the inside of this building, on the inside of our hearts, which is everlasting. Strong enough to withstand the ravages of time, grief, or floods. We can try to cling to the mortar and bricks, but they will not provide security, but this chapel is an example of the One who will not be overcome by time or trouble or sorrow, but who holds us fast in hands strong enough to create the world and tender enough to whisper life into a baby's breath. The One who can restore the broken and bruised."

He turned back to the last remaining beams waiting to be fitted into place. Two. After tomorrow, when he returned to finish up some small pieces of trim work, his work would be done.

"I'll help you finish."

He shot her a look from his periphery. "I do not think you are the best help."

She propped those palms on her hips and narrowed her eyes. "Why ever not?"

"You are a distraction."

"A distraction?" The defensive fire in her eyes died as his meaning became clear. A beautiful swell of rose flooded her cheeks and she tipped her chin in defiance. Ah, he loved her spirit. "You don't strike me as the sort who is easily distracted, Mr. Reinhold."

His stare met hers. "I'm not the sort who is *easily* distracted, Miss Ross."

Her breath caught and she blinked as if stunned for a moment. No games. No coy manipulation. All honesty and fire and loyalty. Yes, exactly what his heart responded to from the first day. The authentic beauty of her heart.

"What nonsense." She cleared her throat and brushed past him. "Let's get on with our work, shall we? I'll take this board out of the way—"

"Jess, wait."

She touched the slanted board, shifting it ever so slightly, and without warning, the massive beam from the ceiling plunged downward toward her.

Jessica's skin still hummed from the touch of August's lips on her hand. If his lips left such a reaction on her hand, all tingly and warm, what on earth would his touch do to her mouth? Her brain blurred from the effort to match her past experience with this luxurious temptation, so different from what she'd expected, but not a surprise. Not from August.

Everything about him proved different than her expectations.

She shuffled forward in a bit of a daze toward the beam, attempting to sort the wild canter inside her chest like a lawn badminton match. "I'll take this board out of the way—"

Everything happened in a flash. She had barely slid the board from its spot before a movement above rooted her to the floor. The beam fell toward her.

"Jess!"

A weight from her right hit her hard, knocking her off balance and to the floor. Arms, strong and familiar with the scent of pine, cradled her fall, but not enough to keep the impact from stealing her breath.

She groaned, frozen in place with August's full weight pinning her to the floor. What happened? She sucked in a thread of air and looked to her left where the rafter beam lay mere inches away.

"August." His name squeezed from her pinned chest and she pushed at his arms. Nothing. A roiling panic rose through her. "August."

Her cry met with silence and his unresponsive body. She pushed out of his arms and held his head and back as she turned him over. His body flopped against the floor and the beginnings of a welt popped red on his forehead.

She pressed her good ear against his chest. The faithful and strong thump of his heart eased her breathing a little, but as she pulled her arms out from behind him, the sight of blood sent a new chill through her. *David.*

Not two years earlier she'd held her brother in her arms, her fingers covered with his blood, in an attempt to save his life from a German spy's attack. Was it another head wound that would take August's memory like it had David's? Would it debilitate him? She turned August on his side and the sight pinched her air to a stop. Bright red blood soaked the back of his shirt.

"Jude!" she called out, praying the little boy had stayed within earshot. "Jude!"

The chapel door swung wide and Jude took in the situation with wide eyes.

"Run to the house. Find Uncle David and Grandpa Ross or Carter. As fast as you can."

With a nod, he turned and fled. Jess began quick work of unbuttoning August's shirt and slipping it from his body. The beam must have struck August as it fell, leaving a two-inch gash between his scapula and spine, clean from what she could tell. But experience had taught her wounds could travel much deeper than the eye could see.

Oh, God, please. Please don't take him. In mind or body. Please... let him stay.

She reached down to her petticoat and ripped the cloth, a mixture of simple lace and cotton, making a poor but needed bandage. As she leaned his head on her shoulder to slip the cloth around his back, mindful of the growing lump on his forehead, he groaned.

She sighed against his hair, a sudden relief washing over her as she tied the cloth in place. David had been unconscious for a week. A minute or two presented a much better prognosis. August pulled back from her and she placed her hands on his shoulders to help him orient himself. Those periwinkle eyes stared back, clearing with each blink.

"Jessica?"

Her name had never sounded so sweet. "Nice to see those eyes, Mr. Reinhold."

He squinted and winced, attempting to straighten his back. "What happened?"

"The rafter beam fell and you pushed me out of the way of it."

His gaze rose to hers. "Are you injured?"

She smiled, softening her hold on his shoulders, and wondered how she ever mistook him for a villain. "Your speedy reaction saved me from any harm, but you? You hit your head, I assume, from coming down hard on the floor." Her gaze dropped to his chest and her makeshift bandaging skills. "And the beam grazed you with enough force to leave a mark."

He touched his forehead, grimacing as his fingers inspected the impressive lump now turning a lovely shade of green, and then he looked down and ran a hand over the cloth across his chest. "You... you did this?"

"I am a nurse, you know."

His smile wobbled into place, and the spark returned to his eyes as he scanned her body. "I am grateful, I'm sure." He examined a loose piece of the cloth between his fingers. "And this? This was from your petticoat?"

She crossed her arms, her face warm. "Desperate times, Mr. Reinhold. Your life was much more important than the welfare of my undergarment."

His brow tipped in that attractive way of his and she prepared for the impish aftermath. "I've been wrapped in your petticoats? I believe a wedding is necessary now."

Jess stood to hide her smile. "You, August Reinhold, are an incorrigible flirt."

He struggled to stand so she braced his arms with her hands and assisted him the remainder of the way. His muscles flexed beneath her touch, budding the awareness of his shirtless form with a bit more potency. They stood close, much too close for a bare-chested man who was unashamedly wearing pieces of her petticoat.

"Only with the right woman who is in desperate need of an incorrigible flirt."

She fought the urge to look away and instead, stared back, drinking in the sight of him, whole and somewhat safe. In fact, besides the knot swelling on his forehead in brilliant colors, his appearance left a feverish wave running through her body. Or perhaps it radiated from his skin, infecting hers with an intoxicating need to feel encapsulated by his strength one more time.

"I think you're going to be fine," she whispered, her gaze dropping to his lips.

"No, I still suffer from an ailment only you can cure, Mause."

"Do you?" She swallowed her fear and edged a step closer into the foggy heat. "I'm afraid your malady requires training for which I'm ill-equipped."

"I suspect you are a quick study." The tenor in his voice reverberated low.

She touched his cheek. "Not as quick about things of the heart, I'm afraid."

"Then take your time. I'm a willing patient."

He didn't hurry her, made no movement to rush but merely stood there, waiting for her initiation, bending slightly to give her more ready access to the items of her fascination—his lips. She drew close enough to feel his breath on her mouth, and she hesitated, flipping her gaze from his lips to those eyes. His brow rose in question, but otherwise, he didn't move an inch, and she smiled, finishing the distance.

His lips were soft and warm beneath hers, sweet and inviting. She waited for the fear to overrun the curiosity, but it didn't. Instead, he gently stroked her lips with his own, ever so slightly. She pulled back to take in a breath and check his status. Did his pulse pound in his ears too? Was breathing becoming increasingly more difficult? He opened his eyes and looked at her with such tenderness, such life, it welcomed her to bridge the gap for another sampling. She cradled his face in both hands and brought her lips to his again.

Those lips took on a firmer quality in response, entreating her to remain right where she was. It was a slow discovery, a sweet caress, pouring over the gaping wounds of a distorted experience with a healing touch. This was altogether lovely.

She lost sense of time as they took turns exploring the gentlest of kisses. Nothing forced, only freely given, welcomed, and wrapped in something beautiful—a direct contrast to her fears.

She pulled back, her eyes closed, savoring the sensations flooding through her. For years, she'd yearned for one taste of such tenderness from a man. Aching for the romance she'd witnessed with others in her life. Resolving to spend her life alone without the taste of such... love?

His warm hand came to rest against her cheek and she looked up, tears framing her view of his handsome face. Now, here she stood, safe and loved in a way for which words fell impossibly short.

"You overwhelm me." He framed her face with his hands. "I... I am intoxicated."

Her breath came in spurts of caught air. "Can you hear my heart pounding? It's a marvel one survives such emotions."

"They've been constant companions for me lately."

"You're quite remarkable, Mr. Reinhold."

The glint in his eyes turned mischievous, a feature she was beginning to appreciate more and more with each passing moment. "I'm glad you've finally seen the truth of it, Mause."

His fingers dropped to slip through a lock of hair at her neck. She reached to cover her scar, a habit born out of her own pride, but he caught her fingers.

"I have heard that the skin healed with scars is stronger than the skin without the scars?" He brought her fingers to his lips, his lashes low.

She stared up at him, tears and breath lodged in her throat. His gentle caress, cool against her warm skin, sent a wave of awareness trembling through her chest with the brilliance of electric lights. "Yes?"

"Is it true?"

Words scratched over a strained breath, gaze caught in his. "It is."

He looked at her, his smile soft. "Then I would wager, the scars on your heart have made your heart strong enough to survive many more kisses, because I have no intention to end what you've begun."

"What *I've* begun?" She couldn't tame her ridiculous smile. "I think you may have hit your head much harder than I thought, because as I recall, you're the one who began all of this."

He shook his head, the glint deepening in his eyes. "I never began the kissing. The kissing changes things."

She felt the truth of that statement all the way through her tingling body. "And exactly how?"

"It confirms all the reasons why being wrapped in strips of your petticoat encourages an immediate wedding."

She laughed and turned to distance herself from the magnetizing draw of his lips. "Speaking of petticoats and head injuries, what do you suppose happened to cause your beam to nearly decapitate us?"

The door to the chapel burst open just as Jess made it far enough away from August to keep the curious eyes of her father and brother at bay.

"Are you all right?" Her father crossed the room to take her by the shoulders.

"Yes, I'm fine. It's August that got the worst of it."

David approached August, examining the hastily made bandage. "What happened here?"

"One of the rafter beams came loose and nearly caused real harm. Had it not been for August's quick reaction, I don't know how serious the injuries might have been." Jess pulled her attention away from August and up to the ceiling. "I'm not certain what went wrong."

"I secured those rafters yesterday. I am certain of it." August shook his head. "This makes no sense."

"I'm afraid I see the problem." David knelt by the beam on the floor, the look on his face chilling away all the previous warmth in Jessica's body.

They all moved closer. He pointed to the edge of the beam where shoddy saw marks slit into the wood. "Someone sabotaged this beam."

"Sabotaged?" Jess joined her brother on the floor and ran her hand over the beam's ragged edge. "That's why August didn't know why a supporting beam had been placed beneath it." She exchanged a look with August and then her father. "But why? Who would wish to hurt us?"

"Not us." August's expression hardened. "Me."

Her father spoke into the wintry silence. "August, do you know of anyone in Hot Springs who wants you wounded or dead?"

He shook his head. "Not with certainty."

"Do you think the sudden outbreak of typhoid in the camp is a mere coincidence?" David asked.

"Typhoid?" Jess stood, searching her brother's face. "In the camp?"

"That's why Dr. Peck called grandfather to the camp after breakfast. He wanted a second opinion, but yes, it's typhoid fever."

Jess' gaze found August's. "Then this... this was no coincidence."

"It seems there is someone who wants more than my death." August's frown firmed, deepening the creases in his forehead. "But all the Germans."

Jess approached him. "You can't go back to the camp. Not with typhoid as a possibility."

"He has no choice, Jess. They've already announced a mandatory recovery of all Germans until the relocation to Georgia." Her father sighed. "Colonel Ames made the announcement as soon as they confirmed the typhoid."

"You could run away."

"Jessica," her father reprimanded. "Would you have him be a fugitive as well as a prisoner?"

She turned on her father, desperate for a way to save this man who'd suddenly filled up so much of her heart. "But... but he'd be safe. Placing him back behind that fence with something or someone causing this deadly disease? Is that the right choice either?"

"I will not run like a coward as my countrymen suffer from someone's evil. I must help discover what has happened." He took her hand and gave it a squeeze. "If I leave, I will not leave from fear or shame, but by choice."

Her hand fisted in his hold. "And I have no choice but to let you go?"

"You have a choice—to trust the God who watches over us... or not."

Chapter Twenty-One

Jessica took her first opportunity, cane in hand, to abate a needling curiosity. She took the sidewalk at a frenetic pace up Broad. Past the mercantile and the pharmacy. Over Bridge Street toward the church. Across the street, the lovely white home of Jane Gentry emerged, elevated a little from the street and surrounded by oaks that promised to stand tall guard in a few years.

Jess took the steps to the front door and prayed her instincts, and those of her family, were wrong. Surely she hadn't fallen prey to blindness yet again? Not after all the thick-skinned suspicions she'd nurtured.

She rang the doorbell and waited for the familiar steps of Mrs. Gentry clicking toward the large wooden door. Most days, the woman insisted on being the first to greet prospective guests. She'd always been an anomaly for most of the women in these parts with her ready friendliness and openness to cultures and people beyond the mountains.

Her small frame, gray hair pinned back in a bun, barely made a silhouette in the massive doorway. "Well, now, Jesse Ross. What brings you to my doorstep?"

"I know you're keeping busy with all your boarders, Mrs. Gentry, but I was wondering if you had a few minutes to talk."

Her eyes twinkled. "You know I always have time to talk."

Which meant 'listen' most of the time. Almost everyone in town shared their secrets, dreams, stories, and desires with Jane Gentry. But when she did talk, it was usually about something worth hearing.

She ushered Jessica in to her home, a small table in the parlor already set for tea as if she'd been waiting for a caller. "Most of the boarders have already come for tea, but I have a pot still warm. Why don't you sit a spell and join me?"

Jess settled into a high-back and accepted the dainty cup from Mrs. Gentry with a thank you.

"Now, what's on your mind?"

"It shouldn't take very long, Mrs. Gentry, but I was wondering if you'd had the pleasure of meeting a Mr. Jasper Little yet? I sent him here a few weeks ago, as you're one of the local experts of our ballads."

"I heard about him arrivin' into town, but I ain't seen hide nor hair of him. Which is a shame since the ladies seemed to think he was worth seein'."

Jess leaned forward, her stomach curling with a growing disgust. No. Not fooled again. "He hasn't been here? At all?"

"No. I even mentioned it to Zepporah, since I heared your Grandpa was sending him her way too. She ain't even laid eyes on him, let alone talked to him."

Jess took a quick drink of her tea and placed her cup down. "Then what I have to say next is even more important. Your boarders need to know."

Mrs. Gentry starting pouring her own tea. "Yes?"

"There are two reported cases of typhoid in the camp."

"Typhoid?" Mrs. Gentry lowered the tea pot to the table and sank slowly into her chair, her hand to her chest. "They don't reckon it's this La Grippe we've heard tell about coming from out west?"

La Grippe? Oh yes, she'd read about it in the papers but no one knew much about it, except that it was highly contagious and incredibly lethal. A new illness, The Spanish Influenza some called it, started in the West, but had spread east following the railway. It attacked quickly and left a steady death trail in its wake.

"Grandfather confirmed the diagnosis along with Dr. Peck, but we don't know the extent or the origin yet."

Her wise eyes steadied their gaze. "And what of Mr. Little? How does he relate to this news?"

That woman was too keen for her own good. "I hope he doesn't."

"Then why is he in Hot Springs?"

A question to which Jessica wasn't certain she wanted an answer. Why, indeed? Either he was a poor researcher or he had something more sinister in mind.

She finished her tea and bid the wise Mrs. Gentry good-day. A breeze wafted up from the street below, through the oaks framing the front porch of Mrs. Gentry's house, and dampened the fire in Jess' cheeks from her internal self-flailing. Had she been wrong all over again? Fooled by someone else in plain sight?

She stepped down to the street and started back toward the camp. Almost in mockery, Jasper Little emerged from Kimp's and saw her. Well, no time like the present. And perhaps all of this conjecture about Jasper Little was mere speculation and nothing more. If he was truly guilty of something underhanded, why would he remain in Hot Springs to be uncovered? But, of course, a more pressing curiosity was... why was he in Hot Springs at all?

She braced herself with a smile as false as his. "Miss Ross, where are you off to in such a hurry on this fine day?"

"I'm afraid I'm returning to the camp to see if I can be of any assistance there."

He halved the distance between them. "Assistance at the camp? What in heaven's name would you do to help a gaggle of German prisoners?"

"I suppose you'll need to know as well, for your own safety of course." She studied him, searching for any shifts in his pristine expression. "There's been two reported cases of typhoid inside the internment camp. I don't know the names of the two men, but I mean to help, if I can."

"Typhoid?" He frowned. "Isn't that caused by some contamination of the food or water supply?"

She held his gaze, challenging him. "Indeed, it is."

He shook his head. "I never expected them to stoop so low."

"So low? What do you mean?"

"Well, it's no secret that the Germans didn't want to leave Hot Springs for the prison camp. Everyone knew that. They're practically on holiday here and Georgia is a work camp for true prisoners. Desperation brings on all sorts of illogical choices."

"Are you implying that they did this to themselves? Suicide?"

He shrugged his apology. "What else could it be? Some nasty scheme from a random villain?" He chuckled. "Now that is a plot meant for a novel."

"Or a plan meant for a devious mind."

His gaze never wavered. "Do you suppose someone with such evil intent lives in your little town? And if so, why wouldn't they have attempted their plan well before now? It doesn't seem very sensible to me."

"Desperation rarely is." She stepped closer, her trepidation evaporating in the face of his extreme arrogance. "Perhaps someone with a festering bitterness planned it? Or maybe someone new in town?"

"I think, my dear Miss Ross, you should stick to your novels and not tamper in things beyond your depth."

"You give me little credit then. I've been tampering in things beyond my depth for a long time. I mean to uncover the truth."

His lips twitched into an unpleasant smile. "Whatever truth your German feeds you isn't going to bring you closer to an answer. You've clearly been corrupted by your delicate German sympathies."

"German sympathies? What of human sympathies, Mr. Little? If someone did purposefully infect the men in the camp, then it is clear to me he's lost all sense of right and wrong. Anger has a pinpointed way of twisting our logic, and I find it highly unlikely they would bring such a vile illness to their own doorstep out of sheer rebellion."

"It appears you're the one with unclear logic in this case. Do you think any one of them would not go directly to the Front and fight against our countrymen if they had the chance? All of them would betray whatever friendships they've developed here to follow through with the Kaiser's murder."

Gone was the English accent and the false charm, and now... now, she stared into a similar face as she had two years ago, one flushed with the maddening purpose of revenge. How had she been so wrong? So blind? All this time. Had she learned nothing from Lt. Snyder?

He took off his hat and pointed it toward the camp. "I know them. They're all desperate cowards who would rather die an agonizing death than suffer the embarrassment of a prison camp. Which is exactly where each and every one of them belong."

"I can't believe I fell for your little façade." She stared him down, unflinching. "Who are you, because clearly you are not here for balladry?"

He opened his mouth to protest but she wouldn't allow it. "I've already been to Jane Gentry. You never spoke to her, and my father noticed your false accent."

He flinched at her words.

"So the real question is, who are you, why are you playacting as an Englishman, and what are you doing in our little town—because if you ask me, Mr. Little, your presence is as suspect as you portray the Germans. If you've lied about your reason for visiting Hot Springs, what other lies have you told? Would you be the type of person who would falsify letters to incriminate the internees? Or sabotage a chapel, perhaps? Or tamper with a water supply?" She searched his face. His jaw tightened to the twinging point. She ignored the warning. "Are you on some vengeful vendetta to redeem the loss of your brothers and your arm? Because, if so, this is not the way to do it."

"You're going too far, Miss Ross."

He towered over her, but she faced him head-on. "Oh no, Mr. Little, or whatever your name is, I've not gone far enough, you can be sure. I'm notoriously stubborn, and I find I have a new opportunity, as it were, to help uncover the origin of whatever or whoever is unleashing all of this hardship. I suggest you either get out of the way or help me, because you're certainly not going to stop me."

His laugh turned ruthless. "You would protect and even befriend a man of the same patronage as the killers who ruined your brother and you?"

She drew in a shaky breath, a sudden revelation buoying her defense. "Mr. Little, my brother is not ruined." She stood taller, challenging him. "And neither am I."

The guards wouldn't allow Jessica into the camp, even though she argued her point for ten minutes, so she'd walked the length of the fence until the wood changed to wire. Her father and grandfather worked behind the walls of those clapboard buildings, seeking to help as best they could against such a devastating illness. Typhoid was not uncommon in the dank world of war, with its nasty trenches and nonexistent drainage.

And Jasper? Something in those eyes warned her that he was much more dangerous than she'd imagined. An eerie light, an unsteadiness... the blind rage inspired by a festering bitterness. Without grace and people to inject reason into her hardened heart, would she have turned to a darker path? She pinched her eyes closed, battling the voice of failure's seething lies. No, God had brought her far beyond the fisted fury and wrath which led her down that twisted path.

But what could she do to discover the truth? To keep people safe. Especially the people she cared about.

Through the crowd of sailors, over the expanse of a lawn cluttered with trees and woodwork, August emerged like an unexpected knight in a fairy story. He stopped his stride across the lawn and time slowed as she took in the view of him with new vision, with a sense of sweet connection.

He walked toward her, strength and grace in his stride, as evident as in all of his actions toward her and her family. His white buttoned shirt and khaki slacks were smudged with bits of dirt from his day's work, and he removed his straw hat as he approached. The coveted golden lock fell over his forehead with its usual distraction, but what held her captive most were his eyes. So gentle and filled with every dream she dared never voice about the desires of her heart.

Somehow, within an expanse of one day, all her childish fancies and grown-up daydreams began and ended in the man she recognized now. Well, it had taken more than a day. He'd gradually etched his way into her heart over the past two months, peeling back her pain and replacing it with hope. She'd been so stubborn and rude to him. So hateful and wrong. How could he look at her with such unshackled admiration?

Before he even reached the fence, her confession burst out. "I'm sorry, so sorry, August. Please forgive me."

His brow crinkled beneath the golden lock and he came to a stop in front of her. "Forgive you? What tragic sin have you committed, Mause?"

She smiled at the tenderness wrapped in his humor. A blush of heat rushed to her face and she ran a palm down her makeshift braid, her breath shallow. "I've been so blind. Too blinded by my own pride and anger to really see you."

He tilted his head, his gaze roaming over her face in pensive observation. "And what do you see, Jessica Ross?"

She failed to waver beneath the intensity of those eyes. He'd cradled in her in his arms during a storm, abated her fury with his gentle humor, and unraveled all her doubts with his unswerving constancy. She stepped forward, gripping the metal fence, and faced him as honestly as he'd done her.

Her breath swirled into a thick, heated knot in her throat, but she would not back down now. Not after all that had happened, all he'd done. He'd forgive her without this declaration. His kiss had already spoken it, but she had to confess. "You are much more than I ever imagined." She sighed, staring down at her fingers clutching the fence. "With more patience than I deserve and a faith I crave."

He stepped close, curling his warm hands over hers against the fence. "Look at me, Mause."

Sweet warmth pooled over her at his endearment she'd once shunned. Tears burned her eyes, blurring her vision, but she lifted her head, staring into the periwinkle tenderness. "Forgive me, August. Please. For being hateful and slow and too broken to see you. Forgive me for... for all of it."

"We are all broken in some way or other, yes? But love binds the broken."

And any final reserve fled under such a beautiful notion. Love. It melted through every choice he made, colored every touch and word, and encased her in a sudden sense of belonging. Safety. Sweet rest, as if he held her in his arms.

Love.

A word much too small for the power reverberating from its bearers. From August. He embodied the love she'd grown up learning about, God's encompassing, covering, beautiful love—a fragrant, comforting balm to her threadbare heart.

A sob caught in her throat and she lowered her head again, his compassion overwhelming and too sweet. "I don't understand why you would still... care about me. I've been fairly horrible to you." She pressed her forehead against the fence, half-praying the fence might disintegrate and half-afraid that if it did... would he let her fall to the muddy earth at his feet?

His palm left her hand and slipped through the fence to skim her cheek. The tears loosed, dripping onto their braided fingers. "You were beautiful in your letters and a lovely challenge in your fury." His whisper breathed over her hair. "But now, in your tenderness, coming to me for... love?" His voice deepened with emotion.

She looked up to meet his gaze, his smile undefinably sweet.

"You are breathtaking."

And she knew, without a doubt. August would catch her.

If the fence didn't separate them, August would have shown her just how much he cared with a kiss to strip all doubt. But here they were again. Not separated by her prejudice and anger, but by a fence neither of them built and a war neither wanted.

"I wish this blasted fence wasn't in the way."

He grinned at her sentence, as if she'd read his thoughts. "If willpower broke wire, it would disappear in a moment." He ran his hand over her cheek, soft and damp from her tears. Tears for him. "But I'm not certain your desire to remove the fence isn't as desperate as mine, Mause."

"I wouldn't place a wager on that statement. You do recall how dogmatic I am, and that carries through to *all* of my passions." She waved her hand toward him and sighed, her gaze taking him in from shoes to head and leaving a radiating warmth. "And now, I cannot get to you."

What sweet torture was this! He'd expected her care, but to have her devotion and her passion too? Blasted fence, indeed. "If I had the power, I would rip the fence out of the ground."

She squeezed his hands through the fence. "I'm so sorry it took me this long, and I was blind about you and then Jasper—"

"No more, Mause. No more. It is enough to have your affections now, as they are." He bathed in the glow of admiration in her eyes—admiration for him. Yes, this blasted fence was a nuisance. "Let us start from today. We have good memories from today."

Her emerald focus dropped to his lips and a fiery warmth followed their target.

"Very good." She looked up at him, the glint from her eyes sending residual sparks. "But I could do with more practice. I'm certain of it. I like to get things just right."

"Do not torment me with a freedom I do not have." His fingers curled around her shoulder, wishing to tug her against him but unable. "For I would gladly oblige."

Her eyes rounded in apology. "If I hadn't been so slow—"

"Your wounds were deep, Mause." He loosened his hold, breathing out the frustration of their separation. "And sweeter the prize is the one that requires effort, yes? For both of us?"

"And God would pick this moment to separate us?"

His grin spread. "Perhaps it is for our protection. If you are as impassioned for me as you confess, then we might very well need separation to maintain our virtues."

She smiled, drawing her face as close to his as she could. "Want to make another wager about it, Mr. Reinhold? On who has the most passion?"

He groaned, appreciating her competitive streak for all the wrong reasons. "There is no way I could lose that wager, Miss Ross."

She lips slanted with her grin and her beautiful gaze revealed a sweetness no woman had ever shown him. She not only admired him, but her expression filled with promises for him alone. Powerful. And for this, he'd waited, prayed, and hoped. This glorious bond of mutual respect, thankfulness, and attraction. He would cherish it with his life.

"Where did you go once you left your father and me?"

"Sunnybank, to speak with Jane Gentry." Her face sobered. "Jasper had never gone to Jane, or several of the other women."

"I am not surprised."

"August, do you think he's responsible for the chapel? For the sickness here?"

He looked past her to the buildings of the town in a vain search for the mysterious stranger. Dr. Cater had taken Jasper on a tour of the camp, and Jasper knew of August's work on the chapel. The possibility turned August's stomach. Why? Was it as simple as revenge?

He captured her gaze again. "Promise me you will be careful."

Her lips tilted. "I will be as careful as I am able." She cupped his cheek before he could reiterate his warning, her soft touch reminding him of their kiss. "You're the one trapped in a camp with a contaminated food or water supply. I don't give my heart lightly, Mr. Reinhold. Never have. You'd better plan to stay on this side of eternity for a good many years."

He covered her hand, sandwiching it against his cheek. "I have your heart, Jessica Ross?"

"From what I can tell, August, my heart went right along with that kiss. There's no going back. I'm either all in, or nothing."

"I love all of you. Every single freckle on your face and glint in your eyes."

"And every stubborn streak?"

"All twenty-seven of them."

She laughed, the sound reverberating through him, deeper and sweeter with each repetition. Her finger traced his bottom lip, her brow furrowing. "I'll be careful if you will." The vulnerability in her look, the break in her strength to entreat him, hollowed out his chest with a need to embrace her. A need he couldn't fulfill. "Please, be careful."

Chapter Twenty-Two

"I hate leaving you like this." Catherine stilled her movements from packing her trunk, her coral walking suit an elegant fit on her delicate frame. "Not when David and Alexander could help tend the sickness."

Jess forced her smile, handing Catherine another garment to place in the trunk and refusing to give way to her grief over their departure. "You've already stayed almost a week beyond what you'd planned. I'd rather you get home before this influenza strikes and you're caught in the throes of it."

"It's a growing concern everywhere, Jess. England too." She sighed and sank down on the bed, tickling Faith's bare feet which she'd kicked free from her wrappings. "It's in these times that we must trust God for His plan and His goodness."

"Even when His goodness isn't what we would choose?" Jess shook her head and offered a weak laugh, nailing that revelation once against to the rim of her heart.

"*Especially* when it isn't what we would choose."

Addie stood from her toys on the floor and toddled over to join the conversation, her dark locks pinned in adorable braids. She held out her ragged doll, knitted together by Granny's loving hands. "Rock baby, Mama?"

Catherine took the threadbare doll, fashioned of feed sack cloth and lots of love, and nestled it in the crook of her arm. "High praise indeed for her to share this keepsake." Catherine shot a crooked grin to Jess. "We've bought a rocking horse, a china doll, and an elaborate doll house, but this baby doll and her dime store building blocks are her favorites."

"Goes to show you that some of the simplest pleasures are the best." And the thought spun alive a kiss she'd carved deep into her mind and longed to replicate with a little added fervor.

"Aha." Catherine's voice pierced into the tantalizing daydream.

Jess slanted her attention to her sister-in-law, a rabbit caught in a sapphire trap edged with a grin. "I know that dazed expression."

Jess could attempt to deny whatever Catherine thought she knew, but her sister-in-law's romantic experience topped Jess' slim, newspaper-sized knowledge with a healthy three-volume novel. "And what expression is that?"

Catherine's eyes narrowed, sifting over Jessica's expression like a blade in search of a weakness. "The afterglow of a romantic interchange, I do believe."

Heat rushed to Jessica's face and she focused her attention on Faith.

"Oh, how delightful. What sort? Words or something a bit... nicer?"

Jessica twinged and cleared her throat, refusing to look up. Surely Catherine couldn't read her thoughts.

"Ah, nicer, I see."

Jess stared up at her. "How do you *do* that?"

Catherine's pixie grin spread to full proportions. "Years of well-honed skill, sweet sister. Was it a kiss?"

Jess refused to look away and add flame to Catherine's mind-reading skills.

"It was." She clapped her hands together. "Oh, this is a good story. And what did you think?"

If Jessica's cheeks grew any hotter, every freckle on her face would instantly pop into the air. "What did I think?"

Catherine's eyes widened. "Of course. You did think something about it, didn't you?"

Jess mouth dropped, unhinged. She thought she'd learned the overt ways of her sister-in-law, but even with Jessica's forceful personality and independence, she couldn't quite combat this conversation. "I... I think it's my particular business."

"I'm so glad it was a nice kiss. My first kiss was only memorable because of how perfectly dreadful it was."

Well, Jessica's first kiss was dreadful, but it was also unwanted and forced. Her kiss with August awakened a longing for another sampling, a desire to share in such an intimate trust, a sudden relinquishing of her fear into his steady hands.

Catherine leaned closer. "When they're with the man you love, they become sweeter, more endearing." Her brow sloped with a coy twist of her lips. "And longer." She sighed and placed her palm over her heart. "Oh, I adore kissing your brother."

"That is delightful to hear." David marched into the room, sweeping Addie up from the floor and nuzzling her neck. He tossed Catherine a grin from over Addie's shoulder. "I assure you, my dear, the feeling is mutual."

Jess stood, waving her hands in the air to end the conversation. "I believe this conversation has delved into territory no sister should endure." She took Faith into her arms and walked to David. "I'm leaving the room before demonstrations begin."

David laughed.

"You're in trouble, Jessica dear." Catherine's voice stopped Jessica at the door. "One kiss from the man of your heart and you're going to spend hours contemplating the next one. Lovely contemplations, of course."

David caught her on the way out of the room. "He's a good man, Jess." He leaned to kiss her cheek. "And a lucky one."

"You're speaking as if we're marrying next week."

David laughed. "Jess, I've known you your entire life. Once you've set your mind to something, there's no going back. And I'm fairly certain you've met your match in both determination and perseverance."

"David and I are strong advocates for quick weddings, aren't we, darling?" Catherine stood and began packing more clothes into the trunk. "Those memories I had with him before he went to the Front? Those beautiful letters?" She paused in her packing to smile off into the distance. "What bliss."

"You'd better leave the room, Jessica." David nudged her out into the hallway, setting Addie down onto the floor. "Would you mind terribly taking Addie down to Granny for a few minutes? I think my wife and I need our own private conversation about kissing." His brows wiggled. "It won't take long."

Jess stared at the closed door, Catherine's laughter melting into silence on the other side, and Addie stared up at her with those bright, blue eyes.

"Come, Addie." Jess offered her hand. "I have a funny feeling your parents kissing conversation is going to take longer than a few minutes. Let's go see if Granny has any apple fritters left over. I'm suddenly hungry for a substantial distraction."

―

Another mournful sound of the death drums accompanied the procession from the gates of the camp. August rubbed his weary head. Only one week since the first diagnosis, and over one hundred men showed symptoms of typhoid fever.

This new development brought a grim reality to the camp's situation. Lt. Col. Ames was not happy in the least. All of his plans to start removing internees met with a disappointing wire from the Surgeon General that no men could be moved at present, to Oglethorpe or anywhere else.

August had become Captain Robinson's, the camp doctor, as well as town doctors, Carter and Peck's, right hand man, interpreting German and providing medical support as needed. Even dressing some of his deceased comrades for burial became a part of his routine.

Jessica visited every afternoon, meeting him at the fence and encouraging him. But each visit intensified the longing to hold her in his arms and wipe the worry from her brow.

As the hollow sound of the drums disappeared down Main Street toward Oddfellow's graveyard, August joined some of his healthy comrades on the trek back to the Inn. Though Lt. Col. Ames' men had replaced most of the civilian guard, about twenty-five remained, including Cliff, and Ruser had issued a mysterious call for both civilian guard and some trusted internees to meet with him and Ames, no doubt to discuss the ongoing investigation.

Rumors swirled around town and even made it into the papers that he and his fellow countryman employed this self-inflicted wound to keep from going to Oglethorpe, and though no one in the camp wished to be associated with true prisoners of war, the reports were false. After watching the agonizing death of two men from the disease, no one would bring such torment on their own. Not for their countrymen. He tossed a look over his shoulder through the wire fence. But perhaps for their enemies.

The men gathered in one of the large meeting rooms in the luxurious inn, where both Ruser and Ames stood at the head. They cut a striking contrast, yet were similar—Ruser with the snowy mane of age and Ames, taller and younger, but both carrying the readied attention and honor of veteran military as well a mutual respect, which August wished resounded beyond the reaches of the camp to any disgruntled—or worse, vengeance-seeking—men.

"You are each aware of the gravity of our current situation," Ames began, his deep voice booming through the room with the authority in his stance. "Captain Robinson and both Drs. Carter and Peck have worked tirelessly to treat the now one hundred and fifty-nine cases of typhoid without targeting any traitor within our gates. Since the water supply for the camp derives from various locations, we've decided to investigate outside the camp for a cause."

He turned to Ruser. "Commodore Ruser and I have agreed that a more covert attempt to capture the culprits is necessary."

"Dr. Peck has informed me that typhoid takes one to two weeks from contamination to the evidence of symptoms." Ruser surveyed the room with his steely gaze. "If this situation was created by an outside force and not from natural contamination of the overcrowded conditions here, the individuals not only devised their scheme over three weeks ago, but could very well be continuing to contaminate despite our efforts with chlorine."

"We have called you together to begin a night watch. Both Commodore and I have selected men on the basis of your virtues, knowledge of the terrain, and utmost discretion." Ames braided his hands behind his back and nodded toward them. "Each of you will be given a six-hour post to watch the water supply systems surrounding the camp. You are to remain in the shadows in the hopes that whoever, if anyone, is responsible for this gross violation, will be apprehended."

"You will be placed in pairs. Lt. Luther has the schedule which begins this evening." Ruser's expression softened. "May this provide a quick solution to this wasteful disability and loss of good men."

They were dismissed and gathered the schedule.

"Our first night watch is tomorrow. "Cliff came to August's side. "They've paired us together."

"No surprise." Cliff's friendship chased the film of frustration to the shadows temporarily, unearthing August's humor. "They need one for smarts and one with the freedom to carry firearms."

Cliff's grin slipped into a frown. "How's that for gratitude? I was just devising a plan to get you and my cousin alone together, but I think I'll change my mind."

August stopped Cliff, searching his face, the words like a ray of sunshine into his daily service with the sick. "Together?"

"I can tell she could use some cheering up since the Rosses left. Besides, people are starting to talk, as often as she sneaks to the fence to see you."

"She's been discrete."

"It's a small town, August." Cliff shook his head, as if the answer alone explained everything. "Which means we'll have to be particularly sneaky to make my plan work."

August held his breath, a smile readied for release if this strategy became a possibility. "You can accomplish this?"

"You wouldn't have much time, but I know what it's like to long to be with someone you love." His expression softened with shared grief and understanding. "Even if it's short."

"I will take any moment. Anything."

"I know. Which means you're going to have to do exactly what I say or they'll ship you off to Oglethorpe on the first train."

"Jess, I'm so glad I found you."

Jessica looked away from Amy as they both opened a new shipment of medicines. Cliff bustled through the clinic door, removing his hat as he came. Her pulse startled into a rabbit run.

"Is everyone well?"

He hesitated and tagged on a smile for minimal reassurance to her frantic heart. Each day brought more victims of typhoid. Each day, the drums alerted the town to another procession from the camp to the graveyard, and each day, she prayed God wouldn't let those drums beat for August.

"Yes, all well, except Mr. Donaldson up at the train depot."

Jess reached to until her apron. "Mr. Donaldson? Is his cough still bothering him?"

Cliff's dark brows rose. "Yes, that's it. And he was wondering if you might come have another check of his lungs."

Jess examined her cousin. Everything from the tilt of his smile to the gleam in his eyes pointed to some act of mischief in disguise. "Hmm, let me gather my stethoscope and I'll be right along."

He nodded and stepped out onto the porch.

Jess exchanged a glance with Amy. "He's a horrible liar."

Amy laughed. "That ain't a bad thing, Miss Jesse. I'd take a bad liar over a good one any day. Keeps back a heap of hardship."

With Amy's painful background and Jess' experiences with a German spy, she certainly agreed. "True, and more often than not, Mr. Carter's mischief is in good humor."

"Well, go on and see what it's about. We're all in need of some good humor around here." Amy nodded toward the boxes. "I can put these away for you to check when you come back."

Jess shot the young girl a smile. She'd been nothing but delightful since her apprenticeship started, and the school proved a wonderful companion for learning, allowing her to read books on medicine as well as the classics for papers and reports. Watching the girl bloom, seeing her grow beyond the stigma of her past, fed Jess' lifelong fight to prove women's dreams held as much value as any man's.

But she'd also learned the value of good men. From the men in her family to August Reinhold, although his attributes took on a very different gleam than those of her kin. No wonder the slang word for courting was 'sparkin' because his touch certainly ignited all sorts of interesting thoughts and desires inside her. What would it be like to have the freedom to kiss him at will, as David and Catherine clearly enjoyed? The idea spread her mind beyond any imaginings and inspired a deepening fragrance of hope in her inexperienced heart.

She met Cliff on the porch and walked in step with him. "How is everyone in the camp?"

"By everyone, I suppose you mean August?"

She slit him a glare. "I meant everyone. It just so happens I have a personal interest in one over the others."

"It's getting worse rather than better. Fifty more reported cases within the last three days."

Jess winced. This outbreak rivaled news she'd read of the growing Spanish Influenza epidemic. Fast, pervasive, and deadly. "And once it starts, we've no way of knowing how long it will last and how many it will take."

"It adds a great deal of gravity to the preciousness of life."

"And seizing opportunities." She stared at him until her vision blurred, then she looked ahead to the approaching depot, searching for some levity. "Which brings me to a rather redundant conversation, cousin."

He raised a palm to stop her well-honed argument. "I know."

"She's waiting to be swept off her feet, Cliff. You must know she's been in love with you for months."

He pulled at the collar of his shirt and added a brisker step to his walk. "Point made. And... and I reckon I need to do something about that."

"Like take your own advice?" She rebuffed his scowl with a saccharine smile. "One good nudge deserves another."

His furrowed brow cleared as they took the steps to the platform. He paused at the top and studied her, his hazel eyes pinning her with their intensity. "You and David are the only siblings I've ever known. You both have been through so much, and I want to see you happy." His grin spread as he scanned the platform. "I suppose you want the same for me."

"We each need someone who is willing to push us beyond our stubbornness, Cliff. It's a Carter family trait."

He chuckled and offered his arm. She slid hers through the crook of his elbow and walked with him. Instead of going inside the station, as she'd expected, Cliff diverted their path around the side of the depot, in the shadow of the tall holly bushes framing the mustard-yellow building on either side toward a lean-to with a door barely visible though the leafy frame.

"What are you doing?"

He swung open the storage closet door and pushed her inside. "Providing one little way to make two of my favorite people happier today."

"What—" He slammed the door on her question. As soon as she drummed down the door to this closet, she planned to skin Cliff Carter for his foolish prank. Some men never grew up.

"Mause?"

She froze and turned, her eyes adjusting to the dim daylight filtering through the slits in the makeshift closet. Her breath congealed into the tiniest gasp. August's silhouette materialized from the darkest corner of the space.

He approached, bringing with him a resounding wave of heat and the warm scent of pine. His gaze penetrated the shadowy film around her, drawing her closer, leaving her breathless.

His lips curved in a playful twist that somehow hit her directly in the pulse, sending a hum of memory over her skin from their first kiss. She'd wanted a second try for over a week, and his mouth looked so inviting. In fact, there wasn't a single piece of him that didn't appeal to her, from the rebellious curl over his forehead to the toe of his shoe that edged another step nearer. Her body melted toward him, responding to his wordless plea.

"What... what are you doing here?"

The hooded stare he gave her only enticed her rather carnal train of thought. Heat scorched the insides of her chest and throat, her gaze dropping once again to his lips as if they might be the only remedy for her internal inferno.

"Cliff had mercy on me." His palm slipped from her cheek and around to cradle the back of her head, tugging her forward. "My heart aches for you."

Her sharp intake of breath split the silence and quivered out on a tremor of air. The warmth of his touch teamed with the smolder in his eyes shot a delicious fire-trail over her skin, teasing every nerve fiber to life. She inhaled his pine scent mixed with soap.

"Yes.' Her hand slid up the front of his shirt, fisting the cloth to bridge the inch between their lips. His touch brought her to life, wiping away the old stains of a malignant kiss with a delicious taste of something infinitely more exquisite.

His mouth moved over hers, firm but pliant, almost as if he wished to massage her wounded spirit alive. It worked with powerful clarity, sending a tingle rushing through her and urging her deeper into his sweet embrace. She slid her palms up to his face, new, hot tears making another vibrant course down her cheeks, but she couldn't help them. This was tenderness, passion, and healing all wrapped in an emotionally charged physical connection.

And she let go of her heart to his hands, no matter what the future wrought.

She'd starved her heart long enough and now, she drank in this sweet abundance, allowing the love he'd offered for months to pour over her stained memories and tangled assumptions with a healing flood.

He encouraged her the freedom of exploration, pulling back from his mouth only to taste again and again with added intensity. No wonder David and Catherine found such pleasure in the practice. What divine gift was this? The very act begged for one minute longer. One more taste.

Her fingers entwined in his hair and she grinned against his lips. "Your hair is damp."

Was that her voice? Breathless in the dark?

His hand slid down the side of her neck as he murmured into her hair. "I bathed before we met to scald away any trace of the illness on my skin." His lips warmed her jaw. "I would not have you sick, but I could not stay away."

She moved to pull her braid to cover her disfigured ear, but he caught her fingers in his. "Do not despise your scars, Mause." The warmth of his breath doused the skin at the juncture of her earlobe and neckline, just before his lips touched the spot. "Your scars? My scars?" His lips moved the length of her mangled skin until his breath disappeared beneath her blouse at the base of her neck. "They have brought us to this place. To each other." He drew back, his palms framing her face and gaze so tender, she had no response except to stare back in wonder. "I will not despise them."

He brought his forehead to touch hers and she traced the sharp contours of his cheek with her fingers. "This is disastrous, you know?"

"I find it rather perfect," came his quick reply.

She kissed his smile and took her time memorizing his face. "I don't know how I'll go back to having a fence between us every day. Not after... this."

"I have an idea." He reached into his shirt pocket and drew out a paper tied with twine. "It is a poor compromise in comparison to your kiss, but perhaps it will provide some solace and comfort in the separation we must bear?"

Would she ever understand his thoughtfulness? His love overwhelmed her in senses, heart, and soul. She'd done nothing to deserve such pure affections, but here August was, loving her in an immeasurable, incomparable way.

"Letters?" She took his offering and slipped it into the pocket of her skirt.

"I have many I've written to you but never given."

"You wrote me letters you never sent?"

He nodded, his thumb smoothing over her chin. "My heart was full of you. I had to find relief in some way. And you were not ready for my letters."

"You... you are just wonderful, aren't you?" She shook her head, unable to pull any more words from her overflowing emotions. She sighed into him, wrapping her arms around him and hugging him close, wordlessly attempting to add depth to her admission. "Can't we stay here forever, away from everything outside?"

He rested his cheek against her hair and surrounded her with his embrace. She closed her eyes, reveling in the cocoon of his arms and resting in this new yet unmatched love. She knew the answer to her question. Others depended on both of them, but here, nestled in the sweet rest and incandescent beauty of his embrace, her restless heart found a home.

The outside world swelled with uncertainty and fear.

A knock at the door invaded their retreat, dousing the moment. Jess gripped August closer and found his lips again, determined to keep his taste, his touch, fastened within her memory for the unpredictable weeks ahead.

August drew back first, honorable man that he was, and pressed his lips to her forehead in gentle benediction. "You have my heart, Mause. It is yours, no matter what happens beyond today or tomorrow. I will not seek it back."

She buried her face into his neck, breathing in the scent of his skin. "It's a fair trade. One heart for another."

He cupped her face and touched his lips to hers in a gentle promise. "A very good trade."

Another knock sounded from the door. "He told me he would give me three knocks for warning before he reached in to drag you out."

She pressed her good ear against his chest, listening to his rumbling voice and failing to tame her smile. "I wouldn't tell him, of course, but he's a secret romantic." Jess looked up, keeping her arms around his sturdy frame. "Do you think he'll ever work up the courage to tell your sister how he feels?"

August's delicious lips tilted. "He has to. He lost the wager twice now." His eyebrow peaked. "If we count every kiss, then he is in immeasurable debt."

She chuckled. "The wager?"

August's spun a loose strand of her hair through his fingers. "He couldn't believe your heart would ever soften to me, so he made the wager that the day you kiss me, is the day—"

"He would admit his feelings to Anna?" Jess gave his arm a gentle slap. "How dare you use me in a wager, August Reinhold?"

"It was a high-stakes bargain. Lots of soft hearts but hard heads in the gamble."

"And how were you so certain you'd win?"

He searched her face with those probing eyes of his, his smile tipping in his adorable heart-fluttering way. "I was hopeful."

"Hope is a good thing, I hear."

"Yes, a very good thing."

A third knock sounded and Jess loosened her grasp, taking his lead. She stepped back and touched his face. "Keep safe, my dear alien."

He laughed at the endearment and caught her hand on his cheek, bringing her palm to his lips. "Alien is better than Mause, yes?"

"They're both equally detestable and perfect, don't you think?"

"Perfect, yes." He squeezed her fingers as the gap between then distanced. "You keep safe, and those children."

She nodded, relinquishing her hold on his hand. Emotions scratched at her words, her heart. She wouldn't succumb to them.

"I will do my best, with God's help." She pinched the tears back with a grin. "And, my dear alien, you're not allowed to die, you understand?"

"I'm not?" His quick response edged with humor.

"No. I've not beaten you at badminton yet."

She pushed open the door, followed by his laughter, a sound she hoped to hear for a very long time to come.

Chapter Twenty Three

August 9, 1918

My dear Jessica,

I claim you as mine on this paper, so it must be the truth. Isn't that so? Your sweet lips have sealed my fate forever. I can go nowhere else for my heart. It is caught and I will not take it back, my Mause. No matter if a fence or an ocean separates us, my heart is yours to do with as you will.

If I attempted to bottle these emotions, I might internally explode, so I pour out my thoughts on this page and cloak it with enough sentimentality and romantic verbiage to make you laugh, at the least, and speak to your heart, at best. Do you like?

Our meeting did not start as I'd hoped. Your pain bound you to caution and suspicion, but blessed be to God that hope and perseverance sought to cover your wounds with this love I wished to offer you. Now, my feelings have only intensified at your glorious reciprocity. It is much more enjoyable to participate in a romance when the partner responds with similar enthusiasm. In fact, your participation proved so potent, I see no way out of my current situation than to enforce your immediate promise to marry me. Yes, that will do.

Would you end my misery? You alone are the nurse who can bring about the correct solution for my malady, Mause.

Your cousin says that men do not speak of such romantic nonsense, but I cannot cease. My heart overflows. I write of love and hopes and futures, because you belong with me in each. Through your grandparents' letters, I became enamored with your strength, resilience, and devotion to your family, and have only become more devoted in my admiration since knowing you in flesh and breath.

Now that I have touched you, kissed you, and felt your passions burn for me, I am amazed at God's perfection in this glorious pairing. Oh, for you to turn that devotion to me? There are not enough pens, nor sufficient ink, nein, not even words, to express my gratitude to the Almighty for this chance to win your heart. You are, to me, vibrancy, truth, and courage.

I dreamed with caution before. I dream with purpose and steady hope now, because you care for me. Know this. I love you as you are and as you will become.

Yours,
The Alien

"Have you talked to her yet?" August's whisper sliced into the darkness of the cloudy night. Slips of moonlight filtered through charcoal clouds leaving a tapered gray hue against the countryside and an occasional glistening on the murky waters of the French Broad.

Cliff pinned his lips so tight they turned white enough for August to make out in the shadowed evening.

"You don't like her?"

Cliff sliced him a glare. "Of course I like her."

"Then why do you wait? I don't understand this."

Cliff sighed back against the tree behind which he hid from someone's approach. "It's not so easy to trust your heart again after you've helplessly watched someone you love ripped from your arms."

"So it is better to keep your arms empty and your heart lonely?"

Cliff leaned his head back against the tree. "It's getting harder each day. Anna Fischer is the type of woman who doesn't go unnoticed, that's for sure."

"Which is why you should make your intentions known, friend. Would you rather her be ripped from your arms by another man?"

Cliff sat up straighter. "What other man?"

Ah, an idea formed with the pinch of a smile. "Who is that man with the ginger hair? I can't—"

"Joel Martin?" Cliff leaned closer, his finger jabbing the air. "He's a bootlegger and bum. There's no way he'd have patience with sweet Sylvie, let alone be a good example for her."

August shrugged, as if the notion hadn't occurred to him. This game provided a perfect distraction for passing the long night and hopefully spurred his reluctant friend into action. He'd seen the longing looks Cliff sent to his sister. The humorous fumbling about in her presence. The protectiveness and gentleness.

"That pharmacist's assistant, what was his name?"

"Reed Parker?" Cliff nearly stood to his feel for that one. "He's outlived two wives and courted half the county. Don't you care about your sister's life at all?"

"I know she's lonely for a man to love her." August stared up at the night sky, searching for some more inspiration. "She's not getting younger, you know. Maybe her hair is fading too."

"You need to get your eyes checked, August. Her hair is fine. Just fine." Then his friend paused. "Oh, I see what you're doing." He released a quiet laugh. "Clever, Reinhold. Real clever."

"And it proved the point, yes? Do not be a coward, Cliff. Life is short. Do you not see it all around you?" August shook his fist toward Cliff. "Take it. Live it. Do you regret loving your wife even though you have hurt from her loss?"

Cliff's silence gave a resounding answer.

"You are my friend. She is my sister. I know your hearts would find homes with each other."

"Men don't talk like that, August. You're always saying things men might think, but they don't say."

"Then perhaps—" A murmur of voices wafted on the breeze from the river.

August drew to immediate attention behind his own tree, using the nearby bush as camouflage to peer from his hiding spot. Two figures appeared from the direction of the repaired bridge, each moving with cautious steps in and out of the shadows.

The taller of the two carried something in his hand. A pail, perhaps.

Cliff slid to his feet, keeping his body behind the tree, so August followed suit. The men's voices remained too low to make out words, but the cadence of one perked August's memory. He knew the voice, but couldn't place the face, the name. Was it Jasper's without the faux English accent?

Cliff motioned for August to get ready. August knew how to fight, and his schoolboy skills had only improved during his few months aboard the *Vanderland*, but Cliff had brought the pistol as a precaution.

The shorter man walked to the well and began to push at the large metal lid while the taller one waited, shifting his attention from the camp to the river behind him, their faces shrouded in some sort of black cloth. Just as the metal lid began to screech loose, Cliff gave the signal.

They both rushed forward, one after each figure. August tackled the startled man from behind, knocking him to the ground. The man's elbow jabbed into August's ribs, sending blinding pain shooting through his middle, but he secured his hold, pinning the man's face into the ground. A strong scent of whisky accompanied the man's groan and the faintest hint of moonlight gleamed like a spotlight on his culprit, but the handkerchief covering the bottom half of the man's face kept his identity uncertain. Dark eyes. Lighter hair.

An explosion of sound blasted from August's left. The other struggling pair split as one stumbled to his feet and the other slumped to the ground. The dark figure ran toward the bridge. Heat fled from August's body.

Cliff.

August released his hold and ran to Cliff's side as the other man limped along after his cohort. The pale moonlight glinted off of Cliff's distorted and pale features.

"Cliff."

"My chest. I think." His words crimped with pain. "Get me to my uncle."

The sound of a motor and flash of car headlamps drew Jess' attention to the window. Lantern light illuminated her clock. Three a.m. It had to be a medical emergency. She'd just gotten Faith back to sleep after her feeding, so it only took seconds for her to grab her robe and race down the stairs. She gave 'the knock' on her grandfather's door as she passed. Years of the routine, living among doctors, had its economy.

She lit a lantern at the end of the stairs and completed the path to the front door just as a frantic knock resounded through the sleeping house. Her breath caught as August's face materialized at the door in her lamplight. She'd spent Faith's feeding time rereading his exquisite letter, so filled with *him*. Usually, such effusion of romance left her squirming in discomfort, but from him? She drank in the beautiful combination of wit and tenderness, her own little secret delight.

"August?" His gaze searched hers and her pulse skittered into a gallop. "What is it?"

"Cliff has been shot."

Her mind filtered through the information, attempting to consume this impossibility. Cliff? Shot? But the faces of the other men confirmed August's concern, and as they moved the body through the door and she saw her cousin's pale face, her body kicked into motion.

"Follow me to the dining room." She rushed ahead and grabbed the cloth her grandfather kept in the sideboard for such occasions as this, separating her heart from her trembling emotions as she worked. *Focus on the task at hand, not Cliff's pallor.*

She spread the sheet, stained with its previous uses, over the table. "Place him here." Her attention focused on August.

The men lumbered forward, sliding Cliff's lifeless body onto the table. He lay too quiet. Too still. Grandfather rushed into the room, his robe hanging loose around his striped pajamas, and made a quick assessment of the surroundings. "What happened?"

"We were on watch for someone who might try to contaminate the water supply," August explained.

"Scissors," Grandpa ordered and Jess complied immediately, grimacing at the wide-spread stain of blood over the top left portion of Cliff's shirt. The cloth slid apart.

"A gunshot wound?" Grandfather looked at her, and they both turned to August.

"Cliff and I were keeping guard on the south well when two men came, their faces hidden behind cloth. There was a struggle in the darkness, and Cliff was shot."

Jess applied pressure to the wound as her father pulled supplies from the closet in the next room. Cliff had lost a lot of blood and continued to lose more from where the bullet lodged in his shoulder. They needed to perform surgery. Jess tensed. And even then, with so much loss, the prognosis looked grim.

Grandfather returned with an unexpected array of tubing and containers. "A blood transfusion?"

"The trip here on the bumpy road encouraged more blood loss, and we still have surgery to do to remove the bullet." He pushed the items on the sideboard to make room for the medical equipment. "It's not an option."

"We don't have Cliff's blood type and we've already used all of the preserved blood from the clinic."

"We will not lose another person in our family if we can help it." The determination in his stare silenced her and evoked a sudden clarity. Her grandfather's grief, swathed with as much pain as hers, buried beneath faith's strength and experience's temperance, but was still there, held within the tension of his jaw.

"What must I do?"

August's voice pierced the conversation and Jessica pinched her eyes closed before facing him. August. Of course. He was the anonymous and universal blood donor.

"Jake and Martin," Grandfather addressed the other guards instead of answering. "Go back to the camp and tell your commander that August is required to stay. He will be under my care. You understand?"

"Commander Ames won't like—"

"It is not up for discussion. I will speak to the commander myself tomorrow, but for now, August is staying here."

Jake backed down, the local boy well aware of the futility in his argument at the out-of-character display in the doctor's tone. He nodded and left the house with Martin at his heels.

"We need three people to complete a direct line transfusion, Grandpa. This will take hours, and Granny's going to have to watch after the children." Jess shook her head, keeping her hands pressed tight against Cliff's back. "We don't have time to get Amy."

"Anna could help," August offered, moving toward the door.

Does she faint at the sight of blood?" Grandpa waved toward Granny as she emerged from the kitchen with a bowl of hot water. "We'll need two cots on the floor—"

"No," August answered. "She has some experience. She took care of our mother during her illness."

"Good."

"Bring Sylvie to my bed so she'll be close if she needs something."

August looked from Jess to Cliff and then ran from the house.

Jess' stomach twisted in knots. Cliff lay unresponsive and August offered his blood, a procedure with its own myriad of risks. Why did she feel as if she was constantly giving up the people she loved to the hand of God?

My love is strong. Sufficient.

Her threadbare faith gripped the promise with both fists. There was nothing else she could do but trust His love. Trust His care. She was powerless to exact any change beyond her medical skills. Only God could manage the intricacies of the future. She had to let go of one more thing... again.

"Help me turn him over so we can extract the bullet." Grandpa gestured toward Cliff, and though cumbersome, they succeeded in getting him turned as gently as possible. "You've had more experience with bullets than I have. I want you to remove it while I prep for the transfusion."

Jess nodded, examining the wound. "It's lodged in his scapula or upper rib, I think. Thank God the bone stopped the bullet from tearing through his lung."

"Granny, assist Jess in clearing the wound site as much as possible so her field of vision stays clear."

They continued in silence.

August entered the house with Sylvie in his arms and marched up the steps without stopping. Anna approached the table, taking in Cliff's body, blood-soaked and still. "Oh, Cliff," she gasped and then steadied her gaze on them. "How may I help?"

Grandpa began explaining the procedure while Jessica drew the bullet from the wound, whispering a quick prayer of gratitude for the speed of removal. She'd honed that particular talent during her time at the Front, proving apt in quick bullet extraction with the least damage.

August reentered the room, rolling up his sleeves as he approached. "What must I do?"

"Once Jessica finishes Cliff's sutures, we will move him to the rolling cot Granny's gone to fetch from the back room." Grandpa moved from one task to another, preparing for the procedure. "You'll lay on the table here. If all goes as planned, we should be able to assist you to a bed within a few hours. Cliff will need to remain stationary for as long as possible."

"The procedure is different than drawing blood for the vials," Jessica added, looking up from her work. "Longer. More dangerous. You'll be placed under anesthesia."

August set about helping Granny and Anna prepare the cot to Grandpa's specifications as Jess finalized the stitching. With careful movements, they all worked to transfer Cliff to the cot and Anna packed a quilt around his body to ward of the chill of shock. His face held an ashen color, the kind to place Jess' nerves on edge with pinpricks of uncertainty. She'd seen worse. Helped save worse. But watching her strong, vibrant cousin lying motionless and frail resurrected visions of her brother's injuries, of her nursing friend who died in Jess' arms after an explosion in their Clearing Station. *Not another, Lord, please.*

"We're ready," Grandpa said.

Jess approached August. "Are you certain about this?"

Those eyes, the unfathomable depths of emotion, searched her face. "Yes."

"A direct blood transfusion brings a risk of infection. You understand the choice you're making?"

The firm press of his lips softened into the gentlest smile. "Yes, Mause, but he is my friend. And he is your family. There is no choice."

Everything fell away except this beautiful man before her, his strength, and his breathtaking nobility. She rocked up on her tiptoes and pressed her lips to his, staking her claim for everyone to witness. *Love?* Yes.

His lips clung to hers, prolonging the embrace for a second longer, and then, as quickly, they drew apart.

She kept her gaze on his but said to Grandpa. "We're ready."

Anna and Granny placed a clean cloth over the table and added a pillow for comfort.

"Lie down, August." Her grandfather gestured toward the table and handed Jessica two masks with various tubing and tanks. Ether and chloroform. Had nitrous oxide-oxygen made it to her remote little town yet? David used it at his hospital, but the apparatus was a newly developed sort. She locked it in her mind to save for the Connell anesthetic apparatus for Grandfather's future use. A worthwhile purchase.

"I'll administer the morphine in preparation, but we can't wait the half-hour for full effect. We haven't the time."

Jess nodded and prepared the masks and canisters for work, replacing this aching agitation with the cold ream of logic.

"Why do you give them morphine?" Anna asked, her voice shaking with a slight tremor.

She'd tightened her expression, pale-faced but strong. Jess offered a comforting smile. "We only administer a small dose. It helps the men rest and reduces the amount of secretions in their body, particularly their mouths." She searched for a clearer explanation to clarify her confusion. "To keep them from coughing." *Among other things, but those particulars need not be voiced.*

"And that?" Anna pointed to the paraphernalia in Jess hands. "Does it help with this transfusion?"

"In a way." Jess moved quickly over the task of attaching the chloroform mask and then the one for the ether canister. "It relaxes the body for the procedure and helps take away some of the sting."

Anna drew in a deep breath, her gaze bouncing from Cliff to August. "And he will be well?"

Jess swallowed. August was strong and healthy. So was Cliff. Both these were truths to bind her worries with optimism. *God, please keep them safe.* "There are always risks, Anna, but August should be fine." Her gaze dropped to her cousin. "For Cliff, only time and prayer will tell."

Jess pivoted from the sideboard, the first mask in hand. Her gaze glided over the man lying patiently before her, the unlikely suitor who'd capture her entire heart.

"I'm going to place this first mask above your nose and I want you to breathe normally, in and out."

"I have a hard time breathing normally when you are so near."

His gentle humor eased over her anxiety like the caress of his hand over hers, guiding the mask forward.

She lowered the mask into place, her gaze locking with his. Oh, the depths of those eyes, the tenderness burrowing deep beneath her cautious disposition and releasing a responsive reply. She leaned close and pressed a kiss to his forehead and then, as his eyelids began to droop, she slipped her mouth near his ear.

"I love you, August Reinhold."

Nausea woke August. He kept his body still in an attempt to keep the nausea from swelling into bile. His right arm ached and his thoughts puttered through a dreamy fog, sloshing to the surface for clarity. What happened to him?

He peeled open his thick eyelids. The nausea intensified so he closed them again until the feeling abated, and then he made another attempt. Dim light fingered through the room from one lantern, casting tall shadows on the pale walls.

His mind began to catch up with his surroundings. Cliff... shot... Dr. Carter... Jessica whispering into his muddled dream. A general heaviness weighed down his body, pressing him into the hard table. He tilted his head at a slow angle to keep the nausea calm, but the swell was worth the view.

Jessica sat in one of the high-back dining chairs in angelic sleep, her head angled to the right. Golden hair flowed from her loosened braid, billowing in erratic locks around her beautiful face. To see this sight each morning, nestled within his embrace? The thought sent the nausea to the very back of his mind, replaced by much more inviting distractions. It was her fault, really. She shouldn't have kissed him so ardently if she sought to keep his imagination under gentlemanly influence.

She stirred, waking as the legendary Sleeping Beauty. If only he'd had opportunity to kiss her awake. His grin perched. Ah, well, there was time for such opportunities. Her gaze, in all its dazzling emerald, fell upon him with a sleepy smile, encouraging his less than gentlemanly thoughts to resurrect with zeal.

"You're a beautiful mause."

Her smile spread into a quiet laugh and she stood to lean over him, her hair spilling toward him, begging for a touch. "I'll take that to mean you feel well enough?"

"I would feel better if you kissed me."

Even the dim lamplight failed to shadow the deepening color of her cheeks, but the sparkle in her eyes poured promise. She pushed back a handful of her golden hair and brought her lips to his, reviving his muscles with a fiery sting.

Her warm mouth blended through his blurry world, igniting his pulse and hands into motion. He forced one arm awake and slid his fingers across her cheek to bury into her loosened hair, cupping the base of her neck. Her lips parted in a gasp. He took advantage of the moment, moving the kiss into more intimate territory and exploring the richness in her response.

She drew back, her breath as shallow as his. "How was that?" Her question breathed out on raspy air, intimate and close.

He took his time, allowing his gaze to roam over her face framed by scattered gold. "Exceptional."

Her tantalizing lips slanted. "Well enough to play an early game of badminton?"

"You will have to spend many more kisses to reach that outcome, Mause, but I am not averse to it."

She swept a palm over his forehead, her gaze glossy. "I think your current weakness might be a providential device to secure our virtue, my sweet alien." One golden brow rose. "I can assure you, since your kiss, my mind's remained fully occupied with thoughts I'd never entertained... before you."

"May it be the last first kiss we ever experience?"

She slid him a sly smile, refusing to indulge in too much romantic talk. What she'd given him already exceeded his expectations.

His mind cleared by degrees and the nausea subsided to a dull hint. "What of Cliff?"

She covered August's hand with her own. "He's resting. Time will tell, but he's young and strong, both truths your sister seems to appreciate."

Jess added another pillow to his collection, elevating him to an almost sitting position. The nausea increased for a moment until he settled into the change. "Your family trait is stubbornness. My family trait is perseverance, yes?"

"Two sides of the same coin, I'd think."

He caught her face as she bent close to tuck the blanket around him. "Then your cousin and I are in very good hands."

She kept her gaze fastened on his. A sudden sheen of tears glimmered across her evergreen eyes. "I have too many games of badminton planned to let you die."

He rolled her a look of mock annoyance and shifted to become more comfortable on the hard table. "Competition over compassion, Miss Ross?"

"Yes." She bent close, adjusting the pillows as he stilled beneath her touch. "It is a much better distraction over the alternative, my dear Mr. Reinhold."

"And what is that?" He groaned from a sudden rush of weakness and fell back against the pillows.

"Being afraid you might not wake up."

Chapter Twenty Four

Grandpa left for the camp directly after breakfast with a secondary purpose of collecting Amy to assist with overnight care for the next two days. The first forty-eight hours remained crucial—not for August, who walked with assistance to the guest bedroom an hour after waking, but for Cliff. He'd not awakened yet, the ether and blood loss taking its toll with a heavier hand.

Jude and Sylvie kept each other company through the morning chores, taking the answers Jess gave them as to the reason for Cliff's injuries as only children can do. Simply, with a childlike trust that sent her into introspection. There was something to its beautiful simplicity. Hadn't Jesus even mentioned having faith as a child?

She'd never pondered on the meaning, but this new gift of motherhood changed her perspective many things. She loved Jude and Faith. With each passing day, this intricate bond deepened in her soul, weaving through her decisions and thoughts as naturally as breathing. Where had she stored this reserve protection and love before she knew them? Before she met August?

Her hand swept over his letter in her pocket. Nothing awakened her heart like his touch and his words. His love humbled and strengthened her. Somehow, it called her to simply trust, to believe, as the children so easily did.

August's love mirrored God's. Her inexpressible connection to these children reflected God's love for her. Air left her lungs in a whoosh as her shoulder collapsed forward as she pulled Faith nearer. A verse from her past surfaced.

You may have power to grasp how wide and long and high and deep is the love of Christ, and to know this love that surpasses knowledge – that you may be filled to the measure of the fullness of God.

How wide and long? How high and deep? If her love for these children or August seemed impossible to fit into words, how much greater did God love her?

She lowered a kiss to Faith's head and her blue eyes twinkled into a smile. Jess' heart squeezed at the sweetness. God loved her indescribably more? Even with the past of what happened to David or Cliff or herself? How could love and sorrow meet like this? How could war and devastation reconcile with this immense love?

Lord, help me trust you more.

August's face materialized in her mind, his eyes staring at her as she placed the chlorine mask over his handsome face. She'd sliced into his arms, leaving him sore, weakening his body, to provide hope for Cliff's life.

Her vision blurred as Faith's little fingers chased a loose strand of Jessica's hair.

All things work together for the good who love him and are called according to his purpose.

In this massive puzzle of life, she saw one piece and God held the entire finished portrait—the dark and light pieces, the sharp edged and the smooth. Each fitted together, relying on one other to complete his work of art. The plan.

Faith, Jude, August, David, Catherine... all of them, each detail, each wound, each joy, were all strategically placed to design something beautiful in His plans. Something for His glory and for her ultimate good. How? Her mind fought to understand but lacked the ability.

Faith.

Even the deathbed name Eliza bestowed on her precious daughter rose to touch Jessica's heart three months later. She fitted the cooing bundle in the crook of her arm and crossed the hallway, careful to keep her steps quiet as she approached August's door. She'd changed Cliff's bandages before moving upstairs to catch a few hours of sleep before Faith woke for feeding. *And I am holding him, child.*

She sighed out the twisted anxiety in her stomach and pushed the bedroom door open enough to peer inside. His smile greeted her.

"Ah, the very woman who held my thoughts." He pushed himself to sit taller. "And you've brought an added beauty with you?"

Oh, that man was too handsome for either of their good, but particularly hers. His shirt hung open to the third button, drawing her rebellious mind to ponder the feel of his chest. Scorching heat planted in each cheek and she lifted her eyes back to his, her smile tight. He'd caught her wayward attention, and his grin inched up on one side with enough mischief to send the heat in her cheeks coursing down through the rest of her body. *Heaven help her.*

"I have another argument for our speedy matrimony."

She pushed down a burning swallow and drew her wavering gaze back to his. At one point in her life, she'd boasted something akin to self-control, but since kissing August... that virtue appeared woefully absent.

"You're establishing quite the list, aren't you?"

He reached out for Faith and Jess relinquished her hold. "A logical argument for each of the rejections you're creating in your head."

She lifted her chin, feigning complete ignorance. "The fact that you're housed behind a fence on the way to being deported to a Georgian prison camp isn't enough?"

"Nein." He smiled down at Faith and her toothless grin responded with matching excitement. "Faith will agree with me. She needs a father."

He patted the bed at his side, but she sat on the edge at a little more distance. "I think I could raise her own my own."

His wounded look brought her an inch closer. "I would take care of you all. You know this, Mause."

She saw him then, as a father and husband. A gentle caregiver to little Faith. A noble example to Jude. And to her? Air thickened around her. Oh, her imagination conjured up all sorts of ways she wanted him to take care of her, and God was probably frowning at each and every one of them.

She cleared her throat and attempted to empty out her embarrassing daydreams. "I do."

His expression turned perfectly rascally. "You say those words very well."

She leaned closer, his eyes darkening into a delicious smolder. "I do?"

"I have many other reasons to marry you, Mause. Reasons I will share after you marry me for they are better shown than spoken."

Her bottom lip loosed and her throat released a tiny squeak of response.

"I have left your mutter speechless, little Spatz?" He pressed a kiss to Faith's nose. "Do you think she needs a kiss too?"

Her body responded to the invitation in his eyes, drawing closer of its own accord, meeting him inch to inch, move to move... touch to touch. His lips cooled hers, sliding over them in slow perusal. She closed her eyes, reveling in the grand mixture of familiarity and newness in his taste and his caress.

Faith's sweet coo brought their gentle embrace to a somewhat satisfied end. She sat back, returning her hands to her lap to nudge the crease of paper in her pocket.

"Oh, yes, I... I have something for you."

"I thought you already gave it to me?"

His faux innocent expression, with a touch of imp, released her grin again. "Well, then, I have another something for you, but I must warn you." She dug into her pocket, his letter to her mixed together with one she'd written. "I am better with facts and arguments, so keep that in mind."

He looked down at the proffered letter and unwound his finger from Faith's grasp. "You should read it to me."

"What?"

"My head is still foggy from the anesthesia. I think you should read it to me."

She pressed the letter into his hand. "No. You can read it when your head clears."

He lowered his lashes, nearly undoing her with the magnetizing appeal of his plea. "I will give you another kiss."

"You will give me another kiss no matter whether I read it or not," she fired back.

"You are right. I will." He nodded, placing the letter back in her palm. "But it will make Faith happy if you read it to me, for I will be able to keep holding her while you read."

Jess rolled her eyes at his ridiculous logic and attempted to ignore the embarrassing fire lighting in her face. Reading it to him? Exposing her heart aloud to the man? It had been difficult enough to place the words onto paper.

She scowled at him as she opened the note, but the fury bounced off his smile without leaving a mark. In fact, his grin only widened. *Insufferable man. Adorably insufferable man.*

"Well, I'll warn you now that I'm no writer. I'm horrible at expressing myself in words." She looked up at him. "Your letter? It... it was like poetry. Mine? Mine won't be."

"Maybe I like your kind of poetry best?"

With an exasperated sigh, she began.

August,

I have no flowery words to compare to your beautiful letter. Though I'm certain I appear to have many things to say, and much too quickly, when it comes to expressing my heart, I am incapable of finding words eloquent or powerful enough to capture the depths of my emotions. Your words, your touch, leave me incoherent but alive. Wordless but rich with feeling.

She refused to look up and gauge his reaction. In her years of nursing, she'd never known such vulnerability. Her hand shook the paper, but his came to wrap around the one she'd placed on the bed, enveloping her fear as much as her fingers.

"Your words seem perfect to me."

"You're hopelessly prejudiced."

"And thus I shall remain, for when you love someone, you ought to see them through such a veil, yes?"

Her shaking hand stilled and her breathing calmed. His love soothed with beautiful devotion.

Life is a constant journey of learning, if we let it educate us—and somehow, through the years, I had closed my head to the instruction of my heart. Your patient pursuit, gentleness, and endearing humor slid beneath the barrier of my hardened will and nurtured hope. I'd lost hope, you see. I'd allowed pain and bitterness to eclipse the knowledge of all I'd been given. I numbed my pain with unforgiveness, but you? You didn't allow me to remain paralyzed by my fears. You would not, despite my rejection and cold return. You shone like sun on a wintry world, and reminded it of coming spring.

Her voice faltered, the intensity pressing in on her chest and tears stealing her voice. He leaned to kiss her lips and then slipped the pages from her hands, dodging Faith's curious fingers.

I'd known love from my family—a mother's devotion, a father's fierce protection, and brother's camaraderie—but you? You touched my soul with fire. That is the only way I can write it. An immense warmth and light burst within my cold world at your kiss, your powerful care. I am wordless, awestruck, and filled with gratitude for God's goodness—a realization I'd refused to see for much too long.

I don't know how God will navigate this convoluted present and uncertain future of ours, but I trust His love and your heart.

Your Mause.

His pale eyes glistened with tears and he handed Faith back to her. Carefully, wordlessly, he folded the letter and placed it in his shirt pocket. He pressed his palm over it and captured her gaze with such intensity, she couldn't look away. "Here is where it will stay, my Mause. Your words near my heart."

She stood, her smile tucked within her embarrassment as she backed toward the door. "I will go and see about dinner." Her hand rested on the doorknob and she turned back to him, his smile following her the entire way. "And August?"

"Yes, Mause?"

"I'll marry you."

August stood, balancing himself against the armoire. Ever since Jess' declaration, he'd anticipated her return, but Mrs. Carter had brought dinner and during the next hour, the house fell into a quiet slumber. Except for him. Despite the weakness, he'd surged to life. She'd agreed to marry him. Surely his muddled mind had not mistaken it.

He pressed his palm against the letter over his chest, evidence that she'd been more than a dream. Then she must have said she'd marry him. He *had* to find her and certainly kiss her—if he could stand long enough to search through the house. Dinner helped restore some of his energy from his loss of blood, but as soon as he stood, the world spun. He dropped down into a chair and waited for the room to right itself before beginning again.

The hallway opened to three more doors. One was closed and two others stood slightly ajar. He approached the first and pushed it wider. The afternoon light fell over Jess' bed and to the cradle beside it. He crept closer and watched Faith sleep, the gentle rise and fall of her chest following the whisper of her breath.

He would be a father. He covered his smile, as if it made a noise, and then backed to the door, his grin spreading with the thought. His daughter. Low voices came from the other doorway. He edged closer and peeked into the shadowed room, one lantern lighting the small space. Cliff lay in the bed, pale and motionless, but with eyes wide and staring toward his companion. *Anna.*

She held his hand, stroking his fingers. August shouldn't listen to their quiet words, but he felt a particular responsibility to the outcome of this little story. He rested his weary body against the doorframe, relieved at Cliff's wakefulness. A good sign. A prayer answered.

"You don't have to speak. I know you must be tired." Anna kept her voice low and gentle. "I'm only glad to have been here to see you wake."

"August?"

"He is well. You were the only one injured by the attack."

Cliff sighed.

"I should go tell the others you are awake. They will want to know."

"No." Came his weak response. "Not yet."

Silence followed his words as Anna relaxed back into her chair.

"August was right. I should tell you."

August smiled and pushed away from the door just as Cliff's long awaited next words released into existence.

"I'm in love with you, Anna."

After years of hurt and sad endings, he and his sister finally found their own happy ending. August sighed out a prayer and made careful progress down the stairs.

As he reached the bottom, the front door opened and in walked Dr. Carter with Commander Ames on his heels. August attempted to straighten to attention for the commander, but tilted back against the wall for support.

"As you can see, Commander, it is as I told you. He's unfit for travel after the procedure."

Jess walked into the room in time to come to August's aid. She slid her arms around his waist. "What are you doing out of bed?"

"Trying to find you," he whispered.

Her face took on a rosy glow and if they'd been alone, he'd have worked to make it a shade brighter. Her grip tightened around him as she moved with him to a chair. "Clearly, our stubborn patient decided to go against our better judgment, Commander, and leave his bed. He's still recovering."

She pinned him with her most warning glare. He barely held back the urge to kiss her directly on her frown.

"How long do you think it will be before he can return to the camp? Besides the important service he provides as an interpreter and medical assistant, the camp is under quarantine and he belongs there."

"Commander, I do not expect August will be able to return to the camp for at least three days."

Three days? That seemed extreme, even with his minimal medical experience. He'd only participated in a transfusion and was without injury or wound. He suspected the recovery to be less than twenty-four hours, not three days.

"His immune system is low from the procedure, and sending him into such a volatile situation without a healthy capacity to fight is practically killing him."

Grandfather shot him a glance with an impish tilt to his moustache. What was he playing at? And the sudden realization had August nearly jumping from the chair to embrace the man. He was stalling. Giving Jess and August time together before the move to Oglethorpe.

Jess looked between them, attempting to sort out the secret exchange. She stood near him, her hands braided behind her back, so he carefully wove his among them, out of sight of their guest. Her body stiffened, her profile tilting in his direction but not turning, and then her lips tugged ever so slightly upward.

"Is Mr. Reinhold well enough to answer questions, then?"

"Yes, sir." August replied, reluctantly slipping his hand from hers and sitting taller in the chair.

"Please, have a seat here, Commander." Dr. Ross offered one of the dining chairs and the man took his seat, never looking quite at ease in any situation.

"I would like a complete accounting of the events last night, even the slightest detail."

August responded, explaining everything to the best of his ability—the two men, the struggle, and what details he could make out of the assailants. Ames listened with great intent, and as August described the two men, he leaned forward, his hands folded before him and his head bent low.

"I believe we found one of the men this morning, based on your description of his clothing and features."

"Where did you find him? At the train depot?"

Ames looked up, grim. "In the river."

August groaned. Would the man who nearly killed Cliff get away with the murders of the camp, Cliff's attempted murder, *and* this? "The river?"

"Someone strangled him and then left him at the river's edge."

Jess gasped. "Why?"

Ames attention shifted back to August. "We can only assume his accomplice thought he was a liability."

Dr. Carter stepped forward. "Did anyone identify him, Commander?"

"Yes, a few of the local guards. Goes by the name of Davis."

August looked to Jess and back to Ames.

"You know him?" the commander stated more than asked.

"His family have lived in this town for generations," Dr. Carter added.

"And he was known for his anti-German sentiments," Jess said. "He'd recently returned from the Front, wounded, after losing his brother over in France."

"Do you know of anyone else who might have partnered with him?"

"Yes, I think I do," Jessica slid down into a chair beside August. She blamed herself. He could see that by her worried brow.

"We could not know," August said, pulling her attention toward him. "Mr. Little acted his part with expert skill. I should not be surprised if he'd played it before."

"Indeed," Ames interjected. "We have evidence to believe this was not the first attack of its kind on these particular men. In fact, three similar situations have happened over the past year—and to German internees alone."

"We've been targeted?"

"It's war, son. Everyone's a target in some way or other."

"What similarities did you find? What information?" Dr. Carter asked.

"Anonymous letters to frame the internees, small 'accidents' which were later discovered to be planned, and then two other incidences of typhoid fever from contamination of a water supply. Once while the internees were housed in New York, and another aboard a train."

"And any leads? Suspects?"

"We have one, but we've never been able to catch him. One disgruntled soldier who'd lost brothers in the war at the hands of Germans. An Englishman, I think."

"An Englishman?" Jessica's hand pressed to her stomach. "In any of these details, these witness accounts, did they mention him missing a hand?"

Ames brows rose, the answer evident before he even spoke. "Yes, as a matter of fact, they did."

Chapter Twenty-Five

Jasper Little had disappeared. She and Grandpa accompanied Ames to the Inn where Birdie confirmed Mr. Little checked out first thing in the morning and left on the 8:30 train. It was all wrong—unfair. Could he get away with all of this evil with no consequences?

"You can't do anything about it, girl." Grandpa pulled the car up to the farmhouse.

Jess slammed her fist into her lap, fury and regret a twisted knife. "But... but I should have done something. Known somehow."

"You heard the commander. This was not Mr. Little's first attempt. He'd practiced his plan well enough to know what to do. He fooled all of us, Jess."

"But I should have known, don't you see, Grandpa?"

"How? How could you have known?"

"I've been fooled before. Shouldn't I know better the second time?"

Grandpa gave her shoulders a little shake. "Oh, girl, this world is steeped in evil. You've been in war. You've seen and experienced it enough to realize war comes with many faces. You can't see or prevent them all." His hold gentled with his expression. "And sometimes, there's nothing you can do but release it to God's judgment."

And again, the same sermon. Same theme. Same struggle to trust.

"Jess, you've been through more hardships in your young life than most women will ever know. You've seen the worst of humankind, watched the corruption eat away at the good and destroy the noble. Our power here is limited, but God is not, and neither is his plan. All of these things, we have to trust to His care or we'll go mad."

All things....

She kicked against releasing the anger. "But we should do something."

"Yes, we should. We fight for the right when we can. We uphold the truth. We show grace and mercy and strive for justice, but when we've done all we can do, we trust."

"And trust is the most difficult things to do."

Her grandfather offered an understanding smile. "We seek control and want our definition of justice. We're like young children trying to tell the doctor how to perform surgery on the brain, furious if the doctor doesn't listen to us."

She sighed. "What can I do?"

"You can go inside that house and enjoy these next two days you have with August."

She searched her grandfather's face, realization dawning. "You planned that? You gave Commander Ames those days so I could... so we could..."

"I don't know what time you've got, Jess, but I know he loves you. Let go of these time stealers, the frustrations you can't change, and hold to the sweet things, the choices that do make a difference."

Jess heard the children's laughter as she exited the car. It rose from the back. She glanced over at her grandfather, his grin urging her to investigate. She took her time, praying through her steps, struggling with the guilt eating away at this sweet opportunity to spend time with August.

Would she always come to God with the same mantra? The same struggles?

"Help me trust you."

I love you with an everlasting love.

And the sweet reminder stirred her heart alive again. The cross. The sacrifice. She rounded the corner of the house and smiled. August sat in the grass, Jude to his left, Sylvie on his right, and

Faith in his arms. God's touch. His fingerprints marked August's love. She walked toward him, toward the truth that trust required sacrifice and risk. God completed the risks and the sacrifices, and her job was only to believe Him... to have faith.

Change the things she could. Trust God with the things she couldn't.

Perhaps Granny could stitch that on a pillow.

―

August caught her after supper and tugged her out onto the porch, sweeping her into a kiss before she had a chance to speak one word. Of course, catching her by surprise gave him the added pleasure of hearing her sharp intake of breath and then feel her body melt into him.

"You're going to ruin my virtuous reputation, Mr. Reinhold." But she made no attempt to retreat. In fact, she nuzzled closer for another kiss.

"I know an immediate remedy for this predicament, Miss Ross. In fact, you've already agreed to it."

Her smile spread against his lips. "You certainly are persistent."

"It's served me well."

She chuckled, her hold on him tightening. "Me too, my dear alien."

"You said you would marry me and then you left the room."

"What else did you need me to do?"

He slid his palm over her cheek and back into her hair, keeping her close enough to kiss at will. "Shout it to the house? We should tell your grandparents, and Cliff. And the children."

Anna already knew. Sisters deserved special secrets as a rule.

"August." Her palmed against his chest stilled his movements. "We can share the news with my grandparents and Cliff, but... I'd rather not tell Jude just yet."

He searched her face, shadowed by the night sky and porch roof. "You doubt me?"

"No." Her fingers slid against his cheek to his hairline. "No, how could I ever doubt you?"

Then he understood. "You are afraid he will be hurt."

"He cares about you so much. We don't know how much longer the war will continue. What if we raise his hopes only to have you gone for a long time... or something happens to keep you away indefinitely?"

"I wonder if you are not speaking more for yourself than for Jude." He pressed his lips to one cheek. "I love you." He kissed the other cheek and she sighed. "I love you still." His lips met hers, gently, slowly. "I love you forever. Jude will have you to help him be strong, even if we all must wait on time."

She braced his face between her palms. "Then let's tell them tonight so we can celebrate tomorrow."

Before he returned to camp, behind the fence, and then... only God knew. "Here is my promise."

He fished for the ring Anna gave him earlier in the day. Their mother's ring. Her favorite. A simple pearl. Perfect for his bride.

His bride.

He felt for her fourth finger and slipped the ring into place. "I cannot see the future. I do not know how long we will be apart, but I can promise you this. My love will remain constant, no matter where I am or where you are. When you look at this ring, remember, and rest in my love for you."

―

Two days sounded like an eternity but drained like a sieve. Jess spent almost every waking moment with August, bringing the children along for walks to the chapel and a picnic by the river, and then she stole a few private interludes with him in the hallway or on the porch, wherever they could find them.

He remained constant, pulling at her smile more than anyone she'd known. He held an infectious optimism and steady faith, reminding her of truths she'd forgotten. And her fears of sharing news of the engagement with Jude turned to laughter at the boy's excitement, even as they attempted to explain the fluid future.

Jude's response was beautifully simple. "It's about time."

Which seemed the consensus of everyone in the family, despite the fact she'd only met August a little over three months ago. Somehow, he'd claimed her heart long before she ever knew him, and all it took was his unswerving love to help her see she already belonged.

She drove him back to town. The drive took much less time than usual, but August kept up a lively conversation for the duration, distracting her, caring for her in his way. How could she love someone with such ferocity so quickly? But wasn't it like God? Once the heart roused, the once murky path cleared of uncertainty, love replaced doubt with a sweet abiding. She looked down at the beautiful pearl ring as she gripped the steering mechanism and smiled. She belonged to him, no matter where he was.

She pulled over to the side of the road before entering town, before the curious onlookers stole their freedom of a lovers' goodbye. He pulled her to him, kissing her until her hat tipped far too crooked to be fashionable and her lips tingled from the exertion. He kissed her to leave a memory, and she closed her eyes, storing the tactile tenderness of his caress deep in her heart for more barren days.

"I will come back to visit tomorrow." She slid her palm over his shirt as if smoothing out imaginary wrinkles, just to touch him. "Around lunch, after I help Grandpa at the clinic."

"I shall wait, though I am much less keen for it than I used to be."

She caught his collar in her fist and pulled him to her, capturing his chuckle with her mouth. "I don't like waiting either."

He groaned and returned the kiss with sudden crescendo until they both drew back, a bit breathless. "One day, we will not have to practice patience so liberally." He ran a hand over her cheek then snagged her fingers in his, placing her palm over his heart, the letter still firmly planted in his pocket. "You are with me, here." He brought her hand to his lips, kissing her knuckle at the place of her ring. "Always remember, Mause."

August 18, 1918

Jessica,

My dislike of fences has magnified throughout the week. They were a mild annoyance when I first arrived in Hot Springs, but when your grandfather gave me employment, they were merely the walls of my temporary abode. Now, I am trapped within them, a cage separating me from you. I miss you. Even though I see you each afternoon, the time is short and the wire keeps me from tasting your honeysuckle lips.

But I must be content, for at least now I can see your beauty with my eyes and touch your hands. In the following weeks, our world will shift again. Commander Ames plans to begin transport of my sick comrades to U.S. General #12 in Asheville, a place once known as Kenilworth Inn. At which time he plans an immediate evacuation of the remaining men to Oglethorpe. I have requested to continue with the sick as long as possible to provide service, of course, but also to remain nearer to you and your family.

Now, as this news settles into an expectation throughout the camp, I am wearied by my own self-interest. I must beg your apology, my Mause. Now, in the daylight of my decision, I realize the selfishness of my choice to pursue you. I have opened your generous heart to grief, for I feel its taunting in my spirit. I was blinded by the beauty of who you are, the promise of your resilient, faithful heart poured out on me, that I did not weigh the ramifications, for now we must be parted indefinitely. Had I not placed myself into your world, you would not grieve my loss now. Forgive me.

I have no doubt my affections for you can withstand the separation. In fact, your letters and your love will provide sweet comfort to breach the distance. You, Jude, and Faith are my family now. Time will tell when that sentence becomes more than words on a page or feelings in my heart, but a physical place of belonging with you, every day.

Forgive my selfishness, Mause.

Your Alien

Jessica slipped down the street beside the wooden fence surrounding the camp. The tall trees of the expansive grounds of the Mountain Park Hotel rose above the planks and shaded her from the late summer heat. Life moved into a quiet routine since the events involving Jasper Little. Death drums kept up a steady reminder of life's brevity each morning as the newest deaths from inside the camp made the short trek from the camp to Oddsfellows for burial. Cliff continued to heal, slowly but steadily, spurred on, no doubt, by Anna's loving presence showering him with attention—and, as Jessica caught this morning, a few kisses. Jude and Faith continued to provide her world with a richer hues of sweetness she never knew she wanted until God brought them into her life, and the ever-present unknown for August hung over the day, waiting to break through the clouds like an impending storm.

August's daily letters attempted to quell the longing his kisses couldn't, but they both knew time grew ever shorter. And then what? Even if the war ended soon, as all accounts proclaimed, how long would it be before he was truly free to find her? How many more letters would replace flesh and blood? A tempest raged to life in her spirit, spinning worries to a fever pitch.

She saw the Old Red Bridge, its steel structure one of the few bridges around to survive the devastation of the flood two years before, a solid structure in the middle of the storm. A surge of realization dawned through her spirit, drawing her feet to a stop—the dark red of the bridge, the immovable steel. *Her hope in His love.* Strong enough to withstand the storms, the ravages of time and pain.

My hope is an anchor for your soul, firm and secure. Trust my love for you.

She looked up into the waning afternoon blue, sunlight shimmering through lush green leaves. Light and warmth bathed her face, her soul, with a sense of gratitude, an awesome understanding penetrating her stubborn will with a renewed sense of grace. She gave into the pull, the hope, the trust, relishing this deep, abiding welcome of peace.

Her palms turned upward. She closed her eyes as the gentlest breeze whispered like a touch of Heaven across her cheeks. *You are mine.*

"I surrender."

She embraced the peace, breathing freedom for the first time in so very long. Her smile spread up to the sky. "I'll need your reminder often, you know? To trust. To hope. I'm painfully stubborn."

"He's not put off by your stubbornness."

She tucked her head with her smile, caught in prayer by one of the most endearing voices. She tilted her face toward the place where the board fence gave way to wire and met August's welcome smile on the other side.

"And neither am I, Mause."

She stepped toward him. "Do you eavesdrop on prayers often, my dear Alien?"

"Do you pray in the middle of the street often?"

She laughed and stepped into the haven of trees to meet him at the fence. "Only occasionally, when I'm on my way to meet a very special man."

"Who desperately needs your prayers." His gaze roamed her face, cherishing her from chin to forehead. She braided her fingers through his against the cool metal.

"Well, I have an excellent wager for you then."

His penetrating gaze lit. "I like your wagers. Each time you pray for both of us, I will kiss you?"

She smiled up at him, wondering if he saw how much she cared for him. Was it reflected in her eyes as it was in his? Did her smile soften with tenderness too? "That would no doubt improve my prayer life."

She sobered, squeezing his fingers into a tighter hold. "August, your letter."

He sighed, looking away.

"Please don't apologize for loving me. Ever." She waited until his attention swung back to her. "I don't think you could have changed anything. My heart responded to yours from the first moment I met you. I fought it, as I do most everything, but I would not change a thing." She drew in a breath, wrestling vast emotions into words. "August, I... I am... found in this love of yours."

He attempted to move closer but the fence blocked his approach. He growled. "But it would have been better for your heart if I'd remained a nameless face among the many here who admire you from afar."

She stood on tiptoe and peered over his shoulder into the Inn's lawn. "Oh, are there others behind the fence who admire me, Mr. Reinhold?"

He lowered his hand to try and snatch her at the waist, but she dodged him.

"Indeed." His fingers finally came in contact with her dress and pulled her back against the fence. "And it's very annoying to fight off an entire group of comrades each day."

Her laughter stilled at his sudden closeness and she slipped her hand through the wire to touch his face. "Well, there is only one you, and that is all I need."

He closed his eyes and snatched her fingers, running kisses over them. His brow crunched into worried lines and he pressed his lips into her palm. "They begin loading men tomorrow for Oglethorpe, Jessica."

The heat in the day cooled over her skin. "So soon?"

"We knew it would be soon."

She nodded, grappling for the hope she'd just embraced. "And the sick?"

"They will try to move them within the next two weeks."

"To Asheville?"

"Yes."

"And will you go to Asheville?"

He hesitated, rubbing his hand over her fingers. "I don't know, but I am hopeful."

"Do you know when you will leave?"

His frown pinched at her joy. "Nothing is certain. One day I will be here, and the next…"

"You'll be gone," she finished on a whisper.

"From this camp, Mause. Only from this camp." He moved her hand to his heart again, reminding her. "But not from here. I will be with you every day. Right here."

"August, you are on the first train in the morning." Cliff pressed a paper into August's hand. "Orders from Ames."

"Cliff?" August took the paper and crammed it into this pocket before taking the man in his arms. "You are here?"

Cliff leaned close, a twinkle in his eyes. "Only today and for a very particular reason."

"I am listening."

Cliff's grin spread across his whole face. "I need your blessing."

And the joy from his friend's expression found its way to August's chest. "My blessing?"

Cliff scanned the empty room and then focused back on August. "I want to marry your sister, and I'd like your blessing."

"You need to ask?"

"No, not really, but I'd like to hear you say it anyway."

August covered Cliff's shoulder with his palm, giving it a slight shake. "I am pleased to offer my blessing and joy. My only reservation is you did not secure a double wedding."

Cliff grin slid into a frown. "You know, I tried, August. I talked to Ruser and then Ames. Neither budged, though I thought I'd hit on Ruser's romantic side with my plea." He shook his head. "I'm sorry, friend. You're a German citizen in America. An enemy during a war. Until you're free from those constraints, nothing can be done."

"I thank you for trying."

"You can thank me for more than that. Ames has given me permission to take you with me for two hours, as your guard. I couldn't get more than two."

August stared, blinking. "I hadn't hope for any."

"You have to be back by curfew." Cliff's grin returned, brighter. "But you're going to walk your sister down the aisle before you leave Hot Springs."

His sister looked beautiful. Happier than he'd seen her in a very long time and clothed in a simple periwinkle gown of lace, she glided down the aisle of Carter's chapel, holding his arm and smiling at her groom with a breathtaking radiance. Sylvie went before them, leaving a trail of white petals to guide their way, her little feet almost dancing with joy.

August found Jessica standing at the front, Anna's matron of honor. Her glorious hair crowned her head in intricate waves of gold, a pearl barrette pinning her wealth of locks in place and matching the ring on her finger. She almost stole the bride's glory as she waited, framed by white roses and wearing a flowing, pale green frock. August released his sister to Cliff, then stepped to Cliff's side as his best man, his gaze drawn back to the woman he wished to make his own.

She shared a secret smile with him, holding his gaze as the vows passed. He couldn't look away, didn't wish to look away. It might have taken months of prayer and persistence to gain her heart, but once won, she held with a passionate, loyal grip. *His bride.* How long, oh Lord?

The notice from Ames brought mixed news. He departed in the morning, but at least his request for Asheville had been approved. Oglethorpe loomed as an inevitable end, but not yet.

The small company, all family, cheered as the bride and groom kissed. Sylvie ran to them and Cliff brought her up into his arms, turning to face the bystanders with a look of sheer delight. The scene gripped August with a mixture of pain and pleasure. His sister's face glowed with adoration for August's friend. It was a perfect pairing. A beautiful beginning.

Jess met him at the altar, taking his arm as they followed the newlyweds down the aisle and out of the church.

"One day, that song will play for us, August," she whispered, keeping her eyes ahead.

He tugged her closer to his side, covering her hand resting on his sleeve. "Do you promise, Mause?"

Her golden brow edged up as she slit him a pixie smile. "I do, without a doubt. I do."

Chapter Twenty-Six

August wiped a hand across his sweat-stained brow and moved to the next cot. Two weeks on the third floor of the U.S. General #12 kept him busier than he'd expected. The nurses complained of the influx of work left to them with so many of their colleagues shipped across the ocean to war, but there was no help for it. Everyone worked to exhaustion.

August shared a closet room away from the sick with another assistant, an American named Thomas Lennox. The young man seemed nice enough, commenting how August spoke so well that he wouldn't have guessed he was German. But there was no time to get to know Mr. Lennox, because they split shifts with the twenty-six men, and occasionally, were called to the lower floors to assist with the care of the soldiers.

"What about those Red Sox, August?" Tom grinned as he passed, taking over the shift. He patted August on the shoulder. "Babe pitched like a dream."

August laughed, looking down to examine Tom's shoes. "Red Sox? Babe?"

Tom's brow crowded with confusion. "You don't know who the Red Sox are? Babe Ruth?" He enunciated the words with such passion, spit flew in the air.

"No."

Tom released a massive sigh. "World Series? The Red Sox played the Chicago Cubs. Won their third series. Babe pitched twenty-nine scoreless innings. It's all over the papers."

August patted his pocket. "I only read this type of paper, and my books."

Tom tossed a hand. "Aww, you and that girl of yours."

Yes, his girl. His beautiful, strong girl.

"If you need help on your shift tonight, find me. A new shipment of wounded soldiers came in the last hour and Nurse Riley from downstairs said a few are in very poor condition. You'll be busy."

"More soldiers? Where are we gonna put 'em?" He shook his dark head, not waiting for an answer before he disappeared down the hall.

August slid into the tiny room and collapsed onto his cot, tugging a coveted envelope from his pocket. Jessica's familiar writing marked the page, her newest letter. He split the seal and reclined back onto the shallow pillow. Suddenly, the distance closed with the first sentence.

September 10, 1918

My dear Alien,

Will you take a walk with me? Take my hand. Do you feel it? My palm rubs across the careworn lines of yours, sliding into a perfect fit as we find our step together. The sky is bluer today—an autumn blue—and the leaves have begun their wintry tilt of color. The trees crowd overhead, arching our path through the forest like a rainbow canopy, and the breeze wakes our faces with the tiny blush of cold.

You tug me closer, warding off the chill with your presence, and I laugh. Can you hear it? I hear yours. Deep, and filled with your effervescent joy. Yes, you are always with me, my dear August. I close my eyes, as I sit on the back steps of my grandparents' home, and see us together, taking in the day with the leisure of a peaceful world and a beautiful life.

The chapel waits, robed in fall roses and welcoming its newest bride and groom.

Some days, I can march through the hours, longing for you but able to crowd my mind with daily duties enough to keep the yearning to a low ache, but then there are days when I need to see you. Feel you. Remember your touch.

And on those days, in the quiet of the evening, you take me for a walk to the chapel and I see you as you last stood—dressed in your beige summer suit, pale blue bowtie, and hair admirably tamed into a stylish wave except for your rebel curl. My favorite. The strand of hair that portrays your true mischief, unrepressed by the rules of the camp or society. It falls over your forehead, a little secret to me of who you are and who I love.

So today, as I long to hear your voice and kiss your lips, close your eyes and join me. Ease the longing of this moment, because one day, we will take this walk with our eyes open, and I want to know the way.

I love you,
Your Mause

"I think you might have to postpone your trip to Asheville, girl."

Her grandfather entered the clinic, his gray brows a storm cloud. Amy looked up from her study of hearing aids and deaf education, a personal goal for the driven fifteen-year-old since she learned of Sylvie's hearing aid.

"What's wrong?" Three weeks! August's train left three weeks ago and oh, how she missed him. How much longer would she have to wait to see him again?

Grandpa braced his hands upon the counter and breathed out a heavy sigh. "Pete Russell arrived home from the War last week, wounded in the leg. He told me Tuesday he wasn't feeling well, so I traveled up to check on him this morning." He groaned and ran a hand over his face, looking every bit of his sixty-nine years. "His whole family was dead."

"Dead?" Jess shook her head in an attempt to comprehend. "The whole family?"

"Was it a feud?"

Grandpa turned to her, weary shoulders bent. "No. Worse. I just returned from visiting Mr. Donaldson."

Jess' chest tightened at the warning in his voice.

"He's... he's down with a severe fever. Delirious. Bloody sputum, bluish pallor."

Her brain refused to acknowledge the growing awareness those symptoms created. "What is it?"

"Our first victims of the Spanish Influenza." His turbulent gray eyes found hers. "We must prepare for the worst."

A chill crept up from her chest into her throat, clawing through her lungs with icy fingers. Rumors like ghost stories traveled the railways, whispering of the dreaded disease. A virulent strain of influenza, quick and deadly. Of course, Mr. Donaldson would be one of the first infected. Even though he was a retired station master, he kept time at the depot, helping as his health allowed. Anything coming from those rails met him first. "I'll go home and prepare Granny and the children. Should I find Cliff too?"

He nodded, the worry lines firming with purpose. "Amy, I need you to take a letter to Dr. Dorland and the school. He needs to prepare his students."

She stood to the ready with a nod. "What else can we do? How can we prepare?"

Grandfather looked back at her, his shoulders stiffening to take the brunt of whatever the future brought. "We cannot prepare for this, Amy. All we can do is pray... and wait."

Jess pressed her fist into her stomach, a nauseous roil nearly overcoming her. She'd kept up with the news in the papers. Only a few days ago, the Surgeon General dispatched advice on how to recognize the symptoms of the flu, followed by a short list of treatments, but the accounts spreading from town to town contradicted the mild response of the government's reaction.

News correspondent Jack Sterling's description from his stay in a camp hospital gave the most vivid and vile first-hand witness, inflaming Jess' concern. Ten men in the camp went from healthy breath to violent death in twelve hours or less. The recent news from Boston, DC, and Philadelphia? The same. Devastating.

And Grandpa had been exposed. She slowed her pace. So had she.

She drew her handkerchief from her pocket and continued her walk, topping the street to where only a month before, barbed wire and wood fencing shrouded the Mountain Park Hotel and grounds. As the internees left, the boarding houses emptied of their associated wives and children, except for Anna Fischer Carter. Jess almost allowed a smile, but her thoughts darkened as she surveyed the drowsy Main Street.

Hot Springs had returned to its quiet, five hundred number population, and sat as ill-prepared for this Influenza epidemic as it had been for its German invasion. Less prepared, actually. The Germans never attacked the Appalachian natives. This Spanish Influenza wouldn't be so kind.

Nurse Riley, August's connection to the lower two floors of the hospital, ushered him forward with a terse gesture. He stifled a yawn. The day brought three more deaths of his comrades and five for the American soldiers. A new threat hung in the air like a dense fog. August overheard the doctors and nurses discuss it in whispered fear. As he'd helped load the coffins of his comrades onto the horse cart, the undertaker and orderly voiced the word with trepidation. Influenza.

An illness that killed with speed, impartiality, and violence. Often.

Already, the doctors reported fifteen cases. He worked the entire morning, directly off of an evening shift. His body ached for a few hours' rest, but two doctors and three nurses lay ill and three more medical personnel worked through exhaustion, just like him.

"I wouldn't ask for your help if it wasn't necessary, but I just don't have a choice," she said, leading him to the first floor. Her gaze shifted from his, and her voice trembled. "Dr. Lippard died a few moments ago and Tom is assisting with emergencies on the second floor. I need help getting his body to the front."

August had little memory of Dr. Lippard... tall, young, with a severe expression.

Her hand paused on the door handle. "There are twelve beds in this room for some of our most severe cases. It is not an easy sight, Mr. Reinhold. Prepare yourself."

A sickening odor hit him first. The air was thick with a sticky stench, hot and heavy with a blend of blood, bile, and death. August closed his eyes and swallowed, stepping over the threshold into the room. The first shocking revelation came with the color of the patients' skin. Faces of various hues of blue, gray, and even ash, contrasted with the stark white sheets. One nurse bent over a young man, holding a cloth to his bloody nose. Another adjusted the pillows for a woman who scratched at the blanket, her breath a rattling squeeze for air.

"Here."

August pulled his gaze from the excruciating scene to the bed before him. A white cloth covered the body, giving blessed relief from the terrifying views on all sides.

"Help me lift him to the stretcher and carry him downstairs."

August looked from her small frame and back to the man's shape on the bed. "Do you have an orderly to assist?"

She tilted her chin up, her bottom lip offering the slightest tremble. "There are no others, Mr. Reinhold."

He scanned the room again, taking closer inventory of the faces and counting the medical staff one-by-one. With a deep breath, he faced her. "What do you need me to do?"

―

August spent the day helping tend tens of men with this 'Blue Death,' along with preparing three bodies for burial, until he had no strength of heart or body to continue. The narrow back steps led the way to his small room, and he dragged his legs up each one to the third floor. Another letter from Jessica had arrived in the afternoon, but his gloomy occupation kept him too busy to read it, and his current exhaustion nearly stripped him of curiosity.

He pushed open the door to the third floor and entered the hallway, dimly lit by a few electric lights. His room door loomed at the end of the hall, promising a few precious moments of sleep. He frowned. From the visions in his head of the day's events, he doubted the dreams would be sweet.

Suddenly, out of his periphery, two men approached. Young and fit... soldiers. He turned to greet them when the first rallied a severe punch into his stomach. August buckled from the impact, pain blinding his vision.

"You and your bloody kin brought the Grippe, didn't you?"

A fist rammed into his face, sending him backwards. "We read in the papers, your kind released the epidemic here. Haven't you done enough?"

August caught the next fist and shoved the boy backwards until he hit the wall on the other side of hallway. "I had nothing to do with the sickness."

August dodged another fist, but felt the full impact of a second against the side of his head. His vision blurred and he crumbled to his knees.

"Get out of here or I'm calling Dr. Stephens." Thomas rushed through the blur as August struggled back to his feet.

"Don't protect him, Thomas." August tried to blink the angry man into view. "His kind need to learn their place."

"You heard what Dr. Stephens said as well I. The sickness comes from the trenches in France, not from Germans." Thomas kept his position as barrier between August, his palms out as an added shield. "For all I know, you could've brought it back with you."

The men exchanged glances and then rushed away. August bent forward, giving way to the moan of pain roaring from his chest.

"I'll fetch some gauze and icings." Thomas ducked beneath August's arm and provided extra support to the room.

August stumbled to the cot. "Thank you, Thomas."

Thomas patted the doorframe on his way out. "And August, if there's a way to keep everyone from knowing you're German, just until this flu passes, I think you'd be smart to make it work. People are scared, and fear makes them dangerous. Be careful."

Thirty cases reported in one week and three deaths. Jess walked from one cot to the other in the clinic, ten poor souls packed within the three small rooms. Kimp struggled for breath in the back room, his wife at his side, their futures in the balance. Mr. Donaldson recovered and even helped bring Miss Jessup to the clinic when the symptoms started.

Jess stretched out her back and then adjusted the mask across her face. Its flimsy cloth felt much too thin to combat the severity of this illness. The simplest symptoms of a headache or sore throat quickly erupted into a deathly fever and suffocating cough. The worst cases died within hours.

Grandfather and Dr. Peck spent their mornings visiting homes to check for more victims and the small town, far from the greater populations of Asheville or even Winston, quietly succumbed to this unseen enemy. A person appeared perfectly healthy one moment and within an hour, lay at death's door.

There was a bone-weariness to the treatment, to the unpredictability.

With a heavy heart, Jess sent Jude and Faith to stay with Cliff and Anna, away from the illness she carried on her clothes every day. She missed them, ached for her children, but the very thought of seeing them suffer as these people did, striving for the next breath, secured her decision. She prayed as she'd never prayed for those struggling, for those dying, and for the survivors left to grieve the sudden loss.

"When do you think I can go home, Nurse Ross?"

Jess stopped by Sarah Ruth's cot, the new widow's pale face gaining more color with each passing hour. "From my limited experience with the illness so far, you should be free to leave by the morning."

She nodded and turned her head away. "I need to take care of Joe's body."

Jessica's shoulders caved forward, her heart gouged by the mere imaginings of such a loss. She remembered Cliff's grief, the daunting and long shadows lost love left behind. Jess took the woman's hand and bent low. "Sarah, I'm so sorry for your loss."

The hard edge in the woman's eyes dissipated into watery pools. "He was a good man."

Jess smiled and nodded, remembering the gentle factory worker. "Yes, he was. Always a kind word."

Her hand moved to her swollen abdomen. "My young'un is going to know about him. You just wait and see. I'll make sure he knows what a good man his daddy was."

Sarah had gotten sick first. Jess would never forget the look of pure grief on Joe Ruth's face when he carried his young bride through the door of the clinic and begged them to save her. He'd sat by her bed for two hours, praying, stroking her hair, begging for God's healing. Finally, Grandpa found him collapsed across her bed, already in the severe stages of the disease. He died within the hour.

To fall asleep ill one moment and wake up a widow the next? Oh, how Sarah must grieve! The room grew suddenly small, death closing in. The coughs and the rattled breaths pressed in from all sides, and she rushed to the door to breathe in fresh air and sunshine.

Oh God, please help us.

The flaming leaves of fall rose above the quiet town, framing Hot Springs with the colors and vitality the streets lacked in the wake of such a devastating blow. The mountains called to her, rebellious sirens urging her to flee the monochrome devastation of the hospital for the freedom of fresh air and heavenly vistas. Her throat tightened with the need to cry.

A lone figure walked forward, her worn, straw hat at a careless tilt on her caramel hair. Amy. She carried a package, one delivered yesterday, but they'd been too busy to retrieve it from the post office. Jess and her grandfather couldn't have managed the influx of needs without the fifteen-year-old spitfire. Her quick wit, energy, and her own self-initiation pushed her to stretch her own abilities. Jess offered the girl a wave but paused, her hand in midair.

Something was wrong with her gait. It was slow... stumbling. The chill of realization crawled up Jess' spine just as Amy's glossy gaze met hers and the young girl collapsed to the dusty ground. *No!*

Chapter Twenty-Seven

August blinked to clear his vision, but the image didn't change. He swiped at his eyes, refusing to believe them, but there she stood, waiting in the lobby of the illustrious inn-turned-hospital. Morning light from the windows framed her, the white mask doing little to hide her astonishing beauty.

Her cream-colored hat, decorated with a lone russet ribbon, shadowed her gaze but couldn't hide the smile of welcome on her face. His chest constricted with gratitude and the backs of his tired eyes stung.

Jessica.

Her presence breathed spring across the barren gloom of his spirit, bringing hope and life.

"Mr. Holden, you have two hours, and you cannot leave the grounds." The guard at the door passed a look between them. "You'll be expected back on duty by..." He checked his watch. "One."

"Thank you, sir." He curbed his accent into a muted version. "Two hours is more than generous."

Jess' tilted brow asked for clarification, but he wouldn't admit to his adjustments in front of the guard. The week since the attack changed many things for him.

He waited until they stepped beyond the doorway and then drew her arm within his, allowing himself to accept the reality of her visit. "You are here?"

She nodded, her evergreen gaze glossy with a teary luster. "I had to come. Five weeks is too long. Much too long."

"Yes. It is." He searched her face, staring in silence, drinking in every nuance of her endless eyes, every flake of gold in her freckles. "Will you take a walk with me?"

Her smile bloomed, her breath hitching on her response. "Anywhere."

He pulled her closer and guided their steps toward a little grove of trees at some distance behind the hospital. It seemed strange to hold her, to plan a quiet walk together, when their days labored with the sick, dead, and dying. The simplest, most natural pleasure radiated a tender frailty, a potent preciousness. Even his steps felt lighter with her by his side—almost dizzying.

"If I could, I would take you into the city to a romantic restaurant."

She shook her head. "I don't need romance or even food right now. I just want to be with you, for however long we have." Her smile twisted with a pixie glint and she tipped the basket in her hands toward him. "Besides, Granny sent a few treats for us to share. It's a beautiful day. Perhaps a picnic?"

He squinted from the sun's brilliance and ran his fingers across hers against his arm, still trying to take in this dream. "How is Amy? And the children? And your grandparents?"

She sighed, her gaze focused forward. "The children are safe at Cliff and Anna's. Granny caught the flu right after Amy, but her form was mild. We almost lost Amy. Her fever rose to such a degree, her beautiful auburn hair turned white and then fell out."

"How is that possible?"

Jess shook her head. "I've heard of it before, but never witnessed it. She was mortified, of course, but her resilience is inspiring. She's taken up a new fascination with hats."

"What will happen to her now that her aunt and uncle have died?"

"Kimp's brother will take the mercantile, but no one in the family wants Amy because of her family history."

August stopped their walk and peered down at her. "So your grandparents have taken her in?"

"Of course they have." Her gaze roamed his face, examining him as keenly as he did her. Her grin tipped. "Should I start calling you Mr. Holden now?"

He chuckled. "I am *your* alien, as always, but I have become Mr. Holden to those at the hospital. German sentiments are low since the negative propaganda about the influenza. I have found it easier to pretend than to suffer the wrath of those who are less welcoming."

She trailed her cool fingers across the cut above his eyes. "This type of welcome?"

He hadn't realized how much he missed her until she stood before him in the flesh. "I would kiss you senseless right now, Mause, if I wasn't afraid of killing you."

"Thoughts that make your face so warm?" Her fingers slid down his face to palm his cheek, as she shook her head. "I'm exposed to the flu every day, August. If I'm going to catch it, I will. Your kiss cannot aid or stop it, but I can assure you, it could do a great deal to improve my overall morale."

He grinned and snatched her hand, quickening his steps until they were safely hidden within the grove. Without hesitation, he gently tugged her mask to her chin, revealing her lovely face and those welcoming pink lips. She drew him like a parched wanderer to a sweet oasis.

He captured her mouth with his own, hungry for the taste and touch. A sob wracked through her at his contact, the long desert finally filling with the tender rain of withheld affection. Her free hand slipped up to palm the back of his head, holding his kiss in place, urging him to give more. He complied greedily, slipping the basket from her grasp and dropping it at their feet so he could take full advantage of her nearness. He pulled her flush against him, tasting her lips, her chin, her cheeks, and the salt of her tears. She responded with a similar need, ending one kiss long enough to gaze into his eyes before beginning another. His eyes watered from the internal burn for her, his body weak with longing. Her hat toppled to the ground, loosening strips of her hair around her face in glorious sprays of gold.

There had been so much loss and grief. So many dark days. This brief reprieve soaked into his lonely soul with a fragrant vibrancy.

They pulled apart to spread the picnic blanket onto the grass but managed to find ways to touch. A gentle press to the back. A twining of the fingers. Neither willing to go too long without the assurance of the other's presence.

"How did you manage it? My leave for these two hours? Our entire floor is under guard."

She sat on the blanket, pulling the basket to her. "Grandfather is a colleague and friend of one of the board members for the hospital. He suggested your medical expertise might be helpful for me to carry back to Hot Springs."

He joined her on the blanket, his fingers braided through hers as she used her other hand to offer him fried chicken.

"I am not hungry," he whispered, burying his face into her hair. "For food."

She leaned into him, filling his senses with her honeysuckle scent. "I won't tell Granny you refused her fried chicken. She might never welcome you back to supper again."

"Oh, Mause, you do my heart good."

She tilted her face up to him. "The feeling is mutual." She squeezed his fingers. "I was very sorry to hear of your friend Tom."

Only a week ago, two days after Tom intervened in the assault of the two soldiers, he'd contracted the flu. August visited him as the poor man writhed with delirium and finally gave way to the suffocating death.

"When we return to the hospital, I have something for you. I meant to give it to you before I left Hot Springs, but my train loaded before you came. I hope it will comfort you in my absence."

They sat talking quietly, occasionally breaking the silence with a word or a kiss. For a late September day, the air blazed thick and warm around him, growing thicker with each minute, stiff in his throat.

The cool lemonade slid down his throat and he brushed the glass across his forehead to douse some of the unseasonable heat of the day before snatching another kiss from his lovely companion.

The world and all of its war and sickness fell away, replaced by a taste of Heaven. August burned the memory into his mind. The way Jessica smiled up at him, her face illuminated by love and sunshine. The fragrant scent of honeysuckle on her skin. The taste of her lips. The way the breeze blew strands of her hair toward him, beckoning him to touch.

They both felt the hallowed moment, the desperate desire to hold the seconds sacred, and Granny Carter's delicious food remained untouched as the hours slipped by.

Jess kept her arm through his until they reached the shade of the hospital. Her kisses had warmed him all over, and even his cheeks tingled from her touch. The heat of the sun followed him into the shadowed building, scorching his face. Had it been so long since he'd felt its light he'd become sensitive?

The world took on a strange, watery hue. He blinked, but his surroundings didn't clear.

"August?" Jess' voice emerged from far away, shrouded in a strange, otherworldly aura.

Her cool palms cradled his cheeks, her eyes two emerald jewels staring into his. "No, please no. August, you have a fever."

The words registered, slow and dense through his head, and the pleading in her voice pushed him to focus.

"Do not fear, Mause."

"August. Fight this, please." Her palms tightened on his cheeks, her gaze drilling into his to emerge from the growing fog. "Fight this for me."

The heaviness in his head swelled into an ache. He dared not close his eyes against it. There was no certainty of opening them again. He fought the drugged pull of his eyelids. "I will find you, Mause. You are my home."

"August, please." Her voice broke. "Fight. Promise me."

He found her face among the swirling world of bright lights and distant sounds, and pushed his words up through his fiery throat. "I'll fight... you rest."

How had Jess ignored the signs? His lack of appetite, his flushed cheeks. The heat of his skin underneath her touch? She knew better, and yet her pleasure at seeing him, touching him, pushed her medical sense to the back of her mind.

He slumped toward her, into her arms, almost knocking her to the ground. The guard rushed forward to assist.

"Is he a patient here?"

"Yes..." She shook her head, uncertain how to answer. "No, he works here. As an assistant. He's been helping with the second and third floor patients."

The guard examined his face. "Mr. Holden?"

Jess nodded, keeping her hands on his arms as they half dragged, half pulled his body toward the elevator. Another guard came to the rescue, along with a nurse.

"No visitors beyond this point, miss."

Jess pulled her gaze from August's liquid-blue eyes to the nurse. "I'm a nurse. I can help take care of him."

The woman's expression firmed, sweeping Jess with a look that took in the limp and the full, delicate ensemble she wore to impress her alien.

Jess stepped forward, watching them half-carry August into the elevator. His gaze met hers before the doors closed, periwinkle and watery. Her stomach lurched into a pincher grip. She turned her full fire on the nurse. "I know you need help here. Medical personnel are needed everywhere right now, and I'm trained to serve in this population."

"*Military* nurses received different training than civilian nurses, miss."

Jess pulled to her full height, adding a proper scowl for effect. "I worked a year in a field hospital in France, almost two years in a war hospital in Derbyshire, and several months in a Casualty Clearing Station. I am well aware of the nature of military work."

The woman's dark gaze took on a fiery glint. "But you have not been approved for our hospital. If you'd like to go through the proper paperwork, we will be glad to take your services, but for now..." She gave her another measured look. "You are a *visitor* and there are no visitors beyond this point."

She slammed her palm against the counter. "I can help."

The nurse leveled her with a severe expression. "We house not only our good American soldiers, but the enemy aliens. We take that responsibility quite seriously."

Jess met her glare for glare. "I respect your professionalism for both our soldiers and guests, I only wish to give one message to

Mr. Holden in person. Please." One glance. One touch. Just enough to check his pulse and listen to his breathing. To imbue her strength to him.

"The rules are in place and strictly enforced as a protection for everyone involved. I advise you to go through the proper channels to gain entrance to the hospital. Good day."

"Miss Ross?" A young nurse called from the elevator, searching the lobby. "Miss Jessica Ross?"

Jessica spun from her argument. "Yes?"

The nurse walked forward, her dark hair pinned back beneath her white cap. "Mr. Rein... Holden asked me to give something to you."

"How is he?"

Her gaze faltered. Jessica's heart plummeted. "He's entered a speedy delirium, which is not uncommon in many cases of the illness."

In many of the worst cases.

"His last coherent words were to take this box from his room and give it to you."

The nurse offered a small hand-crafted wooden box. Intricate carvings of flowers adorned the top, shining with a gloss finish. Jess took the gift, cradling in her hands. "Thank you."

"He has been kind in his service to us, and poorly treated my some." Her golden gaze found Jessica's. "He's offered compassion and prayer for many here, Miss Ross. He comforted my fiancé in the throes of his illness, staying by his side when I could not. I attribute his survival to Mr. Holden." She smiled, soft and gentle. "And he speaks of you."

Jessica's pulse trembled. She clenched the box close. "Does he?"

"Even now, in his fresh delirium, he calls for you."

Jess sucked in a ragged breath. "Take care of him, will you?"

"I will do my very best to bring him safe to you, if I can. I give you my word." She turned back to the stairs, but what was Jessica to do?

I'll fight. You rest.

Rest? Her heart squeezed into a panic strong enough to send her body into a seizure. And they denied her access to care for him? She stumbled out of the hospital, blinking through her tears. *Oh God, don't take him. Please, don't take him.*

"Do you need a car, miss?"

A gentle voice pulled her attention to the face of a driver, his black suit trimmed to reveal his profession. Jess looked back at the tall white building, frantically sifting through all the arguments, and possible illegal action, she could take to get inside to him.

Rest. Trust. Find your hope in Me.

She'd promised Grandfather to return within the day. He needed her. Granny and Amy needed her. Her heart split in two from the struggle.

"Miss?"

There was nothing else she could do for August but pray. Wait... and pray. That was all.

And that is enough.

"I must return home." She blinked the tears away. "Yes, please take me to the train station."

Everyone sat in their seats, as expected. The crowded train car rocked a gentle motion over the mountainous terrain toward home, filled with people from all walks of life, and all wearing the dreaded masks as a reminder of the rampant dread laced through every part of the world. She closed her eyes. She didn't need the reminder of human frailty. She saw it drain from the face of one of the strongest men she'd ever known.

The little box lay in her lap, a problem of labyrinth proportions. A part of her longed to spread wide its contents and reveal the beautiful letters she knew it housed, but another part quivered at the notion—almost as if reading through August's words sealed his fate.

The murky suspicions of her Appalachian upbringing surfaced from the past with a Dickensian vengeance. Would this simple, beautiful gift from him provide a radiant comfort or the wrath of Pandora's Box?

My hope is an anchor. Trust my love for you.

She released a long, purposeful breath and pushed the lid wide. His handwriting greeted her. The top letter brought the first sting of tears, addressed in an envelope and sealed as if waiting to be mailed. Her fingers threaded through some of the loose sheets, letters ranging back seven months. Long before he ever met her, or knew her.

Her lips trembled. Something from her letters, something unfathomable to her, opened his heart to love her, choosing her before they'd ever spoken a word. *Her?* With all of her often thoughtless and fiery reactions? Her obstinate demeanor?

She wasn't gentle and kind like her best friend, Ashleigh. Or passionate and charismatic like her sister-in-law, Catherine. Jess held a more dogged, assertive personality. What was there to love in that?

With a twist of her nail, she slit the seal of August's most recent letter, cherishing it all the more after leaving him in the claws of influenza.

He is mine.

The whisper reverberated through her spirit.

You are mine.

She listened.

I have loved you with an everlasting love.

A hot tear slid down her cheek, dropping on the paper as she read.

Mause,

I have little time to write to you, as my days are filled into the nights with the sick. You understand, I know, but I wish to write more. Please forgive me. If my thoughts could write letters for you, your arms would be filled every day with words from me. I love you, Mause. It seems I've always loved you.

There is a nurse here, Nurse Riley, who has been kind to me. Her fiancé, a soldier wounded and moved to this hospital, recently contracted Influenza. He has been a bad case from the start and I saw in her eyes the same concern I've witnessed in yours for me.

I could not stand by and watch her fret for his well-being without doing all in my power to help. My service comforted little, but I believe God used my prayers to touch her heart in ways my thin words could not. He opened his eyes this morning with clear vision, and smiled to his beloved. Her face, I cannot describe it with any other word but 'radiant.' It is how you looked upon me at my sister's wedding. You in all your beauty and strength, pleased to see me walk toward you.

Radiant.

The vision roams my thoughts, consoling the present pain and dispersing the death shadows on every side. You are my beloved and I am overwhelmed with your love.

As I write these lines, the memory of God's goodness and your love sustains me through these dark days. He is here, even in this, whispering comfort, bridging the gap from one world to the next, wrapping these fragile souls with hope. His fingerprints cover our suffering. Should you doubt his grip, remember this: He is with you, wherever you are, whether I can be or not.

My love follows my words and resides in your heart, but He surrounds you, in joy or pain.

I am called away. Keep these words close to stay the longing, to warm the loneliness, and to remember my love for you.

Forever your alien,
August

She smiled and wiped at the tears on her face. She'd been a skeptical child, scowling at her classmates mooning over Prince Charmings and fairytales, but August's letters, the very man he was, exposed the truth. Love—true love—existed… and found her.

Now she understood Catherine's statement about the right love being worth the risk, because even in this quaking uncertainty, she held the comfort of memory. These letters were a piece of him. As alive to her as his touch, as real as his voice, and a reminiscence this ravaging illness could never steal from her. *His love.*

Yes, it was worth the fear scraping at her faith, because no matter what happened, his love would always be with her. She placed her hand over her heart… *right here.*

August opened his eyes to the dim room, his thoughts floating through a slippery sea of consciousness. His chest ached, sore from his battle for the next breath, then the next. Day moved into night without his knowledge. Sometimes, Nurse Riley stood over him, and other times, emptiness and silence greeted him a second before he succumbed back into a world of mindless sleep.

He snatched at his thoughts and grappled to steady them. The darkened window showed night, but how many nights had passed? How long ago had Jessica been with him? Was it as much a part of his hazy dreams as everything else?

His young kinsman, Maximillian Fiennes, lay on a bed beside him. The poor man had only started to recover from typhoid when the symptoms of influenza appeared the same morning August collapsed, if he remembered correctly. They'd joined the *Vanderland* together as inexperienced sailors and runaways, young, vibrant, and longing to begin anew.

Now, would they also die together?

Max's shallow breath rattled through the room like death chains. So many were sick that cots littered the floor with people waiting to occupy the bed of the next man to die. He wasn't on the third floor, from what he could tell. They'd placed all the men together—soldiers, internees, and staff alike. The dying ones.

His mind cleared a little, landing on a firm memory—Jessica's final plea, her last request of him before his mind fogged into influenza.

Gott, hilf mir kämpfen.

―

God, help me fight.

August drew in a breath, forcing his lungs to comply. He moaned at the sharp pain from the effort but forced another, then another. The sick suffocation in his lungs loosened slightly. He fought for another breath.

Something pinched at his toe. He told his foot to shake. It barely moved enough to slip the sheet free. A tag wrapped around his toe. A death tag. A practice all the nurses began last week to speed the process of body identification.

Max's rasped breath made a noisy response to the silence and then grew quiet. August waited for another. Nothing. The knowledge, sickening acceptance, hollowed August's chest. Wet tears coursed from the edges of his eyes.

May the boy find peace, God. Rest for his restless heart.

August grieved for the boy. No one from home would mourn Max's death, but someone should. A life gone too soon. No one from Germany would mourn August's death, nor care for his future. No, he didn't belong in that world any longer. His home was Hot Springs and his family waited.

He closed his eyes. A vision of Jessica's face strengthened him to pull through another breath, deeper and longer. Her smile tilted, urging him to keep fighting. To come home. The ache curled through him, battling against his will, but he breathed again. His weary soul, his tired heart, desperately wanted to go home.

Nurse Riley stepped to Max's side. Her young shoulders sagged and with quiet dignity, she pulled the sheet over the boy's face. Another bed free. She moved to August, peering close, the white mask in contrast to her dark eyes. With a gentle hand, she lifted his head and placed a glass to his lips. The cool liquid slid down his throat with the taste of bile and blood, but it cloaked the fire and made him more alert.

He attempted to push words through his raw throat, or even air from his useless lungs, but nothing came.

"I promised I would repay your kindness, August," she whispered, her soft palm against his face. "I've done all I can."

She moved to the end of his bed and shifted the sheet back around his foot, fumbling with the cloth for an instance, taking the pinch from his toe.

She moved back to Max's cot and adjusted the sheet around his feet then, after glancing over some of the other beds, she took hold of August's cot and pushed him into the hallway. The place where the hopeless cases were left to die.

Could he truly be near the end? Hadn't she just spoke of chances?

He sucked in another breath, attempting to work out words from his voice to no avail.

He fought to move a finger, a hand, something to let her know he was alive and wanted to live. But the actions drained him, the forceful breaths weakened his already fatigued body, and soon, the darkness flooded back through his mind. *Fight, August.*

Sleep closed in. *Fight.*

Chapter Twenty-Eight

Grandpa took influenza the day after Jess' return, a mild case but enough to employ her waking moments with extra work. News headlines were riddled with the thousands of casualties from the epidemic. The larger cities brought the greatest numbers, but only due to their sizes. Percentages hit highs wherever the flu developed. A new name emerged from the throngs. *The Blue Death.*

She'd made one call to the hospital the day after her return to Hot Springs, only to have her questions dodged from one person to the next. Finally, after a heated conversation with a nurse, she learned August Holden was still alive but in very poor condition.

She prayed through her days as she moved among the patients and on her drive from the farm to check on her grandfather. Those moments, those snippets of conversations and meditations, blanketed her spirit with a powerful peace. A new understanding of God's love for her shone in the smaller reflection of August's. His letters proved a constant reminder and sweeping portrait of a faithful, relentless love.

God cradled her heart in this storm. Though shattered with grief and shaking with fear, her soul found an incomprehensible rest. How?

The truest love.

Unfailing.

Her next call to Asheville nearly shattered her newfound peace.

"We have no one by the name of August Holden in our hospital, miss," the voice replied, indifferent to her plea.

"And what about August Reinhold?"

Papers shuffled and a muffled conversation followed. "No, miss. There is no current patient here by the name of August Reinhold or Holden."

Jess thanked Mr. Leonard for the use of the post office's phone, and her exhaustion paired with her erratic emotions ushered her tears to the brink. She drew the car up beside the farmhouse and gripped the steering mechanism, offering up another faltering prayer before leaving the vehicle.

Grandpa met her at the door. "What did you find out?"

"They have no one there by that name."

Grandpa's frown deepened, his gaze reflecting the darker turn of her thoughts. "You have to find him."

Her throat closed. "You're still weak, Grandpa."

"I'm strong enough to manage, and finding our August will make me stronger still."

Jess immediately set to work for the trip, sending a note to Cliff and Anna to share her plans and to beg for their prayers.

The hospital clerk in Asheville gave few answers when Jessica arrived. Jess' breath shivered behind her mask as the seconds stretched and the woman shifted through papers in search of information.

"I'm sorry, Miss Ross, but an August Holden was taken to Asheville Cemetery four days ago."

Heat drained from her head out through her body. "Asheville Cemetery?"

The woman hesitated before continuing. "One of the local cemeteries. He was buried on the lower side, near the river."

Jess stared, unhearing. Her palm flattened against the counter for support, urgently searching the woman's face for the lie. "No, that can't be right."

The woman folded her hands in front of her, her face impassive. "There are too many losses to count, too many condolences to share. I am truly sorry."

She refused to believe it. Not August. No. She took the first taxi to the shadowed side of a vast field overlooking the French

Broad. She refused tears access. Wouldn't she feel something within her heart if a part of her died?

The gravestones scattered across the earth, as if thrown haphazardly across the green hillside. She followed the driver's instructions to the far side of the cemetery, feeling relief as each stone revealed another name than the one she sought. She crested the hill, the sunlight glimmering off the river below, when gaze settled on a small stone surrounded by fresh earth.

August Holden
German Internee
October 10, 1918

She dropped to her knees into the red-tilled earth, her fingers tracing the letters, attempting to smudge them away. *No, God. Please, no.*

But the sweet name stared back at her, etched in stone much too cold and lifeless for her August. The old, familiar ache surged the trail to her heart. Grief arched out a wretched sob.

"Why? Oh, why August? Of all the men in the world, why him?" She lowered her face to the stone. "What can I do with my heart now?" Her voice broke. "He can't be gone."

She wept until her heart quivered from the effort and tears refused to come, until the afternoon light faded against the horizon. The last train to Hot Springs would leave soon. She pushed herself up and made the trek home. Everything suddenly lost color. The sounds dulled and a chasm of sorrow ripped open every wound from her past, shaking more tears loose.

I have loved you with an everlasting love.

Everlasting? She wiped at her tears and closed her eyes against the passing scenes out the train window.

"Hold me, Father. Hold me together for I'm breaking to pieces inside."

She wrapped her arms around herself, squeezing the emotions tight and her fragile faith even tighter. "I can't... I can't hold on by myself."

Whispers of comfort, threads of the truths that had become her ready companions, bound her trembling heart with immeasurable strength, binding with gentle care. She clung to the strip of peace, threads of promises, filling her mind with truths she repeated to her faint heart until she drew the car up to the farmhouse.

She stared at the welcome home, her feet faltering toward the door. No. She wasn't ready to admit aloud the harrowing truth engraved in stone. No, not yet.

Autumn wind chilled her damp cheeks as she rushed through the back garden toward the forest. The orange hues of coming evening dusted over freshly fallen leaves along her path, creating a carpet of color. The grove of trees welcomed her down the path as a faithful friend, guiding her steps to the chapel. *August's* chapel.

Fall's shades provided a vibrant canopy of golds and reds. She had to make it to the chapel. She could weep there—pray there and touch the wood planks August lovingly set into place for her. *For her.* She stumbled, tears blinding her vision as the chapel appeared through an archway of autumn trees.

She waited for the sound of August's hammering, for his occasional hum of some German tune, but only the birdsong met her, and she quickened her uneven pace.

The sanctuary smelled of pine and sweetness. Her smile quivered. He'd carved each intricate design at the front of the church, personalizing the tiny chapel with his special gift.

She removed her gloves and slid her palm over the wooden walls, placed piece by piece. Her feet drew her to the little closet, the place he'd couched her in his embrace against the storm. The haven where his heart irrevocably touched hers.

Changed and healed her.

And whether in his life or his death, she'd never be the same.

She'd learned how to hope from his love. How to find freedom and joy.

Discovered peace.

She opened the little closet door and pulled her weak body up the rickety stairs until she reached the stained glass window, shattered pieces forged together into a beautiful cross—restored and whole.

That was her.

Her life had been broken pieces, her heart a wrecked collection of jagged edges and blunt corners. August's love, framed by God's grace, pieced her heart and her spirit back together into something... someone stronger than before.

Oh, how she would miss him and the promise of what she'd hoped to have with him, but his love would linger in her faith and remain like fragrance through the rest of her life. She placed her hand over her heart, tears trailing over her cheeks.

Here.

The pain dug deep, to the bottom of her soul, but God's love burrowed deeper still, cradling her to her core, couching her ragged spirit in incomprehensible peace.

Everlasting.

She reached a palm to touch the stained glass window. The sun shone through it, filling the steeple with a glorious halo of color and brightness. All the pieces, the light and the dark, merged together to form something beautiful.

Like her life... and August's life. Each piece in God's hands, no matter the edge, the shape, the color. He linked them together and formed something magnificent that many were unable to see until the sun shone through.

She rested her head against the glass and peered out into a world tinted in gold. A lone figure approached down the path toward the chapel, his steps slow and careful. Her grandfather had probably heard her arrive or seen her furious dash toward the chapel.

She stood up straight, ready to face him and to speak the pain aloud. The stairs creaked beneath her slow decent, feeling the weight of her wounds beneath the weight of her grief. The thick, wooden door of the chapel creaked open. She braced herself with a deep breath and lifted her eyes to the path, but the man approaching stood taller than her grandfather.

His shoulders were broader and hair, blonder.

Each closing step teasing an impossibility.

August?

She steadied her hand against the door frame.

His pale eyes bored into hers, sending her back a step. She blinked and wiped at her eyes, but he kept moving closer.

She shook her head, her breath lodged in a scream or a sob, she wasn't sure which one. Every Appalachian ghost story and superstition she'd ever heard came to mind and inspired a chill down her spine.

He took the three steps to stand before her, his feet making strong thuds against the wood. Real... human... alive?

"I... I saw your grave."

Dark shadows shadowed his eyes and his pale face marked the remains of his illness, but he slipped his warm palms across her cheeks, proving he was either very much alive or she'd gone mad.

She reached for the front of his shirt, gripping the cloth to make certain he was every bit flesh and blood. He seemed to understand the desperation, the irresistible need to touch, because all hesitation fled and he took her mouth and all her remaining senses into his kiss.

His arms captured her, wrapping around her and pinning her against his solid warmth, safe and whole. She sobbed against his lips, but refused to release him. Her palms slid up his back, gliding over the muscles as they flexed and rolled beneath her hands. Alive? She drew back only long enough to examine his face, ensure the nightmare had passed, before meeting his lips again.

His fingers slipped over her shoulders, leaving a wonderful caress of tingles up her neck before burying in her hair. Oh, what blessed grace! What sweet surprise!

This kiss surged with journeys from grief to hope, lost to found, brokenness to wholeness. She couldn't get enough. Her fingers glided over his hair and his face, examining every detail. Yes, he was here, every beautiful piece. *Her* August.

August pulled her down to the step beside him and tucked her beneath his arm. Close. His sigh breathed over her hair as he pressed his cheek against her head.

"How? I... don't understand," Jess' words quivered, breathless. She rested her hand on his chest, pressing her cheek to his shoulder for a deeper scent of pine.

"Nurse Riley exchanged my death tag with a lonely comrade of mine."

Jess pulled back, searching his face. "She what?"

"He was a man as lost to his past as I. She gave him my name so that I could be free to come to you." He shrugged, his grin growing. "August Reinhold is a dead man to this world, and this man before you is free to become whoever he wishes."

She stared up in wonder, attempting to digest this new information.

He ran a thumb across her cheek, his own gaze glistening with unshed tears. "I have no history, no home, no name." He braided his fingers through hers and drew their hands to his chest. "I have great hopes you'll share yours with me."

She laughed and grabbed his face in her hands, kissing him. "Yes." She nodded. "For the rest of my life, yes."

His laugh joined hers with the chorus of birdsong and the applause of the wind. They sat, arm-in-arm, beneath the stained-glass window, another example of brokenness restored.

Epilogue

The chapel door swung wide welcoming Jessica out of the December afternoon and into the warmth of dark wood and smiling faces. Catherine and Ashleigh had been hard at work, using the simple materials available to them in Hot Springs, and transforming the small chapel into a miniature fairytale world. A place Jessica never expected to see.

Holly surrounded white candles in the windows and garland dripped from window to window, meeting a fluffy white boy at the dome of each window. A magnificent wreath hung on the furthest wall, dripping with white and gold. Jessica's vision misted over as her gaze caught on the row of faces drawing her forward down the aisle.

All the people she loved best in the world watched in anticipation as she entered, her father at her side ushering her toward the future. His steady hold balanced her slight limp so that she moved—no, almost glided—forward, shrouded in her mother's frothy white gown.

Perhaps Jessica was living a fairytale, because she and August certainly had witnessed magic and miracles.

Strums of the wedding march reverberated in welcome from the small piano her father had purchased for the occasion. Her gaze landed on her dearest friend, Ashleigh, nestled beside her husband, Sam, who held their four-month old son, Christopher. Their bond of years, shared memories, and secrets, encouraged a fresh sheen of tears in Jess' vision. How they both had discovered truth and healing in their journeys!

Granny held Faith while Jude peeked around her, his grin widening into dimples. He looked dashing in his little brown suit, his hair slicked back to add maturity to his dear face. Jess' heart expanded with so much love for her children. Her gaze flickered to August's as he waited in his fresh, dark suit. *Their* children.

He seemed to read her thoughts, dropping his attention to their little additions with a tender light. *Oh, how I love this man.*

David's smile met her next, the joy in his eyes a matching spark to the pulse of her chest. Love bound them through the losses. He knew and understood. Jess' gaze switched to Catherine at his side, a woman who understood very well the power of love to restore the broken. Jess' grin broadened at the teasing tilt of her sister-in-law's grin beneath her fitted maroon cap.

Kissing practice?

A flush of warmth enflamed Jess's face as she turned forward, her gaze locking with the very focus of her thoughts. *Her groom.* Her prince. Her love. He stood tall in his dark suit, the golden mass of hair smoothed back but for the rebel curl. Cliff stood to one side, Anna to the other, and the minister waited in the middle as she and her father came to a stop before them as the music trailed to a close.

She never expected this fairytale for her life, but, despite her stubbornness and pride, despite her rebellious heart and reluctant love, God filled the hands she thought were so empty with more joy than she could hold. Love to last a lifetime, and much longer.

Her hand slid into August's welcoming palm and his grin crooked in the heart-flipping way she adored. No one could have shown her the pursing, patient love of Christ like this long-suffering, tender-hearted man before her. She gave his hand a squeeze at the thought, stepping with him into a new future and thanking God.

August closed the door behind them as they stepped into the little cottage, the strains of Joy to the World still dancing through Jessica's mind. Joy? Yes. After so much pain and loss, she embraced all of this beautiful joy and peace with a full heart. Her prince charming had spent last month preparing her parents' former home for their newlywed life, even adding an additional room for future growth.

Jess scanned the familiar sitting room and beloved furniture, each with its own story. And now, she could add a new chapter to them. Lights still glowed from the farmhouse as all the wedding guests enjoyed Granny's feast, but August had tugged Jessica away and brought her to their new home.

With Jude and Faith in the safe care of Anna and Cliff for the next week, Jess had little else to do but... love her husband. Quiet greeted their sudden aloneness. She turned to face him and found him directly behind her, slipping his arms around her in the beautiful way she loved best—completely. A cherished hold nestled close to his heart.

"I love you, my dear Mr. Ross."

His smile stretched against her hair, inspiring her own. "And I love you, my dear Mrs. Ross."

She looked up at him, placing a kiss to his chin as she did. "I am a little delighted that you took my name."

His palms smoothed down her back and back up. He kissed her forehead and cheek, then slid a kiss down her neck, sending enough tingles to weaken both of her legs. "I was happy to take your name. You are my family. My heart."

Her thoughts blurred from his attention to her neck, her breath uneven. "You are remarkably forward thinking."

He pinned her against him, face to face, his lips grazing hers with his words. "Oh yes, I am most certainly thinking forward right now, my Mause."

Her lips anticipated his kiss wavering at the very edge of her mouth. Even her body stood to attention, awaiting his next touch. "And what might be on that clever mind of yours?"

His eyes took on a smoky glow and his delicious grin perched with enough of an answer to send a delightful warmth flooding through her from head to toe. "A very intimate wager."

He kissed her soft and long, pearling the air around her into a thick heat, his hold transitioning to a more possessive grip across her back.

She released a quivering sigh, submitting to the aura of his love. "I think, my sweet alien, just this once, I'll let you win."

Acknowledgments

As usual, there are more people to thank then I will remember.

Thanks to Vinspire and Dawn Carrington for taking a chance on this new author and celebrating stories with me. What an amazing journey of my heart!

To Elaina for creating this remarkable cover! Wow! It takes my breath away!

To Julie Gwinn, my agent and friend, who never ceases to believe

To Jacqueline Burgin Painter – an amazing woman and author who brought the history of Hot Springs to life for me. Thank you for discovering the secret behind the German invasion of Hot Springs and sharing it with the world.

Thank you authors and speakers like Jim Rubart, Allen Arnold, Siri Mitchell, Julie Lessman, and Laura Frantz – your inspiration and encouragement has traveled much further than you'll ever know.

To my amazing street team who make this writing journey so much fun with their continual excitement and encouragement. You ladies are fantastic!

Spice Girls! You rock! Thank you for putting up with my self-doubt and occasional neuroses.

I love you my ever-wonderful Alleycats! Thank you for being sisters-of-my-heart! Amy, Angie, Ashley, Cara, Casey, Julia, Karen, Krista, Laurie, and Mary, I am grateful beyond words that God brought you into my realm.

To the aunts – my great aunts – Dee, Ruth, Faye, Edna, and Vatress, who are such sweet encouragements to me and enjoy celebrating the timelessness of romance with me!

To my sweet parents! Thank you for always believing in me. Dad, you're the best book salesman on the planet! And your favorite book will be out soon!

As always – to my family! There will never be enough emoji to express how much you all mean to me. So thankful to be the wife and mother to you. No story I ever write could be greater than the one I live with you.

And lastly, to the great Healer, who binds the broken-hearted with his great compassion and fills those in despair with an inextinguishable hope. Thank you, Jesus, for the power of story to teach timeless truths, and for allowing me to have the gift to share them.

About the Author

Pepper D. Basham is an award-winning author who writes romance peppered with grace and humor. She's a native of the Blue Ridge Mountains, a mom of five, a speech-language pathologist, and a lover of chocolate. She writes a variety of genres, but enjoys sprinkling her native culture of Appalachia in them all.

She currently resides in the lovely mountains of Asheville, NC where she works with kids who have special needs, searches for unique hats to wear, and plots new ways to annoy her wonderful friends at her writing blog, The Writer's Alley. She is represented by Julie Gwinn of Seymour Literary Agency. You can learn more about her at www.pepperdbasham.com.

Dear Reader,

If you enjoyed reading The Thorn Healer, I would appreciate it if you would help others enjoy this book, too. Here are some of the ways you can help spread the word:

Lend it. This book is lending enabled so please share it with a friend.

Recommend it. Help other readers find this book by recommending it to friends, readers' groups, book clubs, and discussion forums.

Share it. Let other readers know you've read the book by positing a note to your social media account and/or your Goodreads account.

Review it. Please tell others why you liked this book by reviewing it on your favorite ebook site like Amazon or Barnes and Noble and/or Goodreads.

Everything you do to help others learn about my book is greatly appreciated!

Pepper Basham

Plan Your Next Escape! What's Your Reading Pleasure?

Whether it's captivating historical romance, intriguing mysteries, young adult romance, illustrated children's books, or uplifting love stories, Vinspire Publishing has the adventure for you!

For a complete listing of books available, visit our website at www.vinspirepublishing.com.

Like us on Facebook at www.facebook.com/VinspirePublishing

Follow us on Twitter at
www.twitter.com/vinspire2004

and join our email list for details of our upcoming releases, giveaways, and more! We give away a themed box every month that includes a paperback book! http://t.co/46UoTbVaWr

We are your travel guide to your next adventure!

CPSIA information can be obtained
at www.ICGtesting.com
Printed in the USA
LVHW091036070419
613252LV00001B/411/P